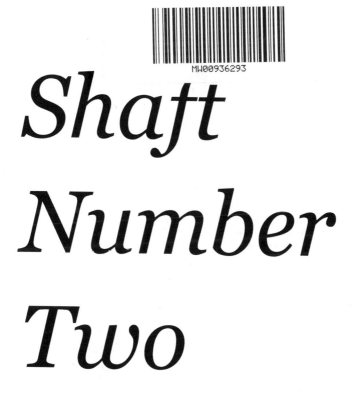

*Shaft*

*Number*

*Two*

*A. A. Wasek*

## Acknowledgements

The author gratefully acknowledges the experience of living on Copper Island, in Michigan's Keweenaw Peninsula, and the wonderful people who inhabit that superior piece of land. Of special note are those who inspired, motivated, encouraged, and appropriately chided the author, as well as provided exceptional editorial and personal support: Richard Buchko, a great writer in his own right, Marianne Tepsa, and Cate Lawrence – acquaintances a few years ago – true friends now.

Paula Wasek provided the (better) traits of some characters, and afforded additional editing assistance. The main character is modeled after Bethanie Hudson, Laura Wasek-Throm, and Sarah Fullerton.

Invaluable Finnish translation and insight into Finnish culture were provided by James Kurtti, Director of the Finnish American Heritage Center at Finlandia University, and Editor of *The Finnish American Reporter*.

The photo on this front cover is an actual Calumet and Hecla copper mine shaft and is used by permission of Michigan Technological University Archives and Copper Country Historical Collections. The photo on this back cover is provided by Wystan on:

*http://www.flickr.com/photos/70251312@N00/8425164400/sizes/o/in/photostream/*

and is used here under the Attribution 4.0 International license at:

*http://creativecommons.org/licenses/by/4.0/legalcode*

*Cover Design by Cheryl Geboski*
*7651 N. Lakeshore*
*Port Hope, MI 48468*
*cgeboski@yahoo.com*

Shepherding this project from draft to completed book, and beyond, is Pauline Glaza at EnhancedPublications.com

*Ad: Jennifer*

*qui nunc habet vocem*

© Copyright – 2014 by A. A. Wasek
All rights reserved
ISBN: 1490501231
ISBN 13: 9781490501239
Library of Congress Control Number (LCCN): 2014902154
CreateSpace Independent Publishing Platform, North Charleston, SC
BISAC: Fiction / Historical

*The church is universal, and so are all her actions. All that she does belongs to all. When she baptizes a child, that action concerns me, for that child is thereby connected to that body which is my head too, and ingrafted into that body whereof I am a member. And when she buries a man, that action concerns me, for all mankind is of one author, and is one volume. When one man dies, one chapter is not torn out of the book, but translated into a better language, and every chapter must be so translated.*

*No man is an island, entire unto itself. Every man is a piece of the continent, a part of the main. If a mere clod of dirt be washed away by the sea, Europe is the less – as well as if an entire peninsula were – as well as if a house of thy friend's – or thine own house were. Any man's death diminishes me, because I am of mankind. Therefore, never seek to know for whom the bells tolls ..... it tolls for thee.*

**John Donne**

# *I*

# *March 3, 1913*

Papa says he can still feel the copper dust in the back of his eyeballs.

I heard him describe it when he finally came home, after the accident, as his *American Justice*.

He's developed a strange habit since the calamity. I see him do it again as I walk into the kitchen, my dress on and my hair tied back, ready to accompany him to work. He slowly moves his head, first to the left, then shakes it quickly to center. Next the other side, slowly moving his head to the right, then quickly shaking it again to center, yet always careful to keep the dark spectacles on the bridge of his nose.

I look to the Papa I love – the man who teaches me so much.

The short haircut along the sides and back of his head tapers to longer hair in front, as he likes it to let his dark hair cover part of his high forehead. The distinct jawlines begin behind his ears and come together to shape a chin that's always set with purpose. His fluid motions and intelligent face on a long, thick neck make him look like he's thinking when he's moving; like he's contemplating when he's standing still. His hair is combed, his face perfectly shaven, and the mirror and razor are returned to their hanging places on the kitchen wall above the washbasin, the blade of the straight razor tucked safely back into the handle.

When he notices that I have seen him shaking his head as I enter, he reaffirms the declaration I have heard from him before.

"It was not an accident," he says. "It was an injury. Good morning, Emilia, welcome to the day," he states in his perfectly enunciated English. Then, as if to deflect my seeing him clear his head, he turns it into a Latin lesson. "*Iustitia*, Emilia," he declares, pleased with himself at the rhyming, and waits for me to complete my end of the dialogue – my Latin lesson.

"First declension, feminine." That's easy.

"And, as you know, there's no *j* in Latin, so it becomes..."

"Justice," I reply with a hint of frustration in my voice. A hint I should have hidden, but it's too early in the morning, and I'm too preoccupied with accompanying him to work to have concealed it. Yet I already know it's too late. The Latin lesson will continue.

"And *injustice* becomes..."

"Iniustitia?"

"That's correct. Now give me a Latin synonym." I need to think about that one. It's clear that Papa has already prepared the lesson, but I can't yet tell what it is. "Also first declension," he states, as if saying that it's a noun will clarify. It doesn't. Latin is full of first declension nouns. "Iniuria," he says, supplying the answer after realizing, as I have, the preponderance of first declension nouns. "Now translate."

"Translation works best on a happy stomach," says Mama, happier than I've seen her in days, happier than I've seen her in weeks and months. I'm glad to see the smile back in her light blue eyes, the same color my sister shares, while mine are gray and brooding like Papa's. Mama's hair is even shining today and, like my sister's, it looks as if it's been milled into fine flour. Mine is still wheat.

Mama has prepared a breakfast feast that our family hasn't seen, smelled, tasted in months. The aroma of pannukakku, always saved for Sunday, is wafting from the oven. I'm even more surprised at the sausage, which joins the panukakku only on very special Sundays.

"On the tick, Kerttu?" Papa asks with deference I hear seldom applied to me or Heli, often to Mama, especially since coming home from the hospital.

"Yes, it's on credit, Henrik, but it's the very first time I've ever borrowed from the store. You're going back to work. You're well. The laundry is up and we have lots of wood and enough kerosene and we even have a bit of coal and the snow has almost stopped because it's almost spring and I have my family back."

Papa doesn't argue with either Mama's logic or her mood, and I am pleased for all the same reasons. And at least one more. I will walk with my Papa, the two of us alone, to his new job. And I will walk back home by myself. Leaving Swedetown with only Papa is novel. Returning home alone will be brand new. I've never been allowed to go that near Red Jacket by myself. I'm nervous and maybe even a little afraid, but this must be the kind of feeling you get when you do grown-up things for the first time.

Heli springs up the basement stairs, two at a time. We've been working the laundry for the past hour, lugging the water downstairs and heating it, washing, rinsing, hanging other people's clothes, and Heli's romp up the stairs when she senses breakfast is ready has lent a rosy glow to her high cheeks, just like Mama gets.

I use both my index fingers to point to her dimples as she hits the top stair, but we have no time to complete our charade, and I move to my place at the table.

My little sister and I tease each other about our appearance "...as only young schoolgirls do," Mama tells us when she overhears us, but we invariably end up giggling as I poke my index fingers deep into my cheeks to mirror Heli's dimples, which she gets from Mama, while she runs her hands over her arms to indicate the dark skin I get in the summer, from Papa. Fact is, Heli, like Mama, is pretty, while

I still feel only tall, another of Papa's traits.

Papa leads with the blessing and we all join in, then Mama reaches for the hot serving bowl with a pad, picks it up and puts a generous serving on Papa's plate, offers to me next, to Heli, then places her usual delicate amount onto her own plate.

As she raises the first forkful to her mouth, we all flinch as we hear Mr. Nelson's raised voice above, swearing in Swedish. "Mikael!" his wife interrupts, also from above, but on the other side of the house.

"At least they're not together," Papa notes, then covers the meaning with a barely discernable smile. Mama sends him a similar, barely discernable look of disapproval, but all our attention re-focuses on the ceiling as the Swedish cursing continues.

We used to be sent outside for both the swearing and the bed-banging. Now, it's just the latter.

Mama is clearly disappointed to have her family's breakfast damaged, but this won't be the first time. I see the expression change in Mama's eyes. I've learned to never be fooled by her dainty chin, for it's her eyes that first become set, and then her chin follows.

"That's it!" she states emphatically as she places her fork back onto her plate. "I'll be right back!" Papa looks surprised as Mama makes one swift move from the kitchen table to the front door, just a few feet away. In moments, she's around to the back stairs, and the swearing subsides as we hear her steps nearing the top landing, in the back of our house. Mr. Nelson no doubt hears the same steps on his back porch, and the look on Papa's face turns to amusement as he tilts his head up to breathe in the fullness of Mama's wonderful breakfast, just as we hear Mama begin with the raised voice she uses only for discipline, "Now you look here, Mikael..."

Papa's mild amusement is our signal that he approves of Mama putting an end to the upstairs diversion, and he returns to his normal morning ritual, today starting with Heli. "Math is done?"

"Yes, Papa."

"English? Biology? And have you completed the Gallic Wars?"

"The Gallic Wars are a waste of time, Emilia can tell you that. She's on Virgil and Seneca and tells me they're lots more fun." It's Heli's way of turning the attention on academics back to me, and this time I don't mind.

"You'll appreciate Latin more when you take anatomy. That's when it's useful."

"If I take anatomy," Heli counters.

"We're still in three-shirt weather, so be prepared, girls, when you walk to school," Papa reminds us as Mama returns through the front door to the kitchen, brushing the snow off her feet that she didn't take the time to put shoes onto as she marched through the door the first time. "Delicious, Kerttu. Please sit down and enjoy the fruits of your labor. And thank you."

Heli and I add our "thank yous" and I think this is indeed a wonderful day, and I'm glad that not even Mr. Nelson's foul mouth will continue to offend it.

After breakfast, Heli and I clear the table and, since it's Monday, Heli washes and I dry the dishes and put them away. It's still new to us to have to clear our blankets and bed shirts off the sitting room floor, but we do so in silent unison, the sadness now mostly gone. Papa goes to their bedroom – the one now carved out of a little space in our sitting room – and feels in the small closet for his shirts, then puts two more on. Mama enters the bedroom and takes over the buttoning. In quiet understanding, Heli's eyes meet mine and we return to the kitchen.

Always the gentleman, Papa offers me his right arm as Mama tucks the brown-paper-wrapped pasty into his left, and I wrap my left arm in his as he feels for the portal with the pasty-laden hand and we're onto the front porch.

"Be very careful on your way there, Emilia, and especially careful on your way back. They'll still be going into work,
and you must keep your wits about you."

"Yes, Mama. Papa will protect me on the way there, and
I have my rosary for the way back."

We thread our way through the high snow banks from
our house to Ridge Street and I just follow my new shoes –
well, they're not really new, but they look almost like it –
down the street as if they're leading the way.

Papa and I both sniffle when the metallic air affronts our
noses at the same time. I'm grateful when I notice the slight
breeze off Lake Superior from the west because it's keeping
most of the smells of the stamp mills and copper smelters
from reaching us. But the mills and smelters that have
already ruined Torch Lake near the city of Lake Linden
merge into smells that rise up the hill here to Red Jacket and
always remind us of where we live during three seasons, and
choke us when the wind sometimes comes from the south-
east in the summer.

"My shoes are leading us," I share with Papa after a
sneeze that brings a rush of late-winter cold air into my
lungs. "Uncle Bear is so clever. They look like they're made
by a cobbler, not a carpenter. And the way he cut the leather
and snipped the soles, and re-fitted them together with the
pretty copper rivets, and fashioned the copper eyelets all the
way to the top, why they're better than brand new because
my toes fit perfectly near the end, and they're only a little
wide because he said he couldn't adjust the width as easily as
the length, and I love the way he told me that he rubbed in
the bear grease. Isn't that funny? Uncle Bear rubbing in the
bear grease, and then baking them in the oven 'until they
were just right' he said, like Goldilocks."

My shoes may be leading us, but my legs don't keep up
with Papa's as I try to calculate how many of my steps
(Eight-tenths? Eighty-five hundredths?) equal one of Papa's,
and I could probably figure it to the third decimal place, but

that would ruin our walk together and I'd rather parley with Papa. "We've been talking in class about Mr. Wilson's inauguration tomorrow, and then we must address him as President Wilson, and our teachers won't say it, but sometimes during lunch we wonder what it would be like if Eugene Debs had been given a chance," and I'm trying to draw Papa into the conversation because I love talking with him even more than he loves talking about politics, but he seems to be in his own state of mind, so as we cross the railroad tracks at the bottom of Ridge Street, I ask, "would you have voted for Mr. Debs, if you could? I mean, you already had three choices and that was unusual, but he seemed to be the only non-traditionalist, don't you think?"

Papa's sudden stop surprises me.

"Two-hundred sixty. Oh, sorry Emilia, my mind was on something else. I've taken this same path for 17 years, and I'm only now realizing how many steps there are. As you know, my eyesight is not what it used to be, so I was counting the steps. Will you join me in an elementary, but useful exercise?"

It's another 260 of Papa's steps from Ridge Street down Osceola Road to Swedetown Road, where we turn right. "That's about what I would have guessed," he tells me. "Although I didn't expect it to be precise. It's 260 to our first turn, and 260 to our second. Let's see what Swedetown Road brings."

Papa takes up the counting again and I allow my mind to wander as we leave behind the blackened, burned, pulverized pebbles forming the road surface out of the discards of once huge rocks from which the copper has been extracted by the crushing rollers of the stamp mills and the blasts of the smelters. A main road, Osceola earns the discards while Ridge Street, where we live and Swedetown Road, with which we are identified, have not.

I love our little village of Swedetown. It deserves to be called Finntown because most everyone who lives here is

Finnish like us, but Finland is still dominated by Russia to the east, and before that, by Sweden to the west, and Papa says that's how Swedetown got its name. He says his Papa, who writes us often from Finland, believes that our mother country is close to independence, and I hope for the sake of our identity both in Finland and in Swedetown that it's true.

I love our place in the Copper Country, though it took me awhile to understand where we live in Michigan. During one of my earliest trips to the library with Mama, I looked at many maps before I located us. Papa had told me that the Keweenaw Peninsula is as far north as you can go in Michigan, but tracing my finger over the names of the cities and rivers and railroad lines, I found nothing that looked or sounded like us on the library map that displayed us in the form of a mitten whose northernmost point is called Michilimackinac.

"We're in Upper Michigan," said Mama, busy with Heli and the children's books, and that confused my young mind even more. It was only when I found another map that correctly linked Michigan's two largest peninsulas together at the Straits of Mackinaw that I could follow it to the left and all the way to the top where we live.

*Kuparisaari* is among the first Finnish words I remember learning. Although Papa and Mama are careful to *not* teach us the Finnish language, Heli and I heard it so often in reference to where we live, that we couldn't help but tuck it into our earliest vocabularies. And it means we're special because we live on Copper Island atop the Keweenaw Peninsula, in the northernmost point of Michigan's Upper Peninsula, and above the mitten of the Lower Peninsula. Papa says that the man-made canal – the Keweenaw Waterway that separates us from the rest of the peninsula – was completed right after the locks connecting Lake Superior to Lake Huron were built in Sault Ste. Marie to our east, even before he and Mama settled here. The waterway that made us into an island, with only one bridge traversing it, was excavated so the huge Great Lakes freighters could anchor right next to the smelters.

All for the sake of copper.

I remember thinking as a little girl that the Copper Country was like Finland and I only had to gaze across the water in the direction of the setting sun to see Sweden. I'd heard comments, too, of the similarities: the long, snowy winters, the short days of winter and short nights of summer solstices, the land that refuses to grow field crops. But, with what the Keweenaw Indians call *miscowaubik* – red metal in the purest natural form ever discovered on earth – the Keweenaw does produce beautiful copper.

The lights from the mines are much closer and beginning to cast dim, dancing shadows behind us. As I lean into Papa to steer him a little left onto Mine Street, he stops.

"Eight-hundred seventeen to Mine Street," he says, with Shafts Six thru Twelve on our right, Shafts One thru Five coming up on our left. At least a hundred men are milling about near each shaft house, waiting for the man engines to take them into the depths. "That's interesting," Papa says, which means that he will turn what's *interesting* to him into a thought-provoking question to me. I look to him, smile, and prepare myself. "Two-hundred sixty, then 260, then 817. Aside from the repetition, what's in those numbers?"

Papa eliminates the obvious, so I add the first two and compare the sum to the second number. "The distance we took on Swedetown Road is about one and one-half times as far as what we walked on Ridge Street and Osceola Road combined," I tell him, certain that I've nailed it the first time.

"That's correct, Emilia," and I smile at him as we stand several hundred more feet from his work site. "Now, what else?" and I'm disappointed. "Compare 260 to 817," he hints.

Multiplication gets me nowhere. "Three..." the mental division of these large numbers is a bit daunting. "Three, point one ... that's ... that's almost pi," I say.

"You've got it!  Now come on, you're making me late for work," and I join in the laugh that begins as he squeezes my hand, and ends in the confidently set jaw of one of his calculating smiles.

Everything is lit now, yet the sun is at least another hour from rising.  We're at the point where Swedetown Road branches into a Y and loses its identity to our left when it turns into Mine Street, and changes its name on our right to the more appropriate Agent Street before crossing Calumet Avenue, the main road separating Red Jacket from Laurium.  Agent Street continues into Laurium, the town of expensive stores and fine homes owned by mine captains and agents.

And a hospital I don't want to think about.

The still morning air has already been shattered into a cacophony of train whistles, steel wheels against steel tracks, steam engines pressurizing, and then releasing their pent-up prisoners as the trains and streetcars do the same.

I hesitate only for a moment to note, on my right, the long lines of horses and wagons laden with supplies as they ply their way in both directions along the main road of Calumet Avenue, which now runs parallel to Mine Street.  As Papa and I head straight up Mine Street, my eyes adjust to the bright lights of the shaft houses.  I can now see hundreds of men in the distance, darkened figures scurrying busily about, heading toward a particular location, a particular shaft, no doubt.  It's only as we get nearer the lights that it becomes clear who is in which group.

The Cornish group mills about closest to the shafts, and Papa has told me they're the only ones allowed to be called *miners*, and will ride the man engines first into the copper mines.  The French machinists, who insist that they always work above-ground, are nearest the buildings.  The Italian stone-cutters are arguing about how to best utilize the poor rock for a small building they're erecting.

"Five-hundred twenty steps again to Calumet and Hecla Number Two," Papa notes quizzically.  "Well, that'll make it easy to remember, won't it?"

I've not seen Shaft Number Two since Mama and Heli and I ran all the way here from home and only caught our breaths in time to watch Papa being carried from it on a stretcher. I try to push that thought out of my head and it vanishes anyway when Uncle Bear calls "Hyvää huomenta, Henrik! And good morning to you, Emilia!" from near the entrance to Number Two. Surrounding Uncle Bear are all Finns, all trammers.

"Karhu-Jussi," Papa smiles broadly as he looks toward the voice and physique and name that describe everything about him, except his temperament.

*Jussi* is Uncle Bear's given name, but only adults are allowed to address him by that, out of respect, Papa says. *Karhu* means *bear* in Finnish, and that describes him better anyway. His dark red beard covers nearly his whole wide face, so I always look to the kindness in his eyes and find it followed by the big smile that, together with his eyes, light up his face.

Uncle Bear lays his tin lunch bucket on the ground, steps away from the man engine entrance and runs to greet us, grabbing Papa's hand in his big paw and shaking it violently. Many of the other men who used to work with Papa, but he hasn't seen in three months now, come over and join Uncle Bear in shaking Papa's hand. I recognize most of them: Mr. Koskiniemi, Mr. Siivola, Mr. Jarvi, Mr. Heikkila, Mr. Onkalo, Mr. Lehto, Mr. Toivola, Mr. Piipo, and our Swedetown neighbors: Mr. Kumpula, Mr. Junttonen, and Mr. Waara. Papa addresses them by their first names as they speak, and they all tell him how good it is to see him, and how they've missed his leadership in the mine.

"Ah, I'm only taking it to a new place. I understand those obscure men in the broom factory need my help. And I'll have them organized in no time."

"Bad choice of words," interrupts Uncle Bear, "but good choice of work site," as he motions for their friends to return to the man-engine. Alone with Papa and me, Uncle Bear looks to me and I cast my eyes down to the tops of my shoes, embarrassed by the furtive glances and outright stares of the other men. "And they fit well?" he wonders aloud.

"Oh, thank you so much, Uncle Bear, they're perfect. And they smell so new and look so new, and I just can't thank you enough."

"Oh, you've done just fine in that territory. I think this is, what, the hundredth time you've thanked me? And you will be fine Henrik, with shoes that won't be eaten up by rock. But what's with the shirts? I expect your new work site to be much warmer than a lousy mine, yet I suppose you still had to walk here," Uncle Bear notes as he answers his own question. "Listen, Henrik, there's a meeting tonight at the Palestra and I'm staying after work to attend, and it would be wonderful if you would go with me. I'll stop by your house just before seven."

"Better yet, join us for supper."

"I had ... um ... other plans ... and Kerttu wouldn't expect me," fumbles Uncle Bear and I'm pretty sure that means Veljetsek's Saloon, but I'm not being spoken to, so I hold my tongue.

"Nonsense, you know that you're always welcome at our home, and Kerttu will be happy to see you again. It's been nearly a month since you finished the project, and it's been too quiet at our home. Please join us."

Uncle Bear nods as the 6:55 whistle blows and Papa barely notices and I nearly jump out of my skin.

"Go," closes Uncle Bear to Papa, while offering a parting smile to me that's part guardian and part amusement over my dismay at being startled by the whistle. "And I'll walk home with your Papa, so you can relax after school."

Papa offers his arm to me again and it's only a few more steps past the Number Two Shaft to his new work site, and he's still counting them.

I feel Papa's entire body become rigid when "Rytilahti,

it's about time!" rings out from the entrance, and a man hastens from the door, grabs my father's arm, and tries to steer him back inside. Without the clean winter coat, clean clothes, and shiny shoes, I'd still recognize him as some kind of boss, just by the way he treats my Papa.

"This is my daughter, Emilia," says Papa, matching the manager's steely tone of voice, but still insisting on manners.

"Oh, yes, yes, pleased to meet you Emily, but we must be getting along now."

"Emilia," Papa repeats, unmoving. "Emilia, this is Mr. Roger Lukas. Mr. Lukas to you."

Mr. Lukas takes a breath, offers his hand in a weak gesture, and shakes my hand just as ineffectually. I notice the lack of calluses, so it all fits. I've heard of this man all my life. He's the shaft boss, and has been Papa's boss, nemesis, daily and nocturnal nightmare for my whole life. This is the first time I've met him and, in a few brief moments, I already detest the reality of the man as deeply as I've detested him by story and reputation.

"The pathetic tyrant," I've overheard Papa and Uncle Bear repeatedly define Roger Lukas, and I now agree with their description.

"A few moments alone, please," Papa says by way of excusing the man who will continue to hold sway over Papa's every action at work. Mr. Lukas returns to the poor rock building while Papa listens for the fading footsteps. "Iniuria, Emilia. Now translate," he adds with a smile.

"Oh, Papa," and it feels good to laugh, to break up the uneasiness caused by finally meeting the pathetic tyrant. It feels good to return to my love for the day and my love for my finest teacher. I would have easily forgotten all about our earlier Latin lesson, but I love how Papa brings me back to it, does it with a smile, and creates a smile in me. "Iniuria," I repeat, and then recalling his first-thing-this-morning admonition about *j*'s, I place them back into the English. "Jinjuria?"

He spreads his hands apart, expecting me to fill in the space.

"Jiniuria? Injuria? Injury! An injustice is an injury. An injury is an injustice," I repeat both for emphasis and because I just couldn't help myself.

"As I've said for many years now, Emilia: when you know Latin, you can easily learn virtually any other language. And now you know why I call it my *injury*. You must hurry back home now, and please be careful."

*And now I know why you call it your American Justice*, I think to myself.

The trip back home – a brief trip I've made many times with my family and friends, or at least with Heli, but never by myself – goes easily once I find my pace and focus on my shoes instead of the wandering eyes of the Frenchmen who still notice me even as they're heading for their work sites above ground.

When Papa got better, yet told us that he wouldn't return to his old job in the mine, Uncle Bear went to work on these shoes. They used to be Papa's, and I remember being with him when he bought them at Vertin's only a year ago. By the start of this winter, I had both worn out and outgrown my only pair of shoes. Uncle Bear had just finished all the work on our house, and said he needed a new project. So he traced my feet on butcher paper, took the paper and Papa's old shoes home to Eagle River with him, and sent my skepticism to shambles when he returned with what I was certain was a brand new pair of lady's shoes from Vertin's.

"How did you know my size?" I asked him, still not realizing these could be Papa's old ones.

"I traced your feet, remember? They're as good as new. The shoes, I mean. Your feet are old and smelly," he teased.

And only then did I understand. I should have known, for I watched Uncle Bear dismantle our inside staircase and re-construct it on the outside of our house, adding a fine landing at the top, where he made an entrance door out of the window from which Heli and I used to be able to see Eugene Field School. I watched him make a kitchen out of our upstairs bedroom in the back, a sitting room and small bedroom out of Papa's and Mama's upstairs bedroom in the front. It was only when he brought two more cast iron stoves – one for the new apartment upstairs and one for the basement – that he needed any help. I watched him as he brought bundles of wood from home, where he had sawn them to size, and nail them to the upstairs floor to cover the old staircase. I watched him put in new lath and mix and apply plaster to the ceiling where the staircase used to be, and he did it so carefully and lovingly, it turned out as nice as the work he does on his own home.

Then the Nelsons rented the upstairs. And Heli and I need to get up an hour earlier to help with the wash that Mama brings in the day before. But we have managed. And Papa is well again. And today he's back to work. Today, I am as happy as I've ever been.

It was nice to go to school at Field, almost next door to our house. Now, Heli and I have to walk to Washington School in Red Jacket. I still feel like a junior in my Junior year while Heli's quiet self-confidence among her friends sways her seventh grade class in middle school, and she will own the class by the time she reaches high school the year after next. Washington School is not far from Calumet & Hecla Number Two, and returning home to Swedetown every day, twice a day to accompany Papa to and from work, will take some time. But returning home and waiting awhile for school to begin will give me another opportunity to review my school work. And I would have wasted the time sleeping if I weren't helping with the laundry.

It's only when I'm near our front door and I begin taking off the first shirt that I find the unsaid rosary. I'll make up for it tonight.

Heli is waiting for me when I arrive home. "To the privy," she announces, not even fashioning a sentence.

This is different, for Heli has always been my athletic, brave sister, always the first in line to do anything, and never, ever afraid to try something new. I don't complain because I have to go too, but it feels silly crowding two people into an unlit one-holer, and standing there, holding her hand, while she just has to go number one. This started right after Papa's accident, or *injury*, as I've learned this morning. She says she doesn't like dark, smelly places anymore because that must be what a mine is like, and Papa nearly died in a dark, smelly place. I've been with her to our outhouse every time she's gone in darkness since December 7, the day of Papa's accident.

Heli does her business and lets go of my hand only as she reaches for the door, opens it, then closes it behind her so I can do mine, unafraid of the darkness, and only a bit uncomfortable with the smell. I hear our upper back door open, the door that's now Nelsons' apartment, and I quickly finish and dash to the house, since it's colder when you just sit there than if you're moving, as I've been all morning.

Home after school feels like we should be going to bed, even with the longer days. It doesn't help that Yvonne made fun of my shoes. She sits behind me in the only class we have together, and would have never noticed that they're reconstructed trammer's shoes except that I tucked my feet under my chair and exposed the reconstructed soles.

Yvonne and I landed in the same class at Eugene Field School when I skipped a grade and she flunked one. Two new pupils in the same class for opposite reasons, I gravitated toward her for only a few days before she let me know in many ways she would not be my friend and I quit trying to become hers. I'm sure our teacher, Mrs. Reynolds, was too smart to have believed the stories Yvonne made up of me, and I learned to carefully inspect my seat for upturned tacks when we returned from recess. Even though she hated me, I used to feel sorry for her because she would hold her breath until she almost passed out whenever someone dared to push her back after she bullied her way around the playground. Then my grade-school misery with Yvonne ended as suddenly as it began when she announced early in the school year that her papa had been promoted and they were moving because Swedetown is no place for a proud French family like the Joliets.

Nothing has changed with Yvonne's sour, snooty attitude, and if she weren't such a liar and cheat, and so easy to ridicule since she's also fat, I'd find a way to get back at her for making fun of my shoes today. But it's just too easy and unchristian, and I won't waste even a little time on making friends or enemies of someone who doesn't care either way.

With the extra time I'll have today, since Papa will come home with Uncle Bear, I'll get some school work done.

I've alerted Mama that we're to have a guest and her initial look of apprehension turns to delight when I reveal it's Uncle Bear. She admonishes us to tidy up the sitting room, which doesn't need it, and take the sheet off the sofa. Heli and I have learned to respect the sofa like it's a member of our family. She re-inspects their bedroom, which also doesn't need it, picks a piece of lint off the American flag hanging on the wall, and returns to the kitchen to make coffee and prepare a snack with the leftover pannukakku and sausage. The soup she's already begun to cook for supper will have to do, and I know she'll add her delicious rye bread with Uncle Bear as a guest.

With the stairwell gone, we've re-gained a little of the space we lost to the Nelsons upstairs, though I still see Heli look up longingly whenever we sit on Mama's sheet-covered sofa, a beautifully crafted piece of furniture she's always been proud and careful of. It was her contribution to the new house, the only furniture they could afford when they first came here to Copper Island and Papa bought the house with some of the savings his Papa gave to him before he married Mama and together they left Finland. Mama said she saved for it her whole life, and Heli and I are careful when we sit on it to read or do our school work, the only time we're allowed to use it. The sheet covers it unless we have a guest coming. We never sleep on it.

Mama does not believe in a neat and tidy house – Mama believes in a perfect house. Only once in a great while do Heli and I ever need to be reminded to fold our sleeping shirts and put them on the small bureau in the bedroom Uncle Bear made for Papa and Mama out of a space in the sitting room, and it is not often we need to be reminded to place our shoes in a neat row of eight, from Papa's to Heli's, near the door in the kitchen. Now, with his poor eyesight caused by those dark spectacles, Papa is even more fastidious than Mama, insisting that everything be in a specific spot, in impeccable order.

Papa and Uncle Bear doff their caps in unison as they enter the front door, though Uncle Bear defers to Papa to allow him through the door first. Heli and I wait in the sitting room, knowing we'll have our turns with the bear hugs.

"Good day, Mrs. Rytilahti. It is indeed my pleasure to encounter your glowing countenance."

"Oh, stop it Karhu-Jussi. But thank you for joining us for supper. Please sit down. It'll be ready soon."

"I'd like to say hello to the girls, if I may."

"They'll be disappointed if you don't."

Uncle Bear enters the sitting room stooped over, stoops even lower to wrap his arms around Heli's hips, then gently picks her up and lays her to the floor, grabs both her wrists in his large left hand and places her pinned hands against the floor over her head, then tickles her stomach with his right. Soon she can hardly breathe, and he looks up and feigns a bearish growl as he spots me in the corner, laughing along with Heli.

Uncle Bear is more careful with me, and he's been this way since one of his bear attacks accidentally landed his right hand on my left breast. He stopped suddenly, as if he just learned that I had grown up. When that thought finally settled in during a long, embarrassing moment, he got off the floor, apologized profusely, went into the kitchen, poured himself some water from a pitcher, and sat down at the kitchen table, stunned and silent. He is also more careful now with Heli since that incident, and she and I both know that the bear attacks are nearing an end. So I'll enjoy them immensely now, for I love his faux fearsome demeanor and his genuine gentleness.

During supper, Heli asks what the meeting at the Palestra is all about, and I can tell her the answer as well as Papa or Uncle Bear.

"Mine business," Mama interjects, for she, too, knows the answer.

The adults will try to keep us girls out of this matter, but I'll hear all about it tonight, when Papa shares it with Mama, Heli sleeps, and I eavesdrop.


"They're talking about a strike, Kerttu," I hear from our sleeping area in the sitting room, right next to their bedroom. Heli gently tugs on the blanket more from habit than intention, for she is asleep. Mama is silent for a moment, then an "it's been coming ... perhaps it's time," tells me what she thinks of the possibility.

Papa continues. "A fellow by the name of Frank Aaltonen was the speaker. What an orator, a terrific presenter of the facts and the emotions and the power and money. He spoke of sticking together, of solidarity and gathering our voices into one unified declaration that cannot, will not be denied. He never said the word 'union' because he knows, as we all know, that everything said tonight, everyone who was there tonight, will be reported to the likes of Lukas and MacNaughton before the dawn. He said there are those who will separate us and use our separateness to fight against us. We already know how they accomplish this. How many

languages can be heard in Red Jacket?  Few of us can
understand everyone else.  No one in management can
understand everyone else, and that's the way they've planned
it.  If we can't talk, we can't stick together.  But he says a
common language is emerging.  It's called dignity and
fairness, and I was just speaking to Emilia about it this
morning: it's called justice.  On our way home, Karhu-Jussi
and I talked about the issues that have been brewing since I
begged to join this company, then helped blast and sledge
and shovel our common path to hell.  I already know most of
them: an eight-hour work day, three dollars a day for
trammers, a fair forum for our grievances to be heard, and
union recognition.  And a new one.  They've been working
with drill manufacturers to develop a one-man drill.  It's
being tested in a few shafts now, and C&H has ordered more.
Can you imagine, working alone, how many men will lie on
the bottom of a drift before someone else comes across
them?  If Lukas hadn't made a spectacle of me, I'd still be
lying there.  Aaltonen says we must stand up for ourselves
and unify our language of solidarity and even learn to talk
management's language – money."

Mama picks up the conversation. "I've heard this all before, and I think I'm becoming even more radical since your
accident in defense of my friends, their husbands, my family,
my husband.  I fear a strike.  We're just getting back on our
feet.  Yet my greater fear is to do nothing.  To let these
mining companies claim that a death a week, two amputa-
tions, and who knows how many broken bones are only the
price of doing business is more than I can stomach.  And a
man's eyesight: what's that worth?  Will you ever be paid for
your time off?  Who will pay the hospital bills?  Tell me,
Henrik.  I don't want to know what Aaltonen thinks, I want
my husband's opinion.  That's the only one that matters to
me."

The long silence in our home heightens the sound of the
faraway trains, steam engines, machinery, and raised voices

in the still night air.

"I told Karhu-Jussi and I'll tell you: I need to think. In many ways, this has been a fine business and a very good company. I have a job and we own a home – never mind the land underneath it – and we live in an area that has good schools, beautiful churches, thriving businesses, and arts with a gorgeous opera house. The Skyhooks are a great baseball team and I'm ... I was a good pitcher. I couldn't be happier where we live. This is Finland without her great forests, and I miss her trees, but I love this water. And I hope to clearly see this water again. I will clearly see this water again. Lukas tells me that they're still trying to figure out a new Michigan law called Workingmen's Compensation. He asks that I be patient, and that's an interesting word for him, for he has none. He's just afraid I'll sue. And Doctor Jacobs says he's still hopeful about my sight."

"Quiet," Mama admonishes. "They took some of your hearing when they tried to take all of your sight, and you don't realize how loudly you speak. Emilia sleeps softly."

"I don't know," Papa says quietly, yet I can still hear him. "I've seen what they do to those who *don't fit* and I still don't know what that means. How can you give your body and your mind and your spirit for 17 years and still not *fit*? I can handle the hurt, but I can't handle the way it hurts my family. I don't love this company, but in many ways I respect it. I don't hate them, but they worry me. I need to think."

"I don't," says Mama with her typical quick decisioning. "Henrik, you said it yourself: you gave your body and your mind and your spirit. Management doesn't want that. Mind and spirit are too much and they don't know what to do with them anyway. That's why you *don't fit*. They believe that their money for the schools allows them to tell the schools what to teach. They tell the preachers what to preach. The opera house presents what the mines want presented, and the businesses sell what the mines want sold. And the politics. Don't even get me started there. Who's the chairman of every Houghton County Board? MacNaughton or one of his cronies at the Miscowaubik Club, or one of his peons if it's a lesser office. We've heard that women already vote in Finland. Will we ever vote here? You can think about it, Henrik. And it's probably best for your body and your mind and your spirit if you're not involved, but I've heard this coming and I've seen what they've done to you, and I will be involved, and I will be fighting for you and for our friends."

A long hesitation. Papa is thinking again, I can tell.

"Hyvää yötä, Kerttu. I must get some sleep."

"Good night, Henrik. And you will pitch again."

*Good night, and good-bye fine day*, I think to myself. I'm asleep before I'm to the third Joyful Mystery.

# II

# *March 23*

It's springtime and not even yesterday's heavy, wet snow-fall will disturb it, for the bright sun on the fresh snow casts a light that makes everything – the roads, the houses, the churches, even the people, especially the people – glow.

Easter is one of my favorite days of the year.

Mama has the privilege of taking Papa's arm on our way to St. Joseph's and I notice as we continue down Osceola Road past Swedetown Road, where we usually turn right toward Calumet and Hecla Number Two and to the broom factory, Papa hesitating to begin a new step count.

Some of my friends say we don't belong at St. Joseph's. We're Finnish, so we should be Lutheran, they say. But today proves Papa's choice when he and Mama first settled here.

He still tells the stories of when he grew up in Helsinki. He tells of how he was raised by his Papa as Finnish Ortho-dox, which was brought to Finland by Russian Orthodox Christians, but he also went to church at the Roman Catholic St. Henrik's a few times as a youth. They didn't know what to do with him because St. Henrik's was built to accommo-date foreign Catholics. But they welcomed him anyway.

Finland is wonderful that way, I've learned. We Finns welcome everyone and even build beautiful structures to invite everyone, including foreigners, into our lives.

Papa says he was curious about St. Henrik's, and his Papa encouraged his curiosity in everything.

My Grandfather, my Ukki, who knows both Latin and Greek, is a thinker, a philosopher and a professor at the great Imperial Alexander University of Finland. He taught Papa that there's room for many religions: Catholic and Protestant, and certainly Lutheran and Orthodox. After all, though my friends may not know this, the Finnish Orthodox Church and the much larger Evangelical Lutheran Church are both national churches of Finland. My Ukki must be a wonderful educator, for Papa is the best in the world.

With his extensive knowledge of Latin, and I'm sure he's only being modest when he describes his understanding of Greek as "merely conversational," Papa taught himself perfect English and he speaks it better than the vast majority of people who have lived here all their lives. He says he and Mama practiced it every night so, of course, they taught me and Heli the same impeccable pronunciations and the same complex rules of grammar. They were careful to *not* teach us Finnish.

"You are Americans," Heli and I have both heard countless times, but we've still picked up most of our mother language with no assistance from our parents, and I'm even better at it since reading *The Kalevala* in its entirety just a few months ago.

Papa says he chose St. Joseph's because it's the union of the two religions and churches he knew best from his hometown – the Orthodox Uspenski Cathedral and the Catholic Church of his namesake, St. Henrik's. "Even the statues are similar," he still mentions. "There's a statue of St. Paul on the outside of St. Henrik's, just as there is on the outside of St. Joseph's. I was glad when St. Joseph's invited me and your Mama in the same way as St. Henrik's," he now says. "If there was a Finnish Orthodox Church on Copper Island, we'd be going there. Yet I experienced a certain *inner peace* at St. Henrik's, and I feel it here at St. Joseph's. This church is so special – it has much of the grandeur of the Uspenski Cathedral, and also preserves the personal feeling, and the sense of *inner peace* I found at St. Henrik's."

I think Papa secretly revels in our religious minority status among our kinsmen. I know he misses Finland, but with Russia's dominance of Finland's politics and also its educational system, where my Ukki teaches at the university named after a Russian tsar, the lack of freedom is what troubled Papa the most. With his Papa's encouragement, it's what caused him and Mama to emigrate here.

I know Papa has found the freedom here that he loves.

We sit together in a pew near the middle of St. Joseph's, with Papa on the far left end, then Mama, me and Heli. Papa fits right in with the dark hair that matches his dark skin in the summer, and Mama, Heli and I fit in even better because our lighter hair is covered in the same kind of hats that cover the dark hair of the Slovenians.

This is the finest church I have ever seen, and I've been to many. St. Mary's for the Pellegrini wedding. St. Anne's for the only concelebrated Mass I've ever attended, with Father Denay and Father Turmell and Father LaSalle reciting their Latin liturgy in perfect unison. St. John the Baptist for the Likovich funeral. And St. Anthony's, a beautiful little church on Seventh Street and oh, how those Poles know how to celebrate a wedding. I've been to Sacred Heart only once because we're not welcome across the big road in elegant Laurium.

Nothing compares with St. Joseph's. I love the towering altars on each side, and could spend the entire Mass gazing at them. Within the altar on my left is a statue of Christ revealing His Sacred Heart. The beautiful matching altar on the right is where we gather in May and sing *On This Day, O Beautiful Mother* and, my favorite, *Hail, Holy Queen Enthroned Above* in front of the statue of Mary, mother of Jesus.

The center altar beckons me even more. Rising easily

forty feet high, the soaring peaks of the sculpted and lighted altar enclose another three statues, St. Joseph, the patron saint of our parish, holding the child Jesus in the center. Clutching the keys to the kingdom, St. Peter is ensconced on the left with the Greek A above him. St. John the Baptist is on the right, with the Omicron above him broken at the bottom and their edges turned outward.

Alpha and Omega. The beginning and the end.

Father Luke Klopcic begins the Mass with the sign of the cross in Latin, and then the *Confiteor* references St. Peter and I glance up to the Alpha.

Since Papa's injury, the next prayer has become my most difficult part of the Mass. It's the only prayer in Greek and requires that we respond three times to Father Klopcic's recitation of the same words.

*Kyrie eleison.* Lord have mercy.

"Kyrie eleison," all the congregants except me respond. Instead, I think of my Finnish grandfather who is so smart he knows Greek, and hope he is a bigger person than me.

*Christe eleison.* Christ have mercy. Three times.

*Kyrie eleison.* Lord have mercy, three more times.

The incredibly beautiful painted mural above the pinnacle of the main altar is another thirty feet of concave colors depicting the final judgment. The angels are awakening the dead, no, the sleeping, who are emerging from their resting places and looking up to a risen Jesus, seated on a rainbow. Those on Christ's left are the damned, and can hardly bear to look at Him; on His right are the just, who are eagerly awaiting their reward. Jesus's left arm is raised, as if He's about to make a declaration, yet His eyes are closed.

I often close my own eyes and wonder when I open them, if Jesus will open His too and look straight at me. He's expecting me to forgive the men who caused Papa's injury.

I still can't. Maybe forgiveness is the Omega.

Even if I weren't Catholic, I'm certain I would know Latin very well anyway, because it's required in school. As I think about it, I probably have learned Latin even earlier, for Papa says it's the root of most languages and he knows it better than anyone, although he defers to his Papa having even a greater knowledge, along with Greek, another requirement for thinkers and philosophers. So as the Latin Mass with its Greek references proceeds, we're all right at home, except Mama, who says she's still learning.

The older boys are the altar boys today, since they're more experienced for all the rites of Easter, but I flinch when one of them stumbles several times over the *Sucipiat*. It is clear that he will have more problems with this prayer when he mispronounces the first word, the title of the prayer, and he makes it worse with every long word, stumbling over *sacrificium* and *utilitate*. By the time the four altar boys reach the end, his voice is missing when the rest of them correctly pronounce *totiusque ecclesiae*, then he re-joins them for *suae sanctae*.

I could easily do better.

"Girls will become altar servers in this church when women will be allowed to vote in this country," Mama has chided me in the past. She would have preferred to remain Lutheran, yet I'm sure she prefers to remain in America, in spite of her complaints, because she believes she can change things.

"Only a woman believes such things," she says.

"Only a Finnish woman believes such things," Papa would say in grudging admiration.

"Which is when hoarfrost covers a very warm place," I would chime in, a veiled reference to an adult phrase I'm not allowed to use, but Mama lets me get away with it in this context because it's our private joke.

I chase this thought out of my head for the Consecration, and carefully follow the prayers in my book all the way to Communion. When the usher gets to our pew, the whole row rises and moves to the center aisle. As Heli approaches the aisle, she moves to the middle and backwards a bit, I do the same, Mama still has room to let Papa out of our pew to lead the way to Communion, as he always does, but she takes his arm and they're the only people who approach the communion rail as a couple. They are such a fine couple that they pull it off as if nothing is awry.

I'm sure something is awry, yet I still can't put my finger on it.

As I begin my motion of kneeling at the altar rail, the heel of my shoe catches on the back of my dress and I stand straight again, tuck the back of my dress in with my left hand, then complete a more graceful move to kneel. I know my family has noticed, but I hope others haven't. I don't like bringing attention to myself, especially when it's awkward.

It's only after Mass, when I've forgotten about my mishap at the altar rail, that Erik Mikkola approaches me and says hello. I used to like Erik because he was smart and always came prepared to class at Field School, and was always clean and well-mannered. I never knew where he lived, only that it wasn't Swedetown, and he was always embarrassed and circumspect when I asked him, so I didn't ask anymore. Erik's family is the only other Finnish family who attends St. Joseph's, and Papa says they, too, were originally Finnish Orthodox. I've seen Erik only occasionally since we all left Field School, and I heard that he soon quit school and got a job at the Quincy mine.

"I'm happy to see you again, Emilia" Erik says, smiling but looking a little discomfited.

"It's been a long while since we were in school together. Where have you been?" I ask as I make a mental note to thank Heli for insisting that I brush my hair and wear my only good dress. She even let me borrow her hair ribbon for Easter.

I'm surprised at how Erik has grown and actually turned into a handsome young man, the gangliness and uncoordination of grade school behind us both. "I'm at Quincy now," and I'm sure I hear his voice drop an octave for that pronouncement. "I'm tramming now, but my boss says I've got great potential and I'm learning about blasting and I'll bet I can be a miner in no time." Erik knows as well as I know that Cornish are the only miners, but I haven't the heart to tell him that he has the wrong looks, by far the wrong name, and entirely the wrong nationality to be a miner. There's no way he'll ever pass for Cornish and I also haven't the heart to tell him he'll likely be tramming the rest of his life. "I saw you at Communion. You look wonderful in that dress," he says.

I can feel the blush rise in my cheeks. Heli nudges me from behind, and Papa and Mama, who were talking with the Wiseks from Swedetown, turn their attention to me and Erik.

Mama used to tease me that Erik had a crush on me when we both went to Field School because he often walked me home. And Papa often commented about the Mikkolas by saying they're a good Finnish family, which is the highest compliment.

"I'd, uh maybe like to come over today, if maybe you're home," he stumbles like an unprepared altar boy. "I, uh, have a book for you that I think you'll like, and I've seen you many times and, uh, just didn't have it with me and, so, uh, here you are today on such a fine day and it's a fine book, and maybe, uh, well, you know."

Papa hears poor Erik stammering and comes to his rescue. "We'll be home today. There's school work to be done and clothes to prepare and shoes to dry and shine, but we may have some time by late afternoon," leaving the acceptance to me.

Erik hears a segue and takes it. "Oh, shoes. That's what I noticed about you today, Emilia. Nice shoes. Trammers' soles and heels, but nice shoes."

I feel my shyness subside, and my anger rise even faster. "I'm very busy today, Erik. I'm behind on my school work and I'll be busy all day."

"Oh," is all he can manage, and that's fine with me, as he

looks around for his family and skulks away.

Leading the return home, Papa and Mama are engaged in their own conversation, and I'd rather be included because I know the taunting I'll get from Heli. She doesn't disappoint. "Are you crazy? He's actually a good-looking boy and he has a job already and he thinks he's going places and it's time you thought about what you're going to do when you graduate from school barely more than a year from now."

I'm not sure where to begin with my response, so I just plunge in with the obvious. "He made fun of my shoes. I don't think he intended to, but he did. I had hopes for Erik. I liked him when we were at Field, and the subsequent years have added to it. Sure, he has a job, but he has no future. Worse yet, he doesn't even know it. I want a life when I graduate. I want a future."

"And that would be what?" Heli counters. "You can be a teacher, and you can work in a store, but only if your husband owns it, and you can work in the library at ten cents a week for the rest of your life, if that's what you call *a future*. But that's it. Except on your back at the Michigan House."

"Heli, on Easter Sunday!"

"Mama is right and Papa never says it, though he knows it too: you have your head in the clouds. One of these days, you need to return to earth."

"I don't know exactly what I want, but I know it's out there and I'll think of it. I just need to think."

"You and Papa," Heli concludes.

We wait until the Nelsons return from the Swedish Lutheran Church and we wait until they eat, and just when Heli and I think the kids will be shooed outside, we ask.

With Mama's permission, Heli and I run around to the back stairs and announce our raucous arrival up the stairs before we even knock on the Nelsons' door. Mr. Nelson greets us with a look like he'd rather be doing something else. Heli won't be discouraged.

"Mr. Nelson, we'd like to know if we can, we all can, I mean your kids too, use our window, I mean your window for snow jumping."

All five kids must have heard Heli as well as Mr. Nelson, since they're behind him in a moment. Mr. Nelson looks around at last night's snowfall that added a couple of feet to the already huge piles leaning most of the way up our two-story house. It'll be a short drop from the second-story window to the snow, and last night's snowfall will make for a luxurious landing.

"Yeah, sure" he says with no conviction, but he opens his door farther to invite us in.

We open the window closest to the door, leaving only a few feet of the floor of our old bedrooms to clean up when we're done, and Heli pushes to the front. She's always the first one out and she's so athletic, I don't mind letting her make the first jump because she'll sink in, but not pack it down for me. I've learned to look forward to her first jump, never certain whether it'll be face down, or back down, or a twist or flip in mid-air, or both a twist and a flip that she's named *the Heli flipper-flopper-flooper-flopper*, but I've also learned that it'll always be graceful and she'll sink deep into the snow like a swimmer.

She hesitates. "Please hold my hand, Emilia. It'll be fun together." This doesn't sound like Heli, but with Anders and Per and Johanna shoving from behind, and the two littlest Nelsons waiting behind them, I indulge.

"Okay. Let's see if we can both fit on the sill." With both our feet perched there, I ask: "What'll it be? A flip or a twist or..."

There are several hands on my back, probably several on Heli's as we plunge unexpectedly and haphazardly into the snow.

A good beginning.

We stand up and emerge from the hole in the snow created by our fall, laughing and accusing and vowing revenge.

It's difficult to move out of the way, but that's how the game is played unless you want to get jumped on. So, our hand-holding unbroken by the fall, we trudge toward the stairs to go up and get in line for the next jump.

With so many of us jumping, and the warm weather and the bright sunshine, the snow packs quickly. At the third jump, Heli approaches the sill solo and this feels more customary. The Nelson kids aren't so bad after all, and at least I'll credit them for keeping a neat house. Not as neat as ours. The downstairs, I mean, but not bad for seven people living upstairs.

We brush the snow off our clothes, stamp it off our feet, and then clean the snow off the back steps from the bottom up, stopping at the landing. We clean our clothes more carefully before we go into the apartment, where we pick up all the snow that's there, and then find a mop to complete our clean-up.

The sun sets quickly on Copper Island in March and yet, even with Erik's pull on the day, I'm content to let it go once I've gone over my school work one more time to ensure my preparation for tomorrow's tests. I even remembered to thank Heli for reminding me about the importance of some special preparation for Easter Mass. I should be tired, but I'm not. Heli's asleep and this is probably a good time to grapple with the questions I can't answer out loud. *What will I do for a future I can't even define? Is Heli right about the limited options? If so, why bother?* Papa and Mama should have had sons who could do more than just dream about being altar boys, and actually had a chance, if they were the right nationality, of becoming businessmen and demolition experts.

"What's going on with that thing called Workingmen's Compensation?" Mama asks from their bedroom as a welcome interruption to my thoughts.

"There's seems to be some confusion over the date of my

injury," Papa answers.

"Confusion? If there's any confusion, I'll be glad to clarify it for them. There's no confusion in my mind and no excuse for any confusion in theirs."

"And you say that I talk too loudly. You should hear yourself when you become irate."

"I'm sorry, Henrik. It's not you. It's Calumet and Hecla. It's a malicious bill collector at that dreadful hospital in Laurium. It's a doctor who offers hope, but no treatment until we're caught up with the bills. It's fear of a strike and fear of not striking because this company won't understand anything else."

"Karhu-Jussi says the men are pressing him to press me to take a stand. He says they'll follow me, as they always have when I do the right thing. But what's the right thing? I know what it is for the men, but it's not the same thing for my family. I've learned some cruel lessons. I should have learned very well when Lukas promised to not only hire me, but to help buy our house for us with the money my Papa had saved all his life to give me..." Papa pauses. Not for emphasis, as is sometimes his trait, but because I know this is special to him. "'To give us freedom,' my Papa said. That was important to him and it's important to me now that I've tasted it. Then, as you know, Kerttu, Lukas bought the house himself, sold it to us at a profit, then turned around and made another profit promising to help me change our Suomen markka into dollars. I was unprepared for this kind of duplicity, this greed, this ... this ... savage capitalism."

"That's a good description, Henrik, though our Indians may be offended by it."

"But *savage capitalism* is only part of it. I've seen the type of vengeance this company has wreaked every day on men for petty transgressions. Then when Lukas referred to me by that name and ordered me to check on the black powder ... that ... that ..." Papa stops. I can hear him choke down his breath, wait awhile, then take a deep one. "Minä rakastan sinua, Kerttu."

"And I love you, Henrik.  Sleep well."

I've heard many of my parents' stories, often told to me and Heli with humor and affection, and sometimes even with a lighthearted admonition to learn something from them.

I've never heard these, and I wish I hadn't.

# III

## June 1

Uncle Bear and Aunt Iiris must be some of the best people in the whole world.

I love going to their home in Eagle River, for it combines many of my favorite things – a walk into Red Jacket with my family, a train ride, the quiet of their countryside home, a wonderful view of what Papa describes as the most beautiful body of water in the world and, of course, waking up Uncle Bear.

It's not really Uncle Bear, just his namesakes, and we don't really wake them up because they've likely been moving about for a few weeks now, but it's now safe to explore their dens, and Papa says this may be the first time that Heli and I can do that by ourselves.

We get off the train in downtown Eagle River, and then re-cross the river on foot, the river we've just crossed as the train pulled into town, and take the road southwest that parallels Lake Superior. It's a twenty-minute walk to Uncle Bear's and Aunt Iiris's house, and with Mama's arm tucked near Papa's vest and the talking and laughing between them, I can tell that Papa is not counting steps.

As I've lately deduced, his eyesight must be improving. I've not as often seen that odd habit of moving his head to each side, then shaking it to center like he's trying to physically dislodge a thought.

The earliest freighters of the season are moving again on the liquid horizon and I sight them first by their smoke, then their sheer size and length as they ply the treacherously beautiful Lake Superior. Douglass Houghton, the famous geologist that the small town a few miles to our south is named after, was drowned right here when he ignored what he deemed to be a trifling October storm many years ago. *The Inland Seas*, I've read of the Great Lakes, and a day like today walking near Eagle River, Michigan makes me appreciate that I'm gazing upon the greatest of them.

The freighters we're seeing in the northwest are the few that are headed around the tip of the Keweenaw Peninsula to Duluth, and will stop here again to pick up copper on their way back. They're dropping off food and supplies and new machines that are too massive to be transported by train, and will return with a whole winter's worth of copper ingots.

I've come to know Uncle Bear's and Aunt Iiris's home as a farm because they have so much land around them. Like our home, Uncle Bear says even the land under his house is owned by the mine – Cliff's, he says, like C&H, who owns ours. It looks like a farm to me because there are no neighbors in sight, and Uncle Bear says he can scavenge for wood to support his carpentry hobby, and even allow a few animals to graze on the land that only structurally supports the house, and refuses to support good crops, in spite of Uncle Bear's efforts. The goats don't venture far in their yard, and neither do the chickens, which Heli and I love to round up and put into their tiny coop at night so the foxes in the area won't take them for their suppers.

Everything about Aunt Iiris is sculpted except her light golden hair. She has a demure nose that separates fawn's eyes, trailing off the edge to a full mouth whose lips reflect the color of seasons. Her chin, unlike the small, shallow square of most of my kinswomen, is round and dimpled in the center, setting off a face that is as finely crafted as the rest of her. Her mama must have named her only after Aunt

Iiris first opened her eyes to reveal a blue that is light as Superior is dark.

She seems hardly a physical match for Uncle Bear, until she surreptitiously sneaks behind me as we enter their home to wrap her arms around my ribs and lift me off the ground so Uncle Bear has clear access to my stomach for a round of tickling that always surprises me in both its intensity and gentleness. Like me, Heli knows their ploy by now, but still acts surprised when Uncle Bear moves behind her and lifts Heli up in the same fashion as me, so Aunt Iiris can tickle her in the same way.

Aunt Iiris adds her signature of placing her outstretched arms on our shoulders – even Papa and Mama – then looking straight into our eyes as she warmly and eloquently pronounces the word "tervetuloa."

This is their way of welcoming us into a home that needs children and has none. Heli and I have talked often of how wonderful it would be to have *cousins* and, better yet, how much Uncle Bear and Aunt Iiris deserve them, but it appears not to be.

"True friendship is better than a bunch of undeserving relatives," I've heard Uncle Bear tell Papa by way of explaining how close our families are, even though we're not related.

Uncle Bear and Aunt Iiris were some of the first people Papa and Mama met here in the Copper Country. It was Uncle Bear who encouraged Papa to join Calumet and Hecla, since Uncle Bear was already employed there right after the Cliffs Mine in Eagle River closed its shafts for good when the copper petered out, after making fortunes for the owners. He still teases Papa about the way it all unfolded.

"I said to your Papa: 'Go and tell them you will work hard for them, and don't say anything more,' because I already knew your Papa's propensity for teaching, even when no one wants to learn. 'Did you get the job?' I asked him the next day. 'No,' your Papa answered, disappointed. 'What did you tell them?' I asked. He said he told Lukas: 'I can help with translating many of your languages because I know Latin.' So I suggested a second time: 'Go and tell them you will work hard for them, and don't say anything more,' and on the second day I asked, 'Did you get the job?' and he said 'No,' and he was devastated. 'What did you tell them this time?' I asked your Papa, though I was afraid of his answer. 'That I have been studying copper mining and I will do everything I can to assist in the recovery of your precious metal.' So I told your Papa a final time: 'Go and tell them you will work hard for them, and if you must say more, tell them you're a Finn. That's all they need to know.' He went to them, told them he was a Finn, and started that very day as a trammer."

Whenever Papa hears the story again, which is often because Uncle Bear loves to tell it, Papa defends his three efforts to work at Calumet and Hecla by explaining that he thinks any employer should ask what a prospective employee knows, and what skills he can bring to the job, and what abilities he has that he can apply to any job to make it easier or smarter or more productive or safer. "But all they want is your back. Your mind is never invited, and your opinion is never welcome," Papa says he now knows.

Uncle Bear puts his arm around Papa and leads him back outside, where "I'll force this city man to breathe good country air," he exclaims. We Finns have a reputation for being reserved and even aloof, yet I know that it's because we're respectful of one another, and especially respectful of our privacy. So the arm around my father is unlike both Papa and Uncle Bear, and it seems like he is steering Papa into the yard. "My home reminds me of Lapland, and his of Helsinki, so we've both landed where we belong, but I've the better of the lot," Uncle Bear says as he directs Papa to his shed and begins explaining his current woodworking project, while Mama and Aunt Iiris busy themselves in the kitchen, so Heli and I have our opening.

"Mama, can we go wake up the bears?" I offer, beating

Heli to the inevitable question. Like Papa, she was born in Helsinki and has never tacitly approved of our spring rite, but understands the importance of it.

"Ask your father and your Uncle Bear," she defers.

Outside near the shed, Uncle Bear and Papa know what to expect, and Heli and I wait respectfully for our opening.

Like a bust of a finely fashioned woman, Uncle Bear's shed features two window openings in the front so you can see inside her and she can look out, an awning in the front to form her nose, neat cedar shingles for her perfectly plaited hair, which streams down along the sides of her head in long wooden planks tucked under her eaves. Her shoulders are shaped by the long tree trunks stacked higher near the sides of the shed and falling away into the woods surrounding it. From the front, you can't see the sauna attached to the back and you can't see the little chimney poking through its roof, which would ruin the effect of my imaginary bust. I wonder to myself if Uncle Bear has planned it this way, or if it's just my sometimes too-vivid imagination.

Inside, there are saws and hammers and clamps and a large framing square and assorted tools hanging on every square inch of one wall, with wood organized by size and stacked on top of old and irregular-sized rotting wood lying on the ground. Piled above the ceiling joists are thin planks probably left over from his floor in the house, for you can see the tongues on one side, the grooves on the other side of the pieces with large knots that didn't pass Uncle Bear's inspection for use in a house, so he keeps them for another project.

"What are you working on now?" Heli wonders aloud to Uncle Bear as she pokes her head inside his shed and spots a few pieces of wood lying haphazardly over saw horses that take up the last remaining space. It occurs to me that not just every square inch, indeed, every cubic inch of space is accounted for in Uncle Bear's shed.

"I'm not sure yet," he responds. "I have some ideas, always ideas, and I've yet to work them out. Don't worry, Heli,

I'll find something to keep me busy."

"Bears are always busy," I hear Papa introduce a syllogism. "Karhu means Bear. Karhu *is a bear*," he clarifies. "Uncle Bear is always busy." Papa pauses at his conclusion, then thinks to add "when he can stay away from the honey," and laughs as he nods toward Aunt Iiris in the house.

The ambient air temperature is warmer this near Superior in the fall, but it's cooler here in the late-spring, and Uncle Bear guides Papa inside the shed when a gust of spring air that has carried over the water swirls around us.

"Today would be a wonderful day for a sauna, were it not for Sunday," Uncle Bear says. "Henrik, the next time you're here on a Saturday, I'll prepare a *savusauna*, and we'll enjoy it the better part of the day."

"I'll count on it, and I look forward to our smoke sauna" Papa says. "Take a bull by the horns and man by his words," he laughs at the Finnish proverb we've heard many times. "For today, though, I have some ideas for your garden. The frost danger is nearly past, and we can begin with the root vegetables. I'll enjoy getting my hands in the soil."

This is our opening. "Papa, can we wake up the bears?"

"I'm not sure I can join you this year, Emilia." It's only now that I realize I had not meant to include Papa and Uncle Bear when I said "we" so I'm glad he interprets "we" as Heli and me only, yet I believe I'm also hearing a "no" coming. "We'll be eating soon and there may not be enough time and..."

"Oh, let them go by themselves, Henrik." Turning to me and Heli, he asks, "You're what, Emilia, 12 already? And Heli, that means you're eight. Henrik, they're both old enough to get into trouble by themselves."

"Sixteen. Last January," I correct him, though I know Uncle Bear knows because he stopped over to our home after work on my birthday and nearly missed the last train back to Eagle River.

"Twelve, soon to be 13," Heli adds, though not with her

usual conviction.

"Be back by four o'clock," Papa states firmly. "We must leave enough time for supper with your Uncle Bear and Aunt Iiris, and time to walk back into Eagle River and catch the six o'clock and get home, and time to review your school work."

Heli and I begin walking quickly, and only slow to our normal pace when Uncle Bear's and Aunt Iiris's home has faded into the distance behind us, and the next bend in the road aligns us closer to Superior with it blue vastness dwarfing the huge freighters in the distance.

"You're already turning dark, just like Papa," Heli interjects, and then vigorously runs her hands over her arms to remind me how she pesters me about my dark summer skin during our charades. I refuse to take the bait.

"Last one there is a rotten egg," as I lead the charge toward another grown-up experience.

It's not far to the spot near the shore where we've found as many as three bear dens in the face of the dirt cliff carved out of the place where the land nestles near Superior, then drops off a good ten feet before coming to rest on a massive outcropping of red rock next to the water. The fat, thick rock stretches along the shore for about a half-mile here, declining gently from the land to the water over the course of 30 or so feet. It's like the rock boiled up under the land and bundled itself into one massive red structure when the lake refused to admit it, and ordered it to stay on the shore instead of a sandy beach.

We walk quietly from the road toward the water, and I'm thinking that our stealthy approach is just like the way Uncle Bear taught us, but Heli's furtive look betrays something else I can't identify. I'm almost certain we're in the right spot as we near the edge of the land, and both Heli and I slow for the sudden drop onto the red rock. We carefully traverse our descent to the rock by sliding on our backsides down the drop-off and, when our footing is secure, I stand up and look for the crevice. I spot it to the east and we walk carefully over the slippery lichen, then up the step carved out of the hardness to the peak. Just in front is our crevice, a crack in the red rock that begins only a few feet wide at the land and widens toward the water to about ten feet, creating a 20-foot deep chasm.

It's as if God looked at this half-mile of rock forming the beach and decided it would make a great place for bear dens, but it needed easier access to the water, so He picked it up and split it into two pieces over His knee, then set them back down again a few feet apart so the bears could move easily from their dens down through the crevice to go fishing in Superior.

With our backs now to the lake and looking up from the rock near the chasm, we can see at least two bear dens in the face of the drop-off. Knowing that she's expected to be the first to enter, Heli still chooses the den farthest away and haltingly leads me toward it. Something is amiss, but I still can't define it. She's way too quiet. She drops to her knees and peers inside.

"No, Meewa." The blood in me stops first, then every-thing else. I haven't heard Heli's reference to me as "Meewa" since I started school. It's my name she couldn't pronounce as a baby, dropping the first syllable and putting a "w" in the place of a rolling "ilia" that she couldn't wrap her baby's tongue around. Something is wrong. Something is very wrong and Heli's relapse to my baby name immediately unnerves me. "I can't," she says simply and emphatically, then grabs my hand. "Please, Meewa. Please don't make me."

I look to the bear den and understand why, because my mind is now in the same place.

News of a mine accident travels fast on Copper Island. Until we arrive at the shaft entrance, no one is sure who is injured or how many or how badly. A collapse most certainly means broken bones. Errant explosions are sure to cause concussion. Air blasts are the most mysterious and most deadly, as I've learned that they literally shook the Minesota mine out of existence. If bad enough, they all mean death. I've seen a good portion of our neighborhood empty as the words "Quincy Number Five" spread like disease from house to house. I've joined most of our neighborhood as we ran as fast as horses when "C&H Number Two" was announced.

On December 7 last year, near the end of Papa's Saturday shift, Mama and me and Heli and many throughout our neighborhood and more, stood at the entrance to Shaft Number Two waiting for word.

As usual, it came in spurts.

An explosion. Not good.

Black Powder. That's not making sense because they've been using nitro for years.

One man down. That, too, is mysterious. What's taking them so long?

We crush in toward where the man engine is spewing out the workers. Only when there's been an accident can anyone other than the workers get so close to the shaft opening, and I'm sure that C&H management would prefer that we not be so close even now, but I'm also sure that they know we won't be denied.

A set of benches rise from the shaft, powered by the man engine. Men step out and are greeted by wives and children.

Another set of benches surfaces. Then another. The crowd of waiting family members thins.

Another set, and Papa isn't there either.

Another set, and Mama recognizes some of the men, who turn their heads when they see her.

The man engine re-starts slowly, and a complete set of empty benches pass through the opening.

The man engine continues, and then into view comes a stretcher laying over some benches, with Uncle Bear holding both lead handles, two other trammers holding onto the two trailing stretcher handles.

We know who lies on the stretcher.

Heli's sobs are convulsing her whole body as she squeezes my hands and draws them to her face, trying to wipe away her tears without letting go of my hands. "I know ... I know... but I just can't ..." she begins, so I squeeze her hands back to indicate that she should not talk for a while, and mustn't try until we both get hold of ourselves, for I am crying also.

*Waking up the bears* every year has meant finding the dens and crawling inside and gathering what we can of the black bristles or small tufts of fur left there, while deeply inhaling the remaining scent of their months-long naps. This year's excursion has caromed off into another meaning altogether.

"It's a bear den, not a mine shaft," I try to reassure Heli after we are both composed. "It can't hurt us."

Heli hesitates, takes a breath and lets it out slowly. "I'm not so sure."

We back away from the bear den and onto the red rock, turn around and look out to the lake. We wordlessly sit on the rock. The sun is coming around the point to our left and the seagulls are the only sounds soon lost to Superior.

It happens again.

When Heli and I climbed the Swedetown water tower a few years ago and I took in the most beautiful sight I've ever seen in my life, I knew that I could see superior. Not just see Lake Superior. See superior.

Now, as the water laps not onto a sand beach, but against the rock and into its crevice toward the bear dens, I hear it. I hear her unfurl just before she caresses the rock. I hear her quiet in the distance, her whisper here on the shore. I imagine her strength against those who did not know her, or who did not listen. I am experiencing her tenderness offered to us who do. I am beginning to understand why second reference to a body of water is always referred to as *she*, and I am hearing her without trying.

This time, I hear superior.

Heli releases my hand only after she rises from the privy and opens the door for a dash back to our house undeserving of this fine early-June weather.

It's been nearly a perfect weekend, what with Decoration Day parades and school is almost out for the summer and our annual trek to Eagle River. I would have changed our exploration of the bear dens, if I could, but I wouldn't have traded hearing Superior for it. I don't want to be alone, but I allow the outhouse silence to enshroud me for a moment of thought before heading back to the house myself. As I open the door, I'm startled by Mr. Nelson, who is standing only a few feet from the privy.

It has taken me awhile to get used to him being at our house, after seeing him all the time at the hospital when Papa was there. That's the first time I met Mr. Nelson, weighted down by a pouch of tools whose contents he constantly wrestled inexpertly. "Handyman," he announced to me proudly one day when I asked what he was doing to Papa's bed, and I was still horrified with Papa's lack of movement. He seemed so ill-fitted for the tools that I came to think they only served to weigh him down and force his already small physical frame closer to the ground. He was always adjusting Papa's bed when I was there and it didn't seem like it needed more adjusting and even seemed like Mr. Nelson broke it more often than he fixed it. "Job security," he confided in me once with a wink.

We didn't talk often, for I never became comfortable with his Napoleonic stature and his Quixotic opinion of himself, but I did tell him about the work Uncle Bear's been doing on our house, and he said he knew someone who might rent our upstairs.

"Eh, Emilia. Didn't mean to scare you. I have something for you," and when he reaches into his left front pocket, I'm not sure what to think, but if it's anything other than a wrench, I'm sure I'm not going to like it. "June rent," he says, and this, too, confuses me. He hands me three, one-dollar bills and, knowing I still need clarification, he continues. "I don't like being late with the rent money. Give this to your Papa for me. And here's something special for you." He reaches into his right front pocket, fumbles around for an uncomfortable moment, takes out his hand, grabs my right hand with his left, and presses a quarter into it. Then he steps back and winks at me. "This is for you. For working so hard to help your Papa, who needs much help these days, and for ... being a good student and for ... all you do around here. Good night. I know I can trust you."

I walk slowly to our house and straight to Mama, who manages the money in our family and will be the one to go to the bank tomorrow. I don't tell her about the quarter. I have an ill feeling about the money, the way Mr. Nelson appeared in the dark, the way he groped in his pocket for it.

Lying too wide awake later, I try to plan.

Ten cents a week from my work in the library had gone to Mama all the time Papa was in the hospital. By the extensive calculations Mama makes nearly daily, I know that our family has many expenses, but Mama said I should keep my ten cents a week when Papa returned to work. Heli and I have enjoyed the candy I've bought, but maybe it's time to start my own account, to save like I know Mama and Papa do. Save where? If this is to be the secret that Mr. Nelson says he can trust me with, where shall I put the money? The money that feels unearned, dirty.

The heavy corded rug that Mama has made out of rags, and added to as she's accumulated more rags since taking in laundry, now covers most of the sitting room floor. I locate my dress by feeling for it in the dark, find the pocket that contains more money than I've ever had at once, and take out the quarter. I can tell by her breathing that Heli is sleeping soundly, and neither Mama nor Papa has made a sound for a long time. Everyone is sleeping except me.

Lifting the rag rug end, I slip the quarter deep under the rug and memorize its place in the dark.

"No!" Papa states suddenly and loudly and emphatically.

How can he know what I'm doing?

"Henrik?" Mama whispers softly and, when there's no reply after a few moments, I can hear her turn over in their bed.

With Mama's quiet interjection, I now realize Papa is unaware of what I am doing. He is only restless, dreaming of things I cannot see, yet I hear from him throughout our nights with an uneasy regularity. I hear since he came home from the hospital his fitful monologues rising up from his sleep against an unseen nemesis. I want to hold him as I did before, when he lay in the hospital. I want to make it better for him.

"I'm not a..." he says as if trying to start a sentence, though it sounds strangely demanding. He has returned to his dream. "I'm not a... You will not..."

Mama must be fully awake now too.

Papa has not gone into Shaft Number Two since December 7. He has returned to work above ground among the French and the injured, at the place near Number Two where they form pulleys and gears and hasps and machined screws that are enormous in size, substantial in strength. The place, too, where they make brooms.

But the haunting that Papa is experiencing in his sleep is affixed somewhere in the shaft, somewhere within the drifts and winzes and overhead stoping of a trammer's bad dreams. I can tell that.

"Don't send in the fin ... the fin" Papa slurs in his sleep. "The finger!" I think I hear him shout.

*"The finger?"* I think to myself, and I want to run to his bedside and comfort my Papa who apparently has someone's accusing finger pointed at him.

"Henrik, Henrik," Mama is cooing softly as I hear her throw off the blankets and turn in their bed to push him awake. "You're dreaming again. You're having a bad dream. Henrik?"

I hear the whole bed move suddenly and it matters not that it is dark, for I am sure that I can see Papa sitting bolt upright.

After a hesitation when Mama again whispers "Henrik?" I hear Papa release his breath in quiet resignation. "You were dreaming. It was a bad dream. Go to sleep again. This time, dream beautifully. Kauniita unelmia, Henrik. And Minä rakastan sinua."

"I love you, Kerttu."

Heli wriggles in the dark, and I fall into a fitful sleep.

# IV

# *July 5*

The only times the mines take a break are on Christmas Day and on Independence Day, opposite ends of the calendar that both seem a fitting time for a respite. Christmas will be special this year, for Papa is back to work and will be home. The day after Independence Day means Heli's birthday and the circus.

Already a busy and crowded place, the train depot acquires an even livelier personality when the cars unload with strange-looking animals and people so colorful and intriguing, you know they belong to the circus. Here in Swedetown, we get a sneak peek when the circus first arrives, and we run to watch the train cars as they pass down the hill beneath us and through the covered area of Tunnel Street, filled with their eccentric and curious contents.

Unloading at the depot on Oak and Ninth, the circus and its entourage start a line that takes minutes to form and hours to culminate straight east for just a few blocks to the only nearby vacant piece of land large enough to accommodate it. Of course, it won't cross the main road into Laurium, for those snoots surely won't allow commoners and plebeians among them. If they could, they would even stop the smell of the elephant dung from reaching them.

Heli and I hurried through the laundry yesterday so she and I and Papa and Mama could all watch the Independence

Day parades together. Today being Saturday, Papa must go to work, and we've already harangued both our parents to permit me and Heli to take Papa to work, and then go to the circus. Sixteen is magical, for I feel all the energy that has been going into growing my body and my feet is done, and now it's helping me grow by letting me try new things.

This also means I'm done with the pony rides. I've gone on those every year I can remember, and it's time I find a big girl, no, a young woman thing to do. The quarter from Mr. Nelson, along with thirty cents I've saved from working at the library, will be plenty to make this the best circus ever for Heli and me. I endure a pony ride for Heli, since it's only a nickel and, after all, it's her birthday.

The big tent in the center beckons me and the main entrance is tended by a man who smiles and collects fifteen cents from each person who enters. Heli and I can see the big show and have a dime apiece left for candy.

It looks like the dark man next to him is guarding him. His eyes never stop, casting knowing glances at everyone who passes, resting for only a second on each person who enters, then scanning left, right, high, low for what I'm guessing would be signs of a thief or some other miscreant.

I could save him the trouble. I've heard of gambling and theft going on outside of Swedetown, but never for long before Calumet and Hecla or Sheriff Cruse catch up with it, usually C&H first, and the culprit is run out of town and never heard from again. I've seen the dark man before. He must travel with the circus because I've never seen him around here except when the circus is in town, and he is not to be missed, having the darkest skin I've ever seen.

The man who is collecting the money takes it from me, and offers a quick smile to each of us, and I glance to the dark man, who lights up with a warm, genuine beam as I pass.

The big tent is even more impressive from the inside, with long ropes hanging from the ceiling and supporting wooden bars high above the ground. The show begins with men and women in perfectly white body suits that look like long underwear, except more elaborate, riding around the center ring on perfectly white horses, not the slack, puny, dirty brown one like Heli was riding. The riders place their hands on the saddle horns and in one swift motion hoist themselves up and put their feet on the small English saddles, riding standing up. Heli and I quickly show how impressed we are by clapping, but not ahead of the rest of the crowd, who obviously know good horsemanship. The horse show continues, yet I'm most curious about the wooden bars hanging from the ceiling. I appreciate the horses, and both Heli and I laugh at the next show – the gaily dressed and painted clowns – but my eyes are still drawn to the ceiling.

The man behind me says those are *trapeze*, and I am astonished to watch the flips, twirls, pumps, somersaults and catches all in mid-air. Heli is mesmerized. We hold our breaths as the drums roll and the lady pumps her legs to propel her toward a man standing high up on an opposite pole. After she reaches the peak of her arc, she returns toward her own pole, and pumps again, this time harder as the man takes off from his opposite pole toward her, but it doesn't look like he'll reach her in time. As she hits the peak of this arc, she's higher in the air than the man, lets go of her bar and flips twice before descending into the man's hands, and they grasp one another by the wrists.

When the long, loud applause finally subsides, Heli turns to me and says, "That's it! At least *I* know what *I'm* going to do when *I* grow up!" On the way out, Heli spies a friend and is gone with "I'll catch up to you later" before I have a chance to object. I've already told her we'll spend the last of our money on candy, so I know she won't go far.

"Lawdy, gull, that be the dahkest skin ahs evah seen in these heah pahts."

I can understand the Romance Languages, especially Italian and French, pretty well. The Uralic languages –

Finnish and Swedish and Danish – are easy, of course. I can translate a few of the Slavic phrases, and can even distinguish between Polish and Slovenian and Croatian and Serbian. Anyone can identify German. There's some English in what the man with the darting eyes and gleaming smile is saying to me, but it's not Cornish and it's not Irish. It's some other dialect I don't recognize, and I can't put it together enough to verbally respond to his comment and kind smile, so I just smile back.

He ambles up to me. "Yooz lahke da show?" I'm still confused. "Enjoy the show?" he says slowly, purposefully articulating the short phrase.

"Oh yes, the horses are beautiful and the clowns are very funny. The people on the trapeze," I, too, slow my speech to articulate that new word, "are astonishing."

"Lawdy, gull, yooz be about the purtiest ahs evah seen. And yo skin be neah dahk as mine."

I'm sure I'm blushing, the flourish to my cheeks slowed by the time it takes me to translate his vaguely familiar language with the foreign dialect. "Thank you," I respond after completing the translation in my mind. "My Papa has skin that gets dark in the summer too. He says he was teased for it as a child and I can expect the same. My sister never misses a chance. I've never liked it because most of my Finnish kinsmen are light. I even tried to change it once."

The dark man's brown eyes turn soft. "Could yooz hep me, gull? Ahs sho could use some watuh. Yooz mind, gull?" and the dark man waits for me to translate.

"Water, sir?" I ask to ensure I've heard correctly, and also because it's a peculiar request.

"Suh? Yooz call me suh? Ahs a niggah. Ahs cain't touch yo fountain and yooz call me suh?"

I think I've gotten the key to his dialect and I think I've understood him, but if understanding this man is difficult, making sense of him now is near impossible. "Niggah, sir?" I ask, not certain I'm pronouncing the word the same as he.

"What's a niggah?"

The dark man looks at me quizzically, tilts his head, and appears to be translating, much as I have been perplexed by him. "Nig-ger," he states phonetically and deliberately.

"Oh, *niger* right? That means *black* in Latin. So you're dark-skinned. You're black. What does that have to do with not touching the fountain?"

The dark man bursts out laughing and others are looking at us and he notices too, so he submerges his laughter in the pool of his warm brown eyes. "Ahs sho could use some watuh, miss. And ahs be much obliged if yooz'd git it fo me." His warm smile, the way his brown eyes soften, and his genuine laugh transcend the words and speak my own language. I walk over to the fountain, take a quart jar sitting near the base, rinse it and fill it to the brim with water. I'm careful to not spill any as I return and hand it to him.

"Thank ye, miz," he tells me, and he motions for me to join him as he sits first on the grass. We are behind the podium that served as the ticket-taking spot where Heli and I entered, just outside the big tent, but out of the way of the criss-crossing paths of mothers and children and men in their *goin'-to-meetin'* clothes, their public finery. His mannerisms and this location tell me it's safe to be sitting alone with this dark, mysterious man from the circus.

"Jaspah, dey calls me," as I take his already outstretched hand in mine and notice the calluses of one who has worked even harder than Papa and Uncle Bear his whole life.

"I'm very pleased to meet you, Mr. Jasper. My name is Emilia."

"Wha choo got 'gainst yo own skin?" he asks me as I tuck my feet in under my long dress.

"Huh?" I reply, understanding what he's saying but unable to place it in our conversation.

"Yooz sed yooz don't lahk yo own skin."

I laugh, for it was four years ago when I tried to change my skin, and it's only been the subsequent passage of a quarter of my life that's enabled me to now laugh about it. "I was young," I say, and his immediate guffaw tells me that was probably the wrong way to start a sentence with an adult twice my age. I try again. "Mama tells me I was just being foolish and impulsive. I tend to be that way. Impulsive, I mean." I don't want to tell him the details, for though time has passed, I'm still embarrassed over it as I think about it while talking to an adult. "I've been teased my whole life about getting dark skin during the summer. Maybe you can understand that. For a while, I thought it would keep getting darker until it was as dark as yours, but every winter it fades, then I look just like everyone else. Now, I've just gotten used to it, I guess."

"Miz, yo special," and as he says this, I wonder how he can do that – make his eyes laugh along with his whole face. "Lemme tell yooz sumpin. Fust, this'n here..." and he rubs his hands on the backs of his arms, like Heli does when she teases me, "...don git no lahter in dee wintuh. Next, be proud o' who yooz is. Ahs understan how yooz was wantin' to change it, 'cause ahs be wantin' to do the same oncet. One day, ahs lookit aroun' and realize ahs special. Miz, in jes a speck o'time, ahs knows yooz special. Be proud o'it. 'Cause yooz purty. No, yooz bootiful," he mispronounces phonetically, but I get it.

"Why thank you sir. Thank you very much," I tell him as I spot Heli in the distance, looking around at the faces of standing people, trying to find me. "I'm pleased to have met you, Mr. Jasper," and I try to match my eyes as he does to the earnestness in my voice, as I rise to leave.

"Pleased to have met yooz, Miz Ameelia" he says carefully and reasonably correctly, at least in my English. "An the watuh, miz ... obliged, miz ... much obliged," he tells me after I've already translated it in his eyes.

Midsummer has just passed and the light still lingers well past nine o'clock. Heli yawns and, our day now nearly complete after we've spent the last hour weeding our meager vegetable garden in the cool of the evening, she heads to the privy. She uses it by herself in waning daylight, and then goes inside our house.

I remain knelt near the row of rutabagas, the root vege-tables being the only crops that are growing well in this rocky, sandy soil warmed briefly by short summers. The light is diminishing quickly now, and I'm holding onto its final dusky effort. I hear the upper back door opening, and look up to see Mr. Nelson walk down the steps and over to the garden.

"Tell your Papa I'm sorry I'm late with the July rent." I'm still kneeling on the ground, resting my body on the back of my legs, and feeling vulnerable. "But you will cover for me, eh?" He fishes for the bills in his left pocket, withdraws and gives them to me. His right hand is still in his other front pocket and he leaves it there, moving it to and fro. "You're a good girl, Emilia. And a smart one. And you know how to keep a secret, eh?" I remain silent. He is frightening me again with his measured words and lurid motions. "This is for you," he finally says while taking his right hand out of his front pocket. I have the three, one-dollar bills in both my hands, resting in my lap. I leave them there. He bends over and takes my right hand and I am forced to unclasp it from my left to hold the bills, then raises my right hand up, brushes my hand against his crotch on the way, and places a quarter in it.

I hear steps from inside our house, marching from the back to the front. I hear our front door open and someone is hurrying around the side toward us. It is Mama and I am first relieved to see her, and then mortified from what she may have seen through the back window.

"What's this Mikael?" she demands in the voice she last used when she found the porcelain vase we cracked when Heli and I accidentally fell against it while tidying up our bed clothes in the sitting room.

"This?  Oh, the rent money, and I've just given it to Emilia to bring to Henrik," Mr. Nelson says in his attempt to exclude Mama.  Still kneeling, I show Mama the three, one-dollar bills in my left hand, the quarter in my right.

"Rent is three dollars," Mama states flatly.

"Certainly, Kerttu.  But I am late with the payment, so I added a quarter and asked Emilia to also bring that to Henrik."

Mr. Nelson does not know how to read Mama, but I do.  He discounted her once and she let it go.  She will not be broomed aside again.

"Mikael, our house is for rent.  My family is not for sale." He turns away from Mama's glare and stops when his eyes reach the garden, holding his gaze there like Lot's wife. "Henceforth, you will deal directly with me or Henrik, and you will leave my children out of it..."  Mama pauses while Mr. Nelson continues to stare at the garden, refusing to face her, "...or you will be picking your belongings off Ridge Street and looking for another apartment."  She reaches her hand toward me and, words unspoken, I give her the quarter. She turns toward the now set sun, away from the school and toward the powder house, and lets the quarter fly into the weeds.  "Emilia," she turns to me with a voice that melts into a vessel containing a lesson I know I need to learn, "it's time we talked."

Heli is lying down, probably already asleep when Mama and I finish our talk whose contents and directions I shall never forget.  While Mama stops in the kitchen to pump water for a drink, and Papa is moving the kitchen chairs but a few inches to confirm that they're near the table and out of everyone's way, I continue into the sitting room, step around Heli, and get myself ready for sleep.  I place the comforter down and put on my sleeping shirt.  Heli and I both use Papa's old work shirts for sleeping and this has become my favorite one for summer because it's so worn and light.  I return to my place beside Heli, pulling the summer blanket – an only slightly worn sheet – up to my chin.

My sleep is light and brief most of the time. Tonight, I know it will be.

Like a new wound, the conversation with Mama is too fresh and sensitive and fraught with too many meanings I've yet to learn. And I find when I've a very difficult thing to learn from school, like five pages of epic Latin poetry, that it's best if I give it some time after I first assimilate it. Besides, I should have known better. I still have so much to learn about adult ways. I make a vow to myself to always try to look straight into a man's eyes before trusting him.

"The windows to the soul," Papa told me long ago with a prescience I have only discovered today.

I want to take the bleach out again and clean the darkness off me, as I tried once when I was 12. It was a week before school. Summer was almost over, and if I had just left it alone, my skin would have returned to its normal lighter shade. Instead, I snuck out of the basement with Mama's bottle of bleach stuck into a pillow case with my swimming clothes, and headed down the hill straight to the Swedetown Pond. It was right after supper so most of the kids were still home, but I nonetheless had to find a private spot in the brush, several feet away from the pond. I took the bleach out of the pillow case and lay it down. Knowing that Mama is careful about adding bleach to our wash to prevent white spots or damage to the fabric, I laid my swimming clothes a few feet from the bleach bottle. I took my dress off and tossed it on the other side of my swimming clothes and sat down naked. Wary at first, I poured some bleach into my left hand and rubbed my hands together, keeping them away from my body as the bleach dripped onto the ground. I turned them palms up, palms down, up and down while keenly observing them for a change, poised to walk to the water and plunge them in when they reached the desired shade.

No change.

I repeated the stratagem, rubbing my hands together as I started feeling a strange, gummy sensation in them. Mama is right, I am impulsive, for I remember then standing up with the bleach bottle in my right hand and pouring the pungent liquid over my left arm, changing hands to pour it over my right arm and, careful to not let it touch my privates, I watched the bleach rivulets run down my body in smug satisfaction, then I rubbed it into my legs. I stood there, naked and bleached, righteous in my beliefs.

First my hands started burning. My arms felt like they were afire. The lines down my legs were the only part of my legs I could feel when I realized I had forgotten my face. Leaning the bottle over with my feet so the liquid gushed into my cupped hands, I closed my eyes and splashed it onto my face with abandon.

That did it. With my eyes closed, my eyelids felt like they were ablaze, but I was afraid to open them.

Wondering where I was, and figuring I was at Swede-town Pond, Heli said I looked like a drunken madam as I zigzagged toward the water and found it only after tripping, rolling in the dirt, then getting up and spitting saliva and the *Our Father* in both English and Latin. She said I got lucky by entering from the shore to the water in a little deeper spot. I was surprised to open my eyes after several minutes and be able to see, for the pain from my eyelids was intense, though soon dwarfed by the burns on my hands, arms and legs, in that order of intensity.

Even as a nine year-old, Heli had enough sense to piece together what had happened when she found the bleach bottle near my clothing and quickly dressed me after I no longer found succor in the cool water of Swedetown Pond.

My backside, one of the few areas of my body not smart-ing from the bleach, was nonetheless not spared reddening when we got home. Mama made the rounds of the neigh-borhood to find enough salve for my soon-blistering body and she told me I was lucky to have done it near the pond, lucky Heli was there to help, and lucky she could find enough salve or I surely would have scarred.

And today, I'm told I'm special because my skin gets dark in the summer. Today, for the first time in my life, I'm told I'm "bootiful."

I'm relishing that comment when Papa speaks. "What was going on out near the garden?" he asks after he and Mama have snuggled into their bed and believe I am safely asleep. "You and Emilia were there for a long time."

"Woman talk." I hope Mama's answer will end Papa's line of inquiry, and it does. There is a long silence. "Henrik, the voting for the strike began four days ago. Have you already cast your ballot?"

"The balloting reopens Monday, and Monday I will vote."

Mama allows the unspoken question to hang in the still night air.

"I will vote *no*, Kerttu. It matters not, for I am a small minority and there will be a large majority voting to strike. But they don't understand those who run the mines like I have come to. Our men have their legitimate grievances, some petty, many not, all begging for fair and ethical and just redress. There will be no redress. My brothers in solidarity believe they can influence management. They cannot."

"Why? What do you know that everyone else does not?"

"It's all about money, Kerttu. No one has a complaint against a fair profit. But if it's a matter of giving many a few dollars more, or giving many, many, many more dollars to a select few men, then 'savage capitalism' will easily tip the balance. We will strike, but we will not win."

"I am for the strike, Henrik. It's a battle that must be waged and much is at risk, but I believe much is to be gained. The mine companies have had their way with everything, banding together to spread their influence throughout this area and beyond. The workers have no voice, no influence. If this is the only way we're to be heard, let us be heard in one loud voice, not the many voices of resignation and surrender."

"Your *battle* metaphor is not lost on me, and I will address it more in a moment. But first this: you have a right to your opinion, Kerttu, and you know mine. We have most often spoken in one voice and I want us to continue. Regardless of this difference, can we agree to discuss this in civil terms, and not allow it to rip our family apart, as I fear it will this community?"

"Agreed," Mama quickly interjects.

"Thank you, Kerttu. I also agree." I hear both their breathing subside, and then he continues. "My greatest fear of a strike is not losing, for much can be learned on both sides in a fair dispute. It's the blood. I've seen how vengeful the Miscowaubik mine managers can be. Vengeance belongs to Calumet and Hecla, with little left over for The Lord."

"*Pax tecum*, Henrik?" Mama says with a quiet laugh, for this is one of the few Latin phrases she knows, and it's the right place for it.

"Peace be with you, Kerttu. And also with your spirit," Papa responds with a calm chuckle that takes us all to sleep.

# V

## *July 23*

"Today may be difficult, Emilia. My friends have called for a strike and today is the day."

Papa is shaving in the kitchen and I have brushed my hair in the sitting room and join him. Heli is hanging the last of the clothes in the basement that won't fit on the clothes lines outside while Mama completes breakfast.

"Are you striking with them?" I ask the question I already know the answer to.

"No. I must work and I will treat today like any other. My friends may not, though, and you and I must be wary. I don't know what they will do because they're not working, and I don't know how they will treat those of us who choose to work. None of us has ever experienced such a day and I don't know how to act on such a day except to follow my conscience and work. My friends do not know how to act either ... on a day they should be working ... and that's what concerns me."

"Is Uncle Bear striking?"

"Yes, your Uncle Bear believes strongly in the ideology of fairness and the principles of the union."

I want to ask more about this, but I have heard Papa's principles and Mama's ideology regarding the strike, and I know I cannot get in the middle of it. Yet there is so much about a strike I don't understand.

"Who else is striking?"

"According to the Western Federation of Miners – that's the name of the union – everyone in the Copper Country who works in a mine. I'm not certain I can believe them but, if it's true, that means every one of the 25 or so mining companies, and that would mean at least 15,000 workers. With over 4,000 workers, Calumet and Hecla is by far the biggest and most profitable, but there's plenty of misery to go around, if that's how this strike unfolds."

"Papa," I say, unable to quickly complete my thought because of the sheer magnitude of a work stoppage that could involve a substantial percentage of our entire peninsula. "Papa," I say, now noticing the side of his neck. "You're bleeding."

Standing at the cast iron stove, Mama has not seen the droplet of blood trickling from the left side of Papa's neck, so I pull up the hem of my dress and tuck a small handful of fabric in my hand, wet it with a few drops of water clinging to the mouth of the well pump, and wipe his neck with the inside of my cotton dress that causes a brief disconcerted look on his face before fading with the wetness on his neck.

"I guess I missed that one," Papa admits sheepishly. "Is it still bleeding?" he wonders, not bothering to check it himself at the hanging mirror.

"There was only a little," I tell him. "Papa, will you ... will we be safe?"

"We will be safe, but there are many other questions to be answered, and we will learn the answers only by engaging the questions. Let's eat."

Heli has hung the last of the clothes and needs no invitation to begin, but waits for Papa to lead with the blessing. Mama reaches for the bowl of what my non-Finnish friends call oatmeal, but we call puuro, and serves Papa first, then hands the bowl to me, I to Heli, and Heli back to Mama before she serves herself. The first warm spoonful seems to cleave to my tongue like it's lost the familiar texture and taste of the breakfast my family shares as a favorite. I'm sure it won't go down my throat, so I let it rest uneasily in the back of my mouth. I turn to Heli, and it's clear nothing is different to her as she swallows after barely tasting it. Ever the lady, Mama is eating slowly and delicately, seeming to savor even the smell. Papa swallows hard.

Offering me his right arm with the pasty already tucked into his left, Papa leads me out the door, down the front steps and, at 23, turns right onto Ridge Street. I've learned to keep silent for the straightaways and offer only brief comments at the turns, when I know the step count begins again, longer comments at the intersections, and truly engaging dialogue with Papa only when he invites it as we're stopped for trains at the foot of Ridge Street or long lines of supply horses and wagons at the intersections.

During the school year, I kept my mind busy as I escorted Papa to work and he assisted me with reviewing my school work and preparing for tests, and at the beginning of the summer it was wonderful to watch the daily progression of light green on the trees and in the yards, to the rich green of full summer when color covers the Copper Country. The grass is beginning to brown now and the leaves on the trees seem to have been muted by the same metallic dust that has now replaced the taste of puuro in my mouth.

The passing of the train just as we reach the bottom of Swedetown hill tells me we have started out later than usual, for Papa and I often talk while we're waiting for it most other days. We move left onto Osceola Road between the long lines of horse-drawn wagons also heading left before curving into Red Jacket, the same direction as the train. It's only as we reach Swedetown Road and begin the walk almost straight into town that I notice something different, surely something wrong. This is where the light from the mines becomes brighter in the early morning of other seasons, yet even with the sun of a warm summer morning, the change enshrouds and disturbs me.

There are a few men also walking toward the mines, with no sense of direction.  In the near distance, more men are strolling nearer the shafts, with no sense of purpose.  No one carries a lunch.  Papa does not seem to notice the lunchless men glancing at us uncomfortably, their eyes invariably settling for a moment on his dark spectacles before resting on his wrapped pasty like it contains meaning rather than lunch, before turning away.

Our many-numbered steps to Mine Street seem tenuous and hollow, their purpose stolen by our uncertainty.  Shafts Number Six thru Twelve stand mute to the aimless workers around them.

I am relieved when Papa notices the sounds of commerce to our right on Calumet Avenue.  The horse-drawn wagons, many with high wooden sides straining outward by their bursting contents, some with wooden crates, others with canned food and even some fresh green beans in piles near the sides of the flat wagons, are a welcome sign of normalcy.

As we continue on Mine Street and Shafts One thru Five rise to our immediate left, a man from behind us wearing a green shirt and carrying a tin lunch bucket on a run passes me and Papa.  He looks to our left at Number Four Shaft and then hesitates for a moment before veering left and trying to run through a large group of about fifty men standing in front of the Number Four man engine.  Papa and I stop to watch as the man in the green shirt is also stopped by a group of men now forming a fence of themselves before the man engine.

The human fence re-forms into a circle surrounding the green-shirted man, who disappears from our view at center.  I can feel Papa's arm flinch against mine at exactly the same time mine flinches against his when we both hear "scab" and "traitor" and "scum," and their Finnish translations.  A burly man fights his way from the outside of the circle to the center, and I watch a metal lunch bucket fly straight into the air and catch a glint of the sun as the green-shirted man is propelled from the center of the circle almost as fast.

He ignores his lunch bucket lying on the ground as he moves away from the group and begins to walk toward us, then breaks into a run again as he nears us standing in the middle of Mine Street. I turn and watch him as he passes us in the opposite direction as he came, then really lets his heels fly down Mine Street.

Papa and I stand in the middle of Mine Street and we are not as anonymous as we usually are in the crowds, our presence announced by the brown package under Papa's left arm.

"We're almost there," he says like he is exhausted and needs to quickly arrive so he can rest awhile before beginning work.

Shaft Number Three is set farther back from the road than the others on Mine Street, and I can't even see its entrance because the distance between us is filled by a huge group of men talking and moving about in all directions. Only a few more steps to Number Two, then Number One, and only a few feet past that, and Papa will be safely to his work site.

At Shaft Number One, I involuntarily stop again as I notice two men shouting at one another, one of them wearing a miner's cap and holding a lunch bucket in his left hand as he gestures wildly with his right hand at a much taller man. The shouting attracts several of the others who are also standing at Number One, and they move menacingly toward the man with the miner's cap and lunch. "Ismo," they call the man in the cap, and Ismo gestures again to the tall man in what appears to be a plea of understanding. But the dialogue between these two again becomes heated, and Ismo now drops his lunch bucket to turn and face the taller man and swear at him before raising both his hands to chest level and thumping him on the chest with his outturned palms. It's apparent to everyone that Ismo, who is now without his lunch, shouldn't be the one to pick the fight, and I fear I will see blood. More of the men move toward Ismo and, when one from the crowd strikes him on the back with his out-turned palm, others join in and propel the man with their thrusts toward me and Papa.

"Ystävät. You were my friends before today. What has changed? Because we do not agree? Because I must work to support a wife and new baby?"

"Best you leave now, Ismo," responds the tall one who was engaged in the first argument. "Our friendship is over. And here's your lunch," he says as he picks up the tin bucket, removes the pasty, drops the bucket to the ground and crushes it with his foot, then winds up with the semi-circled crust in his hand and throws it toward his former friend.

The crust breaks from the force of the throw, and Ismo's wife's pasty recipe is revealed as potato, carrot, rutabaga, turnip and even some smaller pieces of onion in the morning sun before hurtling to the ground like garbage.

I look down at Papa's lunch, the pasty wrapped in brown paper and still tucked into his left arm. I grab it before he can protest, and call him by name before I hand it to Ismo as he is about to walk past us heading in the same direction as the first *scab*. Ismo looks to me initially in an unthinking glance of gratitude, and then turns away when his look changes to fear as quickly as he takes a few steps, runs into more men, and drops the package to the street before disappearing among them. The crowds have stopped nearly all directional movement in the street and most men appear to be apprehensive as they mill about like they're looking for trouble. I turn back to Papa and take his right arm.

"I am afraid," I tell him and I know he must see me walk-ing around him in circles, looking for an opening in any direction through the men.

"Can you see through the crowd?" he asks. "I cannot."

"No," I admit. "I don't know where to go."

"To Depot Street, across to Laurium," he says, the cer-tainty and clear-headedness apparent in his voice.

From Laurium, Depot Street intersects Calumet Avenue, then stops virtually on the threshold of Shaft Number Two, yet I still need to turn away from the shaft and stand here for a moment in an attempt to ground my sense of direction because the street and everything around it is filled by men who mostly appear to be moving toward us. I grab Papa's hand and take him into the crowd of men on Depot Street toward Laurium. It's only one block to Calumet Avenue, the main dividing road, yet with Papa and I locked in each other's arms, it takes us nearly a half hour to reach and cross it.

I look gratefully at the Laurium women who have moved tentatively toward the main dividing road, then stop a few safe feet away. One woman in a pretty yellow summer dress looks first to Papa, to this face, to his spectacles, then to me for only a moment before dismissing us quickly. Behind her are men in business suits and others wearing the ties of mine captains who are walking and craning their necks toward the noisy, inconvenient congestion across the big road in Red Jacket.

This is the only area of Laurium I know well, and the hospital where Papa spent his Christmas and almost died is straight down Depot Street near the cemetery, so we simply stay on this street. Another crowd is gathered as Papa and I near the hospital, my grip on his arm beginning to loosen, then re-grip as I spot Sheriff Cruse standing on the front steps of the hospital in the center of a large group of men, all Laurium men fanned around the hospital entrance and dressed in their daily work clothes that are meant to distinguish them from the rugged apparel of machinists and clerks and common laborers and trammers.

Standing behind him and one step higher is the best-dressed man I've ever seen, and I double-check myself to make sure it's not Sunday.

Everyone knows Sheriff Cruse, or at least recognizes him with a cigar in his mouth and wearing a dark vest and a string tie and badge nearly lost on a broad chest and frame that surely supports over 300 pounds of well-fed self-importance. Sheriff Cruse's right hand is raised and he's looking into a book held open in his left hand, which he appears to be reciting from. The men in the large group forming a semi-circle around Sheriff Cruse and the well-dressed man, whose backs are to the hospital entrance, also raise their right hands and I can hear them reciting something in faulting unison.

Getting closer to the group with Papa in arm, we stop and both he and I lower our arms to rest them as we hear Sheriff Cruse apparently nearing the end of his recitation.

"...and to uphold the laws of the land into which I have been sworn as a deputy."

"And to uphold the laws of the land into which I have been sworn as a deputy," the men answer the brief sentence together fluidly.

"I have enough badges for each of you," Sheriff Cruse says as he leans toward a corrugated box and grabs a handful, setting the book down near the box. "Wear them proudly and walk about your daily business with your badge always on your chest. More badges will be coming and more of you fellows will be deputized. For now, I want no one to openly carry a weapon." He lets that point settle in. "But you will need to be prepared to protect yourselves from renegades and vigilantes and ... and ..." he looks over the men's heads as if some unnamed person in the distance will supply him with the end to his sentence. His faraway glance reaches me and Papa and I first see his hesitation laced with surprise, then comprehension. "...and their ilk," he concludes with a sardonic smirk. Many of the men who were facing Sheriff Cruse turn to me and Papa, and quickly turn back.

We are the only ones outside the semi-circle, and I can't imagine that we pose any kind of threat to Sheriff Cruse and his large group of new lawmen, yet I also can't help but feel that his concluding comment was aimed at us. Perhaps we are "...their ilk."

"One more thing," the well-dressed man says, and I swear he glances at Papa before looking away uncomfortably. I see the men's backs immediately straighten as an addition- al air of respect gravitates toward the man behind Sheriff Cruse. Papa looks like he is also paying closer attention. The finely dressed man looks down briefly and brushes his lapels and, looking to his shined black shoes, he gives them an imaginary brush before returning his hands to lock them into his lapels. "Already the strikers are disrupting our communi- ty. We have all worked long and hard to build this area into an economic and political powerhouse. The Copper Country is known in this state and this nation as the mighty producer of the purest copper in the world. We intend to retain our reputation at the top." And the men cheer at the references to the pride of the Keweenaw. "I also understand," he continues, "that the striking ruffians are beginning to fight among themselves. If they do, let them, but protect your businesses and most of all protect yourselves and your families. Those are our most important assets." And he looks to Papa as if Papa is providing some sort of poetic footnote.

Some in the group of men walk up the few front steps into the hospital, and the remainder of the group turns and looks around before going off in scattered directions. I take Papa's left arm without realizing that's the one I take for the way home, and he speaks for the first time since we escaped from the Depot Street mob on the wrong side of Calumet Avenue.

"Yes, Emilia. It's best we head back home. There will be no work today. Certainly not at the mines of Calumet and Hecla."

"Who was the man with Sheriff Cruse?" I ask.

"Oh, I should have informed you. That is James Mac- Naughton. Mr. MacNaughton to you," and I roll my eyes to myself, for I know very well that I'm always to address all adults courteously. "He's the superintendent of Calumet and Hecla. I've heard him before, though always from a distance, so he's easy to recognize today."

It's nearly noon by the time we reach Swedetown, and Mama is beside herself. She sees Papa and me from the distance of our rounding Osceola Road onto our street, and she struggles to keep her balance as she runs all the way down steep Ridge Street to greet us. When she's near, she says "Thank you, Jesus," and the three of us stand there while Mama catches her breath, looking like she's unsure whether she wants to laugh or cry, and I'm glad that she does neither, for I don't want to be a topic of Swedetown conversation in the middle of Ridge Street.

Papa explains our delay, but shares little detail with Mama, and completes the description of nearly our whole morning by the time we reach home. Now certain that we're safe, and none the wiser for it from Papa's description, Mama offers no objection when he says he'd like me to accompany him to the water tower later this afternoon for a bird's eye view of the happenings in Red Jacket. That will give me time to help Mama and Heli with our basement full of laundry.

It's only a few hundred feet farther up the hill past the cow pasture, baseball diamond and a few holes of the golf course before crossing the Upper Gate Trail to the top of Swedetown hill and the water tower.

Papa says it was built the same year he and Mama came to Red Jacket as newlyweds from Finland, and he remembers thinking that it would surely feed water to the homes of Swedetown when Mr. Lukas volunteered to help us buy our house here. Papa says he and Mama were surprised to learn, after they bought our house, that the water lines run past all the houses in Swedetown to Calumet and Hecla, then to the businesses of Red Jacket.

The water tower itself is a tall, octagon-sided edifice atop the crest of Swedetown hill, yet appears safely squat from a distance. It surely deserves its name as a tower from the top.

I've never told Papa about the time Heli and I scaled it because the boys told us we couldn't. As if we needed further encouragement, they said you can see Lake Superior from there. Heli is a better baseball player than most of the rest of the boys and can climb any tree and will not be left out of any athletic activity. When the boys taunted her to climb it, sure she wouldn't, Heli threatened to kick them so hard down the other side of the hill that they wouldn't stop until they tumbled into Superior. I knew immediately that she no longer just wanted to climb the water tower; she had to.

She climbed atop my shoulders to reach the bottom rung of the ladder that's attached to the side of the water tower, and scaled it like a red squirrel. When she reached the top, she only exclaimed "wow" and came back down to the last step. She turned around on the ladder and wrapped the back of her knees around the last rung, let her upper body swing upside down, then reached out her hands to grasp mine. I still wasn't sure how this would work, but she locked her feet against the water tower and heaved me upward until I could reach out with one hand and grab the rung her knees were wrapped around. I ascended a few steps, looked down at Heli and the ground far beneath us both, and froze there. Heli untangled herself from the bottom rung, ascended past me by one rung and looked down at me saying "just keep your eyes on my butt and follow me." I did not want to go up, but wanted to go down by myself even less, so I did as she suggested, never looking down again. We stopped only briefly when we reached the top where Heli had been, and the ladder continued its attachment from the side to the top of the water tower, so scaling it across the top instead of up was easy. The ladder reached an abrupt end and Heli dropped to the top of the tower and scooted over to leave room for me, but I just flipped my body over and rested my butt on the last level rung, still hanging on.

The hazy piece of land I thought to be Sweden as a child turned out to be Isle Royale, which is recognizable from up here, and it took only a brief recollection of a map of the Midwest I'd once studied to believe we could see Wisconsin to the southwest, Minnesota to the west, and Canada to the north.

If I thought Lake Superior was a sight to behold from Eagle River, it's an azure jewel from up here. It is a gem that cannot be owned, surely not worn. It's as if her existence of a perpetual lifetime is solely for the purpose of being admired, respected, cherished.

That day, I understood what it's like to see conceptually.

"Heli, I see superior," I told her.

"Of course you do, silly. It's almost all you can see from up here."

I didn't try to explain the difference between seeing superior and looking at Lake Superior. I'm not sure I even understand that difference now myself. When I reached the ground after descending the water tower ladder, I understood that I had been given a gift. Ever since that day, I've felt that Lake Superior has always given me more than I have ever asked of her.

Papa brings me back to the present with a tug from his right arm as I slow our pace to look for a comfortable area of ground to sit on. Even though it's the base of the water tower, not the peak, the view up here is lovely. Heli and I come here often, and I always examine our panorama by starting to my left, the west, before sweeping to my right and taking in Red Jacket, a mile in the distance below: the cross high above the roof of St. Mary's, the towering twin spires of St. Joseph's, the cliff in the far distance, whose countenance bears the name of the mine where Uncle Bear began his career before joining C&H and bringing Papa there, the beautiful bell tower of St. Anne's, the huge coliseum under construction and, to our right, mine shafts One thru Twelve silhouetting the tallest structure on the horizon, the Calumet and Hecla smokestack next to Washington School.

"The sun feels good on my face," he says as he looks into the bright orb of a warm late-afternoon July on Copper Island. "My eyes are especially ill-suited for distance. Can you describe what's happening in town, Emilia?"

I focus on the hundreds of ant-sized people I can easily see moving to and fro, for it seems that nobody has taken on a sense of purpose. Then I see almost straightaway to the north the glint of musical instruments in the sun leading one of the few organized movements of people in downtown Red Jacket on Fifth Street. "Ah, that must be the firemen's tournament that I've heard is in town, and they're parading through downtown on Fifth Street," I inform him.

"They're led by a band," Papa fills in, and I feel that I should compliment both his eyesight and his hearing.

"Fifth Street is still crowded in front of them, though not as crowded as this morning," I describe to him. "Sixth Street is packed with people next to all the stores."

"What's going on at the mines?" he asks.

"The ones between Red Jacket Road and Swedetown Road," *which are shafts One thru Five*, I think to myself, "look like they're busy."

"How are they busy?"

"Busy with people, same as the ones this side of Swede-town Road," *which are shafts Six thru Twelve*, I confirm in my mind.

"So the mines are still not operating. Those people you see near the shafts must be Cruse and his new ... law enforcement team" he concludes in some way that I cannot understand, and I am curious how he did it. "They're *protecting* the mines," he notes ironically.

"How can you tell?"

"When the mines are working," he says, "all the activity is underground. It's like a city, and the city is dark in most places, light in some of the places where we men work. It's dusty and dirty, and cool at the top, and hotter the deeper you go. The air sometimes moves well through the drifts and winzes, sometimes not." He pauses and I can tell his mind is in the mines. "We've already taken the copper from the upper streets of that underground city, so the man engines transport us through the shafts past the upper parts to the lower streets, and that's where all the people are truly congregated in our city far beneath the streets you see."

"How far down do you ... did you work?" I trip over my tense because Papa has rarely spoken of his work in the mines and has yet to speak of his work in the broom factory. Perhaps because he's now working above ground, he can talk of his experience in the mines with the objective separation of time.

"In Shaft Number Two, we were well past 5,000 feet..."

"That's more than a mile," I can't help but interrupt.

"That's a quick calculation. Good for you, Emilia. Yes, the man engines and man cars take us as far as they can, but they cannot take us that deep. The copper lodes are some-times predictable, mostly not, so we follow them where they take us. The underground grids are deep and huge and complex. We number them as we descend in pursuit of the copper. Well over 50 levels are not uncommon. We work ... like dogs, but harder. Some of us have joked that we'd like to sneak some cats down there, just to keep the rats at bay. We'd never do it, though. It would be too cruel to the cats. We do what we're told, but many of us have ideas to work smarter, more efficiently. Certainly more safely. Our ideas are like the mines ... they never see the light of day." He pauses again, gathering his recollections of the mine before casting them in the moment. "There were days when we sometimes quit stoping – that means falling the rock from above our heads with picks and sledge hammers and drills ... and tramming – that means picking up the rocks and tossing them into the tram cars ... those are little train cars – a full hour before shift end to give us time to get back to grass."

I wish I could see through Papa's dark spectacles, for I would love to see his eyes light the way his face does as he closes his too-brief rendering of life in the mines and returns his attention to the reality I recognize.

"It's a far busier city down there beneath the busy city you see up here. Is there any activity in Laurium?"

I turn my gaze to the right and squint to try to bring the details of Laurium into view. "Something must be happening at the Palestra," I say to him, for I'm able to barely discern what must be a large crowd of people at Laurium's social gathering place. "I think they're moving toward Red Jacket." The late afternoon sun is nearly at our backs, helping me focus in the far distance. "There must be hundreds, maybe thousands because it's forming into a long line and a thick line on Depot Street, and they seem to be heading toward Red Jacket."

Papa leans back and rests his head on the ground. He lies there still and I am also weary from our harrowing experiences this morning and from his description of the mines, so I join him, nestling my head near his and closing my eyes as I think he has.

We both start awake and sitting at the sound of shots in the distance. The streets of Red Jacket reflect back to me in a peculiar way. I look right to Laurium, whose diagonal streets only stare back at me with the same levitated waves of the summer's hot sun. The large, irregular rectangle filled with shaft houses that help separate the two cities is also filled with a dense crowd of people. There was space, albeit not much space in the crowd when I described it to Papa before, and he opined that Sheriff Cruse and his cronies were gathered there at the mines. Now it is congested with people.

"Tell me what you see," he asks eagerly.

"Everyone is at the mines. The firemen's parade down Fifth Street is over. The line we saw forming from the

Palestra toward Red Jacket is gone. I've never seen the mine area so crowded. There are hundreds ... no, there are thousands there, Papa."

We hear the noise of the crowd rise up in an unintelligible roar. It's difficult to see the people distinctly and we cannot hear individual voices. The certainty in Papa's voice is comforting amidst the uncertainty of what is going on in our community.

"There was a meeting planned by the Western Federation of Miners this afternoon at the Palestra. I fear they'll only form a wedge between managers and workers, so I did not go to the meeting. They say they want to advocate in our behalf and they are trying to organize us so we are a unified voice that will be heard by the mine managers. A voice that will be heard by MacNaughton and ... his ilk," Papa uses a word we both heard earlier.

It sounded strange then. It sounds worse now.

"Today is the confusing culmination of what has been brewing for months, years, even decades here in the Copper Country. The mines have in many ways been good for the area, and they have been especially good for the owners and the managers. I bear them no ill will, for they have borne some of the risk. Yet this continued uneven field of risk and reward is littered with severed fingers, amputated arms, missing legs and dead bodies. And much more." He rises to his feet as another loud concerted sound also rises from the crowd below. "There is blood already. I can tell. There will be more blood," and he takes my right arm as his signal that he's ready to return home.

*School is still a few weeks off, but today feels like the end of vacation*, I think to myself as I prepare for sleep, Heli already lying down and squirming to find a comfortable position.

I will rise early tomorrow, same as always. Put on my dress, same as always. Help Mama and Heli with the laundry, same as always. But I know Papa will not be going to work in this mayhem. I lie here with my eyes open and think. In a few minutes, a plan forms in my mind.

A full week left in July. It would help to have our calendar in front of me, but I know I can do this. Two extra weeks August thru November and four times four is 16, plus the extra two, plus the one left in July, and three in December, plus the dime I have from my work at the library last week equals 230.

I roll over and reach for my dress and feel in the pocket for the dime. I clutch the tiny wafer of money to myself in my right hand as I toss the dress back with my left, then feel along the edge of the rag rug with my left hand. When I've found the spot, I raise the edge of the rug and put the dime deep in its place.

Two dollars and thirty cents won't be a feast, but I'll bet it'll be a pretty good Christmas supper.

# VI

# July 28

Mama warned me last night that I would have to complete this task today, but all the warning in the world, and the fact that I've done it many times before, doesn't prepare me for the unleashed stench that rises freely as we together lift the hinged alcove of wood forming the seat of our privy. It smells much worse in high summer, of course, the one time of year we've never had to clean it. I muck out the privy in the fall and Heli gets the spring cleaning, and that has worked fine for as long as I can remember. *Another benefit of the Nelson inhabitants*, I think to myself.

There's little room inside for both me and Mama shoulder-to-shoulder, so I back out the door first when we've lifted the wide piece of wood with the hole in it, relieved to take a breath of cool, early morning Copper Island summer air.

"Grab the shovel," Mama instructs as she backs out the door. "Keep filling these two buckets until it's empty," motioning to the privy, "and dump the buckets into the pit that Papa and I dug last night, over there," as she points down the hill of our back yard to a hole dug in the underbrush with a bag of lime perched next to it. "Don't fill the buckets too full, and carry one in each hand for balance." I don't know why Mama feels she needs to provide such explicit instructions. "Keep the last two buckets here, and then let me know when you're done. And don't dawdle. We have lots of other things to do today," she again adds unnecessarily.

I take the shovel shared by many in Swedetown that is specially designed for this, with its handle that makes a 90-degree angle at the bottom and attaches to the scooped metal that makes it look like an oversized ladle. I've learned to start this job quickly so I can finish it even more quickly, though I do wonder why I have to save the last two buckets.

A little of the liquid/solid mess gets on my summer dress where the bucket mouths rub against my legs as I try to hold the handles away from me, but they're just too heavy even half-full. The lime gets onto my shoes when I cover the shallow pit with the pungent dust that smells alkaline with a touch of bleach, so I half-fill the final two buckets and head into the house to clean myself off.

"I'll wash my dress with the load Heli is working on." I say to Mama, who meets me at the front door.

"No, she and Papa are in the basement, and they'll be just fine. Heli can make the rounds to pick up the laundry, if there is any, and Papa says he'll help in the basement. Emilia, I want you to come with me. There's something we need to do together today. Go back and grab the last two buckets. I'll get the brooms and we'll meet at the street."

"...if there is any," I understand as I set the buckets down, feeling foolish between the two squat, silent smelly sentinels near Ridge Street waiting for Mama. The beginning of the strike last week has meant there will be little laundry on Monday, usually our busiest day. Papa has never helped with the laundry, though I suppose he's just looking for something to do because nobody is working and he must always be doing something. Even when he is silently sitting by himself, which he does more often since returning from the hospital, I can almost hear the machinations in his head as he looks through his dark spectacles into a syllogism, or some dilemma at work, or constructs, then unravels an

imaginary equation, or solves a problem. But Papa helping
with the laundry is laughable.

My real quandary – "there's something we need to do
together today" – may take awhile before being answered,
for Mama is joining me from the house with a broom in each
hand and a look on her face that speaks of sheer determination and strong will, pillaring a quiet resolve that also
whispers ... *and don't you dare ask me a thing until I'm
ready to tell you.*

We hasten silently down Ridge Street and I'm surprised
when we end up taking the same roads Papa and I take into
work, passing only a few men along the way with Mama's
short and quick steps greased by a specific destination in
mind.

I think of the word I heard only a few days ago to describe the men with their pasties in their tin lunch buckets,
and "scab" seemed like a cruel word at the time, and it has
not changed. We've started out a little earlier than Papa and
I usually do. Still, there are few men going to work and that's
because a strike has been called, and few men dare go to
work.

We finally stop just before Swedetown Road veers to our
right and changes its name to Agent Street before continuing
into Laurium, and Mama motions me to put the buckets
down on the side of the road, our backs to Shaft Houses Six
thru Twelve as we look north across the road at the first five
shafts. I look back up Swedetown Road for the first time and
see more women coming our way with their metal buckets
gleaming in the sun and brooms under their arms. Behind
them I can just make out a few women moving left from
Osceola Road onto Swedetown Road, having taken the
roundabout way here from Red Jacket. Even from this
distance, I can see they are similarly equipped. A few
children are helping with the buckets, as I have, and all the
women have the same look of steely determination, have
taken the same vow of steely silence. They form a single line

across the road from us, and more women also join our side of the road.  In only minutes, both sides of the road are lined with women and some children and buckets and brooms.

Two lunch-laden men who are talking to one another pass us with perplexed looks on their faces as they head toward the shaft houses.  When they have passed the gauntlet, the attention of all the women turns and focuses on a large group of men walking on Swedetown Road toward us.  Mama hands me a broom and, with no words spoken, the women in lines on both sides of the road drop their brooms into their buckets and begin swirling the foul contents.  Unsure what to think, the men drop into single file and move to the center of the road, daring not to get close to either side.  When the few men in the lead reach the front of the line of women and the rest of the men are spread toward the back, I hear a voice from somewhere among us, high and sturdy and authoritative.

"Now!"

Mama and all the rest of the women lift their brooms from the buckets and raise the bristles filled with excrement over their heads and flick the broom handles with their arms and wrists to let loose the manure missiles.

The men look left and right for an escape and when none is offered, for there is no break in the women's lines, they duck their heads over and blindly begin to run.

The immediate sense of victory allows many of the women to now speak, and the expletives fly like the watery defecation.

"Scab" is the favorite, then the volume and curses and oaths and obscenities rise to become interspersed with language more colorful, and in languages more varied than I've ever heard at one time in my life.

The running men trip into one another and a few try to get up, but soon realize their eyes are also fouled, so they fall onto their lunch buckets in the middle of the road.  It is when Mama and many of the others have nearly exhausted their first buckets that I realize I have only been standing here, a little of the runny mess spattered from across the road onto my summer dress.

I have been given permission. The nod of ascent has been conferred upon me by Mama and some of our neighbors and many other women who lugged buckets and brooms from Red Jacket to affirm their beliefs and convictions in a manner I did not know existed.

I join in enthusiastically.

Just as he tries to rise again and open his eyes, I anoint a man with a fierce shot to his mid-section, and he glances at me for an instant before looking down to his stomach like he expects to find a flesh wound. My next shot flies farther than I intend, but reaches most of its target since I am aiming diagonally at the men who are still lying in the road, groveling in a mixture of feces and urine that is turning into a naturally brown mud. Dipping and flicking, I am already reveling in a new endeavor that, like others I've recently experienced for the first time, thrills and astonishes me when I participate. I give up aiming when I notice the near-empty bucket, and swirl and flick my broom handle a few more times to empty it at a man who only momentarily staggers too near me and Mama, then struggles across the road into another volley. I am out of ammunition. As I try to clean out the little mush left in the bucket and only succeed in turning it over, I hear the first muffled laugh rise from a woman next to us who I recognize from Swedetown and often say "hello" to, though neither of us knows each other's language.

That does it. I pick up her laugh and hear it followed with belly volleys that move down the line and across the road to the other line of women. The laughing and gaiety infect us all, and as I look to Mama and see the formerly stern lines in her face now broken with hilarity, she and I fall together backward onto the roadside into a dollop of Mama's clandestine planning and daylight determination, mixed with my wonderfully aching stomach.

Swedetown Pond, which we all must pass on our various paths back home, is a good place to stop and make an effort to get at least some of the stuff off our clothes and hair, and it quickly turns into a story exchange as well as a preparation session for our coterie of female planners, architects, engineers, and outlandish executioners.

This is what must be meant by the respectful disagreement I heard Papa and Mama promise to one another in the night they first discussed the then-impending strike, for when Mama and I return home, barely a reference is made to our urchin-like appearance and animal-like odor. Heli is outside playing, and Papa remains seated at the well-organized kitchen table from which Heli has been excused, her utensils washed and dried and put away. Lunch will wait for me and Mama as we go to the basement and carefully thread our way through the meager lines of hanging clothes. A few others are hanging outside, and for the first time I understand the value of dirty laundry, and wish there were more of it.

Mama takes off her dress and moves among the clothes in her undergarments until she reaches the line with our family's laundry hanging from it. She feels a well-worn dress of hers, and moves to my sleeping shirt and also touches it to determine if it's dry. "Close enough," she says as she takes both garments off the line and hands me the sleeping shirt. Mama moves to the tub of water and takes off her undergarments and begins to clean herself. She swishes the water around and I can hear her lathering her hands with the soap we make from lye and lard and Mama's *secret* ingredient, lavender grown in our back yard. Underneath the hanging clothes, I see her clean dress move near the floor as she steps into it before buttoning up the back and heading upstairs to wash her hair in the wooden barrel that sits beneath the eaves of our house during the summer.

Avoiding anything that floats, I take my turn at the laundry tub when I hear a long train lumbering past. The train is too-long and it's off-schedule and none of that matters because I'm surely not to run to the foot of Swedetown Hill to find out. I wash my lone summer dress and hang it, and put on Papa's old threadbare shirt, my sleeping shirt. It hangs nearly to my knees and is far less modest than I prefer, but I must wash my hair outside.

Papa is talking with Mama as she dries her hair at the rain barrel, then hands me the towel. Draping the towel over my shoulder like Mama, I bend to pick up the bowl Mama has left near the rain barrel, dip it in to fill it with water, and move away from the rain barrel to bend over and dump the water onto my head. Mama takes the bowl I silently hand her. From the window ledge I grab the *upstairs* bar of soap that is scented with our back yard lilac bushes, rub it into my hands and lather it into my hair. I reach out my hand for Mama to place the bowl back into, but she moves to the rain barrel, dips it in, and rinses my hair. Twice more she does this as I make a fist around my hair near the top of my head and run it down the length of my hair to remove the soap. Mama and I walk inside for lunch while Papa's attention turns to the sounds of frolicking robins in the yard.

Papa flashes us a knowing smile when we return outside after lunch, and Mama reaches to brush the hair from near my eyes.

The shouting between two boys about who gets to go first can be heard well before they rush past our house, then Heli comes running up Ridge Street and into our small front yard in a panic. She must have run all the way home from the foot of the hill because Heli is out of breath and barely able to speak.

"Soldiers. Horses. Cav'ry," she falters, frustrated with herself for being unable to pronounce a word, but still too excited to stop and get it right. "Guns. Big Guns. It's the army. Maybe even the cavalry."

"Whoa, slow down and hold your own horses, Heli. Your

Mama and sister were just near town and nothing much is going on there," Papa fibs a little. He watches as Heli takes a gulp of air and is about to start again. "Easy does it young lady. Just relax for a moment and catch your breath and gather your thoughts and start all over again. Where were you?"

"Down at the tracks."

"There's nothing to be seen from the tracks except trains. And nothing that interesting can be seen on a train."

"Yes you can, Papa. You can see through the windows into the passenger cars and tell that they're soldiers because they're all wearing the same kind of uniforms. You can look between the slats of some cars and see the horses with matching blankets over them. And you can't miss the big guns on the open flat cars."

We all look to Papa for interpretation of Heli's unreal sounding sights. All we can see is grave concern spread over his face. "Heli, let's go up to the water tower and you can tell me ... and we can see for ourselves."

I look to him for inclusion but he ignores me and reaches out his arm for Heli to take. I look to Mama, who holds her hands up and points them both at the sleeping shirt I am wearing. The hanging laundry in the basement of only a few minutes ago dawns on me in soundless rebuke, and I return my mind to it to quickly find my only summer dress hanging there and still wet.

"There's a laundry tub to empty and re-fill for our sheets and towels. That will give your dress time to dry," Mama says.

From the basement I hear a second and third and fourth long train move past Swedetown to the station in Red Jacket, sending ominous messages up the hill as their wheels hit the joints in the steel tracks.

My summer dress is dry, then wet again under the arms by the time Papa and Heli return just before suppertime. The last batch of bread is baking in the oven as I pump the water over Mama's hands to rinse the flour off, and she scrubs her arms to her elbows, then works the pump handle for me to rinse, though I only need to scrub to my wrists. Bursting to tell the story, Heli nonetheless comments only on the smell of baking bread while she sets the table. Papa leads in blessing and waits until the kesäkeitto is ladled into our bowls to begin.

"Heli was right," to which, of course, she beams as Papa opens. "The National Guard is here." He ignores the simultaneous gulps from me and Mama, while Heli revels in the attention still focused at least in part on her. "Half of Swedetown was up near the water tower, and the other half was at the train depot, along with most of the rest of the cities of Red Jacket and Laurium, I suspect," continues Papa. "By the time the four trains were unloaded, I'm sure General Abbey had a rapt audience that included most of the populations of Yellow Jacket and Blue Jacket and Tamarack and Raymbaultown and Centennial."

"The National Guard? General Abbey?" Mama wonders aloud, and I'm glad she says it, for I haven't the nerve to interrupt Papa, but I wonder the same.

"I'm getting ahead of myself. I need to clarify. Just before Heli and I returned home, some of the boys of Swedetown who went to the train station had reported back to everyone gathered at the water tower. The boys filled in the details of the information we could only see from the top of the hill. They said that before they left the depot, they saw other boys from Kearsarge and Ahmeek and..."

"That must be three or four miles away," I exclaim, unable to stop myself.

"And they saw other boys who live all the way down the hill to Lake Linden, another three or four miles the other way," Papa says. "Which tells me that we here in Swedetown may have been the first to see, but we were not the first to know." Heli jerks her head in wonder and rests her gaze momentarily at Papa over this last remark, and I can tell that she is as surprised as I sometimes am at what he can truly see. Or at least conclude. "It took only a little while for the word to spread throughout this area. Easily within an hour, thousands were milling about the depot as the soldiers disembarked from the trains. It took a little longer for the soldiers to prepare the horses and gather them into a temporary corral. We were surprised how quickly, though, the flat cars were unloaded. Within minutes, another corral was formed and filled with the cannons."

Neither Mama nor I have to meet Papa's last declaration with a question mark or exclamation point. Our looks state it all.

"How many soldiers?" Mama manages.

"Two, maybe three thousand."

"Good ... grief," Mama allows the last word slowly.

Papa leans back in his chair as if he's letting this thought settle in his own mind, and it gives me a moment to digest it as well, though I can feel it sink to the pit of my stomach and sit there.

Heli looks slighted from being unable to tell the story she has also seen unfold, and I can tell she's gathering her thoughts as Papa pauses. In a hurried fury of words, Heli lets loose: "And train car after train car of tents and food and supplies and even a band, me and Papa guessed from the top of the hill because we could see the brass in the sun, especially the tubas, and even up there, we could see the mountain being made out of the bales of hay for the horses, and I even learned what a red cross means because there were two huge covered wagons and the coverings on them had a red cross painted on their sides."

Heli stops to catch her breath.

"That's the international symbol of friendship and aid for the sick and wounded. They've been instrumental in fighting tuberculosis. Clara Barton founded the Red Cross many years ago and just died last year," Papa explains.

"I've heard of tuberculosis, but not up here," says Mama.

"I believe the Red Cross helps in all kinds of situations where there may be illness or disaster, or...," he thinks for a moment, then adds, "...or victims of any kind."

The summer soup has turned colder in front of Papa and Heli, and Mama and I have eaten nary a meal's worth, so we turn each to our own thoughts and pick at the remainder of our supper.

In the waning daylight, Heli ventures out to the privy alone as I fight for enough light to get to the end of the chapter I'm reading. I've waited for months to get Mr. Baum's *The Emerald City of Oz* and tonight I don't want to stop to even light the kerosene lanterns.

Her steps back to the house come too quickly to have finished her business, and their pace is too fast even for Heli's usual in-a-hurry stride. She barely gets to the front door, and her shout needs no explanation.

"Rats!"

Dorothy and her friends fly from my hands as I race through the kitchen and out the front door. Both of us slow when we round the back corner of our house. My cautious gaze finds only the open door of the privy. As if she needs to prove her point, Heli reaches down to grab my right hand with her left, then points the index finger of her right hand to the ground at the spot where I rested the two buckets before carrying them farther down the hill to the end of our back yard.

I've only occasionally seen rats before, one of the many reasons we give the innumerable bars in town a wide berth when our family has walked through Red Jacket. These two creatures near the privy are the size of cats and I force Heli a little closer to be sure of what we seem to be seeing.

They're rats, alright.

Together, they look up to see us, and return to scratching in the dirt before nonchalantly ambling around the privy and down the hill toward the pit. Looking to one another in silent ascent, Heli and I tighten our grips on each other's hands and sneak after them. Stopped at the privy by a rustling sound near the pit, we squint in the now dusky light and suck in our breaths with a gulp when we spot at least a dozen huge rats scurrying around the pit.

Summoned here by Heli's cry and our joint disappearance from the house to the back yard, Mama and Papa are walking toward us, and Mama stops them both short when they near us and Mama sees what Heli and I already wish we hadn't.

"Come on, Emilia. With this light, I'll need a little assistance to get back there." I hope my look to Papa convinces him that I'm not going anywhere near the pit. "They'll scatter as soon as we get near them, and you'll need to use up the rest of the lime so they won't want to come back here."

When my look to Mama, then to Heli is met with none of the succor I so desperately need now, I walk to Papa and take his hand, unable to move. Heli follows and grasps Mama's hand, the sides having been chosen and Heli obviously pleased with the result.

Papa heads in the direction of the pit and I follow reluctantly behind, still holding his hand. Only when his unsteady gait causes him to falter over a downed branch, am I able to keep pace with him, never taking the lead. The sound of Papa's foot hitting the downed branch gets the attention of the rats, and they all seem to look at us suspiciously for a moment before slithering away in the opposite direction of our approach. I had not known that I was holding my breath and the last of it escapes from my lungs only when we reach the spade and bag of lime left near the pit. I'm glad to see the spade, and I pick it up and hold it like a weapon as I walk the few steps to the edge of the overturned ground.

The smell still lingers.

"The lime first," Papa redirects my work, and I walk the few steps back to him, pick up the lime bag, and form a choke in the neck of the bag with both hands before turning the bag upside down and scattering the lime in a thick dust over the pit. I move a bit farther down the hill and dig into the ground and return with a spadeful of dirt that goes over the new layer of lime. Like cleaning the privy, I hasten back and forth between the new hole I'm now digging farther down the hill, and the dirt's new destination at the pit. In minutes, a thick berm has arisen over the pit.

"That should do it," Papa says when I stop for a moment to check on my work. For insurance, I make five more trips between the newly dug hole and newly risen berm with the largest spadefuls of dirt I can handle. It appears that Heli has held Mama's hand the entire time I've been working, for I see her release it and allow her own hands to drop to her sides when Papa and I rejoin them near our house.

"The mines are filling up with water," he says.

The look on my face seems to be lost on Papa and his pause allows me to sort out my sentiments. I am first surprised by the disparate relationship of having just chased a bunch of rats out of our yard and his comment that the mines are filling up. Then it occurs to me. Papa has come to a conclusion I could not have reached on my own. As creepy as I'm still feeling, I await his inference.

"The rats of the mines seem to be their own unique breed. They have terrible eyes and an exceptional sense of smell and vicious jaws." I wonder to myself what made me feel more secure with only a spade in my hand. "They will tear through a tin bucket if they're hungry enough, so we leave scraps of food behind so they'll let our pasties be. With the mines shut down and vacant, the water is rising and chasing out the rats."

The brown-paper-wrapped pasty that Papa now carries to his work on the surface. The tin lunch buckets of the other trammers. Rats in our yard. The inferences are now apparent to me. Their meanings disquiet me.

# VII

# *August 5*

The ebb and flow of this strike is already beginning to unnerve me, for it's not a gentle ebb and it's invariably a harsh flow. The joy of taking Papa to work versus the pain of watching his friends quarrel with one another, call each other rancorous names, hurt one another. The laughter I share too little lately with Mama on the side of Swedetown Road versus the arrival of the National Guard and our unwelcome back yard visitors.

Papa says enough men have broken ranks with the union to enable them to pump the water from the mines, and he returned to work yesterday. This is good.

Papa is a scab and I still don't know how I feel about that term. This is bad.

I thought of ebb and flow as I wrapped his pasty in brown paper yesterday for his return to work. I think of ebb and flow today after I return from accompanying Papa to work and Mama informs me that Heli and I will join her for a trip to town to greet a special visitor.

Papa is back to work. Papa is a scab.

Mama invites me and Heli along for a special day in town.

I fear what may happen next.

Prepared for a mama near the age of my own, I am surprised to find a woman surely old enough to be my Finnish grandmother, my Mummo, when she gingerly steps from the train and the crowd cheers her every step like she is performing something magical. The cheers continue when she strides across the platform, and grow even louder when a man in his Sunday best reaches out his hand to guide her down the platform steps and she brushes him away with a motion from her right hand and removes her left hand from the railing to continue to ground level, faltering a bit on the way. Her hair is cut severely short, short enough to pass for a man if it were not for the double row of buttons on her dark blue dress that barely seem to be holding in her wide, ample bosom. The knowing, maternal smile that never leaves her face highlights her large gray eyes above and her set jaw below.

I am grateful we have arrived early on this clear summer day, for Mama and Heli and I are only a few feet back from the platform steps and able to see easily over the heads of the mostly shorter women in front of us. Turning around to survey the huge throng packed into a semi-circle surrounding the platform, I am impressed by the crowd and struck by the number of dresses. We are mostly women and children, with but a few men interspersed throughout the hundreds. Then, as my eyes take me all the way back to the far edge of our gathering, I notice a ring of matching shirts and the glint of rifle barrels and bayonets in the morning sun.

The National Guard has surrounded us, and it does not feel like they are here for our security.

The cheering ceases to allow our obvious guest of honor to speak privately to a small group of men who meet her at the bottom of the steps. The impatience of the crowd of mostly women shows itself with a short-lived silence as she continues to speak to the men, and then nods her head. The man who offered his hand for a moment on her way down the platform now offers his arm, and she takes it to re-ascend, the two of them standing and looking out into the crowd.

"Ladies," he shouts, and looks around the crowd in a command of silence. "Ladies and gentlemen, Mother Jones," and the sound of raised female voices commands an even greater attention in applause that lasts a full minute.

"Ladies," Mother Jones begins with both deference to the crowd and a backhanded smite to her introducer. "I am not here to give great speeches. I am not here to support the men who invited me. I am not here for the greater glory of a humble woman by the name of Mother Jones." The cheers move toward us like a wave from the back of the crowd, and the volume feels as if it goes through me as it peaks at the elderly woman standing alone now on the platform. "I am here for you!" and she pauses again for emphasis. "I am here for your husbands who are striking back at the tyranny of managers who say 'to hell with a fair wage.' I am here for your friends who are striking back at the tyranny of managers who say 'to hell with a reasonable workday.' I am here for your friends who are striking back at the tyranny of managers who say 'to hell with safety because a one-man drill means more money.'"

I think her pause here means I should clap and cheer, yet there is no reaction to her reference to the one-man drill, and I quickly realize that her reference to more money for managers will not be acknowledged.

"I have already been told about some of the dirty tricks that mine managers are dealing our men. I have just been told about a union man threatened for daring to exercise his right for fair wages, an eight-hour day and a safe place to work. Well, if I'd have been threatened by a man for daring to speak of this," she raises her right hand and makes it into a fist, "I'd have knocked him to the ground myself!"

Starting from the front of the crowd this time with the women who have the best view of the grandmother with the fist, the crowd erupts with cheers and applause and a little laughter at the image of this elderly mother taking on a man with her bare hands.

"None of us wants violence. None of us wants blood-shed. Tell your men to leave their guns at home. But if a management tyrant comes after them ... if a soldier comes after them ... if some deputy just hired by the mines comes after your man because he dares to do what is fair and right and just..." she pauses long enough to hush this bustling outdoor train station into the silence of a Sunday Mass Consecration, "...then tell your man to blacken both those tyrant's eyes with his fists so he can't see to shoot him."

Mother Jones stands in the middle of the platform to deafening applause as she points to individual women and mouths the same phrase to each of them. As she moves her gesticulating finger across the crowd to the area where Mama and Heli and I are standing, and points near us, I can tell what she is saying.

"I'm here for you."

"I'm here for you."

"I'm here for you," she concludes by pointing to a woman in the front row dressed in a torn, shabby gray dress and holding a baby in her left arm and a toddler in her right.

*Uhh-oooooga!*

Accustomed to train whistles, I am still so startled I jump at the sound unlike a train whistle that comes from behind me. Along with all the other women, I turn to see for the first time a bright black automobile creeping slowly toward us. Mother Jones's face breaks into a wide grin and she stands firm on the platform until the man who introduced her walks up to her and again offers his arm. She lifts her hand to her mouth and cups it as a motion for the man to lean over and lend his ear. His face breaks into a grin that matches hers and he motions to those of us in front to give room as they reach the first step. They stop on the first step, and the man looks at me and others standing between them and the automobile.

"Mother Jones says she's never ridden in one of these machines. Give us a little space, please."

The group in front parts to allow Mother Jones and the man who introduced her to pass freely through, and as they stop at the right front door of the automobile, he opens it and motions for her to get in. With help from the man, she steps both feet up and onto the floor of the automobile, and stands there stooped with her head near a wheel jutting out from the inside front of the left side. Still hesitating, she lowers her left hand onto the seat and, when it gives a little under the pressure from her hand, she lowers her bottomside left and backward onto the seat. Her grin broadens even more at the cheer arising from around her.

Farther back from the automobile, a band that has soundlessly assembled takes the lead and begins marching away from the train station. With instruments at their sides in silence and high-stepping in a smart march, the band leads the way left onto Oak Street. The National Guardsmen fall in behind the band, and the crowd narrows into a thick line to form the parade.

We've lost our advantage of being up front and it'll be some time before the band and Mother Jones in her new automobile and the crowd wend their way down Oak Street for the four blocks to Fifth Street, the unofficial start of Red Jacket's parade route.

"So that's *the most dangerous woman in America*," Mama says as she turns to me and Heli. "I read it the other day in *Työmies*," she volunteers as the answer to our unspoken question. "Our former President Mr. Theodore Roosevelt described her that way."

I recognize the sarcasm in her voice and the wit I've come to respect when Mama adds a mocking gravitas to Roosevelt's already auspicious title of "President" by inserting "Mr."

"Himself a former rebel, President Roosevelt must not have enough to keep him busy, now that he's been out of office for four years. I wasn't sure I wanted to attend today. And I wasn't sure I wanted to invite my own daughters along to an event that seemed to have no purpose," Mama lets slip her disdain for pointless parades. "But when I read that, I knew I had to come today. And I hope you girls learn something from this as well."

I'm still not certain where I stand in the ongoing battle between my parents over this strike. But I did learn at least one thing. Now I know where Heli gets her resolve.

We are held near the depot platform by an incoming train that disrupts any hope I have of parading down Fifth Street with Mama and Heli and the rest of the women. Mama has been content to let the crowd move from the train station to the parade route without her, and that means without me and Heli.

The smell of cigar smoke hits me and I look to see Sheriff Cruse briskly walking toward us, obviously with an agenda and more obviously with a large folded white placard tucked under his left arm, a corrugated box under his right. He almost runs into all three of us at once with his girth that nearly matches his height and an air of holier-than-thou authority propelled by a badge. The same vest and jacket that today do not match his trousers are again stained with sweat as he chomps at his cigar and moves to the center of the platform. His visage presents the other side of an ugly dichotomy when he stops near the same place as Mother Jones stood a few minutes ago. As passengers step from the train to the platform, he bends over with effort, lays the corrugated box on the platform, untucks the placard from under his left arm, unfolds it, and holds it over his head. It's then I realize that the placard has writing on it in a bold, wobbly, barely legible hand that runs downhill from the first letter to the last, and I think to myself that the handwriting fits the placard-holder.

*Waddell Mahon* states the placard, and Sheriff Cruse waves it left and right over his head as if he needs more attention.

A man who looks to be about 30 in a scruffy old sailor's

suit and a scar running from the inside corner of his left eye to the hinge of his jawbone is the first to leave the train, and he saunters up to Sheriff Cruse and stops. They look at one another, but no hint of recognition registers on either one's face, and the ex-sailor's gawp breaks first as he moves to the Sheriff's side and turns around to also face the train.

This guy looks like someone with a name like Waddell Mahon, and he looks like he's trying to deny it by stepping aside and watching for someone else to disembark who somehow better fits the description.

A wad of brown spittle shoots out the door of the train first and splats on the platform before a short man with grease in his long dirty wavy hair steps from the train, glances up at the placard, squints like he can't see it, or more likely can't read it, and joins Sheriff Cruse and the sailor who is denying his surname is Mahon.

The two newly arrived passengers can't be related.

A third Waddell Mahon joins the group with a dirty braided rope holding up trousers that are ripped down the outside seam of his right leg, then on closer inspection I see that the new seam is caused by a clean cut. This Waddell Mahon seems to catch a sniff of air that offends him, and he cups his left hand over a nose that is flattened wide over much of his face, squeezes his nose near the bridge with his thumb and forefinger, and blows snot into his palm, then wipes the snot onto the left leg of his trousers, adding to an already damp area on the unseamed pant leg.

Sheriff Cruse ignores us as completely as when he nearly ran into us, but all three Waddell Mahons leer at us with looks so evil and lecherous that neither Mama nor Heli nor I can abide, and we back away from the platform without speaking, the lechers following us with their stares until they bore of their mutual amusement and we are a safe distance away.

Mama places her arms around me and Heli, and we stand our ground in the safer distance near the railroad signalman and continue to watch this Shakespearean comic tragedy unfold.

The misfits stream through the train door now, onto the platform and over near Sheriff Cruse, a dreadful menagerie of Waddell Mahons who all glower at the sheriff like they'd just as soon cut out his liver as look at him.

The railroad signalman waves his right arm up to his shoulder, then down to his side and the train lurches forward and stops as the last train car before the caboose aligns just short of the platform.

This is not a passenger car. It is an enclosed freight car with a single door in the center that slides open from an overhead rail that, together with the door, take up nearly half the length of the freight car. The signalman moves toward the door to open it and before he can reach it, the door slides aside and men jump out and onto the ground, squinting away from the summer sun. They jostle into one another when they first hit the ground, and a pushing match erupts as soon as some of the men have their footing.

I cannot tell who starts it or who the fight is between or even how many, but I hear the sound of knuckles against skin and I hear a loud pop that I guess is a jawbone moving or a nose breaking.

The entire scene in front of me freezes when we all hear the sound of a gunshot and look to Sheriff Cruse holding a pistol over his head, smoke lazily floating from the barrel.

"Men, you're here to do a job," he shouts. "You're here for protection." None in the ragtag gang seem impressed. "And you'll straighten up and listen up, or you ain't gettin' paid."

That does it. The motley group on the ground stops jostling, the men filling the platform stand a little straighter, and Sheriff Cruse re-holsters his pistol as they all continue to eye one another suspiciously. He bends over and reaches to his feet, then straightens, holding a badge in his left hand. He holds out his right arm at shoulder level and cocks his forearm up and opens his hand, palm out.

"Alright men, raise your right hand."   A few comply. "Raise your right hand!" he commands, this time with better, though not complete compliance.

As Sheriff Cruse glowers at the faces of the unraised right hands, expecting to shame them into compliance, the ex-sailor finds the corrugated box and, standing behind Sheriff Cruse, he lifts the box that is bulging with its contents over Sheriff Cruse's head and steadies it with his left arm.  Then, with a move so fast I barely see his right hand and do not see the knife, he slits the box, and metal badges pour over Sheriff Cruse's head and shoulders and onto the ground.

The Sheriff flinches when the first metal badge hits his skull, then bends over and covers his head too late, for all the badges are now spilled onto his head and onto the platform. Rising now from his bent position, he looks angrily into a sea of laughing faces and turns around at the ex-sailor, turns again to face the group, and then, in a moment of better judgment, allows a half-smile.   He waits to regain his composure before starting again.

My mind takes me back to Sheriff Cruse and Mr. Mac-Naughton deputizing the men of Laurium on the steps of the hospital, and the difference between these two scenes is as disparate as the difference between Sheriff Cruse and Mother Jones.  Today, the sheriff is not even bothering with the formality of specific words found in a book that would be appreciated by none of his audience were it held in his left hand.

"Alright men, raise your right hand and repeat after me."

"And repeat after me," shouts one of the men from the freight car who is standing below the platform.

It is now definitely time to leave.

Papa had already heard of Waddell Mahon at work and waits patiently at supper to hear of today's dominantly female adventure before explaining to us that Waddell

Mahon is the name of an agency in New York City that supplies goons. "Goons are paid strike-breakers," he explains further. "Mercenaries who love to fight, and are sent across the country to supposedly *protect the interests of management*, but invariably pick fights with workers who have gone on strike. Waddell Mahon is based in New York City, where it has the choice of former pugilists and former military men, and all are present-day fighters and misfits."

"There is something disturbingly familiar about the way they look and act. And it occurs to me now," Mama says as she turns to me and Heli. "When we left Ellis Island, Papa and I knew we wanted to come here to this special place in Michigan, for we'd been told when we left Finland that here is where the land and the weather and our kinsmen will most welcome us. But we needed to make arrangements to get here, and we planned to stay three more days in New York City to complete our travel arrangements and see the sights. And after passage on the ship, we needed some time alone on firm ground."

"Terra firma," Papa and I say together in duet, and laugh at the way we harmonize.

"The days were fine," Mama continues. "Papa and I were enthralled by the big city and tall buildings and riches everywhere in our new-found freedom. But the nights," and Mama turns to Papa as they both smile at their now-timeworn recollections. "The nights in our inexpensive boarding house were bad dreams of excesses in every imaginable way. The drunkenness and bile everywhere. The loose women and undisciplined men. The debauchery and blasphemy and fighting. Oh, the fighting." Mama pauses in a state of uncomfortable recollection, and then says, "I brought intense pressure to your Papa to get us out of there. After only two days, with the ink barely dry on our tickets, we left New York City for the Copper Country. For home. And that's why I recognize those men today. The clothes, the behavior, the fighting all say the cheap boarding houses in the ghettoes of New York City."

"Are we safe from Waddell Mahon?" Heli asks, lumping all the men into one name, as I did earlier today.

"We must be careful," and the way he dodges the question tells me we must be *very* careful. "We must stay together, as we have, and be more zealous in the way we look after and protect one another. We are Finns, after all, and our togetherness will get us through the short run, and our love and friendship will prevail in the long run. This strike will be over soon, I'm sure."

With enough men returning to work to pump the water from the mines, but not enough men to re-start copper production, Papa tells us it is safe to venture into the back yard, but Heli is still taking no chances as she motions to the privy and grabs my hand in the waning light of the day of Mother Jones's inspirational encouragement and Sheriff Cruse's deputizing debacle.

The inside of the outhouse becomes lighted and Heli's eyes meet mine when she looks up and we both hold our breath, not from the odor, but in anticipation of the sound of thunder.

The light is gone as quickly as it appeared. My mind refocuses with the clarity of the earlier day on the cloudless start to the parade, the freight train of fighters squinting from the pain of the bright sun.

A minute ago, as Heli and I walked outside and turned left to round the house, I noticed no clouds against the horizon illuminated by the barely submerged sun, now set beneath Superior to the west.

I let go of Heli's hand and back out the privy door to see what I may have missed in the sky, but she is up and straight through the door right after me, so I wait for her to re-grasp my hand and we both look up together. It's dusk now, but we can tell there are no clouds. We look to the west when another flash of light is cast onto all the houses on Ridge

Street in front of us. I sense that the light came from behind, and was so bright I felt it on my back. Heli felt it too, for we turn around and face east together.

In the eastern distance, a powerful single beam of light is now pointed away from us, lighting the top of Shaft Number One. It slowly redirects its aim toward the Coliseum still under construction and continues moving westerly until it hits us again, and both Heli and I duck, but it quickly passes us in a wide sweep south, and then is extinguished by what I think to be a phantom puff of air in the early night.

"What was that I saw?" questions Mama as she and Papa join our now mutually mystified little group.

"I don't know, Mama. I was only sitting there, when suddenly Emilia and I are just lightened up! We looked up and then we saw it again because it lit up everything around us," Heli explains, excluding the part about being together in the outhouse.

We stand together looking in the direction of its origin and the beam is suddenly revived, starting with a shot from on high to the ground, and then moving upward to the east until its destination is lost as it is aimed straight into the sky. Even with nothing to be lighted by it, we can sense its power as it casts a bright shaft of light far into the sky before finally being swallowed by the looming darkness.

"It's only going down and up now," Heli says. "When Emilia and I saw it before, it hit us from behind, and then it swooped over every bit of Red Jacket and every bit of Swedetown and every bit of Laurium."

"Where would you say it's coming from, Emilia?" Papa asks.

"It seems like the light always starts from a few hundred yards past where you work, Papa. Maybe near Washington School."

"Ah, that explains it," and if I didn't admire his logic and intelligence so much, I could get really peeved at him during moments like this. "It's coming straight from Shaft Number

Two, where I used to ... near where I now work. The reason it appears to be emanating from a farther distance is that the light is mounted high at the top of the shaft house. They were working on it today and I heard talk that it's a 'security light,' but no one could really explain what that means. I asked others what was going on, and they only said 'Mac-Naughton's eye.' I still wasn't sure what 'security light' meant and I certainly wasn't sure what 'MacNaughton's eye' meant. Now, I think we all know what both of them mean, and they're both the same."

"*MacNaughton's Eye*, Mama laughs. "That's a good description."

"Isn't it?" Papa agrees. "Frankly, I hate the thought, but love the metaphor."

# VIII

## August 17

A baseball diamond is the place where I belong on a summer Sunday. Every summer Sunday for every year for as long as can I remember, our family has congregated at St. Joseph's for Mass, packed a picnic basket, and set off for the diamond in Tamarack or Kearsarge or Ahmeek, sometimes even as far as Eagle River, and at the top of the hill near our house in Swedetown for the home games to watch Papa and our Swedetown Skyhooks.

This is the year of colossal change, what with Papa's injury, the strike, and my *coming of age*, as Mama describes it, and it feels good to wrap up all this change, tie it in a bow, and lay it aside for a day to watch baseball.

I can think of nothing else in our lives that has crossed the lines of religion and nationality to produce unprejudiced excellence like baseball. The players from first base to third base represent every religious conviction and the catcher to the center fielder every ethnicity. Talent and speed and quick thinking and hard work matter. Job title and who is a good friend with whom and who is Finnish and who is Catholic or Lutheran or Methodist do not.

The Kearsarge Comets are in Swedetown for the final home game of the season and this is indeed the Skyhooks final game, for they are out of the playoffs this year. Edouard Archambeau, our third baseman who was leading the league in homers, is now gone with a broken arm from falling rock, and our best pitcher is out for the season. Many men have tried to step up, I have heard, to replace Papa, but none have the physical attributes or mental toughness or sheer strength of will that define him on or off the mound.

Today, he sits with Mama and Heli and me behind first base, a little up the hill so we can see home plate over the heads of the players on the bench.

I try to ignore the clear picture now in my mind of the scene from only a few hours ago when heavy foot traffic and horses pulling wagons loaded with people were coming toward us as we left Mass at St. Joseph's. The altar veils were being changed from white to black. *I know where the people were heading*, I think to myself now, and it's best if I can forget about it for at least the duration of a baseball game.

When the Catholic players on both teams, and we fans on the sides of the field make the sign of the cross at the end of the Angelus after the noon church bells ring, the game begins.

The Skyhooks score first on a double, a dribbler to second that advances the runner, and a throwing error in the bottom of the third inning, and hold the Comets for the first four innings. Sock Johnson, our young pitcher who is being groomed to replace Papa, starts the fifth by retiring the first two Comets with a sharp groundout to short and a flyout to deep center before walking the next two batters. Sock is too young to be tiring, but has just lost his stuff for the moment, and is struggling to regain it. Our manager, Mr. Hubert Kunnari, walks out to the mound and puts his arm on Sock's right shoulder, says a few words, and returns to the bench.

The next Comet batter, a right-handed hitter who is a little behind on Sock's well-delivered pitch, drills a liner to the opposite field, scoring the first Comets' run and putting men on first and third. Mr. Kunnari sits on the bench and brings his right palm to his forehead, then wipes it over his face before resting his chin in it. With runners on the corners, a left-handed batter digs in at the plate with his bare feet, and smashes a long fly ball over the head of Mr. Emil Frantti in right field, who catches up to the ball after it rolls near the third hole of the golf course, but before it reaches the cow pasture. Mr. Frantti throws it to the second baseman Wilbert Aho, now deep in right field for the relay. The relay from right innocently reaches Gervin Frazier at home plate after the red-headed Comet races around the horn for a three-run homer.

The Skyhooks are behind four to one.

Usually the first with words of encouragement and shouts of support, Papa is surprisingly quiet and only chimes in after one of our fans first calls a Skyhook by name, or Papa clearly recognizes a voice. Earlier in the game, he incorrectly identified one of our hitters because Mr. Kunnari had changed the batting order. With my thoughts of an impending funeral and something amiss with Papa, my package neatly wrapped into the innocence of baseball is becoming undone.

Mr. Frantti remains in right field talking with the golfer who is approaching the area where the golf course converges with the baseball diamond, overseen by the grazing cows. Another contrast, this time in costume, strikes me as I watch our right fielder with his short-sleeved shirt sporting the name *Skyhook* stitched on the back, now in an apparently heated conversation with the knickers-and-jacketed golfer.

I have often seen this man practicing golf before, and I have often wondered how he can afford to golf so much because I've never seen him in town working.

Play on the baseball field stops to watch Mr. Frantti puff out his chest and stick his right index finger near the nose of the golfer like the man in knickers is an umpire who just made a bad call. The golfer stands back and apparently lets fly with some sort of expletive I can't hear. With a well-deserved reputation for being a slow burning hot-head, Mr.

Frantti first shakes his head, and stands back. The golfer sees this as a retreat and stands taller to hurl what I guess is another expletive. Our Skyhook, who we all know is really in charge here, walks around the golfer, bends over and picks up the golf ball lying near both their feet, and puts it in his pocket. The golfer raises his club to strike Mr. Frantti who, seeing it coming, winds up and lands a punch on the golfer's chin before he even starts to lower his club.

The biggest cheer I hear all game erupts from both the first and third base sides of the diamond, everyone on both sides of the baseball field expressing partiality for the man representing the sport they're playing.

Lying on the ground with the club still in his hand, the golfer straightens the shaft toward Mr. Frantti and waves it at him like he's trying to dare the baseball player into a jousting match. He springs to his feet with the shaft headed toward Mr. Frantti's face. Before it reaches him, Mr. Frantti swipes his left hand out and grasps the shaft out of the golfer's hands, grabs the club end with his right, snaps the shaft over his knee, and throws both pieces to the ground. Now standing up but weaponless, the golfer looks at Mr. Frantti for only a moment before turning and walking away from an angry baseball player and a standing ovation from both teams and both teams' fans.

"We've missed you, Henrik," says Mr. Frantti as he joins our family after the game. He is Papa's best friend on the baseball team and they both hail from Helsinki and they both have the same complexion, like mine, that's unique for a Finn because it darkens in the summer. "That game should have been ours, one to nothing with the strength of your pitching."

"Maybe even more than one," Papa counters. "I had a fair eye for a pitched ball and I knew all their tricks, and a decent bat."

"Okay, five to nothing with your imaginary grand slam. A fair eye? A decent bat? Henrik, I was pretty sure you could count the stitches on a pitched ball before you belted it. I wish ... we all wish you had removed those dark spectacles and joined us by now."

"What do we say at the end of every year, Emil? There's always next year. But tell me, what was that all about?" Papa asks, not needing to explain his reference to the altercation in the top of the fifth, out in right field and on the third hole of the golf course when Emil Frantti sent the golfer packing.

"He called me a fin...," Mr. Frantti pauses and looks at Mama and me and Heli. "A finger," and he looks to Papa like he will recognize it as an insult, but I do not. "So I put mine near his nose and told him I was in the middle of our game and willing to overlook that, but he wouldn't let it go. Then I recognized him. He's the crooked banker who tried to *help* me finance my home with a never-ending mortgage. My wife insisted she read it all before letting me sign, and between us we figured the bank would own our home *ad infinitum*, as you would translate into your fancy Latin." He and Papa laugh together as Mr. Frantti puts his hand onto Papa's shoulder like a coach. And a friend. "Needless to say, we didn't sign. His name is Carl Houseworth and he works for First of America Bank and together they make a lot of money on crooked mortgages. I don't know what stopped me from pummeling him into the ground once I recognized him. My sense of fair play, I guess. Certainly not my temper," he admits.

"There was no reason for that," Papa says. We've been sharing the diamond and the golf course for years now. We've stopped a baseball game when a group of golfers stand on number three and put those silly small balls into the hole. They've deferred to fly balls into right field. What was different today?"

"*Putts*, Henrik. They *putt* a golf ball into a hole, not *put* it in. I've been listening to you correct this team's grammar for years now, and it feels good to get one on you."

"I had that coming, didn't I?" Papa says as he and Mr.

Frantti laugh again together.

"Like I said, I was willing to overlook the insult, but he just wouldn't let it go. Then he swung at me and pointed the shaft of his golf club at me, reminding me of how he pointed the pen at me when I refused to sign his mortgage. But I don't play his game and I surely didn't want his golf ball. That reminds me, Emilia, would you like the game ball?"

Mr. Frantti takes the golf ball out of his pocket and hands it to me.

The bells of so many churches toll that I can't tell whether their source is Catholic or Lutheran or Methodist. Probably these and more. A train whistle blows a blast so long that it ends in a descending dirge as if it has lost all its steam. We look down to the bottom of our hill and see a long passenger train moving past Swedetown toward the depot in town right next to St. Joseph's church.

*The funeral train*, I think to myself, and others who are near the baseball field state in words. I have managed to leave the thoughts mostly alone during the game and I can no longer quell them when every player from both teams, and every fan from both sides, stops in respectful silence.

I read the news to Papa from the Finnish newspaper *Työmies* on Friday, and again to him from the *Mining Gazette* yesterday.

Seeberville is about twenty miles south of here and still as dramatically affected as we by the same events. Their workers are on strike, their mines idled by the standoff between the Western Federation of Miners and every one of the over 25 mines in the Copper Country, as well as the seven mines Papa says are being developed.

The *Työmies* account spoke of the Seeberville strikers minding their own business, being confronted and harassed by drunken Waddell Mahon men, then being chased home where they were shot and murdered in cold blood.

The *Mining Gazette* story reported inebriated and belligerent protestors who provoked and dared lawmen to take justifiable action, which they did when they defended themselves after being lured into a trap.

When I was done reading the newspapers to Papa last night, I told him I felt like I had just read two fiction novels with only a few similarities, yet both with the same morbid ending: two wounded, two dead. Both accounts named the aggressors and the aggrieved, though they were switched in either newspaper. There was no dispute over its location in Seeberville, the place of the *incident*, or *murder site*. Both newspapers named the Waddell Mahon men as well as the wounded and the dead.

"As usual," he said, "the truth is somewhere in the middle. That's why I read, I mean I have asked you to read these two. They are both reporting the same tragic incident, and I already know their not-so-subtle biases, so I get the widest possible views. It's my responsibility to sort through the details, ascertain the facts, and get to the truth. I'll tell you, Emilia, I cannot always do that. Let's try this together." Papa lingers for a moment and I can tell by the two different looks on his face that he is first expressing sorrow and regret for a confrontation that took two lives, wounded two others. Then he is trying to make sense of it while trying to help me make sense of it, too.

This strike has hurt his eyes and is approaching his heart, I can tell.

"Let's look at the reported consistencies," he begins.

"John Stimac and a friend were accidentally crossing onto, or got caught trespassing on mine property by a mine boss. They confronted, or were confronted by goons or lawmen," I summarize.

"And they were shot where?"

"At the boarding house of one of the men killed – John Stimac."

"None of the deputies or Waddell Mahon men wounded? ... shot at?"

"Well...," I try to recall all the details of both newspaper articles, "...one of them, I'm not clear from the *Mining Gazette* article whether it was a deputy or one of the Waddell Mahon men, had a ten-pin thrown at him. I do recall that the *Gazette* stated he could have been seriously injured because it nearly hit him in the head."

"Could have been injured? Nearly hit him?" Papa lets his disdain slip. The expression on his face changes and I can tell he is thinking. "Neither account says how far between the mine property and the boarding house, so you and I will need to extrapolate. Let's use this area as an example, and say that the boarding house was at least a few hundred feet away, to as much as a mile. Now, who else was there at the boarding house?"

"The newspapers are consistent on that point: two women and three children."

I see the picture beginning to form in his mind.

"Let's recap what we know of the consistencies so far: two men are leisurely crossing or trespassing, not an egregious crime either way, right? Waddell Mahon men are involved, and that makes me suspicious. I trust your Mama's judgment of those men, none of whom were injured, or possibly even shot at. Two killings occur some distance away. Women and children are tangled in the mess." He stops again. I can tell he is there. "Now read the names of the Waddell Mahon men."

"Arthur Davis, William Groff, Harry...," I begin to recite.

"Just the surnames."

"Davis, Groff, James, Cooper."

"Now read me the names of those shot."

"Stanko, no, I'm sorry, Stepic is the surname. Stepic and Stimac wounded. Tijan and Putric killed."

"I will leave you to your own conclusions," he states with a flat note that I know signals finality. "I have drawn mine."

Papa echoes his morose thoughts of last night when he

says today that it is not right to make a spectacle of a funeral. Yet that is what we are watching from the baseball field not far from our house high above Swedetown. After gathering their baseball equipment and picnic baskets, the players and fans move from the field. The boys who have run to the water tower to view the spectacle return with reports of "thousands" gathered between St. Joseph and St. John the Baptist Churches, where the funeral Masses for Steven Putric and Alois Tijan are being offered. It will take a line from there all the way to Lake View Cemetery nearly two miles away to accommodate that many mourners.

We walk in silence together as a family down the Upper Gate Trail to Fir Street and over to Ridge Street, where we pause in front of our house. A train is departing off-schedule and we stop to watch it pass through the tunnel at the foot of Swedetown. It's another long one and Heli and I continue down Ridge Street to watch the train as Papa and Mama turn to our house.

"I wonder," Heli says, but leaves the thought hanging as our hush from the funeral continues to enshroud us. We can see the train clearly as it exits the tunnel. There are no uniforms visible on the men through the windows, but they're all young men, and the clothes they're wearing are somehow more citified, not of the Keweenaw Peninsula. The enclosed freight cars, like the one from which the last of the Waddell Mahon rag tags stumbled into our world, offer no further hints. We suck in our breaths in unison when three cars with wide slats emerge from the tunnel, and release our breaths when the contents of a flat car hit the afternoon sun, the black cannons seeming to absorb, not reflect, the light. The caboose on the end is not even out of sight before another engine slides from the tunnel into view, and Heli and I remain watching as the scene repeats itself with passenger cars chockfull of what we now know to be departing soldiers, freight cars with supplies, wide-slatted cars for plenty of air for the horses, and flat cars with heavy guns just before the lonesome caboose.

"Good riddance to the National Guard, but good riddance to only the half of you who just left," I say because I clearly heard four long, off-schedule trains from our basement when Heli announced their arrival nearly three weeks ago. But this is a good start, for I often see their officers speaking only with mine managers, while the mine workers have been intimidated by their *peacekeeping* presence, in spite of their claims of neutrality.

The walk back up Ridge Street feels lighter than the walk down, though no more conversational, and I let Heli provide the details to Papa and Mama, preferring to be alone with my thoughts of a strike that has now claimed two lives and caused my life as I knew it to change in ways that I can barely understand, and cannot foretell its consequences.

"You're not allowed to dawdle," Mama interrupts my intention to read a book, and disrupts my thoughts and maybe even a little self-pity when she announces "bread for the upcoming week, fried dough for supper!"

Mrs. Archambeau brought some of her fried dough, with sugar sprinkled on it, to one of the Skyhooks games and passed it around for others to share. We Finnish ladies were all impressed, but Mama was too bashful to ask for the recipe. Mrs. Archambeau gladly shared it with Mama when Papa also tasted it, and insisted that Mama at least try it. Fried dough, with sugar if we have any, has become a favorite since, and even Uncle Bear has taken a liking to this French specialty.

I rinse the metal bread batter bucket, the one we're not permitted to use for anything else except bread and water, but only if it's pumped directly from the well. The water is already warming and the lard is melting on the stove, so Heli gathers the flour, sugar and salt while I look for the eggs and buttermilk, purchased only since Papa is back to work. Heli mixes the warm water, melted lard, and buttermilk in the bucket while I add some flour, then she hands me the big wooden spoon and I stir the mixture slowly until she returns with the sugar and eggs, and cracks the eggs into the batter. I take the wooden spoon and Heli knows how much salt to add and how much of the cake of yeast to cut off and crumble in, how much flour to continue adding, and to mix it into the batter only a handful at a time. When the mixture looks right to her and me, we nod in agreement and I lay the spoon on the counter for the first of three breaks we'll have before putting the loaves into the oven.

That's plenty of time to enjoy more of *The Secret Garden*.

When I've floured our tiny countertop and moved the wooden spoon over, Heli takes the bucket and pours its now single content of heavy dough onto the counter. The small and wispy child who used to struggle with the bucket and force the big wad of dough down the side of the bucket and onto the counter is now a mischievous young lady who lets the dough plop onto the counter in a lump, spraying her and me and half the kitchen in a haze of flour. Armed only with intuition, I could see it coming and still let her get away with it when she raised the bucket and flashed that impish grin at me.

"Well, we both know you're not cut out to stay at home and wash clothes and bake bread. So what *are* you going to do after you graduate next year, Emilia?"

"I'm going to live at home and stay busy trying to keep you out of trouble."

"Can you make money studying?" I respond to her rhetorical question with a smirk. "Can you make money reading all the time?" This option is more pleasurable, so it earns my smile. "Seriously, Emilia, you need to be thinking about what you're going to do with your life. And if you don't, I'll be happy to figure it out for you."

"Heli, I appreciate your reminders, but I don't appreciate your suggested occupations, and besides, I have a whole year to work on it."

"No, you don't. Papa will insist that you at least have a plan in place. You know how he loves to strategize."

I'm impressed with Heli's use of the word. Perhaps she, too, is beginning to take academics more seriously.

"I don't know, Heli. I know I want something with a future and something that engages my mind. Mama is right about me being impulsive, so that eliminates teaching." Taking the wooden spoon off the counter, I raise it like a pointer and leave it hanging in the air. "Mama and you are both right. There aren't a lot of options for women. Mama was lucky to have found Papa, but I don't hold out much hope of duplicating her feat." This is the same discourse I have with myself, and it's heading for the same dead end I always seem to encounter with no help from Heli, so I use one of her diversionary tactics. "I'm going to learn to play baseball even better than you and Papa, and you just watch when I swat that ball," and I spank at her behind with the wooden spoon, "better than the red-headed leftie who hit the homer today."

Heli is content to let it go for a while and I listen to her chatter about baseball as we return to bread-making.

Since my hands are already floured, I take the first shift of kneading, a task I've actually begun to enjoy lately. Heli adds the last of the flour and takes over when she sees my arms beginning to tire. When she's done, she puts the dough back into the bucket and I cover it with cheesecloth and return to a full hour to indulge in the *Garden*. Break number two. I leave Heli to fire up the stove and melt the tub of lard we'll need later for frying the dough.

When I smell the hot lard and heated oven, I return to the kitchen and overturn onto the counter the bucket containing twice as large a wad of dough as before. I punch it down a little, careful to remove the bubbles, but not kneading it as hard as Heli and I first did.

"Don't cut it in half this time," Heli says. "First cut off enough for frying, then cut the rest in half," and I'm glad she reminds me, for my head is still in the *Garden*. I think Heli knows it. The knife is shared between us as we cut pieces the size of about half a bread pan from the lumps in front of each of us, then tuck them into the greased pans and cover them again with cheesecloth.

Break number three.

"No, you don't. We're making fried dough for supper. Remember, the fried dough you cut off and laid aside about five minutes ago?"

Heli is right, of course. We need to deep-fry the dough for supper, an addendum to our bread-making that occurs only infrequently. I cut off a palm-sized piece of dough, roll, then flatten it, pick it up in both hands, and punch a hole in the center with my big finger before placing it back onto the counter near the stove. The lard will be boiling and Heli will let them rise a little before dunking them in. I count how many I'll need to make out of the last remaining wad of dough, and cut and form the numbers and sizes according to what Papa and Mama and Heli and I usually eat. I'll still have a little time before we take the bread from the oven, and Heli makes no complaint when I head for the sheet-covered sofa in the sitting room.

I don't hear Papa come in from outdoors, where he's been since Heli and I started the bread and started frying the dough, but we all know what he's here for. I usually like to have the honor, but I give it to Heli this time and she takes it with another impish grin. She cuts the crust off the first loaf of bread removed from the oven, turns away from him, and pours salt onto the top left corner, then sets it onto a plate on the table in front of him. Of course, he takes his first bite into Heli's well-aimed corner, while Heli turns to the cupboard and brings out the butter and honey.

Papa stops as soon as he's chewed only a little too-salted bread. He looks up from the table as if he's going to comment on the bread recipe, chews some more, and Heli knows she's been tried and convicted as the villain, me as her accomplice.

"Emilia?" Silence. "Heli?" and the three of us burst out laughing together as Heli moves in with her butter and honey to salve a sense of humor that he probably doesn't even need.

We've not yet put away the supper dishes when there's a tentative knock on the door, and Mama opens it to the two eldest boys who live upstairs. Twelve-year old Anders, holding a baseball bat, and eleven-year old Per are the only well-behaved Nelsons, the rest of the children having apparently learned nothing of proper behavior from the parents who also must have given up trying to teach after birthing their first two.

"Sir,"Anders begins by addressing Papa, "we'd like to play baseball. And we'd like you to join us, Emilia and Heli, and ... and ... Mrs. Rytilahti," he adds as an afterthought. "But we have no baseball ... and we'd like to borrow yours ... if you have one ... and we'd like you to play with us."

"I think that's an excellent idea, Anders," Mama replies first. "Henrik, I watched you pining away during the game today, itching to get your hands on a baseball. Emilia and Heli may have forgotten how to play the game you coached them into. You can show the boys the finer points of the game, and it will do Emilia and Heli good to swing a bat, because we don't own one and sharing is the only way to get a game going. I have laundry to sort and plenty to keep me busy here. Let me see if I can find the baseball. And Heli, go outside and get Papa's backstop."

Mama hastens to their bedroom and I can hear her going through bureau drawers and sorting through things on the floor of their small closet, then she returns to the kitchen with a worn baseball and presses it into Papa's hands.

I see the look of angst on his face when Mama is gone and it lessens only a little with the ball in his hands. He looks down, turns the grayed leather of the stitched covering in his hands, stops and looks up through his dark spectacles at nothing in particular. He looks down and again turns the ball in his hands until he aligns the seams with his two index fingers.

Heli forces Anders and Per farther into the kitchen when she returns with a two-foot by two-foot piece of wood in her hands and sets it on the floor in front of her. We learn Papa's answer only after he moves the ball with his left hand a half-turn, palms it with his right, then loosens the grip with his right hand and bends his fingers over nearly the entire ball, seems to dig in his fingernails, but does not, and instead buries the tips of the back of his fingers into the ball up to their first knuckles.

This is the grip he showed to me and Heli once when I asked how he made the ball seem like it jumps both vertically and horizontally on the same pitch to home plate. He called it his "knuckler."

Now, the same impish smile he taught Heli spreads over his face, and we know Papa will play baseball with us for the first time in a year. The smile on Heli's face isn't nearly as subtle as the one on Papa's, nor is the smile I can feel on mine.

"I need to warm up a little," Papa says when I accompany him to the mound, and Heli knows to squat behind home plate like a catcher and hold the piece of wood where it will approximate a strike zone. "Heli, my eyes are sore today. Don't move the wood unless I'm way out of the zone, but do let me know which direction I'm off." He goes from his warm-up half-wind into a pitch that is so far high that Heli can't even move the backstop fast enough to get it in the way of Papa's pitch. Hearing nothing, he asks, "High? ... must have been, because that's what it felt like."

"High and outside," Heli confirms.

"Outside on a rightie, or a leftie?"

"Oh, sorry Papa. Outside on a rightie and let's assume all the batters you're about to mow down are right-handed."

Heli throws the ball back to me, standing aside Papa, and I put it into his outstretched hand.

He smiles and gets the next pitch lower, and smiles again when he hears it hit the wooden backstop Heli is holding with fingers draped over the edges to expose as little of them as possible, bending them over like Papa's *knuckler*. From the side of the pitcher's mound, I can tell he's lost much of his speed, but his accuracy is getting better with every pitch. Anders is standing out of the batter's box and chattering at Papa and swinging in imprecise time with his pitches.

"Go ahead and step in there, Anders. I'll keep them slow and hopefully hittable for you." Anders is intimidated by his next pitch that's nearly a perfect strike, watching it go by like he's sitting at a supper table still enjoying his meal.

*Thwack!* goes the ball against the backstop as Heli yells "Strike one! You'll wait a long time if you're going to wait for one better than that," she warns.

Anders kicks back the dirt with his feet and digs in for the next pitch. It's a little low, but he connects with it and sends a dribbler toward shortstop, which I chase down before it leaves the infield. Papa takes all the speed off, and adds none of his fancy stuff to the next pitch, which Anders hits into short left field. As I head out to retrieve it, Papa says, "Let's have a game. Anders, you and Heli against Emilia and Per. I'll pitch to both sides and we'll have only two fielders against the hitter, so anything to right field is an automatic out. One fielder for the infield and one for the out. The one who's not hitting must catch, if you're not on-base, and then throw it to the infielder, who returns it to me. I'll let the infielder get into place before each pitch. Any hit ball picked up by the infielder or outfielder before the hitter reaches first, and you're out. This will make you place the ball as a hitter. And don't worry, I won't throw smoke. Five innings should be enough for all of us."

"How many angels apiece, Papa?" Heli asks.

"You're big kids now, Heli. One apiece. Throw the bat

for home team."

When I return near home plate, Anders tosses the bat to me with the barrel down and I catch it in my right hand and offer it back to him. He grips it with his right hand atop mine, I put my left hand atop his, and we narrow in toward the top of the bat handle. He has room to put a full hand between my hand and the knob of the bat, and there's no doubt which choice he'll make.

"We're home team," he declares.

"What's the batting order?" Per asks of me.

"Ladies first," Papa interrupts. "I get to make the rules."

I feel like a rusty hitter as I walk into the batter's box and Per settles in behind me with the backstop. Anders has taken the infield, probably thinking he'll get more defensive action there, but Heli can catch nearly any fly ball, though none of us own ball gloves, so it's a good spot for each of them. I connect with a ball that lofts lazily toward Anders, but he drops it, then quickly picks it up and holds it above his head before I reach first base. He walks to the mound and places the ball in Papa's hand, as he has watched me do.

One out.

I catch while Per stands to the plate and drills the second pitch past Papa's left side, but on the right field side of second base for an automatic out.

This is going too quickly.

He winds up into a fuller motion and puts a little heat on the ball, which I meet solidly and lace over his head on the barely safe side of second base for a solid single. There's no catcher now, so Papa grooves one to Per and he drives it into left field and I reach second before Heli chases it down and throws it to Anders in the infield.

"Angel on second," I declare and head into home plate for my turn again at bat. Papa doesn't need to remind me of this rule. With only one angel, and that one angel stranded on second, I need to hit at least a double. If I don't make it safely to second base, the angel won't score. I think he intentionally pitches me a pumpkin, and I smash it over Heli's head for a stand-up double, advancing Per to third.

"Angel on third," says Per as he strides in for his third at-bat of the inning, with two outs. A single would give us a little insurance, but the inning ends when he hits a liner straight to Heli, who stops to rub her stinging bare hands together only after she fields the ball cleanly, walks it in to Papa, and hands it to him.

"One-nothing," I say to Heli with my fingers pointing to the dimples on her face.

"One for the team that just batted in the top of the first, with *the home team* coming to the plate," she emphasizes by moving her right hand over her left arm to remind me of my summer-darkened skin.

I plant myself on the infield before Per can make a stand. I consider myself to be a trusty fielder, but I'm not as comfortable as Heli in stopping line drives dead in my hands and would prefer to knock them down and still have time to pick them up for the out.

Heli strokes Papa's first pitch straight at Per in the out-field, but it takes a bad bounce in front of him and over his right shoulder for an easy double. Anders is behind on the pitch that he connects to right field for an out, so he takes second base to allow Heli to come in and bat again.

*With a runner on second and one out and Heli at bat and not even their first angel on base, this could be a long inning*, I think.

"Papa, let's see if she can hit the knuckler," I suggest.

"The knuckler needs some practice," he says "so let's just see what she can do with a fastball."

Telling her what's coming in advance is no advantage to Heli because Papa's fastball has caused many a grown man to shake his head after missing it, some not even trying to swing. The pitched ball reaches Heli below her chest and near the outside of the plate, the place I know as her favorite spot to belt a long one. But she swings just a little too late and just a little too level and hits it straight back at him.

*Get your hands up to catch it*, I think to myself, but can't get the words out fast enough.

*Not at your face ... not at your spectacles*, I realize in horror, with these words frozen too.

"Duck!" I think, not sure if I've said it or only thought it.

The line drive straight back at him would have been easily caught with a clear-sighted Papa, the Papa I've seen often rising deftly from the half-crouch of his fastball delivered from his right hand to nimbly snatch a liner with his left. The Papa who used to be able to count the stitches on the ball before hitting it, or before having it hit back to him and making an out from a liner most other pitchers would move aside to let fall safely over second base and into shallow center field.

The Papa who used to be able to see.

The line drive strikes him squarely against the lens of his right eye, sending the spectacles flying in two pieces into two different directions as he spins to the ground with both hands now covering his face.

I run to his side and throw myself on the ground as he raises himself to his knees, grasping about with his hands in a vain attempt to find his spectacles. His head is down, his hands grabbing at the dirt while his fingers sift it for lost pieces. Onto my knees, I see the blood begin to drip down his right cheek. I grab his arm and he raises his head to look straight at me. I look at him. I look into his eyes.

Nothing.

Nothing is there.

No color.

No recognition.

No sight.

The gray of his eyes is gone, replaced by a large round dark spot in the center of each eye. A dark spot he couldn't possibly see out of. He closes his eyes with eyelids that are still peppered with small black dots, a thin layer of scarring over them.

*These must be the places where the specks of copper dust pierced his eyelids and punctured his eyes and came to rest in the back of his eyeballs*, I think to myself.

I am so stunned I am unable to even move.

I continue to stare.

"Papa, I am so sorry!" Heli cries as she joins us on the mound. He covers his eyes with his hands and I dab at the slow stream of blood running down his cheek. Heli picks up the two pieces of spectacles. The right lens is intact, but broken into shards that form a sunburst from the center of the lens, and broaden into wider pieces toward the metal exterior frame. The right bow is separated from the rest of the frame. "Here, Papa," she says as she hands the two pieces to him, waits for him to offer his right hand, then places the pieces into it. He covers his eyes with his left. "I am so sorry," she repeats.

Papa leans back and sits on the ground. He takes a deep breath and continues to shade his eyes with his left hand. "It's not your fault, Heli. You hit the ball, as you should have. It was a good pitch, wasn't it? I was just not quick enough to catch it. I'm fine now, but my spectacles are not. I'm afraid the game is over. And since we didn't make the three-inning minimum, there are no winners. No losers. You'll have to demand a re-match," he adds with a forced grin.

Anders and Per look around uncomfortably, then Anders picks up the bat and heads toward the water tower, enough light left for some serious frog hunting.

"Want to come, Heli?" and she looks to Papa, but he does not answer her unspoken question.

"Can I go, Papa?"

He tells her to be home before dark.

I take his left arm and walk beside him in uneasy silence, his face cast downward. He moves the spectacle pieces from his right hand into his left, and uses his right hand to shade, no, cover his eyes.

The hints come rushing at me, daring me to ignore them now. Taking him to work. His counting steps to go everywhere. Unable to see in bright light, unable to see in dim light. No sight into the distance from the water tower, none to read a newspaper.

"Most everyone, including the manager Mr. Roger Lukas, is blind," I've heard Uncle Bear joke.

"Especially the manager, Mr. Roger Lukas," I've heard Papa retort.

I re-create the syllogism. Everyone who works in the broom factory is blind. Papa works in the broom factory. Papa is blind.

Papa cannot see to even deflect a baseball coming straight at his eyes.

Papa is blind.

Walking in silence beside him as we cut across the diamond toward the Lower Gate Trail near Ridge Street, holding his arm, I realize it distinctly.

Papa is blind.

I collapse in tears.

"*Koma* is a Greek word that means *deep sleep*. It may be sleep, it may be a profound state of unconsciousness. In either case, we know little about it," Dr. Jacobs tells me and Mama and Heli and Uncle Bear at midnight of the day we follow Papa on a stretcher through the snow to the hospital in Laurium.

It is less than a year ago on Saturday, December 7, at the end of his shift when Papa emerges from the mine with Uncle Bear's hands on the stretcher near Papa's head and none of us are greeted, no words spoken.

Uncle Bear looks beyond us and asks of no one in particular, of everyone there, "No emergency team? No help? No horses? No transportation?" then leads the way in a frantic pace to the hospital, the two trammers with a hand apiece on the back of his stretcher, and me and Mama and Heli, and Papa's trammer friends, and our friends and neighbors from Swedetown breaking into a run to keep up with Uncle Bear. A nurse who is leaving for the day sees us coming from the front door and takes the lead to the men's ward. She stops our entourage and looks down the long hallway of the ward at the occupied beds on both sides, and then motions for me and Mama to help her get the Cornishman with the broken leg out of the bed nearest us. Papa is laid down gently, the fabric of the stretcher still under him.

Dr. Jacobs gathers his instruments from the bed of the man he is assisting in the center of the ward, places his tools into a worn black bag, and we make way for him when he hurries over to examine Papa.

His eyes are closed and swollen, nose and lips burned and swollen, his face red and swollen, the whole front of him speckled with a greasy black dust. His eyelashes and hair are singed, the individual hairs frayed and crossed in unkempt, wild directions. He makes no sound, offers no objection, does not move a finger. Onto Papa's chest, Dr. Jacobs places a round piece of metal that is attached with two rubber tubes to pieces of thin hollow metal that he puts into his ears. He listens intently for a moment before looking to Mama with the hint of a smile.

I cannot bear to look when Dr. Jacobs begins to force Papa's eyes open with his thumbs. I re-open my own eyes a long time later to watch Dr. Jacobs gently place his thumbs over Papa's eyes and bring his swollen eyelids back down, the hint of optimism he implied to Mama only minutes ago now gone. Continuing his examination for more than an hour, Dr. Jacobs gently taps his cheeks, touches his shoulders, moves his arms, raises and lowers his legs, and whispers into his ears.

No reaction.

Papa's trammer friends and our friends and neighbors try to infuse their looks at us with as much optimism as they can muster. But they must leave for home.

When Dr. Jacobs pulls Mama and Uncle Bear aside, the three of them exchange questions and comments and observations and answers, then more questions arise from Mama as her voice loses its usual restraint and she bursts into tears. Uncle Bear helps to calm Mama, and places his arms on her shoulders like Aunt Iiris, looks into her eyes and says, "It will be alright, we will get through this" before catching the last train of Saturday night to Eagle River. Placing his hand on Mama's shoulder, Dr. Jacobs promises to return as soon as he can with more information. He says he needs to check some material in the medical library, and returns at midnight to re-examine Papa and share with me and Mama and Heli the Anglicized spelling and definition of *coma*.

Near 3:00 a.m. Sunday, Mama walks to the end of the men's ward and back. She leaves the ward and we can hear her in the quiet hours of early Sunday morning softly arguing with a nurse in the hallway. We hear her footsteps turn and she walks past the men's ward again and her footsteps disappear into the night, the nurse's footsteps padding in the other direction. Heli and I sit astride Papa, holding one of his hands in each of ours and praying. We look to one another as tentative steps approach the men's ward. It is Mama with a basin of water and a clean cloth in it. She gently dabs at the raw skin of his face and more vigorously rubs his hair with the cloth, then looks at the cloth. She gives me directions to a faucet and sink around the corner and I find it easily with the incandescent light still on. I dump the basin of dirty water and refill it, find a pile of clean cloths and towels on a nearby shelf, choose three of the best of each, and return to Papa. Heli and Mama have removed his shirt and the three of us work wordlessly to get the stretcher out from beneath him, and we clean the unburned skin of his upper body to his belt.

Mama finds a clean colorful rag to cover her head and,

wearing no extra shirts on a frigid winter day, goes to 6:00 o'clock Mass just down the street from the hospital to Sacred Heart in Laurium. The liturgy feels the same for the Second Sunday in Advent as Heli and I attend 8:00 o'clock Mass, but we do not feel welcome, and are the first ones out of church after freezing near the back door wearing only the one shirt we left our home in. It is best we arrive just before Mass begins, and leave as the last note of the organ sounds on the departing song, for Heli and I feel self-conscious at a different church in an upscale city with no extra shirts, and rags on our heads. Even if we had our extra shirts, we would be the only ones there without coats, for everybody at Sacred Heart has a fine winter coat, while no one in our family has even a shabby one.

The rest of Sunday remains in a fog.

Well before the sunrise and before he is due at work Monday, Uncle Bear returns tired from little sleep and fraught with the same worry as the rest of us. Mama insists that Heli and I go home and get a little sleep, then go to school on a Monday I know will be overcast with a Copper Country sky that alternates between iron gray and brilliant sunshine reflecting off the snow between November and March.

Today, I am sure, will be an iron gray day.

Heli and I go home to a table full of food in the kitchen keeping silent guard over an otherwise vacant house. Our neighbors have slipped into our house all day Sunday and left us with at least a week's worth of meals. Neither Heli nor I can sleep before school, so we eat a little, and then walk to school in the same silence in which we walked home from the hospital. After school, still unwilling to go upstairs and sleep in our own bedroom, we peck at some of the food and nap for a while on Mama's sofa and walk back to the hospital.

We grab one another's hands in dread when Heli and I turn the corner into the men's ward and find the first bed unoccupied, then soon find Mama in a chair near the next bed, in a fitful rest with her head lying on Papa's chest, her ear near his heart. We watch an elderly German man, a butcher Heli and I later guess, being led to Papa's former bed and helped to lie down while he holds his hand over his stomach.

"Is his heart...?" I ask Mama when she raises her head from Papa's chest, unable to complete either the thought or the sentence.

"Yes, I can hear his heart," Mama confirms. "But there is otherwise no change."

Heli and I insist that Mama go home and eat and rest. "We will be here," we tell her. We all stay much of Monday night as well, Mama returning after only a couple hours.

A Scottish man with a frail heart takes the lead bed on Tuesday, as Heli and I join Mama after school for our vigil. Even as she talks with us, Mama keeps returning her head to his chest, listening to his breathing.

"It is getting shallower," she tells us. "And it seems that he wants to cough, but is unable."

We send Mama home and Heli and I take turns with our ears to Papa's chest, hearing the beat of his heart and the confirmation of Mama's concern for his breathing in his slow, superficial puffs. Mama returns again after not enough rest, not enough to eat. Sometime near 2:00 a.m., none of us willing to go home, Papa manages a weak, cough-like sound that shakes him slightly, then movement and sound stop. When Mama bends over to confirm heartbeat and respiration, she shoots from her chair and slaps him hard in the face. Heli and I look at one another in dismay from across the bed. She bends over again and waits only a moment before grabbing his right side and shaking him violently, nearly flipping him onto his side.

When he rolls onto his back again in dead weight, Mama bends over to put her ear on Papa's chest and, hearing nothing, she slaps him again, and again grabs his shirt and belt and starts shaking him.

Heli grabs his leg and I take his arm, and we shake him back and forth, Heli and me from one side, Mama from the other. We are desperate, and Heli and I flip Papa onto his side without realizing that we are more force from our side than Mama is from her side by herself. He rolls onto his stomach near Mama and, in frustration and panic, I slap the palms of both my hands onto his back, creating a noise that reverberates off the wall at the head of his bed.

We stop in surprise at the noise I have made, and as Mama bends her ear to Papa's back, we hear a low, rumbling sigh, like the sound of something trying to evolve into a cough that may clear a throat and chest.

Mama beats his back with the palms of her hands, striking them all over his back. Another sound, this time a clearer cough. Mama reaches to his mouth and wipes something away, looks at it, throws it to the wall and returns to striking his back.

A sound. A groan. Mama glances at me and Heli and, with no words exchanged, we roll him from his stomach to his back. Mama puts her ear to his chest and glances up to me and Heli with a nervous smile. She moves her ear to his lips and, when she hears the breath, she takes Papa's face into her hands and kisses him hard on his lips.

Uncle Bear arrives again before work on Wednesday and we tell him of our panic and our progress. Heli and I cannot endure leaving Papa and going to school, but Mama again insists, saying he would insist if he could, so we do not argue. After school, Mama and me and Heli stay at his side and alternate between checking his heart, offering a prayer of gratitude, listening for his breathing, and quietly sniffling when we hear it.

Mama has wiped away the black spittle from the wall that dripped down and looked like death itself.

On Thursday, Papa is still in his *deep sleep*, but becoming more and more restless, which we all take as a good sign.

Before going to work, Uncle Bear stops again at the hospital and hands me a worn book, and I open it to Finnish words.

"I know my very best friend in the whole world, your Papa, will be alright now. I know he prefers that you read books in English, but I also know you love to read, and Finnish poetry is best read in the Finnish language anyway. You've been here a long time, Emilia, and you may be here for a long time still, and you'll enjoy this and maybe even your Papa will enjoy hearing it. Again."

I admire the lovingly worn leather cover of *The Kalevala*. I open to the first page and begin skimming, then stop at a reference I think I recognize, but I'm not sure if I'm translating into English correctly. I point to the passage and Uncle Bear peers over my shoulder and says, "My Finnish is good, but my translation may not be. I think that means 'the luckless lands of the north.' Finland or Lapland or the Copper Country. Take your pick."

Papa has been moved into the last bed at the end of the men's ward, across from a Finn with a crushed leg that we learn will likely need to be amputated.

"May I read aloud?" I ask the man who is often grimacing in pain.

"Please do," he says. "Anything to take my mind off the pain. And the thought of only one leg."

I read of the earth's creation from the shards of a duck's egg. I read of the Finnish hero Väinämöinen, who names the trees and plants and living creatures. I am saddened when the beautiful young Aino rejects the marriage proposal from Väinämöinen, who it seems was born as an old man. As I read more, I think Papa is taking an unconscious interest by his sighs of agreement at *The Kalevala's* numerous references to copper, and moans of displeasure at Väinämöinen's constant bickering with Joukahainen. Still reading aloud, I am perplexed by the meaning of the Sampo, thinking it is riches or fame or, if I am reading and translating this correctly, the pillar of the world. Perhaps it is only happiness and I already know I will read all this thick text of epic size and scope, and I hope I will learn the meaning of the Sampo.

Papa sleeps less and less every day, and looks like he wants to talk with Mama and me and Heli and Uncle Bear, and our neighbors and Papa's trammer friends who have all visited. When Uncle Bear returns early every morning and after work in the evenings, I ask him for translations of language and imagery and interpretations. He tells me that, even before he left his homeland, *The Kalevala* was already beginning to shape Finland's national identity and was having a profound effect upon the Finn's perception and value of himself.

"Perhaps," I tell him, "there will even be a time when a Michigan community like Swedetown will not be confused with its Scandinavian neighbor and will earn its own true name of Finntown."

"I believe it!" he says with conviction.

On the Saturday of one week following the explosion, with Dr. Jacobs getting about as much sleep as the rest of us, he meets me near the entrance to the men's ward and escorts me to Papa's bed. I cannot tell if Papa is awake, with the new darkened spectacles covering his eyes, but he appears to be lying straighter with blankets rolled beneath his back and propping him up.

"Go ahead and give him a hug," and Papa has perked his head a little at Dr. Jacobs's voice, maybe even at his suggestion.

I move gently to the side of his bed. I wrap my arms between his shoulders and the tucked blankets. I hug his face to my chest. I feel someone's arms upon my back and I dare not move. They are Papa's arms, and he squeezes my back lightly.

"Eh ... eh ... Emilia," he stumbles with a slur.

I dissolve into tears.

The now-broken spectacles in two pieces in Papa's right hand as he looks down at me, slowly regaining my composure a short ways from the baseball diamond, should have been my first broad hint. No, they should have told me the truth that I covered like the scarring now on his eyelids, the scarring I placed on my own eyes to shield myself from a truth I knew in my heart and refused to acknowledge in my mind. The scarring I applied in layers to my own eyes when I walked with him to work at the broom factory, and described scenery and read him the newspapers.

The scars of my refusal.

He slips to the ground beside me and takes his left hand away from his eyes and faces me.

I look into the blank orbs. "Mama knows, doesn't she?"

"Yes, Emilia, Mama knows. And I will tell Heli. These are my eyes, useless as they are. It is my responsibility."

He puts his arms around me and lightly squeezes me to himself.

I weep as I did the last time he held me like this.

# *IX*

# *September 1*

When I read the newspapers to Papa the other day, *Työmies* announced the huge parades and special events planned for New York City and Chicago and the Copper Country on Labor Day, while the *Mining Gazette* printed a united message from mine superintendents that said all striking men may return to work on Monday without prejudice.

Papa has taken the day off, fearful, I think, of crossing the pickets on Labor Day, and he says that no one else will dare to work, on this day. I now understand how I can take him to the broom factory unharassed on most other days.

The spectacles that Mama has patched with masking tape provide a two-way shield, protecting him from strikers who haven't the heart to turn on a blind man, while enabling him to hide at least some of the pain.

I wish I had the same shield, at least for the one direction.

Bankers obviously have the day off, and obviously have no interest in parades or strikes as I see Mr. Carl House-worth in his silly knickers near the third golf hole beyond right field. Bankers also have no interest in miners' children, I can tell by the way he ignores our very existence as he hits a long drive to begin the hole, a shot with an iron club to the green, and putts it only three or four times over the short distance of smooth, low-cut grass to get it into the hole.

Anders and Heli have challenged Per and me to our last baseball game before school begins, and I am sorry it is only our second, for Heli and I would have relished more baseball if we had known the boys were this good. With no laundry to do since it's a Monday and a holiday during an ongoing strike, Mama supplies her easy consent. We agree with Papa's previously stipulated baseball rules and I already regret the absence of a man I will likely never again see on the pitcher's mound.

After earning home team honors when her playing partner again wins the toss of the bat, Heli further insists that she and Anders are named the *Skyhooks*, and I agree only after pausing for a moment to think of a better name, and then christen Anders and me as the *Bears*.

Heli's hitting prowess appears as if it took little time off this summer and I almost wish I had taken the outfield, for she pokes three fly balls over Per's head, one that he could have caught if he had properly judged it soon enough. With each turn at bat, Anders improves, I think, though I'm unsure because my pitching is not terrific to begin with, and even weaker since I'm not concentrating when I pitch it because I'm hurrying to cover the infield.

The newly named *Skyhooks* are ahead 4-2 after two innings.

"The *Bears* are not ready to nap for the season," I announce to Heli and Anders and my imaginary crowd of admiring fans across the third base line. Per and I score three angels in the third inning, and three more in the fourth, capped by Per's long fly ball over second base that falls deep in center field, far from Heli, who is covering the line in anticipation of Per's last two hits. Like Heli, Per is stringy and strong and quick and well-coordinated.

We are leading 8-6 in the bottom of the fourth.

Mr. Houseworth is standing near the start of the first golf hole on the other side of the powder house as if he is waiting for someone. Abandoned years ago with the refinement of nitroglycerine, the roof is caving in, but the thick concrete sides will stand for many more years. Mr. Houseworth looks lonesome.

A single, a double, then another single scores the *Skyhook* angel from third. Our *Bears* force the first out when Per finally catches one of Heli's fly balls, then Anders strokes another single to tie the game. When Heli hits into two outs in a row, it's a major batting slump for her, and she reaches the pit of her slump when she flies out again, this time a high popup which I catch before it leaves the infield. I pitch my version of Papa's knuckler to Anders and scamper over to cover the infield, but I could have easily fielded his weak grounder from the mound before he reaches first base to end the inning.

In the top of the fifth with the game tied, Per and I both hit easy pop-outs to Heli when we try to be heroes with the long ball, and Heli stymies us by taking a few steps back deeper into left field. Then Per hits a single, I hit a single, and Per hits a double down the left field line that Heli leaves uncovered. We are up by one run with two outs and an angel on third and Per on second. I connect on the next one and think I've added two more runs over Heli's head, but she turns to chase it while continuing to watch the ball over her right shoulder, then lifts her left hand to snatch my glory out of the air for the third out.

"Great catch," I tell her as the *Bears* take the field and the *Skyhooks* come in to bat.

"You'll need a lot more practice if you expect to make a living out of playing baseball," Heli says. "But I have a lot of confidence in you, Emilia. Almost as much confidence in your ability to find an occupation as I have in my ability to catch nearly anything."

That's a true compliment, coming from Heli, and I take it in the good-hearted nature she intends.

Ahead 9-8 going into the bottom of the last inning, I

don't let the confidence of a slim lead fool me, especially since I know Heli's batting slumps are usually good for only two consecutive outs.  I still want to win the game, but I allow myself no extra credit for prescience when Heli begins the Skyhooks at-bat with a double and Anders follows with a single.  It will take at least a single to score Heli's angel on third and at least a triple to get Anders in from first base.

*Anywhere but chest-high and on the outside corner*, I say to myself which, of course, is exactly where I put it.  Heli has plenty of time to get under my fastball and belts it far over Per's head down the left field line.

The game is over.

It feels strange to shake hands with my own sister, but she has been a good sport about it, and often models my behavior, so I follow Heli's lead this time and meet her genuineness with a smile.  The boys even join in with appropriately modest, brotherly handshakes that tell me there's a chance they will turn into finer young men than their papa, the underhanded and overzealous Mr. Nelson.

Declining the invitations of Anders and Heli and Per to join them at the pond, I prefer to be alone with my thoughts of the past few weeks as I promise to return the bat and ball to our mutual house.

Papa's trepidation of Calumet and Hecla has taken on an understandable connotation, yet I am coming to admire Mama's strength and courage to take the opposing opinion in the face of the same events.  I've still not developed my own opinion, partly because I've never in my life had to form a strong one, and partly because I'm only now beginning to understand adult ways.

A finely dressed man in attire similar to Mr. Houseworth is coming toward the baseball diamond carrying a small bag of golf clubs.  He has come from the club house behind the water tower and is probably the golf partner Mr. Houseworth was looking for earlier. As I move shyly toward home plate, I am captivated by his cashmere knickers and jacket, and fascinated by the strange holes in the dirt after he passes the infield in a fine pair of shoes with thin metal spikes on the bottom. He glances toward me at home plate and I have the sense he doesn't even see me, and that's when I recognize him.

He is James MacNaughton, the superintendent of Calumet and Hecla. The mining magnate who stood one step higher than Sheriff Cruse during the deputizing ceremony at the hospital. The man who glanced guiltily at Papa after his speech. The mogul who must have a different pair of shoes for every occasion.

He stops to brush the infield dirt off his beautiful black spiked shoes after crossing the third base line, and Mr. Houseworth runs from the starting golf hole near the powder house to join him. Mr. Houseworth treats Mr. MacNaughton like a god, greeting him with too much enthusiasm, extending his hand first to shake it like they are good friends, then placing his arm around Mr. MacNaughton's shoulder as they walk off together like old pals. They return together to the first golf hole, which is on my way home, so I follow from a safe distance.

Mr. MacNaughton hits the golf ball first, sending it toward the roof of the powder house which sits beside the first hole with weeds high around it. From my vantage point, I can see the golf ball wedged under a piece of tin roofing. He laughs and reaches into his pocket for another ball, but Mr. Houseworth holds one out to him, so Mr. MacNaughton quits fishing in his pocket and takes it. His second swing strikes the top of the ball and at least it goes straight, though only a few feet in the direction of the flag flying from the middle of the area of short green grass in the distance.

Mr. Houseworth winds up with the club and misses his ball by a mile, the first time I've ever seen him do that. His next swing hits the top of the ball, the first time I've seen him do that as well, and it settles behind Mr. MacNaughton's.

If the purpose of the patrician game of golf is to overdress and overimpress while pretending to play poorly, I'm glad I play plebian baseball.

Mr. MacNaughton and Mr. Houseworth search together for the golf ball near the powder house. I walk toward them with the intention of telling them where it is, but as I near the powder house and they glance at me in disdain, I stop and look down at the Queen Anne's lace and brush the dirt from the top of my bare feet. By the time they return to hit their next shots after too-quickly giving up the search with no result, I have formulated my plan.

I turn over one rusting metal barrel, then hoist it onto another, rest the top barrel against the concrete side of the powder house and climb up. First looking toward the two golfers who I see are a safe distance away and walking the other direction, I lift my dress and grab the side of the roof and pull myself up. The heat radiating from the tin roof is hurting my bare knees, so I pull my dress back down and gingerly scoot across the caving roof to the ball. It has a slit near the seam and the initials *JM* handwritten in black ink, but otherwise looks exactly like Mr. Houseworth's ball that Papa's friend Mr. Frantti gave to me after the game.

I jump down, grab the ball and bat, and head home.

With the ball and bat still in-hand, I run up the stairs on the back of our house and lean the bat against Nelsons' door, and run back downstairs to return the baseball to Papa and Mama's closet floor. Thankfully, the golf ball Mr. Frantti gave me is on the same closet floor. When I find it and compare it to Mr. MacNaughton's ball I've just retrieved from the powder house roof, I'm disappointed but not surprised to see that Mr. Houseworth plays with dirtier balls.

I can fix that.

Running down the basement stairs with a basin of water in my hands, I grab the scrub brush and bleach and hold them over the basin. Wetting the dirty golf ball, I judiciously pour some bleach on it and scrub the bleach in with the brush. When the bleach has saturated the golf ball covering and I've scrubbed it well, I rinse the ball and bring it outside to dry after rinsing the brush and returning it to its place near the bleach. Then remembering I forgot the basin of water in the basement, I get it and toss the slightly bleached water away, then rinse it and put it away.

My wait for the washed golf ball to whiten and dry is less-than-patient, but worth it when I compare the two and see that they now look exactly the same, though only one of them bears the initials *JM*.

Mama's sewing kit has thread that nearly matches the color of the torn golf ball, but I still don't want the thread to show, so I use the invisible stitches that Mama taught me to close the small slit in the cover. I stare at Papa's pen and ink set, and wish I had studied him more closely when he penned his handsome handwriting.

I wish not for my own sake now that I need it, but for his sake that he were still able to do it.

With Mr. MacNaughton's now-mended golf ball laying up so the handwriting forming the letters *JM* is visible on top, I take Mr. Houseworth's, no, Mr. Frantti's golf ball in my left hand, dip Papa's fine pen into the open bottle of black ink, and write *JM* on it, in handwriting so similar I have even impressed myself. I set it down to allow the ink to dry on the golf ball that was Mr. Houseworth's, lost in a fair fight to Mr. Frantti, given to me, and I hope will be sold to Mr. Mac-Naughton, along with his own lost ball, for a fair price.

Mr. MacNaughton and Mr. Houseworth have golfed nearly all nine holes on our little course above Swedetown. They have made their way back near the club house and I watch from a respectful hidden distance as they conclude their match. When Mr. MacNaughton gets his golf ball into the final hole from a foot away, Mr. Houseworth raises his arms in mock despair, looks at a piece of paper he is carrying and onto which, I am presuming, he has tallied their scores after each hole, and congratulates Mr. MacNaughton with another handshake.

*Big surprise,* I think to myself. *I could have predicted the conclusion without even counting.*

As Mr. Houseworth looks at the sun like it is telling him the time of day as accurately as the winner of the match, he picks up his bag and starts heading toward Bridge Street, on his way toward Swedetown Road, then into Laurium where he undoubtedly lives. He turns to see Mr. MacNaughton walk toward the club house, and Mr. Houseworth changes his path and cuts toward home plate. He nonchalantly crosses the diamond toward the juncture of Air and Ridge Streets, and I know he will revisit the powder house and look for Mr. MacNaughton's new golf ball.

Along with the satisfaction of knowing he will not find it, I have my opening.

Sipping on lemonade and standing on the shaded porch of the club house by himself, Mr. MacNaughton fixes his gaze on me as I approach timidly and reach into my dress pocket for the golf balls. My eyes cast downward, I cannot tell his spike marks from the labyrinth of others on the wooden decking of the porch floor. From the time he first notices me until I am in front of him, he regards me as if I will disappear with the strength of his stare.

"Sir," I manage to force from my uncooperating voice, "your balls," and open my hand and offer them to him.

"What's this?" he asks with genuine surprise, I think not from the golf balls but from the sight of a girl in dusty hair and a worn summer dress with no shoes holding his balls. He takes the golf balls from my hand and I can tell he immediately recognizes the initials, yet examines them both. "Thanks. Now move along, I need to eat lunch and get to work."

This is not going as I had envisioned.

"Sir," I venture again. "A quarter."

"What?"

"A quarter, sir, for both of them. They're just like new."

He scrutinizes them again, this time for only a second.

"Young lady, they're also mine," heavily emphasizing the last word as if he has to say it, but doesn't really mean it.

"But I found them, sir, and I..." about to say "fixed them," I stop myself in time. "I found them and cleaned them very nicely and..."

"Whose initials are on these golf balls? Whose balls are these anyway?"

"Well, they're yours, sir. But you lost them and left them out there...," I point to the golf course, "...and I searched for them and found them and cleaned them and ... and ... I am returning them to you."

I hesitate, then begin anew with a fresh thought. "Are your balls not worth a quarter?" I wonder aloud, now willing to negotiate the price to twenty cents. If pressed, I know I will take less.

I do not see his arm raise. I do not notice his open right hand. I do not detect his open hand near my face. I see only his lips moving and hear only:

"Why, you impetuous little Finnish bitch!" just before the blunt forces of his slap and speech both send me to my knees.

Neither the golf balls nor Mr. MacNaughton are on the porch when I finally look around after rising from my knees. I half-heartedly peer through the window at a man in golfing attire laughing with the waiter as he is handed a sandwich and another glass of lemonade. As I pad over the wooden porch with my bare feet and set a course for home, I stop at home plate, feel my still-burning face, and reverse my path back toward the water tower.

I cannot go home yet.

Near the water tower where Bridge Street narrows into the Upper Gate Trail is a shiny black automobile and I'm sure I know the owner, know him more closely and coldly than I ever intended. The automobile faces Bridge Street's descent, ready for its callous owner to return home and first change his clothes, if indeed he goes to work as he says he is.

A jagged stone hurts my foot and I stop to kick it away as if revenge on a stone serves some retribution value. I pick it up and examine it like a golf ball with initials near the sharp jagged edge. I kneel beside the door facing away from the club house, the door on the other side from where the driver sits. This way, I cannot be seen from the club house and it will take the driver awhile to realize he has the word *scab* etched into the door of his automobile, with an *X* etched over the word, in handwriting he will not recognize.

The water tower still beckons me, and Heli won't be home for a while, and I need to think.

I think of having heard the social strata of the Copper Country referred to as the *Boston Caste System*. I think of the men of Boston, who formed the Calumet and Hecla Company, at the top of the caste, and clustered downward in increasingly greater numbers are the James MacNaughtons of mine superintendents, the larger group of Roger Lukas's and their type who make the workers' lives hell, the Carl Houseworth's who lie to them and cheat them, the German businessmen who profit from them, the Cornishmen who lead the trammers into the mines only because they are Cornishmen, not because they are good leaders, the French and Italian who are treated as skilled craftsmen primarily because of their nationality and not necessarily their skill, the Irish and Poles and Slavs and Swedes who labor. Then the trammers, the Finns. With the possible exception of the black man I met at the circus, the one who cannot touch our water fountain, no one in the caste system is lower.

I think of my Ukki, my grandpapa and teacher and philosopher who I know could out-think all these men, while he struggles for intellectual freedom in Finland. I think of my Papa, who learned so much from him and teaches so much to others, and has spanked me and Heli on our backsides aplenty, but has never hit either of us in the face.

I think of the fracture in the caste dividing those who profit from those who pay. They pay with their talents, with their money, with their bodies, with their eyes. With their self-respect.

Yet like Papa, I have reached my conclusion as he does with experience and observation and a quiet investigation of the facts.

I will fight that man.

I will fight the prejudice he stands for and the animosity and divisiveness he spreads like an infection.

Like Papa, I will use my head and dispassionately cite the facts from which I will form my plans. Like Mama, I will use my wiles and intuition and take action, clandestine if it need be, and laced with laughter if it can be.

But I will fight.

# X

## *September 7*

The burgundy wool coat in Vertin's display window looks like it would fit me perfectly, and it belies the warm early-fall morning, yet foretells the snow soon coming to the Copper Country. Vertin's is closed in Sunday observance like every store, and that suits the Rytilahti family just fine as we often take the long way home through Red Jacket's downtown, tranquil and  hushed as it gets only between bar closing and early morning, or after Sunday Services.

Heli has her eyes on the brown suede dress boots and, unlike the giddy grade-school children of a few years ago who used to start every sentence with "I want, I want," we have since learned to hold our tongues and instead think to ourselves "I dream, I dream."  As she holds Papa's arm, Mama is scanning the school dresses and figuring the math in her mind and, by the look on her face, coming up short.

"My boots would go well with your coat," Heli informs me.

"And either your boots or my coat could buy school dresses for a whole class," I realistically tell her, though I'm sure she knows, and I regret having burst the bubble of our reveries.

Mama steers us all back to reality when she asks, "Henrik, will you show us where *MacNaughton's Eye* is mounted?" and I am peeved by the name but piqued by curiosity of the beam that continues to light up our house at irregular times throughout our nights.

"It's almost directly on our way home, Kerttu. I will be more than happy to take you that way."

We all laugh because even without being able to see the merchandise, we know Papa dislikes shopping. We walk past the front of Vertin's along with small family groups of other churchgoers who acknowledge one another with nods and smiles and a few words in Finnish when Mama recognizes them.

She steps aside for a moment to chat in English with a tall couple from St. John the Baptist, then re-joins us.

Oak Street to Fourth until it joins Red Jacket Road is a short walk, and we stop just before turning onto Mine Street to check out the new Coliseum, which will feature one of our nation's first indoor ice skating rinks. I've loved keeping up with its progress since construction began only a few months ago. According to the newspapers, it will be home to dances in the summer, and bowling in the fall, and hockey in the winter, and weddings in the spring, and its colossally reinforced semi-circled roof should easily hold up to the massive amounts of snow we get here. Best of all, it's even bigger and nicer and certainly newer than the Palestra in Laurium.

Living right next to a town with a Coliseum, which is easily traced to Rome and the Latin language, and living across a busy road from a town with a Palestra, which I've learned is Greek for *athletic training center*, I feel like I'm in the middle of the richest cultures in the world.

"This is among the reasons why I love where we live," Papa says, agreeing with my thoughts. "We have one of the finest libraries I've ever seen in my life, and I have the libraries in Helsinki to compare that to. And as my Papa has described the Finnish Theatre in letters to me because it was built in Helsinki after Mama and I moved here, it may not rival the Opera House here in Red Jacket. And now the

Coliseum. I am so grateful for where we live."

I do not have Helsinki as my basis for comparison like Papa and Mama, yet I share Papa's opinion of our rich community resources, especially the library where my name is on the borrower's cards of many books, and where I also earn a little money. But I do not share his acceptance of whatever scraps the moneyed class deigns to drop from its tables, and permits us to pick off its floors. I still think of his phrase *savage capitalism*, and agree again with him.

Our Sunday walk continues, and the many churchgoers we have seen in downtown Red Jacket thin as we turn onto Mine Street, and I can feel my thoughts darken as we approach the broom factory on our right. Six uniformed National Guardsmen are ensuring the rows of shaft houses in front of us are secure.

Just past the edge of the broom factory, Shaft Number Two rises up on our right, and Mama and Heli and I look to the top, where *MacNaughton's Eye* is unlit but aimed at Swedetown.

Another churchgoing couple appears in the distance on my right, and I turn to spot Sheriff Cruse and a woman I guess to be his wife on his arm, making the corner from Red Jacket Road onto Mine Street and heading toward us. Even in the distance and even without a badge shining from his vest in the Sunday morning light, and even with a woman on his arm, I recognize Sheriff Cruse in his black dress garb covering some height and a lot of width.

Papa is the first to hear the strange sound coming from behind Shaft Number Two; a sound I, too, have heard during a wind storm when Heli and I were near the water tower at night, watching the lightning move in and ready to dart for home as soon as we heard the thunder. The strange sound that I later told myself was *frazzled electricity* reached Heli and I as we saw the lights dim in a whole section of Red Jacket.

Papa is the first to hear the footsteps before we see a

young man round the corner from behind Shaft Number Two, and walk toward us wearing heavy gloves and holding one long handle of what looks like an oversized pair of pliers. He stops momentarily as soon as he sees us, and then walks closer with his head down.

The flash of recognition on his face and mine probably registers with each of us at the same time. He is Homer Jaakkola, and would have likely been named Valedictorian of our class, even though my grades are better but, after all, he is a boy. I remember thinking I was sorry to hear he quit school to get a job at Calumet and Hecla as soon as he turned 16. He bragged to everyone that he would be an electrician, but we all knew he would end up as a trammer. His head still down, he raises it when he's near me and Heli and Papa and Mama standing on the edge of Mine Street, and then only to glance to his right and to his left.

He whirls his head to the right again, and no doubt the Guardsmen have registered in his mind. The six uniformed men are already walking toward us, probably trying to determine the source of the sound of *frazzled electricity*. In a few moments, they will be certain to find its origin from the foul burning odor now reaching us on the edge of Mine Street.

Homer casts the long pliers with their small, sharp snout to the ground first, glances to his left again, and then throws the gloves down as he takes off in a run straight toward Sheriff Cruse and his wife. The Guardsmen break into a run and pass us quickly as they head for Homer who is heading toward Sheriff Cruse.

"Wha ... what is happening?" Papa asks and I feel badly that none of his own family provides an immediate answer.

Running like a terrified deer, Homer nears Sheriff Cruse's right side and the Sheriff looks like he is about to nonchalantly step aside as he nudges his wife, who begins to move to her left. Homer is gaining distance on the guards and turns his head to the Guards behind him as he is about to pass near the right of Sheriff Cruse, whose left arm is still holding his wife's. When Homer looks back toward the Guards and toward us, Sheriff Cruse rotates his shoulders and, just before Homer is about to pass to his right, throws his leveraged right arm straight out at neck level.

I hear a loud, hollow pop, like every boy in class has cracked a knuckle at precisely the same time a split second before Homer's neck snaps back, his feet fly up, and the back of his head hits the street first, then his shoulders, hips, legs, feet.

Neither Latin class nor anatomy class has prepared me for the sound of a collapsing trachea.

I watch the Guardsmen descend upon Homer, then stop and pull a leg back for a kick at the now formless young man on the ground. I hear three grunts of forced exhalation in descending volume a moment after three boots reach his body, then I hear what I'm sure is a rib break, followed by a muffled scream of pain, followed by a low gurgling sound from the now indistinct heap on the ground. When there is no breath left in Homer to echo even the hardest kicks, most of the Guardsmen begin moving away as only one of them steps to plant a final boot thrust. Then they all turn away and lower their heads to the ground after the last Guardsman places a violent kick, and bends over to wipe something off his boot.

My head suddenly feels light and I think my heart has stopped, and for the first time in my life I think I know what it feels like to pass out, for I am sure I'm about to. My legs give out from under me, and Heli's legs are doing the same thing at the same instant because we both fall to the ground as I struggle to remain conscious.

"Please … please, you must tell me what is happening," Papa pleads.

I am grateful for his voice, but unable to answer him and neither can Mama, for her head is tucked into his left shoulder.

"Henrik, a moment," Mama finally manages in a plaintive tone I've never heard from her. She takes a deep breath and sees Heli and I on the ground, our heads turned from the scene up Mine Street, turned toward home. "Emilia, you and Heli go ahead. Papa and I will be with you shortly."

"After what we've all experienced today, we're in this together as a family, whether we like it or not," Papa begins. He stops in the manner I've heard before that tells me he's gathering his thoughts. "I frankly detest what is going on," he says. He turns to Mama, who is seated beside him on our sheet-covered sofa, then to me and Heli, who he has heard as we settled onto the floor to his right with our backs resting against the wall. "I'm sure I can say that for each of us," he says without even seeing the looks on our faces. "This may be a long winter," he says, and Heli and I look out the sitting room window at the beautiful warm early September day, then turn away as I think, and Heli probably thinks too, of the burgundy wool coat and brown suede boots at Vertin's. "The Western Federation of Miners union is on the offensive. With about half the National Guard gone, they are organizing parades and trying to intimidate the workers who are trying to work. It is only Emilia at my side and my dark spectacles, I think, that allow me to get to work. And not because I see through them."

Papa adjusts their weight on the bridge of his nose. The right bow has a thick layer of white, cloth-covered tape holding it to the frame, and the right lens is glued and still looks like it's been hit in the center with a tiny pebble that sends the lens into a sunburst of broken pieces still intact in the metal frame.

"I hear the talk at work and keep up with the newspapers, thanks to Emilia. The union is pressing for a U.S. Senate investigation of working practices here in our mines. They are pressing the Michigan legislature to pass a law requiring only eight-hour workdays. President Wilson and

Governor Ferris are well aware of what's happening here in the Copper Country. The national leader for the Western Federation of Miners is in Red Jacket now. He is Charles Moyer and has been here before ... before the strike. Some fancy attorney by the name of Clarence Darrow is also in town now. He has defended Mr. Moyer in a past legal matter in Idaho."

"Papa, Papa," Heli says like she's unsure where to begin with her questioning, or which question to ask. "President Wilson? Governor Ferris? The union president for the whole country? A fancy attorney ... who did you say, Mr. Clarrow?"

"Clarence Darrow," he corrects, and we'll see how fancy he is, for there are many legal issues here. But Mr. Allen Rees, who represents Calumet and Hecla, and is the lead attorney for the other mines, is very sharp also. I've seen some of his work."

"This is a strike," I say. "What are the legal issues?"

"There are many, Emilia. Let's start at the national level. A new federal agency was created the day after you first accompanied me to work ... when I returned for the first time after my ... injury. The United States Department of Labor was created to foster the welfare of workers, to improve their working conditions, to give men a chance for profitable employment. Though it's still very young, the Department of Labor may be able to help mediate strikes, and there's hope they'll get involved in this one. At the state level, we already know that the governor can send in the National Guard, whose *protection* we can probably do without. But Governor Ferris has also sent a judge here from Detroit to try to peacefully resolve this. Then there's constant legal bickering back and forth about parades and how to form a legal protest, where it can be formed, and so forth. I'm very certain Mr. Darrow and Mr. Rees have plenty to talk about. The legal issues are many and complex, Emilia."

"So there's hope for resolution?" Mama asks.

"President Wilson and Governor Ferris have moral persuasion only, I'm afraid. And the attorneys only bicker. They cannot force a company to change what it pays its workers, or what equipment to use, or what hours those workers will work. Neither can they force them to return to work."

"Meanwhile, the violence continues," Mama states in exasperation.

"The violence continues. We have seen it. We have heard it ourselves," Papa corrects himself. "You have probably heard Emilia read me the accounts of 14-year-old Margaret Fazekas shot in the head last week during a parade near Kearsarge. It erupted into arguments over whether it was a *legal* gathering, and there was pushing and shouting and ... and shooting. Margaret Fazekas will never care about what the argument was, or which side was right. And it was on Labor Day, of all days."

Heli reaches out her hand to me and I take it as we shiver over these thoughts. I know she is thinking of what happened to Margaret Fazekas. I shiver at the thought of something like that happening to my sister only a year away from the same age.

I shiver, then feel my face burn again when I think of what happened to me during my personal standoff with Mr. MacNaughton last week on Labor Day.

Although close already, everything is now coming dangerously close to home.

"The hands of the union are not clean, either," Papa continues. "With one hand, they hold out to the workers the promise of hundreds of thousands of dollars in strike pay, and not one worker has seen a dime. Sorry, Emilia. I know that's your weekly pay from the library and I don't mean to impugn the amount, but it's not much."

"It's not much, I agree," as I think of the ninety cents I've saved so far for Christmas supper.

"On the other hand, union men have shut down all the

mines in the Copper Country, and fought with men trying to go to work, and damaged thousands of dollars' worth of company property and equipment ... and ... only temporarily dimmed *MacNaughton's Eye.*"

He pauses and we are all silent at the thought of Homer Jaakkola. I only hope he is alive. Papa looks like he is about to summarize and wrap up our family discussion. The fatigue shows on his face.

"How have you seen some of his work?" Heli asks. "The attorney for C&H, what was his name?"

"Mr. Rees?"

"That sounds like the man you mentioned earlier. How do you know him?"

He turns to Mama, who first looks to him, then speaks softly.

"Tell them, Henrik. We have been candid as a family. We have seen and heard much as a family. We have experienced much as a family. They deserve to know, and they are big enough to handle it."

Heli and I brace ourselves for a revelation, the tenor of which we do not know, the tone of which we already understand from Mama's last sentence, will not be pleasant.

"A few weeks ago, I learned from a man who came to work at the broom factory that his medical bills were covered by Calumet and Hecla, and he was paid a stipend for the period of time between his accident, no, his injury in the mine and his return to work at the broom factory. The man said all the mines had agreed to participate in a new Michigan law called Workingmen's Compensation. He said the law went into effect just over a year ago, on September 1, 1912. He had learned all this from an attorney he visited after he was told by Calumet and Hecla that he was on his own for the hospital bills and the time off. He had learned all this only after he threatened to sue. And the poor man had lost a leg, crushed in a Calumet and Hecla mine."

"You were injured after September 1!"

"I was, Emilia. But I was in a coma for a week after the injury. And in the hospital for a month after that. And home for almost two months after that, before I could return to work and ask Mr. Lukas, who told me only that Calumet and Hecla would take care of me. I should have asked how. The man who lost his leg received at least a visit from his shaft boss in the hospital. And of course his boss gave him bad news – that he would not be compensated – but at least he went to see him. And that's what prompted Tuomas Tikkanen to seek an attorney."

"Tuomas Tikkanen?" I ask. "Wasn't he the man whose bed was across from you in the men's ward? The man who had his leg amputated?"

"I don't know, Emilia," he says as he lowers his head. "I remember little of my time in the hospital."

"So the law covers you too, right?"

"It should, yes Emilia, but there is more to this tale. I shared what I had been told by the new man at work with your Uncle Bear, who was ready to take me to the C&H office that very day. Your Uncle Bear can be a little hotheaded, and I wanted us to approach this as dispassionately as I knew C&H would. So we waited a few days, and then set off to the office. That was last Tuesday, the day after Labor Day. We talked to a clerk about what had happened – the explosion last December, my time in the hospital, the hospital bills we are still receiving, and my long convalescence. We did not need to explain what has happened to my eyes. I have never had to explain to anyone what has happened to my eyes. These tell the tale," and he nudges the dark spectacles to adjust their weight on his nose.

*Yes, those tell the tale*, I think to myself. They reveal the injury and its consequences to everyone except a child who refuses to see.

"The clerk said he needed some time to prepare *the file*, and told us to come back two days later. We returned on Thursday and ..." Papa readjusts his spectacles, "the clerk told us I am ineligible for Workingmen's Compensation."

"That can't be!" Heli cries, I slap my hands onto the floor beside me, and Mama shoots us the stoic look of one who knows the story, its ending, its horrid emotional and financial consequences.

"Uncle Bear was livid, and again told the clerk when it happened, how it happened, where it happened, and all the details that he knows even better than I. As everyone in this family knows, Uncle Bear was there throughout my ordeal. I interceded just as he was about to leap over the counter and ... and I'm not sure what he would have done, but I know the clerk isn't responsible for the contents of *the file* and probably only assembled it.

"I asked what reports he had, and if they were dated. 'I have a statement from a manager who provides a little detail about an incident last year in which a trammer, that must be you,' he tells me, 'ignored warnings and further ignored direct orders to not go near a load of explosives that was about to detonate.' I asked when *the statement* was received. 'Yesterday,' the clerk told us. I asked when it was dated, and by whom. 'It was dated in January of this year. At least I think it's January, but it's unclear. The day is even less clear, but 1913 is legible,' the clerk says. The poor clerk looked like he wanted to put more distance between himself and Uncle Bear than just the counter, but I kept him there with my questions. 'When does *the statement* say *the incident* happened?' I asked the clerk. He told me the explosion occurred on July 12 last year."

"But, Papa..." I try to interrupt.

"I asked him who signed it. 'Roger Lukas,' the clerk said. So you see, Emilia and Heli, Mr. Lukas simply transposed the date of my injury from December 7 to July 12; 12/7 to 7/12, neatly rendering me incapacitated before the new law of September 1 of last year. And I'm positive he prepared his statement only last week, in spite of an uncertain and suspiciously illegible date in January of this year. At least he was correct about the year we are in – 1913. I'm also positive the clerk is complicit in this, for he had no file early last week and one in his hands two days later."

"How can you be so positive of this? And isn't there still some remedy under whatever law was in place before September 1?"

"That's good logic, Emilia. Logic that works in a fair world, but right now, that's not the world we live in. And that's where Mr. Rees comes in."

He is right. By now, I should know better than to think that logic and fairness will prevail in all I've seen since only turning 16. This is how power works. This is how money works. This is *American Justice*.

"I know the file was prepared last Wednesday, between the first and second visits of your Uncle Bear and I. I know this with certainty because I asked the clerk how he or even Mr. Lukas can decide whose hospital bills are paid and who receives a stipend if they're off work for a long time after being injured on-the-job. The clerk said that Mr. Rees determines eligibility for Workingmen's Compensation, and showed me and Uncle Bear the statement Rees had also prepared and placed into the file. It was dated last Wednesday, which confirmed my suspicions about when Mr. Lukas prepared his statement and when the whole file was assembled. At least as an attorney, Mr. Rees knows better than to incriminate himself by backdating a document."

Heli looks like she wants to object, but holds her thoughts.

"He is also a shrewd attorney. In the absence of Michigan's new law, Rees stated common law that says, as a willing worker, I assume the risk of my work. Then he affixed a couple more legal conclusions to Roger Lukas's report. Rees said that in addition to being negligent in my own work, a fellow worker was at-fault. That would be Uncle Bear."

Papa allows no interruption now. He has heard the reaction from me and Heli when Uncle Bear is implicated. "Emilia, Heli, I recall nothing after the explosion. Nothing for a very long time. Yet I know precisely what occurred prior to it, and Uncle Bear had absolutely nothing to do with it. Mr. Rees was only citing the same legal foundation we in the mines have all heard many times over the years. We can recite it as wholly and accurately as any attorney: I took the risk, I was negligent, another man caused it."

He smiles and blesses himself with the sign of the cross. "We call it *the unholy trinity*."

Mama leads me and Heli with the same sign of the cross, with none of Papa's same sardonic smile.

# *XI*

# *September 13*

The sunrise behind Italian Hall one block away casts shafts of light onto the crowd of women and strikers gathering at Eighth and Elm Streets in Yellow Jacket. Many in the crowd have stayed overnight at the hall so they are ready to heckle the strike breakers trying to go to work on the last day of the week, beleaguered and *broomed* almost daily by the women and strikers.

Even though Papa did not ask why Mama also assisted him to work this Saturday morning, and did not ask why we set out so early, I wanted to tell him that Mama and I are on our way to negate what he is doing, but I did not want to upset what I perceive is a delicate balance between my parents.

Yellow Jacket is the site of Calumet and Hecla-owned boarding house after boarding house of mine workers. A woman by the name of Annie Clemenc advised Mama after Mass last week that she could use the support of more women to march against the workers, and an impending large protest is in evidence today.

I wish we had brought our American flag that hangs on the wall in Papa and Mama's bedroom, for many of the strikers have associated their effort with the stars and stripes by bringing the flag I often see displayed in front windows. Some have brought their brooms and buckets.

Our rally now jams the entire intersection of Eighth and Elm. I look as far as I can see east on Elm past Italian Hall, south down Eighth past St. Joseph's church, and west on Elm littered with boarding houses, and see only raised flags and the heads of mostly women for blocks in any direction. It is clear that Mama and I are in the midst of this crowd, for this is the spot where the women are spilling into the tiny yards of the boarding houses. Mama completes my circumnavigation of the compass as she turns north and looks up Eighth, and something catches her eye because the look on her face changes from a neutral taking in of the scene, to black. I look in the same direction and spot a National Guardsman on a fine horse leading seven more mounted Guardsmen and others on foot in uniform behind them, approaching us from Pine Street.

I want to run. Homer Jaakkola's brutal beating we witnessed at the hands of Sheriff Cruse and the soldiers has kept me awake all week. I relax a little when I think of the size of our crowd, the predominant gender of our crowd, and the veracity of a huge crowd of many nationalities, not a Finnish family of four as the only onlookers.

The protestors open a lane and the soldiers move slowly down the middle of Eighth Street near us, with men toting tin lunch buckets falling in behind.

I hear the jeers of the crowd directed at the workers in the distance. I cannot tell what they are saying and it is just as well, for I've heard the accusations hurled by the other women as me and Mama broomed the scabs near Swedetown Road, and the women's commentaries were far worse than the contents of our buckets.

"You must get off the private property and break this up," the lead man on the fine horse shouts as he stops nearly in front of me, unsheathes his saber and uses it to signal in all directions. The men on horses behind him take their cue from the officer and unsheathe their own sabers and raise them. The uniformed men on foot between the officers and the men with tin lunch buckets raise their rifles from the ground, and point them straight up as if to stab the glistening rays of the rising sun with their razor-sharp bayonets.

The tall woman I noticed talking with Mama in front of Vertin's after Mass last week is approaching the officer on the horse like she owns this scene, not the officer.

"Who's that?" I whisper to Mama, the crowd joining me in a hushed respect I believe is being accorded her.

"That's Mrs. Clemenc. *Big Annie* we call her in accordance with her height and the stature she has earned as organizer of these many marches. She will set the officer aright. Watch."

"These are public streets. We have a right to assemble here and to express our opinions. We will hold firm in our rights and stand firm in our streets," Mrs. Clemenc says as surely as Mama just promised. The crowd agrees with her in cheers, slowed a bit by the seconds it takes for Mrs. Clemec's words to move down the streets and get translated. "These are American streets and you are not the tsar," she states as she jabs a flag-draped masthead toward the officer's face, his saber still in the air.

The cheers erupt louder, little translation needed.

*Both protagonists are fully armed*, I think to myself as I watch the officer move the point of his saber to the tip of Mrs. Clemenc's flag mast.

"Mrs. Clemenc," the officer begins in recognition and deference. "Order your supporters to vacate the boarding house yards. These are the yards and houses of the mines and you have no right to trespass onto their property."

A man atop a black horse and in the clothing of us commoners approaches from the direction of St. Joesph's, and the crowd moves aside to give the horse a narrow alley toward us. The horse snorts and moves its head from side to side like Papa used to do when he was still trying to shake the sight back into his eyes. Prodded slowly by the man atop it, the horse is unaccustomed to this many people and is agitated by the smacks to its flanks that are meant by the crowd to show encouragement. The commoner pulls his reins and stops to the left of Mrs. Clemenc, in front of the officer, and the men and their mounts are stationary in standoff.

"God love you, Arvid Jarvi," Mrs. Clemenc calls up to the new man she recognizes on the mount. "I felt even with the Captain before. Now, we're ahead!" The officer looks at the man, moves his gaze to the man's steed, and dismisses them both with a flash in his eyes as he lowers his steely stare again to Mrs. Clemenc. "My supporters deserve a rest, just as your men do, Captain Blackman. We will not damage the houses and we surely are causing no damage to the yards."

"Damage or not, it's still trespassing. Move your agitators aside while we escort these men to work. They, too, have a right to the streets. Unmolested," he adds.

"I will move my marchers. But you may want to provide some distance between your men and the scabs." She looks away to the twin steeples of St. Joseph's and back to the captain. "We understand they need baptizing," and the crowd in all directions agrees with its roar of laughter.

"Your women must move from the private property," the captain yells in a voice meant to reach the yards of the boarding houses.

Mrs. Clemenc looks like she will acquiesce as she makes a move west toward the boarding houses without turning, and steps square into Mr. Jarvi's horse. She backs up a step and lets out a self-deprecating laugh as loud as she is tall, and slaps the right side of the black horse's neck like the poor beast is at fault for her momentary lapse of presence.

The horse jerks its head to its left, away from Mrs. Clemenc's slap on its neck, then pulls its head back into Mrs. Clemenc's body when she laughs, sending her a few more steps back in surprise from the nudge and from the horse's loud whine of protest.

All the horses are now spooked by one another's familiar

language and the crowd falls away from the panic of the horses. Women's screams pierce the air, adding to the fears of the horses.

Mama and I step backwards together, but dare not look back, for we must keep our eyes on the horses and their intimidating display of anxiety.

Captain Blackman attempts to grab the reins of his horse in both hands, forgetting about the saber in his right, and slashes toward Mrs. Clemenc's flag.

I see Mrs. Clemenc look first to the lacerated American flag, then to her wrist, and then to Captain Blackman, who is now pulling on the reins and forcing his legs into his horse's flanks in an attempt to calm it.

Mama and I are still on the inside circle of the crowd spanning all directions from our middle, but we have successfully put some distance between ourselves and the horses. Mama turns and takes me in her arms and holds me, and the horses, too, begin to calm. The involuntary murmuring and the cries from the crowd begin to subside.

"Look!"

It is Mrs. Clemenc's voice and high above our heads she has raised a masthead and let unfurl a flag that slumps oddly from a slash starting at the stars and ending near the fifth red stripe. Because of the tear, the bottom tip of the flag points to her upraised wrist, with blood flowing from the back.

The horses are calmer now.

The crowd is aghast.

Mrs. Clemenc lowers the flag and detaches it from the mast. She clutches the stars to her chest and turns to wrap the flag diagonally around her body, holding the last shredded length in her right hand before it touches the ground.

Captain Blackman has placed his saber back in its sheath like he is trying to hide the offending weapon.

With the flag now draping nearly her entire body, Mrs. Clemenc looks up at him. "I will not move. Nor will my kinswomen." She turns in a circle to survey her supporters as each woman in the crowd, including me and Mama, straightens her back and gazes at Mrs. Clemenc in awed silence.

"Run me through with your sword, if you will. If this flag does not protect me, then I will die with it. My blood and the blood of my friends is already shed for her."

The horses begin to spook again when the voices of thousands of women raise in salute to *Big Annie* Clemenc.

The horses calm as the noise of the crowd diminishes after several minutes.

Captain Blackman turns and a lane forms toward the point of his arrival from Pine Street, and Captain Blackman and his mounted soldiers, then the uniformed men afoot, and the scabs depart northward, moving away from the mines.

Wide awake with my thoughts, I try to make sense of the major occurrences of my life since turning 16. Make sense of them? I cannot even count the major occurrences! And the ones I would have guessed would be major, like being approached by Erik after Mass when he wanted to come over to our house and court me, I have discarded and turned into minor dalliances.

I toss the blankets off, get too cool, pull them over me again, force a thought out of my mind, and it is replaced with a worse one. I wonder how Papa can take such disparate events and organize them into such elegant thoughts: major premise; minor premise; conclusion. Just like the syllogisms he is so fond of.

All women are brave. My Mama is a woman. My Mama is brave.

This would not stand because, while the conclusion is accurate, the major premise is not. Not all women are brave. *Big Annie* Clemenc certainly is. My Mama certainly is, though not the natural leader like Mrs. Clemenc.

I wonder how you become a leader. Many in school and in the library have tried to emulate me. Some have tried to copy off my papers. But that is not the same as leadership.

Leadership is when you have a vision and you encourage others to take action and you galvanize others into achieving the vision. That's what Mrs. Clemenc did today. That's what Mr. MacNaughton did to lead Calumet and Hecla into the world's greatest copper producer. That's what he's doing to lead C&H and all the mines in the Copper Country toward defeating the union and breaking the strike.

Whether I like the actions or not, they stem from leadership. It's time I show some of my own.

I toss the blankets off, get too cool, and pull them over me again. I am 16. I am not Mrs. Clemenc and I do not want to be like Mr. MacNaughton. I wish to know with certainty what I want to do with my life and I want to graduate first from my high school class.

My class. The school. We talk all the time about what is happening to our papas, what actions our mamas are taking in support. Our teachers' voices are silent on the topic, yet I sense they are in support of the strikers. They know that much of what they teach is dictated by Calumet and Hecla, and they know that their very continued employment hangs in the balance of C&H's bidding.

The schools. The mines have not heard from the schools, from the silent, obedient schoolchildren. It is time I lead. It is time they hear.

From the valedictorian of their class of 1914.

From Emilia Rytilahti.

# XXII

## October 3

It's barely a two-shirter, and Yvonne looks ridiculous in my coat from Vertin's.

The frost from the clear, calm and cold night advised me and Papa of two shirts this morning when I took him to work, and I considered keeping the second one after I returned home and Heli and I continued with the laundry before setting off to school, but I knew I wouldn't need it as the sunny day progressed, so Heli and I walked to school like it's still a one-shirter.

I shared my plan with Heli on our way to school and she was far more supportive than I expected.

"As long as it doesn't involve skipping any classes," she tells me, a rule I didn't need to be reminded of. "You have perfect attendance for almost all your 12 years. No, wait, it's only 11 because you skipped a grade. No, wait, it's only 10 because we just started the school year. Anyway, you know Mama's and Papa's rules. Pay attention in class. No talking back to the teachers. Do your school work. Then the extra credit. And never, ever miss school. Not even one class. I'd love to do that – miss just one class and stay outside after lunch on a perfect day like this, but I've got my own perfect attendance record to defend. How is this going to work again, Emilia?"

My plan doesn't sound as true to me when I tell Heli

about it this morning as it did when I hatched it nearly three weeks ago, but it is easy to muster my confidence when I reveal it to my sister.

"This is what leadership is," I tell myself and Heli, and I am determined to see it through, as determined as I must be now that's it is Friday and it's lunchtime and this means it's time to set my plan in motion.

It figures that Yvonne Joliet is the first obstacle. The girl who hated me as soon as she and I landed in the same class together at Field School so many years ago. The girl who made up stories about me and told Mrs. Reynolds. The one who's wearing my burgundy wool coat from Vertin's.

"Another lard sandwich?" she asks of my lunch sack, the one that has lasted since the beginning of school and will last until at least Christmas because it gets folded and put into the pocket of my dress and brought back home every day.

It's then I realize that I should have eaten my lunch in the usual spot near the maintenance garage, but the sunshine near the Miscowaubik Club invited me here today. That, and the notion that my message needs to start with the most prestigious kids, the ones whose fathers do belong, or hope to. Her father is certainly not a member, and yet this is Yvonne's favorite spot just because she wants to be associated with this club and with these kids.

"Don't you have anything better to do than to dance around in a coat that's too warm and too tight?" I ask Yvonne, ignoring her question about my sandwich and taking the offensive in the new leadership role I've conferred upon myself. I knew the coat would fit me perfectly when I saw it at Vertin's, which means it's too small for her overweight body of lard.

"My Papa is a manager. He's been a manager since we left Swedetown. It's only a matter of time before they invite him into the Miscowaubik. We can afford nice things."

This is going nowhere. Yvonne is snubbing me and I'm trying to rebuff her and other girls are watching and I'm running out of time because lunchtime is when Heli and I must unveil my plan.

"Your papa in the Miscowaubik? When hell freezes over!" That word will cost me when Yvonne surely repeats it to the principal, but if its desired effect chases her away from the group of other kids now interested in our faceoff, it will be worth it.

The laughter hits Yvonne square in the face and I can see the red flush rise. She gapes at me for a moment, and then takes in a deep breath.

I have forgotten about that. I have forgotten about her trick of holding her breath as a grade schooler when she's embarrassed by not knowing any of the answers in class or during recess when anyone would dare to push her back after she pushes her way around the school yard. Her face is getting red. "You look like an embarrassed sausage," I tell Yvonne in a voice louder than I intend. I want to walk away, embarrassed myself by the cruel comment I hurl at her.

She looks around at the group of students watching her, and looks down as the top button of her new coat pops free of its eyelet. She lets her breath go when she walks away from the laughter to take off her coat and regains a little composure and even achieves a small victory when the boys look to her big breasts.

But she will not be back.

"The seniors will parade Monday after school. Pass it along," I tell Bethanie and Laura and Sarah first. The boys look like they're actually interested in what we girls are talking about, or in our dresses, sometimes I can never tell, so I share my message with them. "The seniors will parade Monday after school. Pass it along."

Heli is on the other side of school and probably does not have to deal with the likes of Yvonne and probably has the whole side of the school passing it along by now. I move to the next group of seniors and walk up to a girl I recognize from anatomy class. Eveliina never comes prepared to class and spends most of her time passing notes, so she's the perfect communicator.

"The seniors will parade Monday after school. Pass it along."

My closest friends are near the maintenance building, and probably wondering what I'm up to. They are certainly wondering what I'm up to near the Miscowaubik Club. Many of my high school classmates have quit school and have gone to work in whatever jobs they could find to help support their families now that their papas are on strike. Most of my Finnish friends, even the girls, are still here because we Finns passionately believe in education. I've never even bothered to ask Papa or Mama if I should quit school, for they would be insulted by the mere question.

"The seniors will parade Monday after school. Pass it along," I whisper to Kaisa and Annikki and my good friend Elise, then repeat it to the boys, Nikolaus and Ensio. Elise asks me about the where and the why and, for the first time other than with Heli, I share the details.

My first class after lunch is chemistry and Friday is lab day and the perfect place to share my news easily. I begin with my lab partners Brita and Katariina, and work my way around the lab like I'm comparing the ornaments we're making from scrap tin and various thicknesses of wire, the ornaments we'll coat with copper oxide as we get closer to Christmas. I pass it along. As I head to anatomy class after chemistry lab, a girl from another class stops me in the hall and whispers in my ear.

"The whole high school will parade Monday after school," she says, and I do not have to feign surprise at the message.

"Huh?" is the best I can manage. She repeats the missive.

"I just heard it. Pass it along," she tells me, not realizing I know the message. I should know it. I started it. My question back to her was meant to get an explanation of how the 'parading seniors' turned into the 'whole high school,' but there's no time for that between classes.

Eveliina barely sits down in anatomy class before she glances over her left shoulder and back three rows to me and begins writing something on a scrap of paper. I want to know what it says, but she glances at me again and passes it to the girl on her right.

"Alright, class, let's begin by naming the primary organs in the digestive system," and someone in the class lets out a soft moan of disagreement that the teacher ignores because we all know that the discussion will move from the foregut to the midgut before it ends in the place none of us likes to talk about, the hindgut.

The first person I reach in the hall after anatomy class is a boy who has never said two words to me, but I must know, and ask him if he's heard any news around school.

"Oh, yes," he assures me. "I've heard that the whole high school is supposed to parade on Monday in support of the mine workers. I've heard that we're all supposed to pass it along, so here you go."

After the principal rings the final bell and I begin to walk out of school to join Heli at our meeting spot, a seventh-grade girl who is nearly as athletic as Heli makes an announcement to everyone in earshot. "Some teachers have said there's no school Monday. Have a wonderful long weekend, everyone!"

"What did you tell everyone?" I angrily ask Heli when we meet and separate ourselves enough from the other kids so they won't hear us.

"What did *I* say? *I* said 'the seniors will parade Monday after school. Pass it along.' What did *you* say?!"

"I just heard from one of your middle school friends that there's no school Monday, and her teachers told her that."

Heli is nonplussed. "I just heard that everyone is on-strike, including students. We are to make signs and bring them to carry on Monday. We'll have our own parade."

"This couldn't be worse," I tell Heli.

It's Saturday and I am a little calmer. Heli has convinced me, as I should have known from hearing my own message convoluted back to me within minutes of starting it Friday, that neither she nor I caused the miscommunication. And it is pointless to try to determine who did. The message is out, and I just have to work with it as best I can.

Besides, I have to work at the library.

"Take these to the Doomed Room, Mr. Spencer tells me as he hands me three of the same books. "They don't belong in a decent library, and I surely didn't order them. They're complimentary copies from the publisher, some socialist publisher, no doubt." He concludes his directions and begins to walk away, and stops when he realizes I haven't moved. "Well, what are your waiting for?" he demands.

"Where's the Doomed Room?" I ask. "Better yet, what's the Doomed Room?"

His impatience turns to exasperation. "How long have you been working here?" And before I can answer, he turns again as he says "on the third floor, with the other communist and socialist drivel."

The third floor is the place he told me on my first day of work, and has repeated many times since, that I was to never enter.

I think I'm going to enjoy this.

Entire shelves in the Doomed Room are filled with books by Voltaire and Immanuel Kant. Books by Karl Marx fill other shelves and I do a quick perusal of *Manifesto of the Communist Party*, by Marx and Friedrich Engels. There are also several copies of *The Condition of the Working Class in England in 1844*, which appears to be authored solely by Friedrich Engels. I open this one and read.

*But while England has outgrown the juvenile state of capitalist exploitation described by me, other countries have only just attained it. France, Germany, and espe-*

*cially America, are the formidable competitors who, at this moment — as foreseen by me in 1844 — are more and more breaking up England's industrial monopoly. Their manufactures are young as compared with those of England, but increasing at a far more rapid rate than the latter; and, curious enough, they have at this moment arrived at about the same phase of development as English manufacture in 1844. With regard to America, the parallel is indeed most striking. True, the external surroundings in which the working-class is placed in America are very different, but the same economical laws are at work, and the results, if not identical in every respect, must still be of the same order. Hence we find in America the same struggles for a shorter working-day, for a legal limitation of the working-time, especially of women and children in factories; we find the truck-system in full blossom, and the cottage-system, in rural districts, made use of by the 'bosses' as a means of domination over the workers...*

Footsteps in the distance.

I want to continue reading this book, and consider for a moment smuggling it home, then look at its size and bulkiness, and quash the thought. I return it to its original place on the shelf and take another quick glance around the room. On a bottom shelf is an entire row of *The Kalevala*. My curiosity turns to anger. Finland's epic history, compiled by Elias Lönnrot and recited to my father as he lay half-comatose, is gathering dust on a bottom shelf of the Doomed Room. I want *The Kalevala* more than I want any other book here, but it is clearly the largest one.

The footsteps are getting closer.

I glimpse the title of the smaller books, the three books of the same title Mr. Spencer sent me here with, and slip one copy of *The Jungle* into my dress pocket.

On late Sunday afternoon, after I have read nearly half of

*The Jungle*, by Upton Sinclair, another special train leaves the station in Red Jacket and Heli runs up Ridge Street with the news of what it's carrying.

"Soldiers," she says, this time not with an air of apprehension, but with one of relief. I allow her to calm down and we turn and walk down our street to watch the departing train together. There can be but few National Guardsmen left after this one, filled with passengers in city clothing, horses and hay in the cattle cars, supplies in the enclosed freight cars, and the heavy black artillery again absorbing the sun.

Joining us now is Johanna, the sickly little Nelson girl who has decided that Heli is her hero, no doubt encouraged by Anders and Per, who I think both have a crush on Heli. Johanna puts her arm around Heli's waist and Heli wraps her arm around the little waif's fragile shoulders.

"The guardsmen are just about gone," Heli says, then adds, "if you get your bat, Emilia can find our ball and we'll play pepper with you."

I don't mind being drafted into the game. I know I'm not Johanna's first choice as a friend, yet I also know Heli is doing the right thing and I'm glad to be outside on a sunny Sunday.

"I'd like that," Johanna says. "Nobody at school chooses me for their team, so I'm practicing and pretty soon I'll be as good as they are."

"Pretty soon, you'll be better," Heli exclaims. "Do you like it at Field school? That's where Emilia and I went. And we loved the school because we could come home for lunch every day. And still have time after lunch for some baseball," she adds.

"I like school because you can take a bath there once a week and I just had one Friday and I was only the third one in, so the water was still clean. And it's too bad we won't have school Monday, but we'll all have fun marching in the parade together and me and Per and Anders are making a sign to wave around and..."

"Wait a minute, Johanna," I interrupt. "What's this about no school Monday? What's this about everyone marching in a parade? I thought it was only for seniors. Then I heard it was only for high schoolers, then..." my mind gets lost in the meanderings of the message I started myself. I look at Johanna, who is feeling slighted by a senior whose event is being spun from her own hands, out of control.

"We all heard about it yesterday," Johanna defends. "Per heard about it from his friends and I don't know how they know, but we're all getting ready for the parade tomorrow. There will be no school. Every kid will be there. No parents are even invited. Didn't you and Heli hear about it?"

Heli and I look at each other in horror. Our faces turn to guilt, then innocence, then guile. Heli is the first to flinch and I immediately notice the tiny smirk starting in her dimples. We fall to the ground laughing, and Johanna joins us and laughs too, happy to be included with the big girls.

I think of a small parade of not-defiant-enough looking high school seniors, and only the ones with enough foreguts to be there without either of their parents, and the picture in my mind blurs in contrast to hundreds of kids carrying signs in their own parade and marching in proud support of their papas.

"This couldn't be better," I tell Heli.

# *XIII*

## *October 6*

The mirror remains hanging near the front door on the kitchen wall, and Mama and Heli and I sometimes look into it briefly before heading out the door, but Papa no longer pretends to use it, even while he shaves.

With the strike more than two months old, there is little mine worker laundry to do, so Mama walks into Laurium with her baskets and collects enough to keep her busy throughout the day, but mostly busy with walking, not washing. Heli and I fire up the stove in the basement and carry the water down for boiling, running into each other every time we turn around from the excitement we both feel about the impending parade.

We have learned that our plan to parade with the seniors after school is now transformed into a procession of all school children who are to bring their homemade signs and assemble in a display of youthful solidarity. The location and the time, critical elements to our march, have been left undetermined, and Heli and I hope that Fifth Street at eight o'clock, the place and time of our mamas often staging their protests after discouraging the scabs from going to work, are self-evident.

"*Superare*, Emilia."

A Latin lesson is the very last thing I want to engage Papa in, at this moment. I know he means well, and I know he thinks it's for my own good, and he always mixes his tidbits of knowledge with nuggets of useful information and fun, but not today. Not this morning with everything else on my mind.

I'm sure the look on my face exposes the thoughts in my head, and I change my attitude as soon as I realize he cannot see my look. He cannot see anything.

The long recess of my untidy thoughts causes him to repeat.

"*Superare*, Emilia. Our review of declensions is passé..." He pauses and a look of bemusement spreads over his face. "Isn't that interesting? Only seven months on the surface and I am beginning to talk the language of the French without even realizing it." He turns his damaged spectacles toward me and begins again. "Conjugations are more exciting anyway. Try this one."

I'm certain my impatience will show if I immediately provide the translation, so I wait for a moment as if I'm thinking about it, then give him more than he's asking.

"*Superare*," I repeat. "Pride, haughtiness, arrogance."

"That's *superbia*. You're on the right track, but as you know, you decline nouns; you conjugate verbs. Now conjugate it.

"To prevail, to conquer."

"You're getting closer. Try *excellere*."

"To distinguish. To stand out."

"Now take it to the obvious."

I need to think about what he means by obvious, for it is not to me. "To excel," I blurt out as quickly as it occurs to me.

"That's very good. You're on the right track and, with any luck, we'll be stopped by a train at one of those tracks and be able to complete this lesson. For now, though, it's time we leave."

There are other thoughts in his mind, I am sure because of the bemused look still on his face, and Mama notices too as she tucks the paper-wrapped pasty into his left hand and he takes my arm with his right. I have learned that Papa will reveal those thoughts when the time is right, not before.

Outside, he asks me to describe the colors of the leaves on the trees, and I can provide more detail than I would have been able just a few minutes ago because the sun is almost up.

"The maples are turning splendidly into their oranges and reds. The aspens and birch are yellow already and the oaks, well the oaks have begun to turn their dusky brown and that's the best they will do." I'm faltering at my weak description of a place in time that has to be among the most colorful sights in the world. "I'm sorry. I'm not doing justice to fall on Copper Island. But there are few mature trees around here anymore."

"They're long gone to the mines. I can describe the way they prop up the drifts below, but there would be no color. Do you remember when we went to Brockway Mountain a few years ago in the fall?"

"I remember it well," and my mind quickly changes scenes to our view north of Eagle River, almost to the tip of the Keweenaw Peninsula near Copper Harbor.

"Describe that to me," he suggests.

"Oh, Papa, fall is glorious up there. We're nearly a thousand feet above Lake Superior and a short distance away. The world is at our feet and so are the primary colors because wherever you turn, it's the blue of Superior or red and yellow in the trees. Every other color and every tint is displayed in the lake or the land. The light blue of the inland lakes to the azure of Superior so deep blue in the distance, it seems purple. The greens of the conifers..."

I turn to him and he is smiling broadly. My adjectives are still weak, I realize, compared to the glory of fall in the Copper Country, and yet I know he is filling in my weaknesses of description with his far more vivid imagination. And he will not drill me in Latin or interject his thoughts or opinions while he listens to me and counts his steps and knows to make the turns.

On Swedetown Road, the noise waxes as the colors wane, the trees long gone for the benefit of extracting copper. Their trunks have been used for bracing timbers in the mines, their branches for wagon tongues and wheel spokes, their twigs and leaves for the blast furnaces.

*Everything but the squeal*, I think to myself of Mr. Sinclair's *The Jungle*. In this case, truly everything, including their colors and beauty.

As we near Shaft Number Two, I see Mr. Lukas moving about anxiously between the shaft house and the broom factory. "Rytilahti, I haven't the time this morning for a long-winded discussion, but tell me what you know about a children's parade today. That will be all, Emma," says Mr. Lukas, the pathetic tyrant.

"Roger, this is my daughter Emilia. I believe you've met. And I haven't the time to tell you about it. The men and I have been working on some more improvements to our processes and products. I promised to think them through over the weekend and start them first thing this morning. I'm sorry, but I have work to do right now. We can talk later."

Papa leans over to bid me farewell, and I toss a subtle smirk, meant as a lit match, onto Mr. Lukas's smoldering thoughts.

It works.

"Rytilahti! Rytilahti, re...re...rest assured I'll have the last word on this."

Papa tolerates the last word and turns into the broom factory door. He knows that we are up to something and, by the time our parade is completed this afternoon, he will likely know much more.

I wish I had asked Heli to join my walk with Papa to work, for it would have saved me the time of returning to Swedetown to get her. Heli meets me at our door with the

American flag from Papa and Mama's wall now mounted securely to the Nelson's baseball bat.

"I love you, Heli, have I ever told you that?"

"No, but I know it now. I suppose I've known it forever, though it figures that you would need a favor from me to voice it. Come on, Emilia, we have no time for fraternizing ... or is it sororitizing? No matter. Let's go. And quickly. Mama is still in the basement."

We are among every child in Swedetown who is setting out for Fifth Street, some with their sack lunches in their hands to cover their mutual covert motive, others with a wish for good luck at their front doors, some even with their mamas and a few papas joining them for the march. Many have also brought signs with messages mounted on sticks and decorated and colored like careful school work. Heli leads me onto Ski Street instead of going straight, and drops back when I raise the flag ahead of a group of children converging on the corner of Ski and Tunnel. We are the oldest and we are the ones with the flag, so the children wait for us to take the lead, and another group falls in behind us at Bridge and Osceola. We take the same way on Osceola Road that we take for Sunday Mass, and as I look behind me, it is clear that we have already established a respectable parade, just from Swedetown.

The children from Tamarack are coming from the west, converging with the kids from Yellow Jacket and all heading for the proper starting place. When we reach Fifth Street, we move to the corner of Scott, and Heli and I and all the children stop to marvel at what we have created. All of us are craning our necks to try to get a good view to the north.

Fifth from where we are standing on Scott to Portland is jammed with children. The line is jammed farther north to Oak, and the line breaks only a little in the next block to Elm, but that will soon fill from all the children pouring onto Fifth from Pine Street. This is beyond what I have even dreamed.

"Who's in charge here?"

I whip around to see Sheriff Cruse, a cigar in his right hand, accosting one of the papas. He is interrupted by a man atop a huge buckboard being pulled by a pair of draft horses that is stopped at the corner of Scott and Fifth, unable to complete the delivery of hundreds of cases of beer stacked high on his wagon. *Harold Schmidt and Sons, Distributors of Fine Draughts* announces the arrival of the wagon across the front of the buckboard. It has barely pulled across Scott Street and stands in the center of Fifth, between all the children and our southbound route down Fifth Street to Red Jacket Road to Calumet Avenue, the natural terminus for all parades.

"Good gawd, Harold, can't you see you can't get through here?" Sheriff Cruse yells up to the buckboard driver.

Harold doesn't seem to care, but the two boys beside him, obviously Harold's sons, immediately register the humor of Sheriff Cruse's frustration and the congestion they're causing with grins on their faces.

Sheriff Cruse turns toward the crowd of mostly children and demands again, this time of another man. "Who's in charge here?" The man shrugs, so he starts in on the women. "Who's in charge here?"

"I am, sir," I say as I hand the flag to Heli and sidle up to him.

He looks to me, looks to my left and right, looks over my head, and then sticks the cigar back in his mouth.

"What? What did you say?"

"I said I'm in charge here. What's the problem Sheriff?"

He swallows hard and looks at me as if the acid from my gall is mixing improperly with the base of his incredulity. "The problem, young lady, is you are clogging the streets. You are disrupting business. You have," and he waves his hand toward the buckboard full of beer, "effectively stopped commerce here in Red Jacket. And, young lady, you will immediately call off your scalawags and brats and get them all to school where they belong."

I think of Mother Jones, the grandmotherly woman who mustered a parade with her presence only. I think of *Big Annie* Clemenc, the lady who invited a military officer to run her and the American flag through with his saber. All eyes are on me and I hope my voice holds. Good Lord, I hope my legs hold.

"Sheriff Cruse, I will not."

The voices of the children rise in a cheer I can hear all the way up Fifth Street, and I breathe it in and allow it to straighten my spine before it fades into the distance. "These are public streets and we have a right here. We will be civil and we will be orderly. But we will exercise our rights."

The sheriff looks to my left and right, looks over my head at the cheering children, and turns back toward the beer wagon. "Harold, boys, give me a hand here," he says as he holds his arms wide apart, expecting a case of beer to be handed down to him. The boy on the end of the buckboard looks to his father, who nods at him, and the boy climbs to the top of the stack and hands a case of beer to his brother, who hands it to Sheriff Cruse. The portly sheriff waddles over to the building on one corner and drops the full beer case on the sidewalk next to the building. He moves to the other side of the buckboard to take the case handed to him, then waddles to the building on the other corner and drops it to the sidewalk.

"Boys, let's just stack this beer right here, since it's not going anywhere. Keep the rows going from the buildings on each corner back to your buckboard."

He stands back and lets the boys continue to unload the beer, quickly forming a wall of beer that's three-cases high against the buildings on either side, to a seven-case high fortification on both sides of the buckboard. Taking his handkerchief from his breast pocket and wiping his brow like he contributed all the labor, Sheriff Cruse strolls up and faces me.

"Young lady, yes you will," and he turns back to stand

near the pinnacle of beer next to the buckboard.

Many of the children have moved in to watch our drama unfold, and now crowd in closer as Sheriff Cruse backs away. I hear them muttering in the far distance and I will lose them soon to their homes or to school, and if I lose them here, I have lost.

Heli walks to my side and whispers in my ear while handing me the American flag secured to the baseball bat.

I'm sure my eyes light with her message and I'm sure my whole body is alight with the thought as I step to the row of beer cases and take the top one off the three-high base near the building, set it down, and use it to ascend the neat podium assembled by Harold Schmidt and Sons.

Atop seven cases of beer near the buckboard in the middle of the street, I raise the American flag and shout at the top of my lungs, "To Sixth Street. Pass it along."

As I point the flag to my left, I descend a few cases and stop to view the handiwork of Heli and me, *the result of leadership*, I tell myself: a crowd of hundreds lining the street north to Portland, then to Oak; thousands as my gaze continues to Elm, then to Pine. I watch the message being delivered by the turning heads cascading up the street, and children begin pouring onto the cross streets to Sixth. With only a few cases of beer between me and my resumption of the lead on the next street over, I hand the flag to one of my friends and move the final two cases aside to create an easy walkway.

My glance to Sheriff Cruse finds him walking toward me with a pair of open handcuffs. "Put your hands out. This is going to stop right here and right now."

My momentary panic subsides when I see Heli sneaking in behind him. I hold my hands out to him as Heli slips behind him and drops to her knees. As Sheriff Cruse gets closer, I pull my hands back, lean backwards to leverage my whole upper body, a tactic I learned only recently, and shove both my arms straight into Sheriff Cruse's chest.

He tumbles backward in surprise for only one quickly shuffled step, the backs of his knees hit Heli's crouched body, and the handcuffs fly into the air as the back of his head meets the street, then his shoulders, hips, legs, feet.

Heli jumps up and brushes her hands like she just slid safely into third base for show only, certain of a standup triple.

The case of beer at my feet beckons. I flip the cardboard top up, grab a bottle and walk to the nearby building's windowsill. Holding the bottle in my left hand and placing the edge of the cap just over the sill, I make a fist with my right hand like I've seen Uncle Bear do, and hit the bottle top with my right fist as hard as I can. The slight pain is more than assuaged by the satisfying sounds of a bottle of beer opening and a metal cap clacking onto the sidewalk.

Still on the ground, Sheriff Cruse rolls onto his right side while rubbing the back of his head with his left hand. I offer the bottle of beer with both my outstretched hands. "Here, you look like you could use this."

With none of the musical instruments, yet all the talent in even greater numbers than Washington High School's marching band, its symphonic orchestra, its choir, I take the flag again, and lead by singing the first line of *Amazing Grace*.

*Amazing Grace, how sweet the sound*, and by the time I get to *That saved a wretch like me*, I think the entire parade has enjoined my wretchedness.

Our new parade route has added only one block, and I'm glad that it now takes us in front of St. Anne's, then turns the corner along the side of St. Anne's to Red Jacket Road. Somehow, the thought of nearly encircling a Catholic Church adds confidence to my leadership. Though longer by one block, this path is even better. It'll take most of the marchers through four long city blocks of businesses before joining Red Jacket Road, and then march us past the Coliseum and Mine Street, then past Washington School to the main office of Calumet and Hecla on the corner of Red Jacket Road and Calumet Avenue. That's where I want us to end, and that's where I want us to look our best.

With four blocks of children stretching behind us, our march continues, fittingly, past the area with four churches next to one another, known as *God's Little Acre*. French Canadian St. Anne's towers on our right, then the Scottish Presbyterian and the Cornish Episcopalian, with the Swedish Lutheran church in the background. We're to the third verse, *The Lord has promised good to me, His word my hope secures* when we slow in front of the Coliseum, and at Mine Street I lower the flag and everyone stops for the final verse.

> *When we've been here ten thousand years*
> *Bright shining as the sun.*
> *We've no less days to sing God's praise*
> *Than when we've first begun.*

Crossing Red Jacket Road on our left for a short lane to Washington School is Mine Street, and I've always wondered whether Calumet and Hecla donated the land for the school here so that the street would start here or end here. The teachers look lonesome peering at us from the steps of the school, and some call out to us in encouraging voices and a few wave at us, but most stand there with their arms folded over their chests. As I have learned from listening to Papa late at night, the names of those with their arms folded will not make it onto the list, but the names of the teachers who wave, and certainly the names of those who raise a reassuring voice will be duly recorded. And reported.

I won't fool myself. My name is already at the top of the list.

Sheriff Cruse's less-than-acrobatic collapse was my inspiration for singing *Amazing Grace*. There may not be enough time for all the verses of our next song between here and C&H's main office, but this is the right time for this song so, after a few moments of uneasy silence while the teachers mostly stare, I start our procession moving again as I raise my flag as high as I can, and raise my singing voice as loud as I can.

> *Mine eyes have seen the glory of the*
> > *coming of the Lord:*
> *He is trampling out the vintage where*
> > *the grapes of wrath are stored*
> *He hath loosed the fateful lightning of*
> > *His terrible swift sword:*
> *His truth is marching on.*

Mr. MacNaughton emerges first from his big office building and walks to the edge of Red Jacket Road. Other managers and clerks pour from the same door and stand behind him and cross their arms over their chests just like he does to begin what looks to me like some sort of tragic liturgy. He fixes his stare at me as soon as he reaches the edge of the street and I watch the look on his face change from curious inquisitiveness to cautious concern to complete malevolence when I get close enough for him to recognize me.

I have made it easy for him. My skin still has some of its summer darkness and I am wearing the same summer dress. With only a few feet to where I must stop at Calumet Avenue, I make it very easy as I pass in front of him and hold the flag up in my right hand and extend my cupped left hand like I am offering something to him approximately the size of two golf balls.

> *Glory, glory, hallelujah!*
> *Glory, glory, hallelujah!*
> *Glory, glory, hallelujah!*
> *His truth is marching on.*

The parade is over for me and Heli and the children who want to be in front. Those farther back, and the larger numbers of those four blocks away who have not seen the C&H office workers, are still carrying a good and loud tune. At least a thousand all seem packed to the front now and I

raise both arms to support the flag-draped baseball bat and
keep them there until we reach the final verse.

> *He is coming like the glory of the*
> > *morning on the wave,*
> *He is Wisdom to the mighty,*
> > *He is Succor to the brave,*
> *So the world shall be His footstool,*
> > *and the soul of time His slave,*
> *Our God is marching on.*
>
> *Glory, glory, hallelujah!*
> *Glory, glory, hallelujah!*
> *Glory, glory, hallelujah!*
> *Our God is marching on.*

The strike halting our country's largest flow of copper
has garnered much national attention and complete local
attention in everything except the *Mining Gazette*. A few
reporters and men with huge cameras and blinding flashes
have stopped some of the children and are taking notes and
pictures. Feeling like I am now a contributor to a growing
and worthwhile effort, I relinquish my lead role with an
agreement to meet my sister back home. I hand the flag to
Heli. It is my responsibility to thank everyone, and this will
be a great chance to more carefully examine all our signs.

*C&H unfair* and *Students On Strike* and *Ban the one-
man drill* are among the more popular ones. A huge sign
that must have been borrowed from someone's home is held
up by four children and says *Richest Mines, Poorest Miners*.
Shaking hands and saying "hello" and "thank you" as I move
to the middle of the crowd gathered near the Coliseum, I stop
for a moment, take a deep breath of appreciation, and shout
in both directions.

"Emilia says thanks for coming. Pass it along."

As I back-track past the four churches of *God's Little
Acre* nearly to the place we started, a young boy hands me
his sign and says I should be the one posing for the picture

the photographer wants to take. I hand it back to him with a "no, thank you" and a smile, and try to step into the periphery so the photographer gets a clear picture of the boy and his sign, *Papa Is Striking For Us*.

There's no use in trying to hide our skipped school day from Mama. With much of the school day still left and most of the teachers unbelieving that students could create their own day off, some of the children have gone to school. That was our original thought until Heli and I agreed that we have had enough excitement in our day, and do not want to face questioning students and skeptical teachers.

"I am supportive of you," Mama says when we reach home and tell her of our day and the plans that preceded it. "I have been active in most elements of this work stoppage. I have experienced firsthand the heavy hand of these mining companies over more years than either of you has been alive. It has hurt me, hurt deeper than you'll ever know to see what they have done to your Papa and to Uncle Bear and to our families and friends throughout Swedetown, throughout Copper Island, throughout the entire Copper Country. I could cry. If I allow myself to think of it too much, I just cry."

Mama stops and for a moment I think she will cry, then she gathers herself. "And of course, Papa and I have heard some rumors of your involvement. Last night we already knew many of the details you have just told me about, and we discussed whether or not we should get involved. I felt certain we should. Your Papa did not, and he held firm."

Heli and I know better than to question Mama about the who, what, when, where, why and how of the rumors they heard. We have joked that we could not get away with squishing an ant on the playground at school without all of Swedetown crying in pain by the time we got home.

"But your Papa will want to discuss this. And I expect he'll want to discuss it first with you, Emilia."

As usual, there's plenty of truth to the rumors. I knew that Swedetown would be afire with them and I guessed that they would spread quickly to Red Jacket and Yellow Jacket and Tramarack and Centennial and Blue Jacket and Laurium and Raymbaultown and every town in our area with school children.

At least Mama has provided me warning of the firm lecture I can expect from Papa.

"Tell me what you believe in, Emilia."

This is not what I expect, and Mama's warning and my entire afternoon of rehearsal have not prepared me. Papa has said good-bye to those at the broom factory who still continue to work through the strike, and has taken my left arm and I expect the barrage to begin, but not this. The serious look on his face gives away nothing.

"I believe in God. I believe in life. I believe in Christmas," I tell him.

"Very good. What else," he says as a statement, meaning that he expects more without having to ask it.

"Papa, it was the right thing to do." This, too, was not in my repertoire of witty responses that I rehearsed all afternoon. "I'm tired of being treated as a child" and "you can't tell me what to do all my life" were in there. But they are so feeble now. They sound weak to me, and if they do not pass my litmus test, they will never pass Papa's.

"Heli and I ... no, I planned this whole parade. Heli has been wonderful throughout this, but I bear the responsibility. We spread the word around school Friday. It got a little out of control, but by this morning..."

He stops us both and turns to me. "By dinner time today, most of the details of your parade were known and analyzed and editorialized. Remember, you passed within a few yards of my building. I don't want to hear a recitation of the facts," he says sternly. "Tell me what you believe in, Emilia."

We walk together in tense silence.

"I believe in studying hard. I believe I have the best grades of anyone in my class, though I can forget about valedictorian honors now." He gives me the first hint that I am on the right track, even if I can tell from his face that it is only a nod of agreement, not a smile. "I believe in what our mamas are doing. I believe in the efforts of Mrs. Clemenc and Mother Jones and Mr. Darrow. I believe that Mr. MacNaughton and Sheriff Cruse and Mr. Lukas cannot be allowed to continue what they're doing. I believe that even the children of mine workers can make a difference. I believe that this standoff must endure until it yields fair wages for you. Better yet, safer working conditions. I believe that you should fight for your Workingmen's Compensation and Mama should not have to walk into Laurium to pick up laundry for enough money to pay hospital bills."

As we make the corner onto Swedetown Road, I stop us both and turn to him. "Papa, I believe in justice. A word; no, not a word, a concept; no, not a concept, a way of life you taught me."

"*Superare, excellere,* Emilia." I look back at him questioningly, and realize again that he cannot see the pain nor the confusion nor the conviction I am trying to muster in my eyes. Through his darkened lenses, I believe I see it in his. "You told me this morning it means to distinguish, to stand out, to excel. I'd like you to ascend even above that. I almost gave it away." I do not share with him my experience of ascending the beer cases this morning, though sometimes I think my thoughts are transparent to him.

"Transcend!" he states emphatically. I let the word germinate for a moment in my mind. "In Latin or English, it means to exceed or excel," he tells me. "And it also means to go beyond. Better yet, to rise above. That's the place I have in mind for you, Emilia."

"You asked me what I believe in? I believe in myself now, Papa. I believe in myself more than I ever have in my life. I believe I can do something important with my life. I believe I want to be a leader."

"You will be. I am certain of it. But your enthusiasm may get in your way. You will pay for your actions today. Not because me or Mama will make you pay. But life will make you pay."

"So *life* is defined as Calumet and Hecla?"

"No, life is defined as broadly as I intended it. I encourage you to engage it fully. I encourage you to lead it completely. Just be careful and be smart. I know you can do it, with a little ... maturity. And when you decide to lead, also remember to rise above the pettiness and the games and certainly the traps."

"*Superare, excellere.* I'll remember that, Papa"

"Transcend, Emilia."

# *XIV*

# *October 18*

Uncle Bear hasn't worked since the beginning of the strike, Papa is laid off again, and I am fired from the library.

As Papa and Mama and Heli and I properly settle into Uncle Bear's and Aunt Iiris's sitting room, I wonder what further havoc this strike will wreak on our souls. The strong sense of community that I have always felt here on Copper Island has been re-defined by mine owners and the Western Federation of Miners, and our community has imploded in a bitter battle of class struggle, power plays, politics, ethnic divisions and religious wedges, and always, Papa says, money.

"Savage capitalism," as Papa has described it – and Frederich Engels described it in different words when I read an excerpt of *The Condition of the Working Class in England in 1844* in the Doomed Room – is winning.

It has first taken our bodies, Papa having paid a dear price. Our hearts were wounded by the Seeberville killings, our minds by Margaret Fazekas's shot to the head.

Today, I feel it in my soul.

"I don't know, Uncle Bear, I've been working almost every Saturday at the library since I was 13 and I guess I haven't gotten used to it yet," I say in response to his question about having last Saturday off. Two Saturdays in a row including today.

"And what silly reason did they give you?" he asks.

Yvonne Joliet sized me up in smug self-assurance when Heli and I returned to school the day after the parade. I have never figured her family as feed for the Miscowaubik Club, more like compost, but apparently her father has more influence than I have credited him for, or more likely he knows someone who appreciates a snitch, someone with a daughter who lies and snitches too. I could tell my chemistry teacher, Mr. Schubert, didn't want to have to break the news to me that I was no longer a leading candidate for valedictorian honors, but I also knew I couldn't blame the messenger for the message. Oh, how the message hurt. By the end of that week Papa was told they have enough brooms for a while, and I was told I'm not needed at the library and will likely never be needed there again. I was too stunned to ask why, and yet the look on my face must have begged the question because the circulation manager, who was given the unseemly task of giving me the boot, told me I'm "not a good fit." Whatever that means.

"They said I'm not a good fit, Uncle Bear."

"Ah, the favorite phrase of incompetent operations managers," Papa interjects. "They haven't the leadership ability and they haven't the fortitude and certainly not the management savvy to coach you along if that's what you need. They haven't the guts to discipline you if you're truly performing inadequately, though I doubt that was the issue. So they rely on rumor, don't bother to ask your side of the story, and fall back on that tired old phrase that can't be defended because it can't be explained. Then they fire you. Is the name of your circulation manager Roger Lukas, by any chance?" he asks sarcastically. "In my case, they say they'll bring me back 'when the economics can justify it.' Another indefensible and unexplainable and intentionally open-ended date."

It's nice to be invited over to Uncle Bear's and Aunt

Iiris's house again, but this is already feeling like a funeral in the wake of all our unemployment. Uncle Bear is feeling it too, and looks around at all the morbid faces in his sitting room, and lights up when he reaches Papa.

"*Savusauna*, Henrik! You've forgotten, haven't you? When you were here on a Sunday in the spring, I promised you a smoke sauna the next time you returned on a Saturday, and I haven't forgotten! I got up early and I've been heating the rocks all morning. Let's enjoy the sauna all afternoon."

"I'm sure you've heard the description as often as I have, Karhu-Jussi. *A Finn is a man who works like a dog all week, then sweats in a sauna all Saturday.* We haven't earned the right to sweat there today, especially since neither of us is working, but I won't worry about that. I think that's a great idea."

"Henrik, I'm sure you've heard the description as often as I have, and this one fits you even better: *a Finn is a man who worries too hard*," and the room lights up with a laughter that feels good to all of us.

"A few more rocks, a little more firewood, and I'll be ready to release the smoke. Emilia, will you assist in the final savusauna preparation?"

"I could use some help in the kitchen," Aunt Iiris says, and Heli and I accept our respective invitations and I head outside while Heli joins Aunt Iiris and Mama.

Uncle Bear helps Papa to the sauna and leads me around the back where the firewood is cut and stacked. The first log on top is bigger than my hand and heavier than what I think, and it falls back toward me as I try to grab it and lands on my right instep, scuffing my shoe and inflicting a sharp stab of pain through my entire foot.

"Shit!" I cry out involuntarily. The word surprises Uncle Bear and me with equal force, and sends me to the ground. Sitting on the ground and rubbing my foot and rubbing the scuff mark off the shoe Uncle Bear made for me, I am grateful that we are several feet east of the closed door of the sauna and a long way from the house. The s-word I've heard many times, though never at home, so I'm surprised it has crept into my vocabulary, and shocked it has escaped from my mouth.

The tear starts first in my right eye. It starts by itself. Another one in my left, and they drop down my face in that order. On their own, my feet stretch to the next stack of wood, my back leans against the wood pile, and my hands raise to cover my face. The sobs start in the pit of my stomach and find voice when they race past my lungs into my throat. The convulsions are as involuntary as everything else that has commandeered my actions and sent me into an emotional conundrum.

Poor Uncle Bear does not move. He doesn't know what to do, what to say, how to act.

"It's not fair!" I tell him, lifting the log with both hands like it is the true cause of my breakdown, and smashing it back to the ground. Uncle Bear still does not move. "Papa has paid this company with 17 years and with his eyes, and he is not working and that is not fair! You have trammed your whole working life for two mines now, and you are not working and that is not fair! I have the best grades and the best attendance in my class and I will never be valedictorian and that is not fair! I have worked hard for the library and I have never even been late and I have been fired for no reason and that's not fair! I heard Papa tell Mama that Mr. Lukas profited from selling them the house, then profited again when he exchanged their money back to them at usury rates. That's not fair, Uncle Bear! He probably had something to do with the explosion that nearly killed Papa. They have robbed my Mama and Papa, and robbed my Papa again until he is blind! He is blind, Uncle Bear!"

Uncle Bear's gentleness is as unfathomable as Superior on a beautiful calm fall day like today. He gazes into what I am sure is my tear-drowned face and matches my breakdown with his empathy.

"A moment, Emilia. Let me release the smoke in the sauna and talk to your Papa. I'll be right back."

"I am angry, Uncle Bear," I confess to him in the confidence of a clearing in Uncle Bear's woods far from the firewood pile, the sauna, the house. "I am angry at the Western Federation of Miners for calling a strike with not enough strike pay for you or Papa or anyone else. I am livid over the way the Waddell Mahon men and the deputies and the National Guard have turned the Keweenaw into a battleground. I am angry at all the mines in the Copper Country for deciding that they will not negotiate a penny. I am angry that they have enough money to do it, and we have none. I am angry at all the mine superintendents and at Mr. MacNaughton and Sheriff Cruse."

Uncle Bear is sitting on the ground, as am I, leaning against a tree, as am I, silent as the ground and the trees.

"I am angry with Papa, Uncle Bear. He will not fight for that thing they call Workingmen's Compensation and he is not fighting for Mama and all he can do is advise me to *transcend*. What kind of advice is that? He fears them now, Uncle Bear. He has lost his courage along with his eyesight and ..."

"Your Papa fears no one!" Uncle Bear explodes, slamming his right hand to the ground as he speaks.

His outburst leaves my mouth open in mid-sentence and he keeps his hand on the ground and makes no effort to talk until I close my mouth and the dust settles near his hand.

"The mines are a dismal place to work and the only work we Finns are allowed is the worst kind. We are trammers. All morning we break rock from the ceilings of a drift and load it into the tram cars with our bare hands. We cannot afford gloves and the rock wrecks the gloves in no time anyway. We can barely afford boots and the rock ruins them almost as quickly. We warm our pasties in shovels held over candles and throw a few scraps to the rats and break more rock and load it all afternoon.

"Your Papa brought light to Shaft Number Two when he joined us. A light none of us knew existed and none of us knew we even missed. He talked of logic and philosophy and dreamed up silly syllogisms and made us laugh and made us think. In no time, he figured out a way for us to work smarter and safer. Has he ever explained to you about retreating drifts, and who invented them?"

"No, but what..."

"I didn't think so. We used to take out rock by following the lode in an advancing method, causing the hanging walls to collapse on us as we did. Your Papa thought about that for a while, and then talked Lukas into trying a retreating method. We left the hanging walls to collapse behind us and fewer men have been hurt. We all encouraged your Papa to tell the other shaft bosses about it, but he was self-conscious about his English. Guess who told the others about it, and took the credit?"

Uncle Bear looks at me, but doesn't wait for the answer.

"Your Papa would have learned impeccable English on his own, but that motivated him. As I understand it, every mine in the Copper Country now uses the retreating method. We had no faith in Lukas anyway, but your Papa became our leader. It hurt us to lose him to the broom factory. The explosion – or what your Papa describes only as his 'injury,' – hurt in more ways than you'll ever know."

"So how about ...?"

"In just a few days, he had the broom factory cleaned up and organized so that everyone knew where everything was, without being able to see it. He had tried to borrow some of the processes that he had read about from that Ford fellow down in Dearborn and bring them to the mines, but Lukas wouldn't hear of it. He said they were too socialist. But Lukas spends little time in the broom factory, so your Papa broke down the processes on his own and re-built them into steps each blind man could accomplish. Then he paired the lame with the blind into teams. He has the legs of tree trunks, and works with the eyes of a man with only one leg."

Uncle Bear stops and locks eyes with me, and the windows to his soul reveal a depth and vastness and richness that will never be matched in Shaft Number Two. "Emilia, I'm proud to say that I worked with your Papa in the mines. I've seen his work in the broom factory. He is a genius."

"My Papa is the finest teacher in the world. He has always been my mentor. But something happened to him after the explosion, Uncle Bear."

"Yes. I have seen it too, though it is not what you think. He is even more thoughtful now. He analyzes and plans even more than he did before. Before the explosion."

"But he fears, Uncle Bear. He fears..."

"He fears black powder. A sight, when it's burning, every man in his right mind should fear."

"I thought the mines have been using dynamite for years. I thought Papa was a trammer, and didn't work with explosives. This whole ugly episode of the explosion confuses me and I have wanted to hear it from Papa, but he never talks about it. I want to ask, but I am afraid to ask. I know he lives it. I see it in his face, and I wish I could see it in his eyes, but I never will and he never will. So I see it in his face by day and I hear it in his dreams by night."

I work up my courage to ask. "Please, Uncle Bear, tell me what happened. Tell me of the explosion."

"You're right, Emilia. Our Swedish friend Alfred Nobel is a true friend of miners. Working in the mines for over twenty years, I have experienced both black powder and nitroglycerine, or what Mr. Nobel has patented as dynamite, and the days of black powder are gone, thank God. It attracts moisture and burns erratically and has only a modest charge. But on Saturday, December 7 of last year, the last day of the work week, that's what Roger Lukas required us to use."

Uncle Bear's long hesitation tells me he is forcing himself to think again of the day.

"The powder house behind your home on Ridge Street? That's where he found it and he brought the whole keg to Shaft Number Two just to use it up. None of us wanted anything to do with it because we know how fickle it is. He thought that was funny. He laid a thin trail of the stuff around us during lunch and lit it, and it fizzled and raised a terrible smell and ruined our pasties. He used up half the keg playing games and raising a stench and having fun at our expense."

Uncle Bear is structuring his thoughts and the look on his face shows that he's not editing them like Papa. He focuses and continues.

"We are struggling with a small stream of mass copper – that's nearly pure copper that we rarely find. Sometimes we'll run into a lesser amygdaloid lode – that's Latin for *almond-shaped* – your Papa taught us that – but mostly we mine the conglomerate stuff that's stuck in the rock and needs to be crushed and smelted. Even though it's a small lode, mass copper is sticky and tough to mine. We cut out underneath and around its sides and are about to break it out and load it into the tram cars, but Lukas insists we blast it out. He empties nearly the whole keg at the point where the mass copper is still stuck to the rock, and uses the rest to leave a little trail of black powder to ignite. To ignite and run. Lukas lights it and joins us around the nearest corner. We hold our hands over our ears and turn our backs and wait. We wait for a long time, Emilia."

The sadness in his eyes is palpable.

"Then I make the mistake of smirking at Lukas. We should wait longer, but I think my smirk is what causes Lukas to send someone in to check on his folly. If only I had..." Uncle Bear stops and rubs his eyes. "'Eenie, meenie, mynie, mo,' that childish fool counts on his fingers, then looks around as if he's deciding who to send in. Your Papa steps forward."

Uncle Bear turns his head and looks into my eyes.

I want him to stop. I cannot bear to hear the rest, yet I cannot talk to beg him to stop.

"'Ah, just the man I was thinking of,' Lukas says. 'Just the man my finger has settled upon. I'll send in this finger. I'll send in the fin...'"

Uncle Bear looks from his hand to my face. "I cannot say that, Emilia. I cannot tell you what Lukas calls your Papa. It's not important anyway."

"Yes it is, Uncle Bear. I hear Papa in his sleep at night and he mumbles something about a finger. Mr. Frantti said almost the same word at a Skyhooks' baseball game. What is it that haunts his dreams? What is it Mr. Lukas calls him? What is it that Mr. Houseworth calls Mr. Frantti?"

"It is a name I will never repeat. To anyone. Last of all to you."

My argument is over, but the explosion is not.

"You can figure out the rest, Emilia."

I don't want to hear it, and indeed I *can* figure out the rest. Just as I suspected, the pathetic tyrant, who stole from my parents from the time they arrived on Copper Island, stole his eyes as well. There's little left for him to take.

"I told you before and I'll say it again now. Your Papa fears no one. He fears nothing and I will defend him to my dying day. I will defend him if it kills me."

Uncle Bear hangs his head. "I should have defended him more. Even if it *had* killed me."

He raises his head and his eyes lighten. "But here's something else, something very valuable I also learned from your Papa: *you can't kill for friendship*, Emilia. He taught me that, too, though I'm sure we all know it in our heart of hearts. Books, Shakespearean plays, history is full of examples of men killing for love. Your Papa is philosophical. The day he became my best friend is the day we talked about friendship and he explained that you can kill for love, and men often do. But you cannot kill for friendship. You must earn friendship. You must be honest and fair and ethical.

And you must be willing to sacrifice for friendship. You must earn it."

The love and trust I have learned to see in Uncle Bear's eyes are now shining at me.

"Your Papa earned my friendship long ago. I hope I have earned his. And fear? He does not fear, Emilia. He *transcends* it."

"That's what Papa was trying to teach me only days ago. That's the word he used. But the lesson is not complete. It is trying to inhabit my head, but it's not there yet."

"I know exactly what you mean. The lesson your Papa is trying to teach us both will never inhabit my head. But you will learn it, I am sure of that."

"What's the lesson, Uncle Bear? Help me understand it."

"Sometimes I think your Papa is too philosophical for his own good. And the reason I will never learn it is because it is certainly too philosophical for me. It is best described by his favorite phrase. I'll share it with you because you have already used one of the words in the phrase. But don't tell him."

I don't need to hear that to pay close attention to Uncle Bear. But, just in case, the admonition to not tell Papa gets my attention every time.

"Transcend the bullshit!"

"Wha...?"

"Transcend the bullshit! That's what he does, Emilia, and I wish sometimes I had his same ability to do it. Isn't that a wonderful phrase? *Transcend* ... such a lofty word, and every time I hear him say it, I envision that word floating in breathless air, kind of like a soft, low cloud. Like a soft, low cloud rising above a big heap of dung. He rises above it. He rises above the money and the power and the greed and the pettiness and lets all the rest of them wallow in the bullshit. He assigns all the worst of human traits to mere triviality. Pure bullshit. Then he transcends it. God love him for it, Emilia. I wish I could do that as easily and as philosophically as your Papa. That's what he wants you to learn. That's what he wants you to do."

The breeze shifts and I can smell the change from the savusauna to something on Superior. I raise my head and take a deep breath through my nose. "What's that, Uncle Bear?"

"Firewood. I figured as long as we're going to smell the smoke from the sauna, the sauna I should also be enjoying right now, we may as well have a fragrance, so I chose the wood of a choke cherry tree. It's nice, isn't it?"

"Yes, it was nice. But what I smell now is from the direction of the wind change. I'm sensing something from Superior."

Uncle Bear's eyes soften. "Describe it to me, Emilia."

I take another deep breath. "I'm not sure I can. It's not the fragrance of cherry wood. It's just a whiff. It's a smell. No, more like an aroma. No, those are all associated with food. I sense the water."

"Oh, you've caught a whiff of..."

"No, I've not caught it. More like it's been offered to me."

Uncle Bear's eyes reflect the soft light of the late afternoon. His beard widens and his mouth opens and his lips fashion a big, wide grin. "Emilia, you will understand this. Come with me."

He takes my hand and leads me away from their house on a narrow, well-worn path far behind the sauna, a path I've never seen. We bend over and duck through the dense underbrush and I can feel the air turn warmer, so we must be getting close to the water. Just when I think I can't continue to walk at Uncle Bear's pace while stooped over, he straightens and we emerge onto a sandy beach on Lake Superior.

"Uncle Bear, I didn't know you owned this."

"I don't. That's why you've never seen my secret path. I sneak out here on the private beach owned by the mines, and no one is ever the wiser. Except me. I love Superior and now

I know, Emilia, you're a hopeless romantic like me, and you understand and appreciate this incredible body of water."

Uncle Bear takes off his boots and I take off my shoes and follow him to the shore. I pick up my dress and pull out the hem with both my hands and tie the bottom of my dress into a loose bow. He wades into the water up to his knees.

"Here," he shows me. "Lean over and cup your hands and take some of what she offers you." I cup my hands and stoop and plunge my hands into the water and bring her to my face. "Now bring her near your lips. Don't smell it. Breathe it." I take a deep breath through my nose as I did a few minutes ago when she first offered it to me on land. Uncle Bear understands. "Now taste it."

I raise my hands and bring the water to my mouth, then rub my hands over the dried salt of my tears now gone.

I didn't know you could smell pure.

I didn't know you could taste pure.

Wondering if he can articulate it better than me, I ask, "what are you sensing, Uncle Bear?"

The water clinging to Uncle Bear's beard looks like luminous jewels. "I smell superior," he says. His tongue pauses on his lips. "I taste superior."

The mid-October sun is straining hard to warm the Keweenaw Peninsula and to warm Uncle Bear's farm near Lake Superior for a few final days before it gives up in what I know will be a blast of white. The thought sends a shiver through me as Uncle Bear wades with me to the sandy shore and we both sit down and put our footwear back on. He gets up first, looks at me with the kindest eyes I have ever seen, and holds both his hands out for me to grasp. He lifts me to my feet like I am a low cloud that deserves to be lifted to the sky.

"Come on, Emilia. Your Papa is still in the sauna. Your Finnish father has worried hard enough for today."

Only a dollar and twenty cents. A dozen dimes. Twelve

weeks of work at the library since I started saving it as the strike began.  Eleven more weeks to go before Christmas. Two dollars and thirty cents would have been enough for a few nice things for Christmas supper. I've been fired from the library. A dollar and twenty cents won't go far.

I return the dimes to my hiding spot under Mama's rag rug.  Heli turns over and sighs, and Papa and Mama are both breathing the deep breaths of sleep.

*Transcend the bullshit.*  I am already learning to love that phrase as much as Uncle Bear tells me he loves it.  Now, I must learn to live it.

*A Finn is a man who worries too hard.*

*A woman too*, I think, according myself a title and a maturity as a young woman that I am beginning to relish.

A Finn is...

A finger.

No, I don't want that thought.  No matter.  It dominates anyway.

A finger.

A fin.

A Finn!

There are more syllables I have heard Papa mumbling.  I work the sound, the cadence in my mind.  It's a dirty word, for Uncle Bear will not repeat it, at least to me.

A finger ... fing..er

Try it again.

A finger ... fin..ger.

Try it again.

A finger ... fi..nger.  Nger.

Niger.

Latin for *black*.

What did that man from the circus, the man with the wonderful smile and warm eyes and dark skin – Mr. Jasper – call himself? A *nigger*?

A dark person is a nigger.

Why did Mr. Jasper ask me to get a drink of water for

him?  He said he can't touch our fountain.  Why?  Because
he's a nigger?  The man from the circus with the skin darker
than mine tells me to be proud of it.  The man with the skin
darker than mine used to wish he could change it, though he
probably wasn't as impulsive as me when I took bleach to it.
Then one day he realized that his skin made him special.  He
said I should be proud of my skin.

That's the first time anyone ever told me I am beautiful.
He told me I'm beautiful and unique because of my skin.

Papa's skin gets dark in the summer and so does Mr.
Frantti's.  So does mine.

Are we niggers?

Yes, a person with dark skin is a nigger.

Niger.

I'm a Finn.

I'm a nigger.

There are more syllables.

Finger.

A Finn.

A nigger.

I've got it.  This is what Papa says at night.  This is what
Mr. Houseworth calls Mr. Frantti.  This is what I am.

Finnigger.

# *XV*

# *November 8*

There's no use going to the store. We have no money. Papa is up early as usual, but not to go to work. He's just completed the third week of what he calls "lay-off" and I am suspicious that it started a few days after the children's parade. That's simply too coincidental.

I am up early as usual and I should be getting ready for my job at the library. It's Saturday and I still miss working there, so today I'll return some books and take out some new ones, and maybe even sneak back into the Doomed Room. I know there is nothing coincidental about being fired from the library as well as losing my chance at valedictorian honors right after the children's parade.

Mama and Heli are up early as usual, with no laundry to do. Mama says there may be enough flour for bread, and we're luckier than most of our Finnish friends who have neither a garden to grow rutabagas and beets and carrots and turnips, nor a root cellar or basement to store them in. I'm not sure I understand how we can own the house and not the land, but I have come to appreciate the garden Heli and I weeded last summer and the crops that Mama says may get us through some of the winter.

She and Heli start the bread.

Papa says he can sense a big storm coming, and the growing banks of clouds that seem to be accumulating in my head confirm his forecast. He gives me permission to go to the library, but says I must hurry back before the storm hits. Dinner will be carrot soup and supper will be rutabagas and maybe a little fried dough, and I am grateful for what little we have.

I think the Doomed Room will become my favorite place in the library. Now that I've been fired, I feel like I truly belong here among the manuscripts and speeches and books of great people and great writers who will never be circulated from the Calumet & Hecla-influenced library of Copper Island. It's where I found *The Jungle*, by Upton Sinclair, and where I read transcripts of speeches by a lady named Susan B. Anthony. I'd love to smuggle them out for Mama. Mrs. Anthony is fighting for women's right to vote and Mama says that, from the letters she receives from her homeland, Finnish women have already become the first in the world to earn the right to vote and to stand for election, and she may never have it here in America.

The circulation manager, Mr. Taylor Spencer, is as brusque with me when he checks out my books as he used to be when I worked here. A question comes to his face as he looks at the name of the author of the first book. He turns the book over to a sketch of the author on the back of the dust cover, and says "humffh" as he stamps the card and places it into the back of the book. He does not comment on the next, apparently believing that *The Red Cross in Peace and War*, by Clara Barton, is more appropriate for me. Mr. Spencer picks up the first book again and inspects it more carefully.

"What do you want to read this for?" he asks me more as an accusation than a question.

"It's a big world out there, Mr. Spencer. And I plan to see and smell and taste and touch as much of it as I can."

"Have you ever been out of the Copper Country? Have you even been south of Copper Island? Those are pretty big ambitions, Miss Rytilahti."

"That's why I read, Mr. Spencer."

When I worked here, Mr. Spencer admitted to me that he hates reading and I always wondered what he was doing working in a library, but he keeps an impeccable accounting of the books and I assume the finances, so that explains it.

"I've never heard of this writer. He can't be any good."

I had to look carefully in the Doomed Room before I could find a niger, or black author, and reading the first few pages after I found the book immediately told me that the dialect of Mr. Jasper at the circus was just like the characters in this book set in the American Deep South. Although I am yet unsure of this author's writing prowess, Taylor Spencer will never know. "W.E.B. DuBois is a unique author, Mr. Spencer. And *The Quest of the Silver Fleece* is a wonderful book."

When I get home, the American flag is waving on Papa and Mama's bedroom wall.

Our house groans and complains and we listen to its monologue tell us what the weather is doing without ever having to look outside. It is especially informative at night or when we're in the basement. A slow waltz on our roof is the summer rain. Dancing to the beat of a Finnish folk song means hail. When the beat moves to the side of our house, it's the fall winds throwing leaves and twigs at us. We learned last winter after Uncle Bear built Papa's and Mama's bedroom out of a little space in the sitting room, that when the wind whips through the chinks in our siding and the American flag on their wall waves, it's a blizzard.

Even without the benefit of a view from the top of the water tower, I know that Superior is whipping herself into a white frenzy and is flinging herself onto a shore thirty feet farther inland than it was yesterday. From our home in Swedetown, I know the water near Uncle Bear's farm in Eagle River is rhythmically bursting through the crevice in the rock beach like it is trying to shoot at the bears napping safely in their dens on the earthen face of Superior, oblivious to its threats. This I can see only in the clarity of my mind, for nothing is seen outside our windows except white.

Heli takes the north window in the kitchen, and I go to the west window in Papa's and Mama's bedroom, and the volume from the wind's whistle is dampened a little and the pitch changes a little when we tuck the snow from the sills back into the gaps around the windows. We have strung the clothes line from our house to the privy and we are grateful for the pile of firewood we brought in yesterday, and I stoke the kitchen stove while Heli does the same for the one in the basement, and neither of us will complain much when the bugs crawl out from under the bark and come looking for us when we sleep on the sitting room floor tonight.

It's Saturday and I'm not working at the library; will never work there again. The strike is grinding on. The storm is striking. There is no laundry to do.

It's a perfect day to read.

Sitting on Mama's covered sofa with two shirts on against the wind moving through our house, I find that Bles Alwyn is a character I can relate to: young, loves to learn, impulsive, a nigger. The Creswell plantation owners are my MacNaughtons. Cotton is copper. Bles's description of the bolls bursting with cotton reminds me of the blizzard blasting outside. The silver fleece of the quest in Mr. DuBois's book is as mysterious as the figurative Sampo of *The Kalevala*.

Heli teases me that I must have at least two books open at the same time, and *The Red Cross in Peace and War* beckons me. I learn how the Red Cross organization was formed and I read of the twelve nations that signed the Geneva Red Cross Treaty of 1864, and how the crowned heads of Europe backed up their signatures with substantial contributions. In the first few pages, I can't find the original twelve signatories, but I'm pretty sure the United States is not among them. Miss Barton is probably being kind in her book by not naming them, which would shame the U.S. by its absence. Later, I find that the U.S. ratified the original Red Cross Treaty eighteen years later, in 1882. After Peru, Argentina, Chile, Bolivia, Serbia, Montenegro, San Salvador, Persia and Romania back to 1874.

Perhaps there is still hope for Mrs. Anthony's cause and hope for Mama's right to vote, and my own right to vote in a few years when I reach 21. Perhaps there will even be girl altar boys in the Catholic Church.

*Girl altar boys?* I'll need to work on that title.

The importance of women like Clara Barton in the formation of the Red Cross, like Susan Anthony in advancing women's right to vote, reminds me of my own quest for what I want to do with my life. A Civil War passage from Miss Barton's book seizes me:

> *"I thought of the Peninsula in McClellan's campaign of Pittsburg Landing, Cedar Mountain and Second Bull Run, Antietam, Old Fredericksburg with its acres of gun-covered glace, and its fourth-day flag of truce; of its dead and starving wounded, frozen to the ground, and our commissions and their supplies in Washington, with no effective organization to go beyond. Of the Petersburg mine, with its four thousand dead and wounded and no flag of truce, the wounded broiling in a July sun died and rotted where they fell."*

I think of the Keweenaw Peninsula overrun with rats chased out by the risen waters in the mines; of what Papa says is an average of one death a week as *the cost of doing business* or, as Papa also describes it, the *savage capital.* I think of the National Guard bringing wagons with red crosses on them in anticipation of some carnage; of the wounded and dead before the mines were shut down by strike; of the wounded and dead after the mines were shut down by strike; of the two men I helped just before their deaths at the hospital, and the one man I helped just before, and for many days after they amputated his leg.

I never learned the name of the first man I cleaned as Mama taught me, in the back of the men's ward at the hospital in Laurium, where they put Finns who are in a coma to recover and other Finns to die. It was just before Christmas last year and, with some hope of recovery, Papa's bed had been promoted from the very end of the ward to one bed closer to the hallway.

The left side of the man's head was crushed, his ear gone, blood and brain dripping from the opening. Some cloth bandage was wrapped a couple of times around his head, a weak barrier to the huge wound. Unable to move a limb, his body shifted slightly during involuntary spasms.

My heart hurt for him.

With the thin skin and wrinkles of an older man, he has little gray hair and few lines and no deep creases in his wide face. He is clean-shaven and I want to believe he is poetic and articulate, and I have no way of knowing.

Late Saturday night – it must be Sunday the week after Papa's injury because I insist on staying after he has hugged me earlier in the day – the man utters some words. I position my ear next to his mouth.

"Auta minua. Ole hyvä ja auta minua," he mumbles. "Help me. Please help me."

His eyes are closed and his face is clean, but the spittle on his mouth is dry and his lips and mouth cannot move far enough to crack it completely, and he cannot wipe it away. I lay *The Kalevala* aside and look for a nurse, but none is in sight. A pan is in the closet with the water and sink, and I already know where to find the pull cord for the incandescent light as well as the wash cloths and towels.

His hands are filthy and this is the proper place to begin, so I wring out the wash cloth and hold it in my hands to warm it, wipe the filth off the back of his left hand, pry his hand open and dab at the cuts and rub at the calluses until it is clean. There is no wedding band on his hand, and I imagine a poetic and lonely man, which explains why there is no family here beside him. I lay his left hand at his side and expect it to close, but I think that this unconscious old man is willing it open in gratitude. The water in my pan is dirty and I go to the little room with the light and rinse the pan, replace the water and return to the other side of his bed. A more noticeable spasm shakes him gently and I hold the wash cloth to my breast to warm it even more. When I take his right hand, it opens, no, he helps me open it and I see that this man is left-handed, for there are fewer cuts and fewer calluses here. There is a deep mark in the pit of his palm and I am almost done and the water is dirty, so I move the wash cloth over in my right hand and lick the spot on the cloth above my index finger and rub the dark purple mark until it is gone.

With his right hand still in my arms, another spasm hits him, this time violently.

There is no doctor here. Where are the nurses?

Laying his arm to his side and still holding his hand, I begin to get up from my chair to find a nurse, and feel his hand gently squeeze mine. I soothe his right arm with my left as I let go of his right hand. I place my hands on his shoulders and look into his eyes, even though they are closed, like Aunt Iiris does.

The lines in his face from the convulsion smooth and seem to disappear.

There are no nurses in the hallway and I do not want to go all the way to the women's ward to check. Returning to the chair beside his bed, I am about to take his hand again, and instead pick up *The Kalevala*. Opening it to a random page and holding the book with my left hand, I take his right hand to my chest.

"*You have not reached the end yet!*" the Finnish words say.

"*While you were on your way*

*There were great marvels*
*Three incredible wonders"*

He smiles. He tries to talk, but is unable.

*"Three ways for a man to die,"* and I wish I had found any other segment.

He smiles again, this time as if he can see heaven from his closed eyes. I think he hears. I know he understands.

A third violent spasm, but no involuntary grimace.

I need not put my ear to his chest like Mama trying to hear a heartbeat. I need not even look to his chest, for there will be no gentle rise and fall. I have felt his life ebb from his hand against my breast.

Only when his hand turns cold in my own am I able to set it down at the side of the bed. Looking into his face for a moment, I move his left hand over his own heart and place his right hand on top and find a nurse casually sipping tea near the women's ward.

"That's the coroner's job," she tells me when she notices the pan of water at the side of the man's bed. "We don't bother with that for lost causes," and she leaves the ward and returns with a gurney on wheels, slides it into the space between the dead man and Papa's bed, and grabs his feet and pulls the weight of his lower body onto the gurney. I squeeze into the tiny space to the head of the bed and put my arms under his shoulders.

"No, not like that," the nurse scolds and motions for me to get out of her way. She shoves the man's head to his left side, leans her chest onto his face, puts her arms around him and lifts the dead weight of his upper body and heaves it onto the gurney. She moves to the foot of the wheeled gurney and pulls it into the narrow aisle between the beds against both walls. The gurney's head is not cooperating with the nurse's attempt to exit the ward, so I put my hands onto my dead friend's shoulders and keep the head of the gurney from flying around corners as the nurse leads us backwards to the morgue.

"Close enough," the nurse says when she jiggles the morgue door handle and finds it locked. She leaves me alone again, and returns in a minute with a sheet that she drapes over his body. "Time for lunch," she declares and walks to the little room near the morgue and searches among the row of paper bags on a nearby shelf. She grabs one off the shelf and sits down at a table and takes out a sandwich, then looks up at me.

"That'll be all," she says.

Caring for my kinsfolk and reading *The Kalevala* to Papa were the only things that kept my sanity amidst the death and suffering and insensitivity of that hospital in Laurium.

Väinämöinen is a charismatic character, and I am impressed with his boat building skills and especially with the song and magic he brings to each of his tasks. The trochaic tetrameter of the original Finnish text feels unusual at first, but when I embody the beat, it makes me resist my urge to translate everything into English, and helps me to feel the lines as easily as reciting them. It seems that Väinämöinen will be a perpetual bachelor, for his trip to Pohjola does not win him the Maiden of the North, who chooses Ilmarinen.

Tuomas Tikkanen has also taken an interest in *The Kalevala*, and I am glad because he needs much to take his mind off the loss of his right leg. His two young sons are not allowed inside, but his wife visits often and his mood improves when I open a nearby window and we hear his boys call out to their papa.

The nurses are accustomed to me and Heli, and their first attempt to bar our entrance once Papa is clearly recovering is met with such stern retribution from the rest of the men in the ward that the nurses give up in defeat, especially after Dr. Jacobs sides with me and Heli.

At first, Mr. Tikkanen grieves the loss of his job greater than the loss of his leg, but his shaft boss assures him there will be a place for him at Calumet & Hecla, and his boss returns one day after the amputation with the news that there will be a place for him in the broom factory.

"This one good leg will lose all its strength just lying here," Tuomas says. He asks his wife to help him lift it, and it's clear she is doing all the lifting. She visits as often as she can, but she tells me that she takes in laundry for a little money and has her hands full with the two young boys who are not allowed inside the hospital.

Papa is beginning to converse and will need some of the same therapy, so I help Tuomas by lifting his leg and I can see by his face that he is trying to help, but I can feel the weight of his whole leg for many days.

"Eureka!" I tell him as he grimaces when I lift on the seventh day.

"What?" he asks and I feel the weight of his whole leg that I'm now accustomed to, as the expression on his face changes from trying to lift a leg to managing to lift a question mark.

"Eureka. It means *I've found it*, and I haven't found anything, but I think you have. Let's lift again."

His expression changes back to a grimace and I take the back of his left ankle and lift it with one hand to the peak of the arc we've formed, then I take my hand away.

His leg hangs in mid-air for a second, and then falls to the bed.

"Eureka!" he says. "I've found it. I've found some strength. Emilia, I have some strength back in my leg and I can hold my leg up, if only for a second. Emilia, I'll hold it up longer in no time. I'll hold it up by myself. I'll walk again!"

I feel Tuomas's joy almost as much as Tuomas feels it himself.

He asks me to stay near him during his first trip down the narrow aisle of the men's ward on a crutch. With the crutch under his right arm, I feel useless behind him as he takes his first tentative step, then feels himself falling forward, so he shifts his weight backward and falls into my arms when we both fall to the floor under his weight. He and

I are embarrassed and he is still lightheaded, so I begin to move my arms away from him, but he falls back into them in a moment of unconsciousness. His chin is barely onto his chest when he suddenly raises his head and turns to look at me and grins.

"I guess I passed out. I'm sorry. Let's just stay here for a minute, though, and I'll be alright."

The color is barely back into his face when he rolls onto his left knee, raises his upper body straight and grabs the crutch in the middle to get up. I help him to stand on his left leg and he re-positions the crutch and we both just stand and look at one another.

"Grab his belt," the man in the middle of the ward with a broken and swollen ankle says. "Tuomas, tighten your belt, and Emilia, move around to his back and grab his belt there. You'll be able to feel if Tuomas starts swaying like a drunk, and you'll be able to halt his drunkenness."

The belt around Tuomas's waist is already to the last notch from the weight he's lost since his accident, no, his injury, no, his injustice – his amputation. He smiles at me as he pulls on his belt to no more notch holes, and tells me there's much leather to grab behind him. Grasping the belt in my right fist, I turn my hand and take up enough slack to hold my wrist up and feel my knuckles in Tuomas's back. When we make it to the front of the ward near the opening to the hallway, the men with two hands clap them together in approval, and the man with no left hand smacks his right hand onto his leg in dull applause.

Though still behind Tuomas, I feel him beam with pride.

Both Papa and I are enthralled with *The Kalevala.* Ilmarinen gets married and has a wedding celebration the likes of which I would love to have some day, but can only dream of. It seems, though, that his wife is a bully and she torments the young boy Kullervo, who has her killed by a pack of wild animals. Ilmarinen returns to Kalevala and tells Väinämöinen about the beauty of Pohjola and its peoples because of the Sampo.

I am still perplexed by the meaning of this strange and wonderful and beautiful thing, and I wish to know what it is that makes flour, salt and gold out of thin air. There is significance, I am sure, to flour, salt and gold.

It is after Christmas when I see death for the second time and I'm glad it is after Christmas and I hope I never see death again like this. Tuomas Tikkanen is home, and will be there for a long convalescence. Papa is talking now, and he and Mama and Heli and I watch as a drunken young man is escorted to the back of the men's ward and tossed into an open bed across from Papa. He has a bullet wound that has removed a line of hair and scalp and reveals his skull like a perfect part in his hair on the right side of his head. A streak of blood marks a path from his left foot that he is dragging behind him. His loud and off-key rendition of *There's No Sabbath West of the Sault* sends the whole ward into commotion.

"Just stay there and sober up," the nurse tells him. "And be glad it was only a small-caliber bullet. We'll get a doctor in tomorrow to take the lead out of your foot. And your head, well, there's nothing we can do about that." She spins around and leaves the ward and ignores both the men and the gestures of the men who are lying in bed and thumbing their noses at her.

With the nurse gone, the young man's face contorts in pain as he moves his body slightly to his side, reaches to his back pocket, and produces a brown pint bottle. He removes the cap, smiles at the bottle, takes a long pull, and then notices Papa across from him. "Care to join me?" he asks.

Papa is progressing nicely, but is self-conscious of his slow and halting speech, and just slowly shakes his head.

"Don't mind if I do," Mr. Nelson interrupts, and I have already learned that he is nowhere to be found when the nurses need him, always here when they don't. Mr. Nelson takes the bottle that was offered to Papa, guzzles a generous swig, and tucks the bottle into his back pocket. "No liquor allowed at Calumet Public Hospital. At least, none by the patients. And that's too bad because this is good whiskey, young man. But don't you worry. I'll take good care of the rest of this bottle for you," and his disappearance is more dexterous than the tools he handles.

Heli can't stop staring at the young man in the bed and I also notice the rugged good looks of an Irish laborer who is too young to be a man, far too young to try to drink like one. The boy begins singing again.

"Stop it already," "you dumb drunk," and "how long do we have to put up with this?" have no effect on the boy, until a verse of the song reveals something about "a bawdy lass" and Mama looks straight at the boy's face like she will finish the job with a well-aimed shot between his eyes.

Heli turns to me and grins when she notices Mama taking aim.

"That will be quite enough!" Mama says with an evenness of temper and volume and control that is clearly heard, and is immediately understood. Turning to Heli and me, she mutters, "a toiskielinen, a drunken English-speaker."

Shooting to a sitting position in his bed and casting an evil stare back at Mama, the guise lasts only a moment until he looks down, tries to tear the front of his shirt open, looks up and vomits whiskey and blood straight out to the foot of Papa's bed. Heli remains frozen to the chair beside Papa and I nearly slip on the vomit on my way to the boy's left side while Mama moves to his right.

"Where does it hurt, boy? Where does it hurt? And what's your name, son?" whispers Mama at the face now ashen and sunk deep into the pillow.

"Ma gut, ma'am. Ma gut and me heart feel like dares lead in 'em. Hallagan, ma'am. Richard."

Grabbing the shirt that Richard tried to tear, Mama unfastens the two top buttons and, when he gasps for a breath of air, she rips the remaining ones and the buttons hit the floor and rattle away. A small patch of blood has dried around the opening on the left side of his stomach and begins to flow again from the opening. Another small hole looks like it leads straight to Richard Hallagan's heart.

Some of the men move from their beds and are gathering around, and the nurse fights her way to the front, but stops short of Mama, who is now holding Richard to her breast.

"Tell my Ma, ma'am. Tell her I love her."

Mama lowers his head from her arms and looks into his eyes. "No, Richard, no. Hold on, Richard. We can get through this together."

He makes a fist with both hands and flails his arms to his side and I can see that his face has already lost most of its color. The hole in his side is bleeding profusely and he is trying to cough, but seems like he can't bring himself to do it. He raises his right fist and thumps himself on the chest.

The small-caliber bullet, which must have lodged right next to his heart, now must have pierced it. The blood bursts through the hole in his chest like a dam.

Heli falls back in horror. I stare in shock. This is all happening too quickly.

Leaning straight into the blood from his heart and his side, Mama takes the boy back into her arms as the remaining life drains out of him.

I have seen Mama change from astute and objective observer to stern disciplinarian to the most compassionate person in the world. I have often seen this at home and I think she would be a wonderful nurse. She continues to hold the boy until the soft convulsions of her sobs fade and she lays his head back onto the pillow and turns to the nurse, clear-eyed and angry.

"Did you ask? Did you even ask him where he was shot? Did you look? Did you even look where he was shot?"

"No need to. I knew what the problem was, and I don't understand ..." and Mama leans out of the way and points to the bleeding hole in his stomach, the one near his heart.

"Emilia, please help me clean this boy. No mother should see her child like this. Nurse, clean up the blood and the ... and the bile. It stinks in here."

The metaphors of *The Kalevala* now speak to me in terms of loss and bereavement. The Sampo is destroyed and lost at sea when Väinämöinen and his sometimes-friends, sometimes-foes sail together to Pohjola to get it; the only redeeming value of their trip being the invention of a stringed musical instrument, shaped from the jawbone of a giant pike. The distinctive, bell-like sound of the kantele's strings I will always associate with a young man's death. When the Sampo is lost, all manner of ill-fortune strikes the people of Kalevala. But Väinämöinen restores it and sails away, leaving only the kantele and his songs as his legacy.

The Sampo, like youth, is never recovered.

I am grateful for *The Kalevala's* contribution toward the mastery of my Finnish tongue, a language I would not know nearly as well without Uncle Bear's loan of an epic tale sung to me in beautiful poetry. The men of the ward have thanked me as they have left the hospital after invariably hearing at least a chapter of the book. When I close it for the final time, Papa is still weak, yet anxious to go home. The hospital accommodates him when they say that another Cornishman needs a bed, which will be moved to the head of the ward, no doubt.

During a January snow storm that's not a blizzard like today, but has already dumped two feet of snow since it started two hours previous, Mr. Kumpula from Swedetown pulls his horse and wagon to the front of the hospital and we place Papa in the back with pillows and blankets around him to keep him warm and keep his neck and head firmly in place. Uncle Bear has completed the renovation of our house and Mr. Nelson has confirmed that he and his family will move in by the first of February.

Mama and Heli and I are tripping over one another to help Papa, and he tries to taste small portions of every one of the dishes that our Swedetown neighbors have showered upon us. For the first time since December 6, the day before his injury, Mama sits down at the kitchen table and eats a full meal.

"We will need to nurse Papa back to health," Mama says with a lilt in her voice we have also not heard since December 6. "Emilia, you have learned much at the hospital about physiotherapy and you and Heli and I can take turns helping Papa. I will manage by myself when you girls go to school tomorrow, and over the course of the day we can develop a regimen. Then it's your turn, Emilia. And Heli, don't look at me in that tone of voice. You will have your turn with the rest of us."

"Where's your head now, Emilia?" Heli asks as she glances at the two books beside me. "Don't tell me, let me guess," and she lifts the books and opens the one by Mr. DuBois. "Let's see, you're in some warm place with cotton and with people talking a strange brand of English." She looks at only the cover of the next, *The Red Cross in Peace and War*, by Clara Barton. "No, you're nursing someone back to health after a bad accident. No, you're saving someone's life on the battlefield."

Heli knows my propensity to place myself in the middle of scenes for every book I read. "Wrong, Heli. I am nursing Papa back to health. I have already seen too much death at that deadly hospital, but I am pleased with Mr. Tikkanen's progress with one leg. Papa is my next patient in the archives of my mind, in the annals of my memory from last winter."

"Can you come back to the present? My present needs to go to the privy."

My brief dialogue with Heli reconnects me with the day. The trip to the privy finishes the task by brutally reconnecting me with the blizzard. We walk around the east side of our house to give us some protection from the wind howling at us from the northwest. When Heli fumbles to the back corner, she reaches up to grab the clothes line and disappears after her second step. The snow whips around the corner and I put my head down as I feel up the side of our house for the start of the clothes line. When my right hand finds it, I walk past the edge of our house into the white that is nothing, the white that is everything and everywhere. This is the first big snow of the year and no path is yet cut and a slow trudge is necessary to keep from falling, a fear I've always had on days like this. Walking purposefully with my head down and my left hand clutching the third shirt I have thrown over my dress, I let my right hand slide over the clothes line and feel its pressure to take me a little right or a little left to the privy door. I allow myself no time to celebrate reaching the privy without falling. With the door hinged right, I whip it open and join Heli and she grabs my hand and turns around and continues to hold my hand even when she pulls up her dress to sit down. At mid-afternoon, it may as well be nighttime in this blizzard. Heli pushes the door open with her foot and reaches for the clothes line and is gone in one step. My exit isn't nearly as quick and graceful, for I must first find the stick of wood nailed in the center to secure the privy door, then find the clothes line. The slow trudge back through the snow past my knees is as uneventful as I had hoped.

Heli is nosing through my books again. "So you're a nurse, right?"

The words hit me like the breeze I felt in the Alabama summer when I started Mr. DuBois's book. The warmth of our home spreads over me. I am immobile for only the moment of the present. Heli's words have thrust me into the future.

"Heli, I do believe I truly love you."

"What else do you believe in, Emilia?..." Papa's words from the kitchen are lost on me as I dart into their bedroom, a place I rarely go when my parents are home, and grab

Papa's white Sunday shirt. Carefully buttoning it while standing in the center of the sitting room, I let the long tails flow to my knees and stand and envision myself. I need a white hat.

"Heli, hand me..." and I needn't finish the sentence because my hand is out and Heli places the book by Miss Barton into it. The binding complains when I open it to center and balance it on my head, the words blurred in white background. "Is this a nurse's cap, or what?" I reveal to Heli. Mama is up from the basement and Papa is up from the kitchen table and they stand in the doorway between the kitchen and sitting room and look at me in a white shirt with a book balanced on my head. I can tell they don't know whether to scold me for the shirt or admonish me to not ruin the book or just laugh.

"This is a nurse's cap. This is a nurse's uniform and the red cross goes on my shoulder and ... " I feel the book falling off my head and hold out my hands and catch it as it closes with the sound of an exclamation point.

"I am a nurse!" I declare emphatically.

Papa claps first and Mama and Heli join in and I clutch the book across my waist in a deep bow.

"You are indeed a nurse, Emilia. You have been a nurse, and with further nurse's training that you can get right here at the hospital in Laurium, you will be the finest nurse this hospital has ever seen," Papa says as the first to follow my charade and my logic.

"Oh, Papa thank you. Thank you for understanding me and encouraging me and helping me face my future with a career I didn't know I knew."

He holds out his arms and I glide into them and Mama smiles as she looks to my shoulder displaying the imaginary Red Cross, and Heli joins behind.

"I love you, Emilia. As big sisters go, you're one of the better ones."

"And now what?" He asks through his dark spectacles

with the broken right lens.

"Now what?" I wonder aloud. The satisfied look on his face reveals nothing, but I am learning to understand my man-of-few-words Papa, and I am beginning to interpret his questions and decipher his logic.

"Why, Papa I am going to sit down today and write a letter. The letter will be addressed to the head of the nursing school at the hospital and it will state my qualifications and request admission after I graduate from high school." Looking up to him, I see the expression on his face turn to approval. "Will you help me?"

"Emilia, I will be proud to play a small role in your assured acceptance into nursing school, and the début of your career as a nurse."

As I look into his face, the broken right lens conveys something back to me. "Papa," I begin.

"What? What's wrong, Emilia," and I know he has heard my disappointment in only my one word of his name.

"I cannot go to nursing school. I have no ... we have no ... none of us has any money."

His expression remains firm. "We will find a way. And that is not your concern now. Your job now is to write a letter that will get you accepted. The rest, we will ... we will find a way."

We spend far more time disagreeing over the greeting than I prefer, so I finally defer to Papa's insistence upon *Dear Headmistress*, more out of fatigue than agreement. We toss each sentence back and forth as I've learned to do when he helps me write. He waits for me to fashion the phrase, works it a little for sense and sound, and tosses it back to me for inclusion in the letter, cautioning me for grammar and punctuation and spelling and syntax in the completed sentence:

> *My name is Emilia Rytilahti and I am desirous of admission into your School of Nursing for the class beginning next fall, 1914.*

*Some of your exceptional Nursing personnel may recall the days I spent assisting my Papa as he was admitted into your fine facility in a comatose state, and eventually recovered from his injury, due in large part to your Nurses. While he was there, I was pleased to provide an extension to the assistance of your excellent staff when I tended to his physical, emotional and spiritual needs as I helped him in therapy, comforted him, and read to him.*

*The rich experience of nursing the ill and injured has made a meaningful impact, and has caused me to want to become a Nurse so I can continue the quality of care you have already begun in our community.*

*I have studied diligently at Washington School, and carry a good grade point average. Much of the Greek and Latin terminology used in medical science is already committed to my memory, and I expect to successfully complete the anatomy course I am now taking.*

*Your serious consideration of my request is sincerely sought, and your ensuing approval of my admission into your Nursing School next fall is greatly anticipated.*

"Very Sincerely," and I look to him for final, final approval.

"Yours Truly in Christ," he suggests.

"Do I get extra credit for complimenting them, or do I lose credit for pandering to them?" I ask.

No longer able to look into his eyes for clues, I have learned to translate the expressions on his face, and this one tells me I may have gone too far, especially since I asked for his assistance and he willingly, anxiously accords it. Without saying it, he first tells me I am being the impulsive and opinionated girl Mama has raised. When the wry smile appears on his lips, I wonder if I have earned some of the insight and maturity he wants of me.

"Those are not the only choices I have for answering

your question, young lady, and this is not a question or a test in class. This is life, and this is how we must approach it if we ... you are to be successful. This is a very good letter. Nice work."

"Yours Truly," I write before giving him a chance to change it.

# XVI

# November 15

The draft horses strain against the weight of the road roller and their huge hooves break through the packed snow nearly up to their knees as they make their way down Seventh Street. Last night the temperature dipped below zero, but it'll be a few more weeks before we can count on the winter weather remaining so consistently cold that the snow freezes solid enough for the horses to walk atop the packed crust and not break through. Seventh Street and all the main streets in Red Jacket are now about a foot high with the snow crushed down by a few packings of the horse-drawn road rollers. Last week's blizzard added only about four feet to the couple feet already on the ground. Another 15 or 20 feet of snow, with a few warm spells thrown in, and the roads will be packed to five or six feet by spring.

Spring? What am I doing allowing my thoughts to turn to spring when winter has just begun?

The lack of conversation between me and Mama has caused my mind to wander as we trek toward the newly established union commissary just past Italian Hall on Seventh Street. The testy look on Mama's face as we pass the Great Atlantic and Pacific Tea Company on the street level of Italian Hall tells me she is trying to balance the family ledger, and I know she is worried over too much expense on the one side, no income on the other.

The Western Federation of Miners must be feeling guilty for the little strike pay they're providing their workers, and the commissary at Seventh and Pine, like the strike pay, is too little, too late. I'm probably better off thinking of spring, for this thought is depressing, and I can tell Mama feels the same way as we enter the door and she displays the union card Papa just received after his *lay-off* from the broom factory. Mama always travels light to buy groceries so she can carry them back home unencumbered, but today she doesn't even bring her handbag, for it contains no money and Papa's union card can be carried easily enough in the pocket of her third shirt.

"Emilia, you get the flour and sugar and a little salt. No, wait. We can do without the sugar, and be sure you get Gold Medal flour and get the coarse salt. It's less expensive and we can grind it ourselves."

Kellogg's Corn Flakes were not a consideration before the strike because Mama believes in a more substantial breakfast, and does not believe in pre-packaged food products. The corn flakes are out of the question today and I can tell that most other mamas feel the same way because the bright Kellogg's boxes are one of the few items still displayed in quantity on the union commissary shelves. Mama is loading up on canned vegetables and stops at the meat counter. It is peculiar to see this in a grocery store because meat markets are a separate stop, but I guess the union is having some success at making their little store as convenient as possible for its cardholders.

Mama asks about the prices and the butcher tells her to not worry about that because everything is *on the tick*. Credit is a foreign concept to my family, though most retailers have allowed their good customers to buy things that way, knowing they will sell much less if they don't, and knowing that they will be repaid. The prospect of repayment at some future undefined time when Papa is back to work discourages Mama and she walks away with no meat, but with more knowledge than most mamas after finally finagling some of the prices from the butcher.

"This should get us to Christmas," Mama tells me of the small armload I am carrying and the twenty-pound bag of Gold Medal flour she is toting out the door. Still in no mood to talk, Mama just hugs the bag to her chest and marches straight south on Seventh Street. To avoid the Atlantic and Pacific grocery store, it would have only been a block or so out of our way to take Pine to Eighth Street and down to Scott and a little jog to Osceola Road to Swedetown, and I want to suggest this to Mama as we leave, but if discretion is the better part of valor, I should get a gold medal for valor.

"We should have taken Pine to Eighth, then home," Mama says, and I mentally remove my medal for valor and replace it with a reminder to myself that I should feel as free to challenge Mama as I am now feeling to question Papa. But she has been the face of courage and backbone during this strike and I see her courage acquiesce only a little when we walk past Italian Hall. Giving the cold shoulder to Vairo's Saloon, also on the first floor, will not be a problem for Mama, but we first must pass the A&P grocery store and its manager, Mr. Meyer, is out front and watching us go by.

"Good morning, Mrs. Rytilahti. Good morning, Emilia," sings Mr. Meyer in the same voice he uses for all his good customers. "Fine day, except for the snow. The price we pay for living in God's Country, I guess. Or is this the reward we get?"

The "reward we get" changes each season with Mr. Meyer. Next spring, it'll be the slush, next summer the heat and next fall the wind, but he'll always say we still live in "God's Country" and nobody ever disagrees with him.

"Good morning, Mr. Meyer," Mama and I sing back in unison and I know she would trade me the flour for the lighter load of groceries and stop and chat for a while if we had just purchased it all at A&P, but we barely break stride.

"Did you see the button on Mr. Meyer's apron?" Mama asks when we are a safe distance away.

"I did, Mama. It says 'Citizen Alliance' on it. Did you hear me read the article in the *Mining Gazette* to Papa the other day?"

"Yes, I did. This strike is so divisive. But the identity of those who support the strike is discerned only in the face of a Finn. Beyond that, you almost have to come right out and ask which side someone supports. The Citizens Alliance is smart to produce pins to wear. I'm saddened, but not surprised that the business people are taking sides with the mines. How does that old axiom go? *They know which side of their bread is buttered.* I'm disappointed, though, that support for the union must be concealed in a card in your wallet, while collusion with the mines is championed with a button on your breast."

This is more conversation than Mama has permitted all morning, and I want to engage her. I know what she says. This is my opportunity to ask her why.

"A mere button doesn't seem like it should have that much influence. It is making a powerful statement, though, isn't it? I wonder what the Citizens Alliance has in mind. The newspaper article said the group was formed to 'destroy the destructive seeds of socialism.' The Alliance clearly sides with the mines. I wonder what actions they intend to take."

"I don't believe that belonging to a union equates to being a socialist," Mama says. "I'll accept that the union is trying to sow its seeds. But they are the seeds of progress, the seeds of transformation, and the seeds of change."

She has taken the direction I was hoping. Now I must ask if I hope to truly know.

"What needs to change, Mama? And why are you such a proponent of it?" Discretion has prevailed again in my mind, and this time I am grateful because I was about to ask her why she's so militant.

"Something is wrong when money is the primary motivator to getting things done in government. Where is the consideration for justice? Something is very wrong when half of the citizens cannot vote. Where is equality? Something is wrong, Emilia, when companies can send its workers into places like a mine, pay them whatever they feel like, work them for as long as they feel like, with no attention to safety, and then cast them aside when they're done using them. Where is fairness?" Mama stops and exchanges her bag of flour with my groceries as we reach Osceola Road. "Fairness? I am asking too much. Where is basic human dignity?"

She is on a mission in our trip to the union commissary and she is on a mission in her explanation of her convictions. "Notice I did not say that this country is immoral, that this government is broken beyond repair, and that the mining companies are all wrong. I said that things are wrong within them. You don't tear it apart and start all over again. Many countries and many companies try that, and most fail. That's called revolution, not change. You try instead to fix things. That's what I'm trying to do, Emilia."

The incline up Ridge Street to our home now feels almost insurmountable. Mama's quick steps have tired me and perhaps even tired her a bit, for we both stop at the entrance to our village and look up the hill. Mr. Kumpula's horse is not in his little barn behind their house, and looks from our vantage point to be hitched to his wagon, backed up to the front door. Mama begins the incline like she's again on a mission. As we near their home, two doors from ours, Mr. Kumpula is securing a rope across bulging canvas as Mrs. Kumpula helps him tuck in the corner behind her side of the wagon.

"What do you think, Kerttu? Will it be warm enough and comfortable enough to get us to Marquette?" she asks as she points to the lump in the canvas that reveals the top of her rocking chair.

"Marquette? Oh, Pauliina, please tell me no. Please tell

me you're not moving away."

"We have no choice, Kerttu," Mrs. Kumpula says with the sadness of parting from a neighborhood where she knows everyone and shares everything. Mrs. Kumpula and Mama long ago gave up on keeping track of who borrowed sugar, who borrowed molasses and how much, and even who originated some of the recipes. With their children married and moved to homes of their own, she is Swedetown's most reliable source of recipes for the other mamas, and bisketti – cardamom bread – for their children.

"We've been evicted."

"Oh, Pauliina. Oh, Matti. Please tell me no." For as long as I live, I will never forget the shame on their faces. "Why didn't you tell me? Why didn't you let us know? Why didn't you let me and Henrik help? We could have helped. We could have done something. We could have..."

"We couldn't make the payments, Kerttu," Mrs. Kumpula says after first looking to her husband's crumpled face and realizing he cannot speak and, if he could, he would not say these words. "For the first time in our lives, we cannot make good on a commitment we have made. For the first time in our lives, we are indebted beyond our ability to repay. For the first time in our lives, we have accepted charity when we stocked up on food from the union commissary to make the trip. We have been made to ask, Kerttu. We will not be made to beg. And really, what could you have done?"

"But we have a place to go," Mr. Kumpula begins with a hint of hopefulness. He recovers enough to talk and saves Mama from making an offer we have no wherewithal to make. "The iron range in Marquette needs workers. Pauliina's sister lives there and their children have married and are doing well. They have much space in their home and have invited us to join them. Her husband works in the iron mines and says I can get a job there in no time."

"And my sister Marita is a nurse at St. Luke's Hospital in Marquette," Mrs. Kumpula states with pride. "Their house is paid and they will not charge us for rent until we get our feet back on the ground. We have much equity in this home and maybe we'll even be back."

Some of the Kumpulas' dignity is returning. It is a loss I have never seen before and a loss I understand because we are experiencing it ourselves. Now I even know what dignity looks like. And what it looks like when it's lost.

"Matti, in this weather?" Mama asks, and I am grateful she is not pleading.

"We will be alright. I have enough hay and oats on the wagon for old Bucky here. We can find melted water along the way. Marquette is only about a hundred miles. We should be there in five days. A week at the most."

"We have been communicating by letter," Mrs. Kumpula enjoins. "They live near St. Luke's Hospital on Ridge Street. Isn't that wonderful? Just a few changes to the numerals and the city and it's just like home. You must write us, Emilia."

I'm glad Mrs. Kumpula has asked me to join the conversation, for I've wanted to say this as soon as I heard about St. Luke's Hospital. "I'm going to be a nurse! I've already applied to the hospital here in Laurium and I hope to start ... I will start next fall. I'd love to write, Mrs. Kumpula. And may I also write to your sister?"

"Emilia, you must write to me and my sister!" Mrs. Kumpula reaches to the seat of the wagon and takes something covered with butcher paper and I smell the wonderful aroma before she gives me the platter I know I will recognize, containing the suomalais puikot I know I smell. "Here, Emilia. I was going to bring these to your house so you can distribute the cookies around Swedetown and so your Mama can use my wedding plate. I'm afraid to take the plate with me for fear of breaking it, and I was planning to ask your Mama to hold it for me, if we should ... until we return." Mrs. Kumpula looks at me and I lay the big bag of flour on the ground. "I am now entrusting you with the plate because

I trust you and I trust every woman who is a nurse. You must write to us. Are you working, Emilia?"

My temporary loss for words is because I don't anticipate the question and I also don't know how to answer it. "The reason I ask, Emilia, is because my sister heads up the Nursing School at St. Luke's and there may be something you can do there next summer before you begin Nursing School here. It will also assure the return of my plate," she adds with a smile. "Let's see if I have a pencil in my handbag," she says as she opens it and begins rummaging through it.

"Hold on a moment, Pauliina," Mr. Kumpula says as he ambles to the back of the wagon and unties the corner. He feels under the canvas and takes out a tool box and removes a big carpenter's pencil and walks back and hands it to me.

*127 E. Ridge Street. Marquette, Michigan* I write on the bag of flour, right on the Gold Medal insignia.

Their departure is wordless and Mr. and Mrs. Kumpula and Mama and I let our eyes and our faces say the farewell as old Bucky trots down the decline of old Ridge Street.


"On the tick, Kerttu?"

Standing up from the kitchen table, Papa asks precisely the wrong question as we arrive home.

Breathing an audible sigh, Mama musters a smile and places it into her voice. "Yes, Henrik. But we will be alright. We still have a little savings and I'm keeping up with the bills. Half a lifetime of you and me managing a financially conservative household has served us well during this time of challenge. We will be alright."

"Are you sure? We still have the hospital bills and we need kerosene and coal, or at least another cord of wood and that's getting more and more expensive because the mines have used so much for timber supports and..."

"And we need food the most. If you're so concerned about the money, why haven't you pressed Calumet and Hecla for the Workingmen's Compensation for your injury?"

Heli and I retire quietly to the sitting room. We do not hear loud disagreements in this family, in part because Mama mostly agrees with Papa, and both Heli and I know she will not back down this time.

"Because I am trying to protect my family," he says loud enough for our neighbors to hear. Surprised by his own volume, he lowers his voice. "You know how vengeful this company can be, Kerttu. The union calls a work stoppage and the company calls in the National Guard. Trespassing cost two people their lives. *Quid pro quo*. Emilia, tell your Mama what that means."

He does not realize that Heli and I have silently walked away from their tiff, and we look to one another as if to determine whether we really want to get back into the middle of it.

"*This for that*," Mama answers for me. "And don't drag our children into this. They know everything about the strike, but they don't have to be placed into the middle of our disagreements."

Silence.

We hear the long scuff of chair legs scraping on the floor as a chair is being pulled away from the kitchen table, and a shorter scuff means Papa is sitting down. The lighter scuff means Mama is now sitting down.

"*Quid pro quo*, Kerttu," he says from the kitchen as Heli and I settle onto the sofa in the sitting room. "The union establishes commissaries for its members to get food, and a Citizens Alliance is mysteriously organized. Do you think the Citizens Alliance is done?"

We have not told him about the buttons we have seen at A&P and at other businesses Mama and I passed. I am not surprised he has extrapolated the newspaper article I read to him about the creation of the Citizens Alliance into the offensive that the mining managers have now obviously organized.

"*Quid pro quo*. The women's brooming of the scabs by

day is countered with a peek through their bedroom windows with *MacNaughton's Eye* by night. A parade in Kearsarge is countered with a 14-year old girl shot in the head. Emilia has already paid for the children's parade with her job at the library and she will pay more when they rob her of the valedictorian honor. I am protecting my family the best way I know, Kerttu."

"You are, Henrik, and I am grateful. I will not challenge you on the Workingmen's Compensation issue again. As you and I agreed, I am entitled to my own opinion and I plan to follow through with my own convictions. I will not repeat those to you because you know them already, and Emilia knows them as well. But suffice to say that I will continue to fight."

Heli looks at me like I possess information to which she, too, is entitled.

This strike has divided and fractured my community. It has gone beyond a union fighting with mine managers and their hired minions. It has gone too far. It is dividing and fracturing my family. It is trespassing onto some private property in me that I now know I own, including its foundation and the land around it.

It is hurting my soul.

I hear Papa's spectacles being laid on the kitchen table and I envision him rubbing his eyes and his face like he sometimes does before quickly putting his spectacles back on so we can't see his eyes.

"Look at these eyes, Kerttu," he whispers.

Heli and I look to one another and avert our glance without meeting eyes.

"These are the eyes of *quid pro quo*."

# *XVII*

## *November 27*

I dare not open the letter from Calumet Public Hospital that I received yesterday. We picked up the post after school and, when the man behind the counter handed the small bundle to me, I buried this letter under my shirts and moved it to the pocket in my dress as Heli and I bounded out the door.

This one is different than the bills that Papa and Mama continue to get regularly. The paper within is folded into an envelope smaller than the ones containing bills. The return address says Calumet Public Hospital, just like the bills, but the envelope is addressed to me.

Last night, I tucked it into my hiding place beneath the rag rug near my spot on the sitting room floor where I sleep, and felt it with my hand throughout the night, wanting desperately to know what it says, afraid of knowing what it says. It will be safe next to the twelve dimes I have saved for Christmas supper. It will be as constant as the dimes that do not magically multiply as I wish them to.

Uncle Bear and Aunt Iiris are coming over for Thanks-giving supper. Better yet, Uncle Bear and Aunt Iiris are bringing Thanksgiving supper. They bring the fresh meat with them every year and I am so thankful that they are, for this is the first meal of meat that we will eat in weeks. Every year, Uncle Bear insists that he enjoys more than he brings because he loves Mama's homemade sausages, and she has also dried some meat and saved some especially for him. He says no one makes fried dough cakes like me and Heli, and I often wonder how such a big, burly, bearish man can be so kind.

The chickens are freshly plucked and still warm when Aunt Iiris hands them to me to cut up while Heli works on the relishes and Mama begins the täytekakku, a Finnish cream cake with apple filling that Mama just made this fall, for our traditional Thanksgiving dessert.

Aunt Iiris places her arms on our shoulders and looks into our eyes and thanks us for inviting them, and Uncle Bear seems to be ignoring us. He and Papa retire to the sitting room and I can hear them discussing something as they sit on our now uncovered sofa. They are still in conversation when Heli and I venture into the room after completing our cooking tasks and finding, as we do every year, that the kitchen is too small for four females.

*Four women*, I correct myself.

Uncle Bear spies us from the corner of his eye as he pretends to listen to Papa. Heli and I have agreed to initiate the attack. Papa must somehow sense it, because he leans back to stay out of the fray with a smile on his face. Just as Uncle Bear is about to spring from the sofa and send me and Heli into our welcome delirium, Heli reaches in to tickle his chest and, when he bends over in mock pain, I cover his back and neck with what I'm sure is electricity emanating from my fingertips. When Uncle Bear complains that his stomach hurts too much from our attack, me and Heli wordlessly move to Papa and give him the same rowdy, loving treatment. We are careful to allow him to hold his dark spectacles in place, and Heli and I take turns attacking him from the front and back. This he does not expect, and we can tell he is pleased to be so intimately included in our customary game with Uncle Bear.

"Well, ladies," Uncle Bear says when he takes his hands

from his aching stomach and finally stops laughing. "You have grown up, haven't you? All these years I have gotten away with bear attacks, thinking I will always be able to get away with them. Now the old bear will have to learn to play defensively."

Mama and Aunt Iiris join us in the sitting room and they are both wiping their hands on their aprons, a sign they're just about done.

"The relishes are ready, and the potatoes are cooking in the oven with the chicken," Mama announces proudly. "The dough has risen for its final time, and the lard is heating on the stove and will be ready in a few minutes, and you know what that means. Ladies."

Mama emphasizes the final word as a tribute to Uncle Bear's reference to me and Heli, and I am truly beginning to feel like a woman.

"What that means, ladies," Uncle Bear jests, "is you are being banished to the kitchen and will not be released until my fried dough cakes, and supper, are done."

"But Uncle Bear," I protest. "If we have indeed grown up, then we deserve to know what you and Papa are talking about."

Uncle Bear looks to Papa and tries to discern the un-committed look on his face. Finding no answer, he looks to Mama.

"Is it about the strike?" she wonders.

"Yes, it's all about the strike, isn't it Kerttu?"

"Then my young ladies can hear it. They have been living it at least as much as everyone else in the Copper Country." She turns to me and Heli. "I am proud of you for your leadership of the children's parade. It's important you know this and it's important you hear it in front of our dearest friends."

"The lard can wait," Papa says and I am so proud I can burst.

"When Aunt Iiris and I..." Uncle Bear begins by addressing me and Heli, "...as Iiris and I came into the train station from Eagle River, there was a strange formation of train cars coming in from the other direction. It was led by an engine, of course, but right behind the engine was a caboose, then several passenger cars and a few freight cars, then the final caboose."

"I've seen that same formation at the foot of our hill," Heli enjoins.

"You have? How many times?"

"At least twice."

"And did you see anything from the cupolas of the cabooses?"

"No, I didn't notice anything."

"Well, when this train came in today, we saw rifle barrels sticking out the cupola windows."

"What?" Mama says with an alarm that sends our whole house into a momentary silence. Papa is sitting on the sofa with a discerning look on his face and I know he is assessing the implications of the trains and the rifles.

Uncle Bear continues. "There were a few of our more militant strikers waiting at the train station, but they were unarmed, and when they saw the rifles sticking out the windows, they talked to one another for a few minutes and left. The doors of the passenger cars and freight cars opened, and men, mostly young men, spilled onto the platform and into the snow. They all remarked about the snow. They were not as motley as the Waddell Mahon men, but they certainly were not from around here."

"They are scabs, aren't they, Karhu-Jussi?" Papa states.

Uncle Bear is the only one who registers no surprise at his inference. "Yes, they are scabs, Henrik. The men sniping from the cupola windows were the only ones dressed appropriately for our winters, and I'm pretty sure I recognized some of them. They gathered the other men into a large group and when one of the newcomers, one of the scabs tried to bolt after asking the whereabouts of the nearest bar, the snow around his feet exploded with lead from the rifles."

"So what was the purpose of the armed men?" Mama asks. "Were they there to protect the others, or to herd them like animals?"

"Both I suspect, Kerttu. They marched them under guard toward the C&H boarding houses in Yellow Jacket. As you know, that's the scene of the now famous standoff between the National Guard and Annie Clemenc."

"Yes, I know where it is," Mama says and I want to say the same, but discretion wisely interrupts.

"Many of the boarders – those who have not paid their rent, so I suspect that means most of the boarders – have been evicted."

"That is so unfair!" I cannot help myself now. "Mr. and Mrs. Kumpula have also been put into the snow and we haven't heard from them and we don't even know if they've made it to Marquette yet. Where will all the boarders go?"

"I don't know, Emilia. Some have knocked on our door in Eagle River and asked if they can sleep in my shed for the night. If there are only a few, I let them sleep on the floor of our house. If there are more, I stoke up the sauna and open the partition between the sauna and shed and let them stay there. Most have gone the other direction. Some have risked their savings to buy the eighty-acre stump farms in Rock or Bruce Crossing or Watton. Many have left the Copper Country altogether for Chicago or Detroit if they believe they can get a job in a meat-packing plant or an automobile factory."

The lard is boiling on the stove and I want to continue to be included in this conversation, but the facts have all been stated, and Uncle Bear and Papa and Aunt Iiris and Mama will be left only with inferences and implications. There will be many.

Heli and I made bread last night in anticipation of the stovetop and oven being full with Thanksgiving supper today, so we smuggle a little sugar into today's batch of fried cakes. She takes her place at the countertop and I size up the wad of dough for dividing it eight ways.

"Emilia, I'm scared," Heli admits to me in a whisper. "We have little food and no money and maybe enough kerosene to get us to Christmas, and then what? Papa and Uncle Bear are not working. Nobody is working except those who want to break the union. And Christmas, Emilia. Christmas will be here soon."

Struggling with Heli's observations, I want to skirt my newfound role as an adult. I am now comfortable with responsibility. Leadership I think I will always grapple with, but I have already learned some of its traits and I will keep working on more. Accountability and obligation and trust are as deeply ingrained in me as my nationality and my gender. After all, I am a Finn, I am a woman. But how do you assuage fear in your little sister? And Christmas? Sometimes I think these are beyond the traits of woman-hood, and learned only in motherhood. How would Mama do it?

"Yarn."

"Huh?"

"Yarn," I repeat.

"What book do you have your head in now, Emilia?" and we both laugh, and I love my little sister with the dimples that show beautifully every time she laughs.

"Have you noticed Mama's supply of yarn? She has skeins and skeins of it and she's already begun knitting sweaters for Papa and me and you. Let's knit socks for each other and extra ones for Papa and Mama. I'll take the heels because they're hard and I know you don't like to do those. Mama was saving the yarn for after Christmas because she wants to do the sweaters first anyway. I'll bet we could do two pair for each other and four pair for Mama and Papa. I know there's plenty of yarn for it. We both have the knowledge and talent. Do we both have the will power?"

"Well, I won't speak for you, but ... " and I can't help bringing my fingers to my cheeks and poking them in where Heli's dimples go, and she slathers flour on her arms that causes the opposite effect of teasing me for the darkness of my skin in summer, and we both dissolve in laughter.

When they come in from the sitting room, all smiling, Mama and Aunt Iiris take over at the stove while Heli and I set the table. Uncle Bear helps Papa to his chair and my sister and I are wondering what sort of confidential information we've been excluded from.

Papa leads in the blessing and Uncle Bear and Aunt Iiris bow their heads in respect while the rest of us make the sign of the cross to begin and end our prayer.

Sitting on the bench so Papa and Mama and our guests can have the four chairs, I notice that Heli's and my forearms are more comfortably perched on the kitchen table than ever before. Our bench is lower than the chairs, and for years we've struggled to keep the food off our laps, sometimes unsuccessfully.

Along with growing up, a straighter back also comes with adulthood, I surmise.

The topics of our conversation take the typical routes. Aunt Iiris asks how Heli and I are doing in school and I now know that she does it to encourage us to showcase our academic achievements. Papa and Mama beam with quiet modesty. Then the weather, and whether our new Democratic President Wilson will have any power against influential business interests.

Uncle Bear's and Aunt Iiris's compliments of the food begin with their first forkfuls and they save their finest tributes to Mama's dessert of täytekakku. When I taste it, I know she deserves it.

"Family and friendship. This is what I am thankful for," Papa begins the tradition that I should have prepared myself for, but I've forgotten again this year. I will need to be spontaneous. Mama usually offers her own thanks, but today reaches across the table and Papa somehow senses it because his hands meet hers over the few pieces of chicken left near the center of the table.

"Family and friendship. And for having my husband back," Mama says.

Uncle Bear and Aunt Iiris join their hands in the center of the table and they say "ystävyydelle" and repeat in English "friendship" in unrehearsed unison.

It is only when Heli takes my hand that I realize she wants me to offer thanks along with her. "For a big sister who takes my hand when I need it," she begins.

"For a little sister who trusts me enough to offer it," I continue. "And for family and friends who have taught us everything we need to grow up."

"We've come to a decision," Papa says.

I have been wondering what they were talking about in the sitting room, and why it took four people, and how they managed to emerge with smiles after Uncle Bear's explanation of another setback for the union.

"Aunt Iiris knows an attorney in Eagle River who will take my Workingmen's Compensation case, and charge us only if we win it. Mama will gather the hospital bills and calculate my lost wages. Uncle Bear and I have too much time on our hands and will provide the bills and correspondence to the attorney, and explain what happened. And when it happened. This will take some time to resolve, but the attorney has already advised that we stop making payments on our bills to the hospital. This will give us some respite from our debts and allow us a few more weeks before we exhaust our savings. And the hospital won't even know that we plan to enhance our cash flow instead of theirs until after they make their determination of Emilia's acceptance into Nursing School."

There's no escaping now. Now, I must open the letter and read it. If it says what I hope, I will be pleased to share it with these, the most special people in my life. If it does not, I will never live it down. All the others look to me when I get up from the bench and go into the sitting room, and they won't even know my secret hiding place because I find the letter and return to the kitchen in a trice.

"Dear Miss Rytilahti," I say. "We don't believe you are a good fit..."

There is nothing more to say. There is no place to escape to hide my shame. It's too late to regret not having read it yesterday, or regret waiting until tomorrow. It's only regret. And shame. And tears.

"Kerttu, read that letter please," Papa says and I cannot believe he is doing this to me. Doing this in front of everyone.

Mama looks to Uncle Bear and Aunt Iiris for support, and then looks at the firmness in Papa's face and picks up the letter and reads.

"We don't believe you are a good fit for the Calumet Public Hospital School of Nursing. Thank you. Sincerely, the Calumet Public Hospital School of Nursing."

"So the hospital and its school of nursing have plagiarized the Calumet and Hecla language of cowardice."

"Papa, please," I beg him, unable to take this humiliation still standing in the same spot from which I was hoping to deliver my acceptance speech. I look at him again. That look. The one that tells me he has already moved on to another province. He is there, I can tell, but I don't know where *there* is. I am unfamiliar with its terrain, unsure of its place.

"What are your plans now, Emilia?"

"Plans? I wipe my tears with my dress sleeve. "I have no plans. I am devastated. I don't know."

"Do you remember when you fell from Mr. Kumpula's horse?"

Of course I remember that. I was nine or ten, and Bucky was grazing out near the golf course on a summer day, and Mr. Kumpula came out to bring him back to his little barn behind his house. Papa and Heli and I were playing baseball. Mr. Kumpula offered me and Heli a ride, and I let Heli go first and Papa held her hand while Mr. Kumpula led Bucky around first base and stopped at second. Heli and I traded places and Mr. Kumpula handed the reins to me and I wanted to take Bucky into home and flailed my legs against his sides as we rounded third and Bucky took off and I slid off his unsaddled back and laid there and cried.

"I remember, Papa. You made me get back on."

"All I did was make you tuck in your lower lip so you wouldn't trip over it. You bit your lower lip in confidence and got back on that horse and rode it to home plate and rode it the rest of the afternoon until Mr. Kumpula asked you to ride Bucky to his barn so he could feed him." The recollection, and Papa's telling of it with pride, returns a little beam to my face. "Just like old Väinämöinen, who learned to ride on the back of an eagle to get to Pohjola, you need to get back on, Emilia. And ride. Or fly."

"This time, I don't know how. What am I riding? Where am I riding to?"

"Mama has told me about your conversation with the Kumpulas. You're riding Bucky. You're riding to Marquette." He looks at me like he is about to toss me back the completed sentence I have tossed to him as a phrase. "According to Mama, Mrs. Kumpula said her sister is in charge of the school of nursing."

I may be in the place with Papa. "Mrs. Kumpula said I could ask her sister if I can come to stay with them next summer. And her sister may be able to help me get a job. Mrs. Kumpula said she trusts me with her wedding plate." I land squarely in his province. "I can apply to their school of nursing. I will write to Mrs. Kumpula to make sure they have arrived safely. I have her address right here in the kitchen," and I look around for the bag of flour and here it is, with 127 E. Ridge Street, Marquette, Michigan written on the Gold Medal insignia. "I will write to her sister and apply to the school of nursing, the St. Luke's Hospital School of Nursing she is in charge of..."

Mama gets up from the table and I look to Papa and her in gratitude, and continue around the table with what I hope will be a look of both apology and thankfulness. Returning with her handbag in her hands, Mama opens it and fishes around, and I can see her counting something. She hands me four pennies. "Here, Emilia. This will cover the post for your two letters."

"I'm taking an eagle this time," I tell Mama and Aunt Iiris and Papa and Heli as I cling to the pennies with the talons of one. "I'm taking Väinämöinen's eagle because he knows the way to Marquette. I'm taking Väinämöinen's eagle because it's a long way to the St. Luke's Hospital School of Nursing in Marquette."

It's a new moon and this feels right to me as Heli and I change into our sleeping shirts on the evening of a tumultuous Thanksgiving. I have written the letters and will mail them tomorrow with the last few pennies Mama probably had in her handbag. The letters are next to my hiding spot on the floor so I can find them easily tomorrow and bring them to the post office. I'm already looking forward to putting the two-cent stamps on them and handing them to the man behind the counter. I have far more to be thankful for than I said earlier today.

So much has happened in our lives. So much is ahead.

"Good luck," Heli says, and we lie on the floor and bring the blanket atop us without tugging for more this time. Papa is in bed and Mama blows out the kerosene lamp and treads to their room.

We feel the floor quiver and Heli and I are both sitting up when we hear the blast.

Mama stops in her tracks and the windows rattle as it seems the tremors and the sound move southward over Swedetown.

Papa is getting out of bed and I know Mama takes his hand in the dark. We all go to the front door and outside in our bare feet. Some of our neighbors are already outside and lanterns are aglow through a few of the windows.

"Papa?" we ask.

"I don't know," he begins. "That was surely a blast of nitroglycerine and it was a charge the likes of which we don't use in the mines. It was too ... too much."

We sometimes feel the blasts of the night shift from shafts Six thru Twelve and we can always tell if the blast comes from deep within the shafts closer to Six or closer to Twelve. This one felt like none of those because it felt like the whole earth moved. Even when we feel the blasts at night, we never hear them.

"It felt like it came from the north, didn't it?" Papa says.

"That's what it felt like to me," I answer. "And that's also where the sound came from."

"That would be Wolverine. No, it was so huge, it would be farther north. Maybe Kearsarge or Allouez. Maybe all the way to Ahmeek, and that would make sense. Ahmeek is about five miles, and there are plenty of mines around there."

"Who would be blasting at this hour on Thanksgiving night? And why? What are you thinking?" Mama asks.

"It's not a mine blast, I can tell you that for certain. It's probably not even a blast set by the hands of a shaft boss. Even Roger Lukas wouldn't be that crass. At least not that crass on Thanksgiving. That leaves some sort of union statement for the who. The why, I don't know. And on Thanksgiving night, I don't want to know."

We go back into our home and close the door and Mama leads Papa to bed.

*This will make for a night of fitful sleep,* I think to myself, and I don't tug back when Heli pulls more of the blanket to her side.

The tumult of our lives continues.

Mama pads to the kitchen and checks the kerosene lamp again.

I had already checked it when we came in the house, and the wick was not even smoldering.

Something near Ahmeek is.

# XVIII

## December 10

The burial was yesterday. They were murdered early Sunday morning and the *Mining Gazette* announced "not a wheel will turn all afternoon Wednesday" when "citizens of the Copper Country will rise up in righteous indignation" against the "foreign agitators" and "those socialists responsible for their deaths." Even *Työmies* covered the story of the murders in an appropriately funereal tone, though it gave short shrift to the planned mass demonstrations today in Red Jacket and Houghton.

There is no escaping the facts or the consequences when both papers cite the victims as boardinghouse owner Thomas Dally and two miners, brothers who were planning to return to work here: Arthur and Harry Jane, Cornishmen.

Papa listened intently when I commented that the *Mining Gazette* seemed thick for a Monday and we both soon found that the extra pages were all dedicated to the murder story, statements from witnesses who all had an opinion about the nationalities and whereabouts of the still-at-large assailants, and bolder opinions and editorials from the publisher. The newspaper said the Jane brothers, both in their early twenties, had worked at the Champion mine near Painesdale and left immediately after the strike began to seek their fortunes elsewhere. They were encouraged to return here from Toronto because they had heard the mines were operating again.     Around 2:00 a.m. Sunday, the Jane brothers were instantly killed by a barrage of bullets from somewhere outside the Dally boardinghouse and, by sunrise, Mr. Dally was dead and his wife seriously injured by the same gunfire.

*Työmies* didn't come right out and call the Jane brothers *scabs*, but it didn't have to when it stated they recently returned to the Copper Country on a special train arranged by mine managers.

The long reach of this strike has again seized us, this time twenty miles to the south in Painesdale. Painesdalc is near Seeberville, and that significance is lost on neither Papa nor me, nor anyone else who has been following the major events of the past few months and knows that Seeberville is where Alois Tijan and Steven Putrich were killed and two others injured when the Waddell Mahon men surrounded their boardinghouse and riddled it with bullets.

An eye for an eye.

*Työmies* made much of the connection.

A tooth for a tooth.

The *Mining Gazette* did not mention it.

I hate that allegory.

Papa does not invite me to assist him with sorting out the facts or examining the consequences, nor does he ask me to express what I have learned in reading both accounts. He does not use the full phrase of *quid pro quo* and instead wonders aloud how much *quid* will need to be paid in recompense; how much *quo* in retribution.

The massive snow piles are not dissuading the massive crowds gathering just down the road from Washington School at the Coliseum that the carpenters are about to complete for the start of hockey season. We have heard the bands all morning and at noon the teachers read to us from notes they have taken earlier today that we are excused for the afternoon if we attend the rallies. Those who eat their lunches near the Miscowaubik Club are already heading to the Coliseum. Some of my friends take off for home or will hang around Red Jacket. I will attend my afternoon classes and I hope Heli will do the same.

"Well class..." our chemistry teacher Mr. Schubert begins after I walk freely down the nearly deserted hall to my first period of the afternoon. "Class dismissed," he says with a smile as he and I peruse the classroom of two people, my gaze hoping to fill some seats, overruled by his gaze that takes in unoccupied desks and his brief comments that echo off the walls. "How's your Christmas ornament coming, Emilia? We're only two weeks away from Christmas Eve and we have an entire afternoon of quality lab time that you're welcome to use. Now that we both have the afternoon off, the lab is where I plan to spend it."

The socks that Heli and I have begun are progressing nicely. We'll have socks for each other and more for Papa and Mama, and the ornaments will be splendid decorations.

"Done, sir. I love working with copper, and the copper oxide was pretty easy. I hope you don't mind, but I made one for my sister and one for my Mama and the big copper snowflakes turned out beautifully and I think they'll both like them."

"How about one for your Papa? We have the time and I'll be happy to help you with it."

"You'd really help me with it? I'd love that, Mr. Schubert."

"Emilia, I'd be pleased to assist."

If there's one thing I've learned about Mr. Schubert, it's that if you show the interest and enthusiasm and only a little bit of inquisitiveness, he's always happy to help you, and is happier with your finished product than if he had done it himself.

The lab is just around the corner from the chemistry classroom and I lay my books near the door so I'll remember them when I'm done. Mr. Schubert rummages through the scraps of brass that we've made from copper and zinc, and some of the bronze that we've mixed copper and tin and sometimes a little phosphorous for samples of bronze with varying properties.

"Let's see, we have plenty of copper wire in different gauges," and lays the spools onto the lab counter. "This may be too thick," he says as he holds up a sheet of copper about a foot and a half long, and a few inches wide.

As he examines the thickness, I remember Papa's same look through unspectacled eyes when he would pause and look at the papers from my school work and correct them more thoroughly than any of my teachers. Over a year ago.

"Mr. Schubert. I have a better idea for my Papa. He needs a new pair of spectacles and that copper is perfect for the frames."

"You're right. Copper spectacle frames are the fad in fashion nowadays, and we could create them with just the tools we have here. But we don't have your Papa's lens prescription and even if we did, we don't have the tools to form the glass to fit it. I think once he sees the beautiful work we can do on a Christmas ornament, he'll like that even more."

"Mr. Schubert..." I stop. I can't say it. I've never said it to anyone. "Mr. Schubert," I begin again. "My Papa, you see, had a very serious accident, no, I mean injury at work, and he can't see very well and, you see, he may not even be able to see a Christmas ornament, and he doesn't see very well at all and..." I know I sound like a blundering fool. I muster my courage. "My Papa is blind." I stop again, unsure where to go from a place I've never been. "He has a pair of dark spectacles, Mr. Schubert, but the right bow is held on with masking tape and the right lens is broken, though the pieces are glued into the frame, and it happened last summer and we don't have the money to fix them and..."

"Emilia," he says as he looks me straight in the eyes, "we will make your Papa the finest and most fashionable pair of spectacles in the Copper Country." He hands me a ball peen hammer and I hold out my hand with a question mark he sees on my face. "We'll start by pounding the side of the spectacles that will show. It'll strengthen the copper and also give it a finished look."

"I like that. Copper spectacles with a Finnish look. That sounds like my Papa," and both Mr. Schubert and I laugh at the way the word works in both contexts.

"Alright," he says after I have pounded little dents into the metal and he hands me a wooden ruler and pencil and paper. "Octagon lenses are the most fashionable today, and for those you will need to apply some math. So figure out what size you want for the frames, calculate the lenses proportionately, then draw a template we can use for both the frame cuts and the lenses."

"Will you hold still a minute, Mr. Schubert?"

He glances at me, and then steadily fixes his gaze as I hold the ruler over his nose and write down the measurements. Adding a little to the distance between his eyebrows and the little bags under his eyes gives me the vertical numbers.

"Now let's trace the center frame, leaving a little extra for the nosepieces. We'll flare out the inside of the frames to create a malleable edge to hold the lenses in place, and trace the cut-outs for the lenses, determine where to make the corners..." He is ahead of me in envisioning the project, yet I understand exactly where he's going. "I'd love to give you this part of the task, Emilia, but this will take only a few minutes and that'll give you time to complete your calculations."

Mr. Schubert rolls up the sleeves on his shirt and takes a large pair of snips and begins cutting the copper along the lines I have traced. I can't see his biceps under the rolled-up sleeves of his shirt, but his forearms must be at least as large and I can't help admiring the way his supple wrists and massive forearms cut such an intricate design. He has told us in class that he works summers as a carpenter, and is also obviously a hockey player whose wrist shot I would not want to be on the receiving end of. "Now trace the design onto the place where you want the lenses," and I've forgotten about my obligation to do the math and must do a quick recall of the Pythagorean Theorem and apply it to my measurements.

He drills two holes in the center of the location for the lenses, and uses a small pair of snips to cut from the hole and remove the copper. With the newly cut holes for the lenses, these are beginning to look and feel like handsome spectacles. Perfect for Papa. He bends ninety-degree angles at the two spots I have marked on either side of the frame, then snips away the soft metal to make the temple arms. Carefully placing the rough spectacles on the bridge of his nose, he looks through the large holes that should contain lenses to help Papa see.

"What do you think?"

"Mr. Schubert ... Papa's eyes are damaged," I stammer, "and he is a little self-conscious of the way they look to others ... and..."

"Didn't I say we would make lenses? Have you been paying attention, Emilia, or are you distracted by the background noise of all your classmates?" and the question he frequently asks during class makes me laugh in our private lab. "Here," he tells me as he slowly removes them from his face. "You know where the files and emery paper are, and you know the different grades of files and emery paper, so I expect that you'll have all these sharp edges removed when I return from the cafeteria."

After seeing all varieties of solids, gases and liquids spring from the unlikeliest of sources with Mr. Schubert, I don't even bother asking how he'll find spectacle lenses in the school cafeteria.

Returning with two sandwiches and two bottles of Coca Cola, he adds only a roguish grin when he hands me half the loot from his trip, and sits on a stool and puts his feet on the lab counter. This would earn any of us seniors a swat or a trip to the principal's office or both, but Mr. Schubert is really enjoying his charade, and gives it away only when he tips his brown bottle toward me, says "cheers" and holds it to his mouth for a long swig.

The bottoms of the Coca Cola bottles will need only a little trimming with the glass cutter we've all used, and the color is perfect. I can already imagine Papa wearing them outside like they were made especially for him, especially for such a purpose.

As Mr. Schubert fits the cut glass into the lens openings, I look for the copper cleaner we've made with lemon juice, vinegar and salt. When he's done, he tries on the spectacles and they look wonderful on him and I know they will look even better on Papa. He hands them to me to scour, and when I'm done cleaning them I add a little cream of tartar to the solution and use it to polish them.

"Emilia," he says to me as I find a box to transport them with, and will use to wrap them in, "as you know, I was a member of the committee that disciplined you for your leadership ... er, your activism in the children's parade. You've shown me a lot of resolve this semester. You've always had the intelligence and the self-discipline of a great student. Today, I've found you've also learned perseverance. And maybe even a little forgiveness. I'm not the only one who votes for valedictorian honors, but I want you to know that mine is one vote you can count on. Perhaps there will be others I can ... influence."

I'm almost surprised I have remembered my books because I don't remember touching any of the steps on my way out of school. It's a good thing we have an agreed upon meeting place because I would never find Heli in the huge crowd spilling all the way from the Coliseum into the school yard.

"What did you do this afternoon?" I ask her.

"Went to classes, what else? What did the lucky high

schoolers do?  And what do you have in the box?"

She takes it from my hands, opens it and looks inside, but can't tell what's there.

"Go ahead, take them out and try them on."

Heli reaches into the box and correctly guesses that its contents are delicate, and slowly takes out the brown-lensed spectacles.

"My goodness, Emilia.  They're beautiful.  Can I try them on?" already forgetting I've just invited her to.  "Do I look as stunning as these are?"

"No, you look like you're too small for them.  Let me try."

The copper frames and glass lenses from the bottom of Coca Cola bottles are heavy, but comfortable on the bridge of my nose where I sanded them for a long time to get the nose tabs smooth.

"You look like Helena Modjeska, but they're too big on you, too."

"They're perfect then," I tell her.  Miss Modjeska was the beautiful and incredibly talented Polish actress who came to the Calumet Opera House, and if they would look good on her, and they're too big for me, they're perfect for Papa.  "They're for Papa for Christmas," I proudly announce.  "Do you think he'll look like Douglas Fairbanks?" another great actor who regularly comes to the Calumet Opera House who is not nearly as handsome as Papa.

"My goodness, Emilia, they're not only beautiful, they're perfect.  Where did you get them?  Better yet, where did you get the money?"

"I made them.  Well, Mr. Schubert and I made them in the lab and it took us all afternoon, but everybody in high school had the time off to attend the rally, so I made these instead."

"With all your books, wouldn't it be easier if I carried the box for you?"

"No Heli, I'll let you carry my books, though."

"Have I ever told you what a rotten sister you are?"  Heli

disguises her mocking remark, yet I sense its playfulness in the smile of her dimples as she takes my books, jabs me with the corner of chemistry and adds impish injury to mischievous insult when she stoops over to take a handful of snow and tosses it at me.

"Are we going to attend the rally or go home? Because we're not going to stand out here and freeze and I'd like to check out the Coliseum, so let's go," and I grab Heli's hand and lead her through the crowd before she can answer.

We thread our way through some of the crowd near the door, and Heli tugs on my hand and we stop when we can see a well-dressed man in the distance who must be standing on some kind of platform. The rally at the Coliseum is a marvel of leadership and organization.

I count the heads in a defined area and estimate the number of consistently defined areas and multiply the two and add another thousand for the undefined areas and come up with just under 8,000 people jammed on the inside, with more than that number milling around the outside all the way over to the school yard. The Calumet and Hecla Band is fanned out behind the man who stands atop a newly made stage and, thankfully, he is winding down his speech.

I wish that we had stopped anywhere else but in front of the two men with beer on their breaths. Then, worse yet, they begin talking to us.

"Well, girls, you just missed Mr. Allen Rees and you didn't miss a thing," the taller one says. "He spent much of the afternoon on anti-union tripe and we wouldn't bother being here, except Calumet and Hecla paid for our tickets on a special train into Red Jacket and we couldn't resist the opportunity for a free ride to the bars."

The men look German and I'm pretty sure I could even narrow their dialect to the specific part of their mother country.

"Most of the men you see here are Calumet and Hecla scabs who have the day off at C&H expense," the shorter man says. "All I can say is, they'd better have free tickets for out of town, or there'll be a riot."

Heli takes the box with Papa's new spectacles and hands my books back to me.

"I'm glad we went to the Coliseum and glad we stopped where we did," I tell Heli on the way home. "We'll have much to share with Papa."

And he'll know how to assess it.

# *XIX*

# *December 15*

Another foot of snow fell last night and we're already up to about eight feet this winter. With a few days of sun and more days of wind, it has packed down a bit, but if this keeps up, we'll be snow jumping from our former, Nelson's current second floor by Christmas vacation.

As Heli and I head home from school, I note that my shoes are holding up well, but Heli needs new ones because her toes are beginning to wear through the ends and I can see a bit of sock coming through on her right foot as we meet after school on a gloomy Monday. We're almost done with the socks for each other, and for Papa and Mama, so after Christmas vacation her toes will still get wet, but her feet should stay warm.

Perhaps Papa will be back to work then.

The tide of the strike has changed and today's parade by the strikers, set against the backdrop of last week's Citizens Alliance rally, makes it obvious. No bands, no speakers firing up the crowd. Really, not much of a crowd today. A couple of hundred workers are parading; I estimated well over 16,000 among those filling the Coliseum and others outside at last Wednesday's anti-union rally, the day after the Jane / Dally burials.

At least the strikers get credit for pluck, if not organization. Their march has begun where the children's parade ended, in front of the Calumet and Hecla offices at Red Jacket Road and Calumet Avenue near Washington School, and they'll be headed in the opposite direction. Better yet, they have pinched a supply of Citizens Alliance buttons and are wearing them on the seats of their pants.

Heli and I usually take the path they are on, up Red Jacket Road to the post office, then on to home. We are handed Citizens Alliance buttons when we fall in line, so we attach them to the backs of our dresses and join the march toward the post office.

There's no singing. No chanting pro-union slogans. Little solidarity. The length of this strike, the snow, an almost endless violence, and the approaching merryless Christmas have all combined to bring a somber effect to what began just a few months ago, in the warmth and optimism of summer, as disagreement gone awry.

Heli and I are silent in our grave procession.

We march only a couple of blocks past the Coliseum to *God's Little Acre*, and the parade leaders must know that they haven't enough marchers to go much beyond into downtown, so they stop and mill around the churches.

Another flaw in planning. The Swedish Lutheran Church would have required only another block of marching to arrive at a favorable setting. St. Anne's wouldn't have been as far, and would have been neutral at worst. The little yard between the Presbyterian and Episcopal churches, where the Scots and Brits are waiting, is the worst possible setting to disband a bunch of striking marchers with Citizens Alliance buttons on their behinds. The men in the churchyard are brandishing riot sticks the size of baseball bats; turned on the lathes, Papa tells me, of the Calumet and Hecla wood shop near the broom factory.

The pushing and shouting and shoving and name-calling in the name of God erupts in the yard between the two churches, and Heli grabs my hand and we try to escape toward the Presbyterian Church on the corner.

"You're not going anywhere, girl," the Cornishman says to her as he puts his right arm around Heli's neck and forces her toward the church steps. He mounts the first wide step and, with his back to the church entrance, turns Heli to face me and grabs at her butt. The cross above his head, and the words *Community Congregational Church*, swear back at me from behind him at the church's entrance. He takes far too much time groping for the button, and I hear the thin fabric tear when he rips it from her dress.

"What's this? There's a lesson to be learned here, and I'm about to teach it."

"No, you're not," I tell him and take one step toward him and three back onto the ground when he meets my advance with his left arm. From the ground, I watch him change his chokehold around Heli's neck from his right arm to his left. As I get up to charge him again, he re-wraps his right forearm tight around her neck, and in his hand is a pistol pointing in the air.

I immediately regret my glance to the churchyard as I hear the dull thud of wooden clubs against flesh and see a patch of snow turn red.

Heli is between me and the armed Cornishman, and her face is growing redder by the second with his chokehold.

"You're just going to stand here and watch this," he tells me with a dark scowl on his face, a low snarl in his voice, a pistol in his hand. "And then it's your turn."

The Cornishman's voice is lost in a gasp from Heli, and I realize she has taken a quick breath when the man's grip momentarily diminishes as he snarls at me. Her eyes are fixed on mine as she makes a fist with her right arm, then moves her fist toward me and bends her arm. Heli's look, and the angle of her arm leading to her elbow, tells me where she is aiming. She has not seen the man's pistol.

Mrs. Clemenc's American flag would not protect me now, for our standoff is under the same one, backed by a cross.

*Blacken those tyrant's eyes so he can't see to shoot you*

streams into my mind in Mother Jones's voice.

I slowly and purposefully move my right arm behind my back.

Heli's face reddens more.

My forefingers turn over at the knuckles and I spread my index finger away from my middle finger as far as my turned-over knuckles will allow.

The gaze between Heli and I is unbroken.

As he turns his head and a stream of brown spittle shoots from his mouth onto the church steps, Heli's eyes soften and I am ready.

"Now," I whisper.

She raises her fist near her chin and moves to her left and drives her right elbow directly into the man's groin.

*Strike one*, I think clearly and calmly.

A shot fires and I see the man's pistol aiming into the air just before he lurches over Heli's right shoulder in pain.

*Strike two*, I think of the pistol shot.

His eyes bug out like a catcher flashing me the sign.

"Strike three," I yell as I hammer my knuckles into the man's eyes.

The pained scream from my blow to his eyes is a fitting crescendo between the grunt from Heli's elbow to his groin and the dull thud produced by his head bouncing off the first concrete step of the Presbyterian Church.

Heli could not have missed the single shot fired into the air next to her head, but looks at the gun lying in the snow like it's a snake. She glances at me with red horror still in her eyes, then reaches over and grabs it before leading the way down Wedge Street between the site of our standoff and St. Anne's. She applies the full force of a left fielder coming in on a short fly ball when she winds up near the corner of the church and barely breaks stride as she pitches the pistol through the last stained glass window.

The throw is perfect.

Safe at home.

We get a brief break when Heli stands guard at the post office as I run in and offer a quick invocation of thanks for no line, and another "thanks" to the man behind the counter when he hands me the two envelopes. I tuck them into my dress as my shirts fly over the envelopes when I dash down the post office steps and we run down Sixth Street and over on Scott to Osceola Road toward home.

When we slow our pace near Swedetown Pond, I remember the envelopes because one of them drops into the snow. Picking it up, I glance at the return address.

"It's only another bill," are the first words I proffer Heli since the third strike. I enjoy the sound of the ripping paper when I tear it in half and give Heli the clean half. Calumet Public Hospital disappears in shreds in my hands and the other half of the bill suffers the same fate in Heli's. We look to one another and toss the pieces into the air at the same time.

"About as worthless as more snow," I comment, and put my hands under my shirts to warm them, and set out home again.

The other envelope sends a pulse of warmth back to me. Stopping again, I take it out from under my shirts and Heli looks impatiently at me, sees the surprise on my face, and walks back to me to read the return address.

"Oh, Emilia, you must open it."

My fingers are trembling and I almost drop it and Heli takes it from my hands, opens the envelope, and gives it back to me.

"Dear Miss Rytilahti: Congratulations..."

I can't scream. I can't talk. I can't even whisper, so I hug Heli and she does the screaming for me.

"Oh, Emilia, I knew it. I just knew it," and I put a little tear in the letter when I pick her up off her feet like Uncle Bear would do. She wraps her arms around me so hard I nearly choke and it feels wonderful. "Now Emilia, just stand there and read it to me like you're giving an acceptance speech. Emilia, you *are* giving your acceptance speech."

*"Dear Miss Rytilahti: Congratulations on your acceptance into the St. Luke's Hospital School of Nursing. Your reputation as a student, an upstanding Christian and an outstanding community member has preceded you, and St. Luke's is pleased to accept a young woman of your caliber. Stories have also been shared of your leadership as well as your compassionate care of the ill and injured.*

*These are the qualities we seek in St. Luke's Nursing School applicants, and qualities we expect to nurture even more into an exceptional Nurse.*

*A place is held in your name for the class beginning September, 1914, and you may also want to consider working with us upon your high school graduation next spring. We will be happy to have your assistance for the summer and it will provide you with an opportunity to earn enough money for the cost of books. Your tuition will be covered by your work at the hospital throughout the academic year. Room and board will be your only remaining cost, and I understand that those arrangements can be equitably made. I look forward to working with you.*

*Yours Truly in Christ.*

*Marita (Mary) Thompson*

*Director, St. Luke's Hospital School of Nursing."*

I can barely talk with the tears streaming down my cheeks.

Heli is patient enough to let me wipe my tears, but not patient enough to just stand here. She walks a few steps, turns to me with a smile that lights up her dimples, walks a few more steps, and then stops. "That was Papa's pitch, wasn't it?"

I'm not sure what she means at first, and then the smile on her face brightens even more when she shows me her right knuckles and brings her arm back into the start of

Papa's pitching motion. I'm glad she puts my feet back onto the ground.

"Yes, Heli, that was Papa's knuckler. How did you know?"

"I watched it come into home plate a little wobbly, then split the strike zone."

"It was high."

"That's what I mean."

# XX

## December 21

The Fourth Sunday of Advent candle will be lit this morning. I have stoked the coals in the kitchen stove and put more wood on the fire and Heli has done the same for the stove in the basement. There is no laundry today, but the basement stove will keep the floors warm and Mama lets us burn a little more wood on this clear and cold Sunday morning that is revealing the moon in its third phase.

Papa and Mama are talking in the basement as they bathe themselves to get ready for Mass. Heli is in front of the mirror in the kitchen struggling with weaving her long hair into French braids and I'll volunteer to help her as soon as I check again to make sure everything is ready for Christmas.

Papa's new copper spectacles are hidden behind Mama's sofa and I check to ensure they're still there. The socks are done and Heli wanted to hide them under the sofa, but that's where the copper ornaments are, so I talked her into helping me position them above the braces of the rafters in the basement. Double check. Mama has been gently preparing Heli and me for a Christmas supper of fried cakes and some carrots from our garden, now stored in a corner of the basement.

*It still won't be a full supper*, I think to myself as I stick my hand under Mama's rag rug to feel for the twelve dimes tucked deep within, *but I can augment the bread and carrots with some additional food.* I'll let Heli help me pick it out on Christmas Eve when we go to the party at Italian Hall. The A&P grocery store is right there, and...

What's this?

Just under the edge of the rag rug is a piece of paper. With the heat now rising up from the basement stove, it feels warm and familiar and somehow intimate. I keep my hand under the rug and try to discern the feeling I'm getting from the piece of paper that is curious to my touch. Grasping a corner of the paper, I slide it out from under the rug to reveal a sheet of onion skin stationery folded twice. It is the paper Papa and Mama use to write to my grandparents and some of their dearest friends in Finland; the paper Heli and I are never allowed to use.

I unfold the delicate document and Papa's handwriting greets me in amazement. Mama had asked to borrow my slide rule before I went to school the other day, and this letter explains the ink marks when Mama gave it back to me, for Papa's writing is a little too tall in some places, and some of the letters are squared on their bottoms where his pen met my slide rule. The words are tiny, and the front page shows the ink bleeding from the back page of the letter written on both sides of the onion skin stationery. It is dated December 25, 1913. I squint at the diminutive, yet exquisite penmanship with the little light from the kerosene lamp trickling in from the kitchen.

*My Dearest Emilia:*

*Enclosed are your wings. Oh, don't worry, they didn't fall out. Look to the folds of this letter and you won't see them. Look to the ground and you won't find them. They're inside the space between the lines and within the meanings of the words. You're already wearing them. All I am doing today, as your Christmas gift, is helping you see them. For I see them clearly. I could see them forming on you as a little girl and I wanted to*

*clip them when you tried my patience with bleach; I wanted to brush and groom them when you played baseball. They're as delicate as a butterfly, strong as an eagle. They can be damaged, perhaps even broken, but they will fail you only if you do not use them. There's little chance of that. Among all your terrific traits and talents, the one I admire most is your curiosity. Your intellectual inquisitiveness is a gift from your Ukki and I hear his voice in the satisfaction you derive when you prove a theorem or construct a perfect syllogism. Your wings will help you pursue the things that will satisfy your curiosity. Keep flying and you will always keep the strength in your wings, for the beauty of flight is in the quest. Mix your curiosity with your leadership and your ready smile. Others notice it and appreciate it. They make remarks to me and make me feel proud to be your Papa. I may not agree with your direction, yet I respect that you must be the one to set it. You've earned your wings. You've grown up beautifully and it's now time you take to wing, Emilia. Enclosed are your wings. Now fly!*
*All My Love,*
*Papa.*

If Heli hadn't poked me, I would still be kneeling for the opening hymn of the Mass. I remember nothing of walking to St. Joseph's and, although I obviously walked here, I'm sure my feet did not touch the ground.

I shake my head like Papa used to do, and look to my left to notice for the first time that Mama looks radiant and Papa distinguished except for his damaged spectacles, which will soon change. As I shake my head to the right, there's not a hair out of place in Heli's French braids, which must be Mama's work. I bring my hands to my own hair, and feel Heli's only hair ribbon set perfectly into the spot where I like it. Heli must have placed it here, since I only remember putting a letter back under the rag rug and digging a little farther to touch twelve dimes.

And flying.

If Heli hadn't poked me for the opening hymn, I'd have knelt through the entire Mass. It's only when everyone else in church except me responds to *Kyrie eleison*, in the Greek language my Grandfather knows, that I bring myself back to reality. Perhaps I will one day be able to say it – *Lord have mercy* – myself.

During the remainder of the Mass, I envision myself not serving as an altar boy, but leading as a nurse. I am beginning to see my future in front of me, and I am pleased with the picture. Mrs. Kumpula has written back, and her sister, Mrs. Thompson who is in charge of the nursing school, has offered to let me stay at their house so I can work at St. Luke's Hospital in Marquette next summer. Mrs. Thompson says that my fee for room and board at her house will be the return of a Finnish wedding plate. I think I can afford that.

It will be a brief walk after Mass through downtown window shopping because it's so clear and cold, and we haven't any money anyway. Yet the lack of money doesn't bother me in the least because it's a beautiful, brilliant day on Copper Island. The sun is dancing off the snow, and Papa must feel the sun on his face as he walks toward Vertin's with his chin held high. Since most of the churches in the area are ending their early morning services near the same time, our ecumenical spirit and Red Jacket's community atmosphere mix with the Christmas Season and you can barely tell there's still an ongoing strike if you listen to the people greet one another with "good morning" and "Merry Christmas" and "have a wonderful day, Mr. and Mrs. ..."

We move briskly on Oak Street toward the store and Heli and I have time for only a few longing glances at the Christmas displays and gift ideas in the window. Mama keeps her head down and Papa seems to be listening intently. As we reach Fifth Street, Papa slows our gait as he turns his face to the right. He quickly resumes the pace to cross the street with his chin held a little higher.

Papa must recognize the steps of Mr. Lukas, who is on the sidewalk heading north on Fifth Street with his well-dressed wife and a boy who must be their son. The boy is showing off his black patent leather shoes instead of boots. They are coming from somewhere near *God's Little Acre*.

"Rytilahti, good morning and good news! All you have to do is..."

"Good morning, Roger," Papa interrupts. "I know you've met my daughter Emilia, and this is my beautiful wife Kerttu and my youngest athletic daughter Heli."

"Yes, it's nice to see you again, Amy, and nice to meet you ladies," glancing down at Heli and glancing over Mama's head. "As I was saying Rytilahti..."

"And who do I have the pleasure of meeting?" Papa interrupts again, for he has heard other footsteps.

Mrs. Lukas moves her glare from me and Heli and raises her chin, but it only serves to point her nose farther into the air.

"Yes, this is my wife and my son," Mr. Lukas says, yet Papa's eyebrows still arch behind his patched spectacles with the broken lens. "This is my wife Chastity and my son Kermit," Mr. Lukas finally proposes, and Mama offers her hand to Mrs. Lukas's glove.

"I haven't much time, Rytilahti, so I'll make this quick. There have been some, er, mishaps in the broom factory and we're way behind in production and we'd like to have you back to work after the first of the year. The first week of January is, let's see..."

"The fifth," Papa fills in.

"That's correct Rytilahti. All you have to do is turn in your union card and..."

"How do you know I even have a union card? I was *laid off*, remember?"

"Well, come on Rytilahti. You're Finnish and ... and you

have to eat and ... and the union commissary..."

I am embarrassed by what Mr. Lukas is saying in front of the other families who are gathering around us and staring.

"Lukas, what's on my table is none of your business and the strike is no decent business to be discussing on a Sunday morning right after Mass in front of my family and yours..." Papa spreads his right arm upward in a circle, "...and other families."

"Mass? You go to Mass?"

"That, too, is none of your business."

"Rytilahti, I'm inviting you back to work."

"I'll think about it," and Papa pauses for emphasis and slowly and perfectly enunciates: "Mr. Lukas."

Knowing that he now has an audience, Mr. Lukas raises his voice like he is ignoring Papa and addressing the other families standing here in uncomfortable attention. "This is Red Jacket, Rytilahti," and Mr. Lukas mocks Papa by mimicking the same motion Papa just used to indicate our community. "If you want to live in Finland, why don't you just go back to Finland?"

"This is not about wanting to live in Finland. This is about wanting to change things so it feels as true as living in Finland." Papa lowers his voice. "I said I will think about it. Now if you'll excuse us, we're..."

"Think about it? What's to think about? The union is whipped, the strike is effectively over and you Finlanders are ... you're done. That's your trouble, Rytilahti, you think too much."

"If my family and other families weren't here, and it wasn't Sunday, I would tell you everything you think in about ten seconds."

Mr. Lukas raises his fist and nudges it under Papa's up-turned chin. "I ought to..."

The crowd is pushing in, for what will surely be two men coming to blows on a Sunday morning between church services.

"If you believe your manhood depends upon beating on a blind man on Sunday morning after church, and in front of others, then give it your best shot. But know this, Roger Lukas..." Papa points his right index finger to his head... "this is the way I fight!" he shouts.

The crowd of Sunday onlookers stands in rapt attention. Papa's face fixes on Mr. Lukas's and I know he is seeing him through his damaged spectacles with the dark lenses.

"This is the way I fight..." he repeats as he taps his right finger against his right temple, "...and if I thought I had a worthy opponent, I would gladly fight you, but it would be in my arena. You have already seen the way I fight. This is my arena," he says with his finger still against his temple. "I told you I would think about it. And I will. Yet, if you so much as touch me or my family, I will fight you, Roger Lukas. I will fight you in my arena and...

...I
Will
Crush
Your
Soul
Like
A
Grape."

"It's probably a Pyrrhic victory," Papa says when we return to the security of our home and somehow the heat from the stoves seems to have escaped. "Yes, I won the *battle*, but if the *war* is my job at Calumet and Hecla..." and he lets that thought linger in the now cool air of our sitting room.

Heli feels it too, and escapes outside to play with Johanna Nelson.

"Papa, I'd like to go down to Superior," I ask in more of a statement than a question. Mama looks to me and sees the need in my expression and silently takes Papa's hand.

I need to be alone. I need to be alone, and with Superior

I will not be lonely.

"Fine, Emilia. Be back by dinner," Papa says. "I want us to be together as a family today," and I feel some of the warmth restored.

The walk from Swedetown to Waterworks Road is less than two miles. Near the corner is Lake View Cemetery and I don't even realize I've slowed my pace until I'm past it on Waterworks Road. When I see Superior another two miles and a good 600 feet downhill, I break into a run.

I run to her. I am running *to* her. I am not running away from Red Jacket because everyone in attendance at the fight, at the argument, knows the victor. I am not running away from the home and family I love; I just need to be alone for a while. I just need Lake Superior right now.

Her blueness from the top of the hill begins to turn green at the shoreline when I'm to Fisherman Road. *Her blueness.* I like that, and work the phrase in my mind and imagine Papa working it too.

Superior dominates the horizon from the top of the hill. Here at the bottom, where the road turns to hug the shoreline, Superior owns the horizon. Her soothing christening of the sand on this clear and calm day is a gentle invitation to me to walk her shoreline. A wintry crust is beginning to form where the water first meets the land, but she's a long way from freezing. That will be much later.

I feel her flow through my mind, cleansing my thoughts and drenching their meanings in her vastness; the pleasant ones, she clarifies and crystallizes; the hostile ones drown and she holds them to herself and never sends them back to you.

What does it mean to touch superior? I have seen and heard superior; I have smelled and tasted superior. I wonder what superior feels like. Maybe Latin will help. To feel is *tangere*, something tangible, something you touch. That's not what I'm trying to describe.

Not *superbia*, proud and haughty and arrogant like Mr.

MacNaughton. Instead, the conjugated verb of *superare*. Superior, the transcendent state that Papa describes.

*Transcend the bullshit*. Transcend the strike and leave all its pettiness and even its cold-blooded murder on the ground like so much bullshit. *American justice*. Shaft Number Two. The savage capital of a death a week. The savage capitalism that drives it all in the name of profit. President Wilson and Governor Ferris. Waddell Mahon. The National Guard, the Department of Labor. Clarence Darrow and Allen Rees. Rent payments with a tip. The Boston Caste System. Niggers and Finniggers. Shaft bosses and sheriffs. Rats. Golf balls and MacNaughton's Eye. Guns and riot sticks. Citizens Alliance buttons. *Quid pro quo*.

Don't let them contaminate the water. Superior will not abide.

"Go beyond. Better yet, rise above," Papa tells me. How would he work the phrase, the concept, and give it back to me in a completed thought?

I sigh.

Her blueness. Her greenness here on the shore.

My sigh is lost in Superior.

All Superior feels beautiful. I am of Superior. I feel beautiful.

All beautiful birds have flight. I am beautiful. I fly.

Quit trying to describe it. Feel it.

I bend over and touch the clear, cold water of Lake Superior.

*Sensus, tactus, percipere*.

Superior translates it and sends it back to me in the language of my sentiments.

Sense, feeling, emotion.

My soul begins to rise. I am regaining my flight. My sigh is found in Superior.

I've found it. I feel Superior. I feel her intuitively.

She is Mama's resolve, Aunt Iiris's beauty, Mother Jones's passion, and Mrs. Clemenc's bravery. She is lithe and acrobatic like Heli when she bends over to touch her toes and instead rolls in to stroke the shore. She is the modesty of St. Mary's, the majesty of St. Anne's. She is the pride and spirit of mamas with weapons no deadlier than the brooms in their hands; she is the enthusiasm of their parading children. She is the dignity of Mrs. Kumpula, the insight of Mrs. Thompson. She is the wisdom of a philosopher, the perseverance of a teacher, the resilience of a nurse. She is Papa's arm locked in mine.

Sunday Mass and St. Joseph's mural. A sauna. Uncle Bear's tickles and Heli's dimples. Spring melts and fall colors. Snow jumping and climbing the water tower. Circuses and kind black men. The poetry of *The Kalevala*, the prose and metaphors of a golden fleece and a secret garden. Fried dough and baked bread. She is baseball and angels on second and third with no outs and Heli at bat. *Amazing Grace*. She is the meaning of the Sampo.

And I feel her.

I feel every bit of her.

She is the smile that comes to my face every time I'm near her, and she always gives me more than I ask of her.

Timeless. Priceless. Ageless.

She is whatever was here before we were here and is still here and always will be.

I have touched superior.

# XXI

## December 24, 1913

"Ten," Heli says just past St. Anne's on Fifth Street as she beats me to the lone snow flake we both see floating in the distance, and sticks out her tongue to capture it. "I told you I could get to ten before you."

We started our contest only as we reached the back of St. Anne's, and there are few lake-effect flakes lazily descending from the clear, early afternoon sky, yet it figures that Heli would taste the sweetness of ten before I even got to seven.

The John Green block begins right after St. Anne's, and Heli insists we go two blocks out of our way so we can take in the incandescent wonder of Fifth Street on our way to Italian Hall on Seventh Street. Even the cigar store has all its lights on for Christmas Eve. Holding my breath as we pass it, I don't mind when the thick foreign smell of tobacco invades my nose, because Smith's Confectioners is right next door and I exhale quickly and take a deep breath when Heli and I stop. On their own, my fingers go to the piece of scrap paper I found in which to wrap my twelve dimes so they won't escape from the holes in my dress pocket.

"Emilia, look how much a dime will buy," she tells me like she knows the denomination of all my coins.

I still haven't told Heli of the effort I started last summer to save enough money for a Christmas feast. She will soon know when we get to Italian Hall. For the hundredth time, I calculate what a dollar and twenty cents will buy in Christmas food, praying I have made a mistake somewhere that will enable us to walk in the door to Smith's. For the hundredth time, a Christmas feast re-defines itself in my mind as a little Christmas food.

We are soon joined by a few older children as well as younger ones with their mamas, many of whom are also on their way to Italian Hall. Smith's Confectioners doesn't even need its lights on or its big sign over the entrance because the glorious aroma of all its candies and confectioneries are a better way to advertise to all us sidewalk customers.

Yesterday marked the fifth month of the strike between the Western Federation of Miners and every one of over 25 mining companies in the Copper Country. There has been much strife and little strike pay. Some of the workers have crossed the mamas and the parades and the picket lines, but few of us Finns have. Papa says the mines have tons and tons of copper in inventory, and continue to take in money from their accounts receivables.

We have stopped paying the hospital so we can eat, and Mama says our savings are now exhausted.

For the thousandth time, I think ahead to nursing school and of becoming a nurse so we can afford little things like this. I haven't decided where I will live when I've completed nursing school, yet all my dreams include Papa and Mama and Heli.

The fog on the window from our mouths dissipates quickly, leaving the little smudge marks on the windows from our noses as we turn to continue to our event. No one enters the candy store.

"Oh, Emilia, I bet you can't wait to be a nurse so you will have your own money. I have it all figured out for you. Your husband will be a doctor and you'll live in a big house and you'll own an automobile and..."

"I was just thinking of that, Heli. And I don't know who I'll marry and I don't care about a big house or a noisy horseless carriage. I think after I complete nursing school in Marquette, I'll just move back to Copper Island and take care of Papa and Mama and try to keep you out of mischief."

"Dream, Emilia! Dream big!" she tells me as we approach Ulseth Lumber. "Here's where you can buy what you need to build your beautiful house, and I've already decided you want a Ford automobile, and with all the cute boys at the party, I'll have you a husband in no time."

Heli's interest in boys is becoming more pronounced, and I think she also believes that I should feel the same way. Earlier today, she again loaned me her lone hair ribbon as Mama also helped us get ready for the big Christmas Eve party. Mama allowed us to primp and dawdle in front of the mirror, and I again wished Papa could use it himself. Mama saw the look in my eyes: the longing look I sometimes see in her eyes when she briefly peers into the same mirror. After she inspected us carefully, her own eyes lit up and she said, "Emilia and Heli, you'll be the prettiest young women in the whole hall."

Sitting at the kitchen table, Papa turned his head toward our conversation. He appeared as if he could see through the damaged spectacles he'll need to wear for only a little while longer. He smiled and, touching his spectacles, said words neither Heli nor I have heard from him.

"Never mind these," he said. "Emilia and Heli, you're beautiful."

*He has no sight*, I think. *Better, Papa has insight.*

I find the fabric behind the women's hats at the millinery store to be far more interesting than the hats, and I examine the calicos while Heli picks out the satin for my wedding dress. We've barely reached any decisions for our respective dresses when another unfair advertiser greets us with its aromas. Baer Brothers Meats is just ahead and our noses are exquisitely confused by the rows in the window of turkeys, geese, ducks, kielbasa, pot roasts and steaks.

"Emilia, Thanksgiving was the last time we had any

meat. When do you..."

"I think I have Christmas supper planned out, Heli," I tell her as a means to complete her sentence and complete my own thoughts. I was planning to save my surprise until we got to the Atlantic and Pacific Tea Company store where Mama likes to shop for groceries. A little of my impulsiveness – or is it just kindness to my little sister? – escapes, and I'm glad it does. "Heli, I've saved a little money. That is, I used to save it before they fired me from the library. Anyway, I have a dollar twenty and..."

"Will that be enough for a pot roast?"

"No, it won't. But it'll be enough for some potatoes and flour and I want to buy some coffee for Papa and Mama and maybe even a little sugar. I think I've got it worked out in my head, and it's later than I wish because I wanted to be to the hall by now, but you know where the A&P is, at Italian Hall?"

"Sure." Heli's eyes light up when I mention food as both our mouths are watering in front of a meat market.

"Then let's get moving and let's pick out our Christmas supper."

Heli takes my hand and starts to run, but I hold her back as I spot a stray snow flake drifting toward us. She sees where I'm looking, halts suddenly and our heads meet when I lurch forward with my mouth open. The snow flake comes to rest on the top button of my third shirt.

"What a special day! What a special sister you are, Emilia. You're the best big sister in the world."

"And you're a brat," I tell her, rubbing my head.

"Bratwurst. Maybe we can afford German bratwurst or, better yet, our Finnish sausage, some makkara," Heli says, and we both take off together this time and keep running past the children with their mamas and past the stores and the lights and the decorations to our party and to our purchase of Christmas supper.

Mr. Meyers is surprised to see me, then perplexed by Heli's presence, and finally disappointed when we walk to the back of his store and I take out my scrap of paper, unfold it, and show him the money I'm about to spend.

"Hello, Dominic, what can I do for you?" he calls over my head when a man in an apron and no coat and smelling of beer walks in from a door near the front, but on the side of the store, and joins us in the back.

"Charles, can I bother you for a round of change?" and Mr. Meyers doesn't even have to alter the look of disappointment on his face as the man in the apron hands him a twenty dollar bill.

Heli is eyeing the small meat counter that's been added to the back of the store since I've last been here. *It's probably been added since the union commissary down the street opened with a full selection of meats*, I think to myself.

"Vairo's Saloon is obviously doing a brisk business on Christmas Eve, Dominic. That's more than I can say for A&P."

"Come on next door, Charles. I'll be happy to buy you a beer," the man who must be Dominic Vairo tells him with a smile. "And you may not come next door, young lady, for it's no place for a pretty lady like you, but what brings you here?"

His apron smells like beer and his breath like pickled eggs, but his eyes have the kindness that I've learned to read in a man. They are gray like Uncle Bear's and generous like Mr. Schubert's and have the soft lines radiating from their sides like the black man, Mr. Jasper, at the circus.

"Sir, my sister and I," and I point to Heli still stuck at the meat counter, "are buying some things for Christmas supper." I stop to hold out my hand, and when I realize that the twelve dimes pale in comparison to the twenty dollars he just handed Mr. Meyers for change, I quickly take it back and feel the rash of embarrassment rise in my face.

"Young lady, you saved that money, didn't you?"

"Yes, sir" I say, and a quick assessment of the twelve dimes tells me how he also figured it out.

"Here's a roll of quarters and a roll of dimes and a roll of nickels, Dominic," Mr. Meyers interrupts and hands Mr. Vairo the change. "How do you want the other three dollars?"

The potatoes are stacked in bags next to the meat counter, and I pick up a small bag and touch the potatoes through the burlap like Mama to check their freshness.

Thirty-four cents.

The flour is stacked on the bottom shelf along the wall. Ten pounds will have to do.

Twenty-seven cents.

The coffee is back to the center aisle and Mr. Vairo is standing in front of Mr. Meyers, but looking at Heli like he would rather be talking with her.

I take out the metal coffee scoop and dig it into the coffee beans and listen to them jangle onto the scale until I have measured out precisely one pound.

Twenty-nine cents.

Mr. Vairo is gone when I look for Mr. Meyers to measure out the sugar he keeps hidden behind the counter, so I ask about the price per pound and he tells me 60 cents.

"Perfect!" I exclaim and his face lights up too. "A half a pound."

Mr. Meyers works the math and nods.

Heli is back and she looks at the potatoes and flour and coffee and sugar, and then looks at me as I count my dimes for the final time. Mr. Meyers is adding the numbers on the paper bag he put the sugar in.

"Emilia, this will be the finest Christmas supper we've ever had," she tells me, and I am so proud of my sister for understanding.

Mr. Meyers steps over to his little meat display and reaches in toward the steaks and takes out the four largest ones.

"Sir," I protest. "We can't buy any meat and we don't have the money and..."

"Let's see," he says as he wraps the steaks and returns to

his addition. "That's three dollars for the steaks and..."

"Mr. Meyers, sir, I don't have enough money..."

"and a bag of potatoes and a bag of flour..."

"No, please sir, we can't afford..."

"and a pound of coffee and a half-pound of sugar..."

"Sir, my sister and I..."

"Emilia, that'll be a dollar and twenty cents."

"we only came here because it's right below ... how much?"

"Twelve dimes will cover it. What do you call the Christmas elf in Finnish?"

"Joulupukki," Heli tells him.

"A Christmas elf magically came up with the steaks, though he's likelier Italian than Finnish. Merry Christmas, Emilia. Now you and your sister go on upstairs and enjoy the party. I'll hold this for you until I close the store at 5:00 o'clock. You can pick it up on your way home." Heli and I are so stunned, neither of us can speak. "Go," Mr. Meyers laughs and shoos us away with his hands.

We walk out the front door and turn right a few steps and look up to the front door of Vairo's Saloon and I stop. The Italian Hall covers the entire second floor over both the A&P and Vairo's Saloon.

"We can't go in there, Emilia. It's a bar. Papa would tan our behinds on Christmas Eve and Mama would die of embarrassment."

We walk a few more steps to the entrance to Italian Hall, and go up four steps from the street through the big front doors and into the vestibule that stretches for about ten feet before the stairs begin. Heli looks upstairs. The staircase is dark and she takes my hand. There's a small door immediately on our right that leads into the side of the saloon and I stop again. This is the door through which Mr. Vairo walked into the A&P.

"Heli, we must go in there," and I grasp her hand even tighter than she's taken mine, and drag her into the saloon.

We are barely through the side door and I stop and Heli bumps into me from behind and we both sneeze at the same time from the smell of beer and liquor and cigar smoke. When I look up, Dominic Vairo is smiling at me from behind the bar, barely visible to me between a room full of men smoking and men drinking and men talking too loud.

Two young women in the front of a saloon, sneezing in harmony, must be quite a sight for them because all the men quit talking and freeze there along with the haze from their smoke. They are all staring at me and Heli.

"Sir," my smoke-chastened voice manages. "Mr. Vairo, sir. Thank you. And Merry Christmas."

"Young lady, I said that you weren't allowed in here," and every face in the room turns to Mr. Vairo. "And you came here anyway. Young lady, you..." he points to me like Dante giving a tour of hell, "...and your sister..." his gaze shifts to Heli "...are very welcome!" And I can see his eyes light up from our distance through the haze of smoke.

*And what a perfectly Divine Comedy*, I think.

"Buon Natale," he adds with a laugh that lights the bar.

Heli and I are still unable to move. The laughter passes and everybody's eyes are back to us.

"Hauskaa joulua," we say in unison.

"Joyeux Noël!" a man who looks to be French exclaims.

"Wesołych Świąt," a Polish man adds.

"God jul," and that one I can translate because it means *Merry Christmas* in Swedish.

The entire bar erupts in "Merry Christmas" in as many languages as are represented in a saloon in Red Jacket, Michigan on Christmas Eve.

And that's a lot.

There's an incandescent light at the top of the stairs and it looks too far away and too dim for Heli when we pass through the saloon doors and return to the vestibule at the bottom of the staircase and look up. Heli looks left to the double doors back onto the street like she would rather leave than climb the dark stairs on our right. She has been so understanding today that I take her hand without complaint, and she picks up her dress and I grab mine and we bound up the stairs in only eleven steps, two at a time.

The smile returns to her face and she digs into the pocket of her dress to pull out Papa's union card and hands it to the woman at the top of the stairs. The woman looks at it and hands it back to me, and Heli looks disappointed, so I give it to her when we turn to our right into the big open hall.

The staircase has taken us almost halfway into the hall and we walk to the center and just stand there and try to breathe in this beautiful party in a hall that must be forty feet wide and eighty feet long. The theatre seating above us and stretching almost the entire wall to our left looks like the balcony of the Opera House, and it is open except for the railing along the front, providing a wonderful view to the raised stage that fills the wall in front of us. In back of us are the windows looking down from the second floor to Seventh Street, and Heli and I make our way there because all the chairs are taken nearest the stage.

It's clear we're among the last to arrive, yet I don't regret our walk through the business district of Fifth Street, and I'm ecstatic over our little shopping trip to A&P and our adventure into Vairo's Saloon. Heli and I recognize many of what must easily be 500 children's faces from school, from Swedetown, from St. Joseph's and from the families of our kinsmen, for many, many are Finnish. Better yet, most are children, and when Heli looks to me and smiles, I know we have been made to feel right at home in an Italian hall above an Italian bar.

Visually cutting the room in half, then in half twice more, I estimate the number. Eighty times eight is 640, and the ticket office and bar room and stage will be another 80, and that's 720.

What an incredible party!

There are three Christmas trees on the stage and I can

see the sparse tinsel sparkling back at us. The trees and a little bunting along the railings of the theatre seating and the children's chatter and the piano tuning up for some Christmas carols are all I need.

*Yes, this is all I need for Christmas*, I think to myself. My family has given me their love and warmth. Mama has given me courage, Heli empathy. Papa has given me wings.

A man with a perfect pitch tenor voice begins with *Cantique de Noël* and I strain to hear him above the talking, then he increases his volume when he reaches the line, *For yonder breaks a new and glorious morn* just before the refrain. He notches his voice even higher.

> *Fall on your knees! O hear the angel voices!*
> *O night divine, the night when Christ was Born;*
> *O night, O holy night, O night divine!*

Heli and I are too embarrassed to drop to our knees, but the young children aren't. I sweep our view from the back of the hall to left and right. *Ah, to be a child again*, I think. *Just last year*, I think again and laugh at myself. I read the Charles Dickens book about three years ago, just before Christmas and did not feel as poor and as rich as Tiny Tim then.

I do now.

All the children are asked to join in singing *Silent Night* and every child knows the tune, if not in the same language.

> *Silent night, holy night*
> *All is calm, all is bright*
> *Round yon Virgin Mother and Child*
> *Holy Infant so tender and mild*
> *Sleep in heavenly peace*
> *Sleep in heavenly peace*
>
> *Silent night, holy night!*
> *Shepherds quake at the sight*
> *Glories stream from heaven afar*
> *Heavenly hosts sing Alleluia!*

*Christ, the Savior is born*
*Christ, the Savior is born*

*Silent night, holy night*
*Son of God, love's pure light*
*Radiant beams from Thy holy face*
*With the dawn of redeeming grace*
*Jesus, Lord, at Thy birth*
*Jesus, Lord, at Thy birth*

Mrs. Clemenc looks to be in charge of the party and she's near the stage trying to get the attention of some of the children. My estimate of the number of people in attendance here is a tribute to her and to the mamas who planned and organized this.

"Heli," I say, "there's another *thank-you* that you and I need to extend," and she looks at me curiously, but doesn't object this time. As we walk to the front of the hall near the stage, I explain to Heli how I recognize Mrs. Clemenc.

Heli has heard of her. Everyone has heard of her stand-off with the National Guard, and how she invited the Captain to run his saber through the American flag and into her.

"But she's famous," Heli finally manages. "Are you sure we can talk to her?"

By the time we meander through the crowd, Mrs. Clemenc has reappeared on the stage and is seated at a table. I lead Heli up a few steps of stairs to the raised stage and we make our way through more children and stand next to her.

"Mrs. Clemenc. I just want to say thank-you for your bravery. You have been a real inspiration to me and you have changed my life in more ways than you probably know. Thank you again."

"Annie!" a lady carrying a cake calls above the singing and noise and confusion of the children. "We have a few saffron cakes that I made from the Sizer recipe tradition. Between these and some more white cake in the kitchen downstairs, there should be enough for a slice for everyone.

And you should be the one to cut and serve it."

"Thank you, Theresa. I'll be honored."

"Saffron?" Heli says in a voice that's not intended to be heard by anyone other than me.

"Please," and Mrs. Clemenc motions to chairs across the table from her. "Sit down, young ladies. Since you're older, you get to be the ones to have the first slices." Heli smiles and takes my hand and we move to two seats across the table. Mrs. Clemenc cuts two large slices and hands them to me and Heli. She looks at me again, and then looks to Heli and back to me. "You were there, weren't you?"

"Yes, ma'am. I was there with my Mama."

"I remember now!" she exclaims. "I know your Mama and I asked her to attend the parade and you were both near the front of ... our little temporary impasse."

"Yes, ma'am. My name is Emilia Rytilahti and this is my sister Heli."

"Emilia Rytilahti? Heli Rytilahti? *The* Emilia and Heli Rytilahti? The Rytilahti ladies of the Children's Parade fame? I am *so* pleased to meet you. The children are pressing in for a slice of cake. "I had been thinking of some way to involve the children," she continues. "And Theresa Sizek and I and a few others just couldn't come up with any good ideas. Then one weekend, we heard that the children had organized their own parade, and on Monday, you pulled off a stunt that I heard Sheriff Cruse will never forget, and a parade that was nothing short of phenomenal! Thank you. Thank you Emilia and Heli. You have been wonderful!"

The children are tugging at Mrs. Clemenc's sleeves and I again think of Tiny Tim as some of them look like they have not eaten carrots, let alone potatoes or bread, let alone saffron cake in many months.

"I'm sorry, Emilia and Heli, but you'll have to excuse me now. There are some other special guests I'd like to entertain. But will you two come back? I'd like your help in giving out some Christmas presents we have for everyone here."

"Mrs. Clemenc," Heli says for me, "it will be our privilege."

Heli and I eat the last of our cake and walk back down the steps from the stage to make our way to the back of the hall, meandering again through the children forming lines for cake. We stand at the east window and gaze out.

We have said "thank you" to two people and, like casting my thoughts and thank yous to Superior, Heli and I have been blessed more than we have given. All my fears of the past year and my recollections of Papa's stay in the hospital last Christmas are cast away the short distance to Superior.

She will know what to do with them.

"Oh, dear," Mrs. Clemenc says when we re-join her on the stage after all the cake is served. "Some of the children have prepared a *Mother Goose* play, but I'm afraid it's just too confusing in here, and we're running out of time. And we have to get a gift into the little hands of each child. We have a pair of mittens for everyone, I think." She looks to some boxes on the stage and motions to us. "Emilia and Heli, as the children come onto the stage, will you pick out an appropriately sized pair of mittens for each child?"

Some of the children have heard her and a disorganized line is soon fashioned. Heli opens a box and I do the same and begin anticipating the sizes and Heli and I take turns handing them to Mrs. Clemenc, who hands them to each child. We have a wonderful view in front of us of the little faces who light up with gratitude and little voices softly saying "kiitos" and "danke" and "grazie" and "thank you" in almost as many languages as we've heard downstairs say "Merry Christmas."

I've lost track of the time and remember that there's a Christmas feast, wrapped in brown paper, and awaiting me and Heli downstairs, and we must be at the A&P before 5:00 o'clock to pick it up. There are still children with no mittens, but we have attracted a number of helpers. Heli knows what I mean when I motion to her, and together we walk down the stairs from the stage and make our way along the wall beneath the theatre seats. There's a set of double doors swinging toward the landing at the top of the stairs and we move through the doors and onto the landing where we showed Papa's union card for our admittance. A man with a cane begins to descend the stairs ahead of us, leaning against the wall with his right shoulder and using his left hand to feel the cane on the dark steps.

Heli stops.

The incandescent light above us casts a glow that lights the first few steps, but the man with the cane is only about halfway down the stairs and we can barely see his back. It is dark near the bottom and the late-afternoon light is not piercing the doors at our feet.

Heli looks to me with the fear I first saw when she refused to enter the bear den. It looks like we are about to descend into a mine. She takes my hand.

"Fire!" We hear in a loud voice – a man's voice coming from somewhere inside the hall.

The din in the hall drops.

"Fire!" we hear again, and the expression on Heli's face changes from fear to terror.

We glance from the landing at the top of the stairs through the doors opened to the hall, and children are rushing toward us. They want to get to the stairwell and down the stairs and out of the building.

Heli looks to me and must read my dread.

I see the panic in her eyes.

She squeezes my hand as we descend the first step and my feet feel like lead.

Some children are screaming.

I move to the left side of the staircase so we can get past the man with the cane, who is nearing the bottom. The weight from my feet shifts to a force that is coming behind us, and I don't have to look back to know from the crying and the sound of many feet on the steps that children are shoving to get past me and Heli.

Her grip on my right hand tightens. My grip on her left hand is as tight as I can make it.

Our grip is broken and Heli and I and the man and the cane plunge to the landing at the bottom.

I've fallen onto my right shoulder and can see through the little space beneath the doors leading into Mr. Vairo's bar. I try to get up.

I can't move a limb.

I can't move a thing.

The noise from the hall above us sounds like 500 children on roller skates, except some are crying, some are screaming and all are headed in the direction of the stairwell. Our stairwell. The stairwell my sister and I cannot move from.

I hope Heli is alright. I want to hold her hand. I try to move my right arm, but it's pinned beneath me. I try to move my left arm, but it's pinned above me by other children who have fallen on me. I try to move my hands. I try to move my fingers.

Nothing moves.

My body is being pummeled with weight from above, and it seems like it's being added in increments of a big flour bag that Mama and I take turns carrying. The screaming now sounds like it begins from here at the bottom, but I can't tell its direction or where it ends. It does not end. The timbre transforms from screams of fear to cries of pain.

And panic.

I cannot move, yet I am thrashing within my mind.

*Cogito, ergo sum.*

I think, therefore I am ... I am ... *I am terrified.*

Through the foreboding darkness of my dread, I try to discern the cries. Can I hear Heli? The only adult voice I heard was a *huhwhoosh* from the man after his cane clattered to the landing. These are children's voices now.

Heli! Where is Heli?

"My leg, oh God, my leg" from a boy.

"No. Please no. Please no. Please no," from a girl.

It is not Heli.

"Mama. Help me, mama" from a child.

"Mammaaaaaaaa" from a child farther above me.

The voices I hear are children writhing in pain.

I smell bile.

A momentary silence.

No, I hear sound.

It is not voice. It is breath squeezed from children.

Then a word, a name.

"Meewa," Heli pleads in the plaintive breath of a closing sigh.

My sister.

My sister is afraid, no, my sister is petrified.

My heart reaches out to her as my hand cannot.

I feel my heart racing. There is terrible pressure upon my head. This is indescribable pressure within my head. I cannot direct my own thoughts as they tumble down a mine shaft. There is no light. This is the place of Papa and Uncle Bear and Dante. No one else, save a trammer, a poet, a devil may abide.

I try to force myself to return to the surface, to grass. I cannot.

I am trapped in Shaft Number Two.

A sense of dread, but more. Sight and sound and smell and touch of terror, but more.

Pure panic descends upon me.

I am losing consciousness. I am losing it. I am losing...

*I am leading the children's parade and wielding a riot stick like a majorette's baton. Sheriff Cruse is coming toward me holding a stick of dynamite and lights its short fuse with the cigar hanging from his mouth. "Please join us," I say to him. Mr. MacNaughton is pumping his legs up and down from alongside Red Jacket Road and is holding a pair of spiked golf shoes in his right hand, and falls in line when we reach him.  He gives the shoes to Heli.  The children behind us are shouting, "Emilia, Heli, your Papa is blind!"*

The door leading into Vairo's Saloon opens with my eyes. I see feet.  I see nice shoes that I would like for Heli.

"Jesus, Mary and Joseph," I hear in Mr. Vairo's voice.

I move my shoulders a little and take in a tiny wisp of air.

Mr. Vairo's face now looks into mine.  He is on his hands and knees.

"Jesus, Mary and Joseph," he repeats as he reaches in toward my left arm.  I feel his hand around my wrist and I hear the sleeve on my dress rip from the stress of the weight above as he pulls my arm toward him.  He has my left arm. He pulls it hard.  The rest of my body does not move.  He sits on the floor and puts his feet against some of the weight above me.  He strains and pulls and strains and pulls, and I feel my left arm pop out of its socket with a hollow report like Homer's trachea collapsing.

Mr. Vairo returns to his hands and knees and peeks in and tells me with his eyes that he apologizes.  He does not speak.  Tears are streaming down his cheeks.  His face, then his hands, then his knees and feet move away and disappear.

It is quiet above me.  To my left and high above me, I can still hear the sound of feet on the second floor of Italian Hall. Farther above me is faraway crying.  Some screams.

Directly above me, it is silent.

I try to move my hips this time.  No.  I try to move my shoulders and receive only the response from my left that the pain is too great.  I try to move my legs.  No.  My feet.  No.

There is no breath left in me.

My right ear is crushed against the floor.  The smell of bile returns.  I taste it myself.  I am losing consciousness again.

I close my eyes.

This is the first time Heli and I are allowed to attend

Midnight Mass on Christmas Eve at St. Joseph's, and Papa and Mama are with us.

Father Klopcic begins the Mass *In nómine Patris et Fílii et Spíritus Sancti. Amen.*

I follow along in silence, unable to speak.

"*Sicut erat in principio, et nunc, et semper: et in saecula saeculorum. Amen,*" I say the part of an altar boy.

I am only mouthing the words. I have no speech. I translate in my mind.

*As it was in the beginning is now, and ever shall be, world without end. Amen.*

*Confiteor Deo omnipotenti,* I say to myself.

The translated conclusion of the *Confiteor* comes to me without voice: *and I ask Blessed Mary ever Virgin, Blessed Michael the Archangel, Blessed John the Baptist, the Holy Apostles Peter and Paul, all the Angels and Saints, and you my brothers and sisters, to pray for me to the Lord our God.*

Now comes my most difficult part of the Mass.

Forgiveness.

I look to the mural above the main altar.

Jesus opens His eyes and looks at me from atop His rainbow.

I am trying to get my breath to join in the next prayer.

No breath.

Nothing left.

I force myself to focus.

Nothing left.

Jesus is looking only at me. The halo above His head is as pure in its whiteness as Superior is in her blueness. His whiteness moves toward me. He calms me.

I fix my thoughts. I can breathe. I can talk. I take Heli's hand.

I shout:

**Kyrie eleison**

# Epilogue

Emilia Rytilahti and her sister Heli are crushed by the panicked Christmas Eve revelers, and die in the stairwell of Italian Hall, along with 71 others.

There is no fire.

Within days, an investigation releases its findings:

"The Houghton County Coroner's Inquest concludes that the 73 victims came to their death on the 24th day of December, A.D. 1913, at the Italian Hall, in the Village of Red Jacket, by the evidence we find, of the witnesses, that the cause of death of the below-named persons was by suffocation, the same being caused by being jammed on the stairway leading to the entrance of the Italian Hall, where a Christmas celebration was being held by the Women's Auxiliary of the Western Federation of Miners..."

| Name | Age | Relation | Sex | Descent |
|------|-----|----------|-----|---------|
| Sanna Aaltonen | 30 | Mother | F | Finnish |
| Sylvia Aaltonen | 5 | Daughter | F | Finnish |
| Wilma Aaltonen | 7 | Daughter | F | Finnish |
| Herman Aura | 50 | Father | M | Finnish |
| Lempi Aura | 12 | Daughter | F | Finnish |
| Will Bin | 7 | | M | Finnish |
| Ivanna Bolf | 9 | | F | Croatian |
| Katarina Bronzo | 21 | | F | Italian |
| Victoria Burcar | 12 | | F | Croatian |
| Joseph Butala | 8 | | M | Slovenian |
| Nick Cvetkovick | 33 | | M | Croatian |
| Jenny Giacoletto | 9 | | F | Italian |
| Katarina Gregorich | 10 | | F | Croatian |
| Edwin Heikkinen | 5 | Brother | M | Finnish |
| Eino Heikkinen | 9 | Brother | M | Finnish |
| Eli Heikkinen | 7 | Brother | M | Finnish |
| Aina Isola | 30 | Mother | F | Finnish |
| Päivä Isola | Baby | Daughter | F | Finnish |
| Barbara Jelić | 25 | Mother | F | Croatian |
| Rosie Jelić | Baby | Daughter | F | Croatian |

| | | | | |
|---|---|---|---|---|
| Uno Jokipii | 13 | | M | Finnish |
| Anna Kallunki | 9 | Daughter | F | Finnish |
| Briita Kallunki | 42 | Mother | F | Finnish |
| Effia Kallunki | 8 | Daughter | F | Finnish |
| Johan Kiemaki | 7 | | M | Finnish |
| Christiana Klarich | 5 | Sister | F | Croatian |
| Katarina Klarich | 7 | Sister | F | Croatian |
| Mary Klarich | 9 | Sister | F | Croatian |
| Johan Koskela | 10 | | M | Finnish |
| Anna Kotajarvi | 4 | Daughter | F | Finnish |
| Anna Kotajarvi | 39 | Mother | F | Finnish |
| Mary Krainatz | 11 | | F | Croatian |
| Hilja Lantto | 5 | Daughter | F | Finnish |
| Maria Lantto | 40 | Mother | F | Finnish |
| Sulo Lauri | 8 | | M | Finnish |
| Mary Lesar | 13 | Sister | F | Slovenian |
| Rafael Lesar | 5 | Brother | M | Slovenian |
| Arthur Lindstrom | 12 | | M | Swedish |
| Lydia Luomi | 5 | | F | Finnish |
| Alfred Lustic | 7 | | M | Finnish |
| Elina Manley | 26 | Mother | F | Finnish |
| Wesley Manley | 4 | Son | M | Finnish |
| Ella Manttanen | 8 | Sister | F | Finnish |
| Mathias Manttanen | 10 | Brother | M | Finnish |
| Yrjö Manttanen | 13 | Brother | M | Finnish |
| Agnes Mihelchic | 3 | Cousin | F | Croatian |
| Elizabeth Mihelchich | 9 | Cousin | F | Croatian |
| Paul Mihelchich | 5 | Cousin | M | Croatian |
| Walter Murto | 9 | | M | Finnish |
| Edward Myllykangas | 3 | Brother | M | Finnish |
| Johan Myllykangas | 5 | Brother | M | Finnish |
| Abram Niemelä | 24 | Husband | M | Finnish |
| Maria Niemelä | 22 | Wife | F | Finnish |
| Annie Papesh | 6 | Sister | F | Slovenian |
| Mary Papesh | 14 | Sister | F | Slovenian |
| Kate Petteri | 66 | | F | Finnish |

| | | | |
|---|---|---|---|
| Saida Raja | 10 | | F | Finnish |
| Teresa Renaldi | 13 | | F | Italian |
| Elma Ristel | 6 | | F | Finnish |
| *Emilia Rytilahti* | *16* | *Sister* | *F* | *Finnish* |
| *Heli Rytilahti* | *13* | *Sister* | *F* | *Finnish* |
| Yrjänä Saari | 5 | | M | Finnish |
| Elida Saatio | 16 | | F | Finnish |
| Mamie Smuk | 7 | | F | Slovenian |
| Antonia Staudohar | 7 | | F | Croatian |
| Elisina Taipalus | 6 | Sister | F | Finnish |
| Sandra Taipalus | 5 | Sister | F | Finnish |
| Edward Takola | 9 | | M | Finnish |
| Lydia Talpaka | 10 | | F | Finnish |
| Kaisa Tulppo | 10 | Daughter | F | Finnish |
| Mamie Tulppo | 42 | Mother | F | Finnish |
| Johan Westola | 48 | | M | Finnish |
| Hilja Wuolukka | 8 | | F | Finnish |

# Afterword

Many of the events cited in this book are historically accurate to the best of this writer's ability, and they include: the passage of the Workingmen's Compensation Law in Michigan on September 1, 1912; the creation of the United States Department of Labor on March 4, 1913; the sequence and prayers of the Catholic, Latin *Ordinary of the Mass*; snow-jumping from second-story windows;   the circus in early July; the strike of the Western Federation of Miners on July 23 against all the mines on the Keweenaw Peninsula of Michigan (the mine superintendents prevail, and the strikers, emotionally devastated by the Christmas Eve Italian Hall disaster, eventually acquiesce and overwhelmingly vote to end the strike on Easter Sunday, April 12, 1914); the women's *brooming* of the *scabs*; the arrival and departure of nearly 3,000 National Guardsmen; the presence of rats so large that cats would not them take on, resulting from the mines filling up with water as the strike began; the arrival on August 5 of Mother Jones, who former President Theodore Roosevelt actually described as "the most dangerous woman in America"; the presence of Waddell Mahon-hired *goons* or *strike-breakers*; the single large spotlight which came to be known as *MacNaughton's Eye*; the Seeberville murders and woundings, as well as the actual names involved on August 14; the standoff between *Big Annie* Clemenc and Captain Blackman of the National Guard on September 13; the Children's Parade of October 6; the blizzard of November 8; the huge explosion near a mine in Ahmeek on Thanksgiving night, November 27; the Dally / Jane murders on December 7; the formation and initiatives of the Citizens Alliance; and, of course, the Italian Hall disaster, in which 73 people, mostly Finnish, mostly children, perished on Christmas Eve, 1913. That a man twice cried *fire* is well-documented, yet there was no fire and all deaths were caused by vital organs being crushed, or suffocation in the stairwell. Neither the identity nor the motive of the man who yelled *fire* has ever been definitively established.

Much of the mining terminology is accurate to the best of this writer's ability, including descriptions of: trammers, who were predominantly, if not exclusively Finnish; shafts, the vertical main entrances to a mine; drifts, horizontal byways; winzes, vertical air passageways; air blasts; man engines, used to transport men into and out of the mines; *advancing* and *retreating* mining; and the depths of the mines – far exceeding 5,000 feet, or more than one mile – was not uncommon.

Many of the places cited in this book are historically accurate to the best of this writer's ability, and they include: Red Jacket, which is modern-day Calumet; Swedetown, a vibrant community in the era cited in this book, located on a hill, near a water tower, and still existing today (feel free to climb near the water tower and check out the view); the baseball diamond and golf course / club house near Swedetown; Eugene Field School, near Ridge Street in Swedetown; the Calumet and Hecla broom factory to employ the blind and disabled; Lake Superior (with which this author is obviously enamored); the Miscowaubik Club; the names of the streets in Red Jacket and Swedetown; Yellow Jacket and Blue Jacket (right next to Red Jacket, within modern-day Calumet); Laurium, Osceola, Raymbaultown, Centennial, Tamarack, little communities near (the former) Red Jacket; Eagle River, Kearsarge, Ahmeek, Lake Linden, Seeberville, Painesdale, which were historically accurate in the era of this book, and still exist today; all the mine shafts noted, including their numbers and locations; St. Joseph's Catholic Church (present-day St. Paul the Apostle Catholic Church), including the description of the altars, the mural, the statues and their placement (and if you want a real treat, please visit this incredible church!); St. Mary's Catholic Church; St. Anthony's Catholic Church; St. John the Baptist Catholic Church; Sacred Heart Catholic Church; the Churches of *God's Little Acre* – the Presbyterian Church, Episcopal

Church, Swedish Lutheran Church, and St. Anne's Catholic Church, which is the present-day home of the Keweenaw National Park - Heritage Center; Vairo's Saloon and A & P; Italian Hall; and, of course, the number of steps that Emilia and Papa took to the locations mentioned.

Many of the names cited in this book are historically accurate to the best of this writer's ability, and they include: U.S. President Woodrow Wilson; Michigan Governor Woodbridge Ferris; the Western Federation of Miners President Charles Moyer; James MacNaughton, Calumet & Hecla Superintendent; Father Luke Klopcic of St. Joseph's Catholic Church; Sheriff Cruse; *Big Annie* Clemenc (inducted into the Michigan Women's Hall of Fame); Margaret Fazekas; Clarence Darrow, the attorney who actually defended the Western Federation of Miners and visited Red Jacket a number of times in attempts to settle the strike, and went on to further fame when he, among other legendary legal proceedings, opposed William Jennings Bryan in the Scopes Monkey Trial; Allen Rees, primary attorney for Calumet and Hecla; the Skyhooks Baseball Team of Swedetown, including the names and positions of some of the players; the *Mining Gazette* and *Työmies* (Finnish for *The Working Man*) Newspapers; Dominic Vairo, owner of Vairo's Saloon, and Charles Meyer, manager of the A&P, both businesses on the first floor of the Italian Hall; and, most certainly, Emilia and Heli Rytilahti, who actually perished in the Italian Hall disaster.

The use of Finnish words and expressions and general terminology, and references to Finnish culture are accurate to the best of this author's ability and, to the extent that they are accurate, due in large part to James Kurtti of Finlandia University and Marianne Tepsa.

To the extent that they are accurate, the events, terminology, places and names were established as a result of the author's reading and research, and the author gratefully acknowledges the following sources, which were invaluable to the research: *The Kalevala*, an epic Finnish poem of oral tradition compiled by Elias Lönnrot; *Cradle To Grave*, by Larry Lankton; *Rebels on the Range*, by Arthur Thurner; *Italian Hall: The Witnesses Speak*, by Larry Malloy; *Swedetown*, by James Medved; *Tinsel and Tears*, by P. Germain; *Death's Door*, by Steve Lehto; *Strike Investigation*, by the Committee of the Copper Country Commercial Club of Michigan 1913; Woodie Guthrie's song, *1913 Massacre;* the Calumet Public School Library; the archives of Michigan Technological University; as well as numerous editions of Latin/English – English/Latin dictionaries; Finnish/English – English/Finnish dictionaries; English dictionaries; and English thesauruses.

The remaining events, terminology, places, names, businesses, organizations and incidents either are the product of the author's imagination or used fictitiously. Any resemblance to actual persons, living or dead, or actual events is entirely coincidental.

Finally, the author gratefully acknowledges the influence of Ernest Hemingway, and his book, *A Moveable Feast*, which contains advice this author would recommend to any writer – advice this author appreciated in attempts to *make*, rather than *describe*, what can be seen, heard, smelled, tasted and touched of the phenomenal body of water, body of life called Lake Superior.

AAWasek@gmail.com

58823613R00183

Made in the USA
Charleston, SC
19 July 2016